EXPOSURE TO A *Billionaire*

Praise for

EXPOSURE TO A *Billionaire*

Fasten your seat belt and get ready for the adventure of a lifetime! In *Exposure to a Billionaire*, Ann Menke takes readers on an exclusive journey around the world with an elite set of rich and famous. Both hilarious and heartwarming, Menke's debut is filled with opulent wealth, sweet romance, and stunning scenery. I wish I could have read this while jet setting to Venice or Phuket, but alas, I'm quite happy to live vicariously through Menke's endearing heroine and her international quest for love and laughter.

—**Melanie Dobson**, award-winning author of
Chateau of Secrets and *Shadows of Ladenbrooke Manor*

In *Exposure to a Billionaire,* the reader is quickly swept away into a world that only a privileged few get to experience. Live the lifestyle of vast wealth and power vicariously as Ann Menke accurately brings situations to life in their lush settings. Add to that, amazingly accurate descriptions of some of the finest destinations in the world. AND, be prepared for fast moving adventure.

—**Casey Powell**, CEO of Sequent Computer Systems, Inc.

Ann Menke and I traveled the world over the years through our careers with a front row seat to many exotic locations few will ever experience and a list of passengers one could only dream about. In *Exposure to a Billionaire* she has achieved an irresistible and beautiful story...romance, adventure and a rare look into the world of the fabulously wealthy. A must read.

—**Kristina Bauer Selten**, Corporate Flight Attendant

Exposure to a Billionaire expertly weaves a witty tale woven together beyond a glance, but with a true inside view into the world of vast power and wealth. This is a world most can only dream about, yet we together have seen it. Dazzling, fun and what an adventure!

—**Chris Weidman**, Director of Aviation

In the news business, reporters are often asked what celebrities are *really* like. They want a behind the scenes look. In *Exposure to a Billionaire*—a fictional account based on Ann Menke's fascinating career as a corporate flight attendant— you'll jettison to the rarified air where A-list movie stars, corporate titans, musicians, athletes and political leaders are pampered beyond even their wildest dreams. Heroine Anna St. James, invites you onboard the latest Gulfstream, to a world of Cristal Champagne, Louis Vuitton, Stella McCartney and Chanel wardrobes, and travel to exotic destinations around the globe. The story unfolds with Anna flying to adventures in Venice, the South of France, overnight to Cairo—to see the Pyramids at just the right light, of course—onto a 5 star safari lodge in South Africa, and a wedding in Mauritius. You'll read wide-eyed, at her required tasks: Creating gift bags worth $3,500 dollars, plotting scavenger hunts where the prize is a four karat diamond (to each member of the winning team), and the general care and feeding of the world's most colorful characters. All this while Anna finds love, and she and her billionaire help save children around the world. Enjoy the ride!

—**Shirley Hancock**, award-winning journalist
and former CBS affiliate news anchor

A story of captivating secrets, torn relationships, and love strong enough to circle the globe. I could not put it down....it's that good!

—**Pam Vredevelt**, LPC, best-selling author of
Angel Behind the Rocking Chair and Empty Arms

There are many ways to see the world. In *Exposure to a Billionaire*, author Ann Menke 'jets off' delivering an entertaining tale in this delightful read. The locations come alive while unexpected twists and turns keep you guessing what's next. It's been fun to share in the adventure.

—**Rod and Carol Wendt**

Traveling the world as a Photographer, I learned about another Ann Menke who is a Corporate Flight Attendant and Author. We have become friends over the years sharing out latest travels and celebrating our achievements. She is the author of *Exposure to a Billionaire*, a novel I couldn't put down. All I can say is, "Big dreams, deep longings, lost loves…A great getaway novel!"

—**Anne Menke**, *See the World Beautiful*,
World Famous Fashion Photographer (Yes, the other Anne Menke)

EXPOSURE
TO A
Billionaire

To Janet—
May the adventure come alive—

ANN MENKE

New York

EXPOSURE TO A *Billionaire*

© 2016 ANN MENKE

Published in New York, New York, by Morgan James Publishing. Morgan James and The Entrepreneurial Publisher are trademarks of Morgan James, LLC. www.MorganJamesPublishing.com

The Morgan James Speakers Group can bring authors to your live event. For more information or to book an event visit The Morgan James Speakers Group at www.TheMorganJamesSpeakersGroup.com.

Shelfie

A **free** eBook edition is available
with the purchase of this print book.

CLEARLY PRINT YOUR NAME ABOVE IN UPPER CASE
Instructions to claim your free eBook edition:
1. Download the Shelfie app for Android or iOS
2. Write your name in **UPPER CASE** above
3. Use the Shelfie app to submit a photo
4. Download your eBook to any device

ISBN 978-1-63047-758-5 paperback
ISBN 978-1-63047-759-2 eBook
ISBN 978-1-63047-760-8 hardcover
Library of Congress Control Number:
2015914084

Cover Design by:
Yvonne Parks
www.PearCreative.ca

Interior Design by:
Bonnie Bushman
The Whole Caboodle Graphic Design

In an effort to support local communities and raise awareness and funds, Morgan James Publishing donates a percentage of all book sales for the life of each book to Habitat for Humanity Peninsula and Greater Williamsburg.

Get involved today, visit
www.MorganJamesBuilds.com

**Habitat
for Humanity®**
Peninsula and
Greater Williamsburg
Building Partner

DEDICATION

For my husband, Doug, who has walked this story with me and supported my every move, believing in me as I pursued the wonderful career of corporate aviation while raising a beautiful family. What a journey we have had, and it just gets better. We serve a beautiful and mighty Father. Thank you for encouraging me throughout this adventure. I couldn't have done it without you. My love for you grows each day on this adventure, called life.

CONTENTS

Once you have tasted flight, you will forever walk the earth with your eyes turned skywards, for there you have been, and there you will always long to return.
—Author Unknown

Chapter One

THE GLAMOUR OF IT ALL, OR SO I THOUGHT

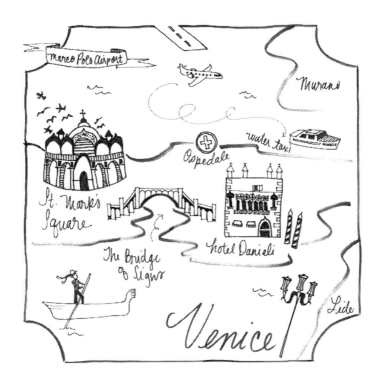

Once you have traveled, the voyage never ends, but is played out over and over again in the quietest chambers. The mind can never break off from the journey.

—Pat Conroy

*V*ENICE! I was really going to Venice. Pinch me. I, Anna St. James, was about to arrive in Venice for the first time in my life. My heart had been racing in anticipation from the moment I had first heard our next trip would take us there. I had been propelled into a new lifestyle of flying for Mr. Stuart Manning over the last few months, seeing the world in nothing but the luxury afforded a billionaire. Yes, I was certainly getting used to this way of life in a hurry.

Descending upon this floating city of romance, I could see what looked like highways in the water below; boats were speckled throughout, racing to where, I could only imagine. *Soon,* I thought to myself, *I will see the city I have heard so much about!* We would only be here for a little over a day, but I didn't care. We would be landing in a few minutes, with the sun shining brightly overhead and Brian, my trusty pilot, ready to be my tour guide once we got settled at the famed Hotel Danieli.

Getting here, however, had not been so wonderful. Mr. Manning had a business associate on board. Yes, two of the richest men in the world together on this one airplane. The contrast between the two was evident from the beginning. Mr. Manning was kind, compassionate, and thoughtful, while Mr. Allister Cummings was aloof to the point of rudeness. He also did us the favor of bringing his administrative assistant/mistress along for the trip. Precious, if that was her real name, was a petite firecracker from the moment she boarded the airplane. That's a polite way of saying she was high maintenance. Both men had meetings scheduled in the afternoon, followed by an elegant dinner party on the island of Murano in the evening, and Precious wanted to shop until she dropped. It looked like she already had all that money could buy, but there were deep pockets in the company of Mr. Allister Cummings.

Precious boarded in Paris as if she owned the airplane—bags and suitcases along with luggage carts full of her shopping purchases in tow. Yes, she and Mr.

Allister Cummings deserved each other. The first words out of her mouth were, "Stewardess, can you get me a blanket?"

Stewardess? You've got to be kidding me! I reluctantly gave her one of our beautiful cashmere throws, dyed to match the leather seats and soft as silk. "Stewardess, this blanket is not warm enough. I want something warm and soft, not this thing. I forgot my skincare kit in my suitcase. I assume you have La Mer products on board?"

Oh, I would give her a warm blanket and La Mer all right. Thankfully, I had stocked the airplane with the luxury toiletries of her liking. I approached her seat again with a soft Restoration Hardware blanket I used for our beds and an overnight La Mer kit for women. She took the items quickly, without a thank you but with some sort of affirming grunt. "This will do."

Mr. Manning looked over, imploring me to hang in there. Almost on cue, Precious said, "I use the lifting and firming mask but don't see it in here. Where is the lip balm? At least you have the mist."

Ignoring Mr. Manning's silent look and knowing I would probably never have darling Precious on board again, I leaned over, opening my mouth with the biggest phony smile I could work up and summoned a voice to match. "I'm so glad we have the mist for you. If you need other items, please, next time, send your shopping list to Mr. Manning's administrative assistant, Linda, who will forward it to me. That way I can have exactly what you would like on board."

Not missing a beat, she demanded, "I need a hair brush and comb, too."

Did this look like a Neiman Marcus department store? I was on to her little game as I went to fetch her comb and brush. She took them from me with a shrug, "Well, at least you have Mason Pearson brushes on board. You know, they are the only kind I use."

Good to know. I was just out of her sight, and feeling relieved, when I heard the service button activate just before takeoff. Her head was leaning into the aisle as she called me: "Stewardess? Stewardess?"

I have been known to get a little agitated when called *stewardess*. Up until this point, I had shown great self-control. In the phoniest smile I could possibly muster I asked how I could help her. Her response, "What kind of champagne do you have on board?"

"You can ask Mr. Manning more about the champagne from his Sonoma SMS winery. I think you will find it an excellent champagne."

"Well" she said, "I guess that will have to do. I personally like Cristal."

"Good."

I tossed Mr. Manning an eye roll on my way back again to the galley, wanting to slip arsenic in her champagne. My Jimmy Choos were already hurting with the repeated trips back and forth to fulfill every request of Miss Precious. We hadn't taken off yet, and I was exhausted!

Mr. Cummings finally spoke, but it was as if I wasn't standing there in front of him. In retrospect, I wished he hadn't said anything. All I heard was, "I want eggs Benedict for breakfast."

That was it! No "please" or "may I have?" All he gave me was a command: "I want eggs Benedict." Did he not see the menu in front of him? Eggs Benedict most certainly was not on the menu. I gave him that awful, fake, flight attendant smile, walking back to the galley to make a quick call during takeoff to Nancy, our chef back home, asking how to make eggs Benedict. She laughed, putting me immediately at ease with instructions on how to pull off this miraculous feat while taking off from Paris. I thankfully had the exact ingredients on board.

Serving Mr. Allister Cummings his requested eggs Benedict, my frozen, flight attendant smile was plastered on my face. I know my expression was not lost on Mr. Manning!

It took all my restraint during the flight to remain civil. The minutes until we landed in Venice couldn't go by quickly enough. If Precious wiggled her champagne flute in the air one more time for a refill, stop me; I wouldn't be responsible for what I might do.

Descending for our final approach, I checked with Brian and Chris in the cockpit. They told me in just a few minutes we would be on the ground and ready for our day in Venice. *Okay, Anna,* I thought to myself, *you can do this.* I had just seated myself for landing when she did the wiggle, not even bothering to look up as she committed the act. My only visual was picturing her neck between my hands. I caught another plea from Mr. Manning's eyes, so I went over with my best flight attendant's voice and asked Precious, "When you wiggle your glass in the air, does that mean you would like more champagne?

You do know that we will be on the ground in less than three minutes, right? Can you wait?"

She ignored me, so I sat down. I felt nothing short of relief when we landed and pulled up to our FBO (Fixed Base Operation), Venice General Aviation, for VIP services. I knew my time with Precious was almost done and Mr. Manning would be my only passenger the following day. That's when I heard her ask Allister for eye drops out of her purse. I wondered why she couldn't get them herself, but then, I watched as Precious wiggled out of her seat and onto Allister's lap. "Allister, sugar, can you put my eye drops in for me?"

I wanted to gag! With a flare for drama, he dropped the liquid into her eyes, sealing the act with a kiss. Within seconds, the screaming began. Now what was the problem? In full-fledged panic, with arms flailing wildly about, she screamed, "I CAN'T OPEN MY EYES!"

Yes, Mr. Allister Cummings had just put superglue into his precious girlfriend's eyes—instead of her eye drops. It really was an emergency but, oh, never mind. I raced back to the galley for wet compact cloths to put over her eyes—anything to stop the screaming. "Precious," I implored, "You need to hold still. If not, it could cause further complications. Let's get you to the hospital immediately."

I looked up at Mr. Manning and Mr. Cummings, expecting they would escort her to the hospital. That was wishful thinking on my part. Already late for their meeting, the two seemed rather inconvenienced by the entire ordeal. The pilots proved no further help in assisting the eyes-closed-shut Precious. Of course, it was up to me.

Precious's intermittent moans narrated my first journey through Venice as the water ambulance whisked us off to the nearest Italian hospital. The city's vivid colors welcomed our approach, even in the oddest of circumstances. The wind drew color to my cheeks and a few splashes of cool water awakened my senses dulled from the flight. The city was breathtaking.

The Hotel Danieli glowed with pink-orange hues of paradise in the distance as we made our way to the Ospedale Civile di Venezia at Scuola Grande di San Marco in Campo Giovanni e Paolo. The building was enormous, and my romantic vision of Venice soon evaporated in a sea of white scrubs. Ever since the ambulance boat pilot had indicated the whereabouts of the Hotel Danieli, I had wanted to make a run for it. Precious must have sensed my eagerness to run as she grabbed my hand and begged me not to leave her. She knew my name after all. "Anna, please don't leave me here alone. I can't do this without you!"

I, Anna St. James, was stuck in Venice, in an *ospetale* with a woman named Precious, mistress to one of the richest men in the world!

Bedside to Precious, I transcended my surroundings by remembering how I found myself on this journey with Mr. Stuart Manning. I had always known I wanted to be a flight attendant. Wasn't it the stuff all little girls dream of? It certainly was for me. Anyway, I wasn't into figure skating. Aviation had won my heart completely. I was born Anna Lauren St. James, with "aviation flowing through my veins," as my father would say.

At the ripe old age of three months, I had boarded my first aircraft. Our family moved frequently, but it was at Andrews Air Force Base in Maryland where the passion really stuck.

My earliest memories of takeoffs and landings happened right there in our backyard. On special days, my dad would leave work early to pick up my older sister Jesse and me in our family SUV. With two girls in tow, he would drive to the end of the runway, quickly park, so we could jump out, throw a blanket on the ground laying flat on our backs to watch the airplanes come and go. laying flat on our backs to watch the airplanes come and go. If we were really lucky, Colonel St. James would spring for a few bottles of A&W Root Beer, or maybe an Orange Crush, to enjoy with our Lay's potato chips and Good & Plenty. It was the best show on earth.

How I loved lying on that blanket, hearing the engines whirl, smelling jet fuel in the air, and being the first to call out the plane overhead. It was more than a game to me. I could name just about anything in the air. Dressed in my Kids Gap play clothes, I romanticized all the destinations those planes were going to and dreamed how maybe, just maybe, I would go too.

No airfield fails to stir this childhood memory. The smell of jet fuel is like going home for me; its nostalgic, heady perfume overwhelms my senses. Yes, this was a world I most certainly was born into.

Elementary spring breaks and vacations were greatly anticipated adventures with my family. My favorite recollection was passing the beautiful "flight attendants" in Ronald Reagan International Airport, complete in uniform pulling their Travelpro crew bags. They looked just like the Barbie doll that I had scrimped and saved to purchase. Dressed in my very best, with French braids to neatly capture my hair, I readied myself to board what I thought was the most luxurious airplane in the world.

At the gate, my childlike fascination continued as I ran up to the windows and plastered my face against the glass. Mouth open, I stared at the sleek, silver airplanes stamped with the red and blue American Airlines logos until an "O" print formed on the window.

On board, sometimes Jesse and I were invited up to the cockpit for a tour. I would sit there, pretending to fly the airplane and channeling every ounce of good-girl restraint not to touch the buttons. Yes, Jesse had the desire too, but she was shy in comparison and better at concealing her emotions. Not me! I could barely contain my thirst for adventure.

Returning to our seats in a daze, I knew that I, too, would fly around the world someday. I just knew it. There was more glamour and culture on an airplane than any place I'd ever been. This was my Hollywood, the little auburn-haired girl's definition of adventure.

Once we were in flight, I waited for the exact moment the fasten seatbelt sign was turned off. Grabbing Jesse's hand, we would make a mad dash for the flight attendants with our little kids backpacks in hand. There we filled our bags with all the goodies they could possibly give us. Surely these items would get us one step closer to becoming part of the exclusive club of American Airline flight attendants! My hands were full, and my heart was nearly bursting wearing my new plastic wings proudly. If only I could have known that this was just the beginning.

Our family moved to the Canal Zone, Panama, with Colonel St. James, continuing to fuel our experiences of travel. Arriving in the tropics at Howard Air Force Base in the dead of night, our welcome was complete with a tropical storm aboard the C-124 cargo airplane carrying us. Despite bucket seats made out of canvas, a curtain for a bathroom door, boxed lunches for food, G.I.s who needed showers, one engine out, crazy turbulence, and one horrible ear infection, I still couldn't have been happier!

Once I was stateside again, I had only to finish up high school before my dream of flying the world would begin. I was practically counting the days. The Colonel, however, had other ideas about my education. He thought the Air Force Academy was a perfect fit. I won this battle, being far too social for the academy, and I became a UCLA Bruin. An undergraduate education was a means to an end in my quest to travel the world. Falling in love was another thing.

Yes, my first week at the university, I met Cade Williams. He was dressed in tennis clothes, just off the courts and carrying the most enormous bag I had ever seen. So enormous, the bag knocked me clean over!

He put his hand out to pull me up, and I looked into the most vivid blue eyes I had ever seen. On that first encounter, he won me over. Or, as he later said, "I was checking you out, trying to turn around for a better look when I flattened you with my bag. You did fall hard for me!"

We stayed up talking that first night until morning, not wanting our time to end. Cade was the number one player on the men's tennis team with a coveted UCLA scholarship. When he wasn't playing tennis, he was with me. We were inseparable, falling into a steady rhythm in our four years at UCLA. Our plan was to graduate in four years so Cade could go on the ATP tennis tour while I worked for the airlines. My job would provide us with travel passes until we got married in three years. We had it all mapped out.

Cade played tennis year round, even in Normandy where he'd spent every summer of his life. I was his biggest cheerleader at every match. Born and raised in Southern California, he looked more like a surfer than anything. He made me laugh hysterically, and his silly humor won me over. He had a big heart and loved kids, working for Athletes in Action and serving the Westwood community. The kids adored him.

Cade's mother was from Normandy, France, and he always talked about their beach home with a passion. On my first trip with him, we pulled up in the dark to an illuminated thirteenth-century chateau, complete with a tennis court and a *chapelle*. What I loved most there was the beach with a view of the Channel Islands. That first trip sealed our summers together.

After we graduated, things went as planned. I was hired immediately as a flight attendant with American Airlines, based in San Francisco. Jesse and her husband, Turner, lived in Tiburon on a sailboat and let me crash with them in between trips. It was a fun way to be together, even in close quarters. My supervisor, Melanie, quickly became one of my best friends in my first three years on the job. I loved my job, and I loved Mel, who was not only kind but also a voice of reason.

I was elated when news broke that Cade had earned a spot in the top tier of his sport—ranking among the one hundred best tennis players in the world! The timing was perfect for us to celebrate over his few days' visit to San Francisco. He was finally making money on the tour, and I couldn't have been more proud. Melanie thought he would pop the question soon. I couldn't resist daydreaming about it on my way to the airport.

My ringing phone interrupted my dreamlike state. "Cade, I am almost there—"

"This is Dr. Phillips from the UCLA Medical Center. I saw your number as next of kin. Mr. Cade Williams has just been admitted into our hospital after suffering a horrific car accident. A semi-truck hit his car."

All my worst nightmares came alive in a moment. I felt like life was spiraling out of control. I hung up and immediately called Melanie. "Mel, this is Anna. Cade's been in a car accident. I need to get to LA now, before he goes in for surgery. I'm requesting a leave of absence. Can you please help?"

All she said was, "Go!"

The doctors didn't know if he would survive the night, and I was a mess trying to get to him. Five minutes after speaking with Mel, she called back, just as I was pulling into the airport parking lot. "Anna, my boyfriend Brian is in San Francisco right now, getting ready to leave in a few minutes for Van Nuys. Can you get over to Signature Flight Support?"

"I think so."

"Hurry, Anna. He flies for a man named Stuart Manning, and he said if you hurry they can give you a lift."

"Mel, are you sure it's okay? I don't know how to thank you."

"Just get to Cade and be by his side. I'll take care of things here."

"Seriously, Mel, thank you, thank you again and again!"

How I ever made it to Signature that day is a mystery to me. Brian was waiting there to escort me to the airplane. I think I said "hi" and "thank you" as he introduced me to the passenger on board, but I really don't remember. My mind was already at Cade's bedside. I just sat there in a trance, knowing Cade needed me.

On the ground in Van Nuys, a car was waiting to take me to the UCLA Medical Center. I breathed out an apology in disbelief, "What? Thank you Brian."

"Don't thank me. Mr. Manning took care of everything."

Inside the car, I sat alongside Mr. Manning. He looked over at me with sadness in his eyes. "Anna, I wish we could have met under better circumstances, but please know we are all here for you if you need anything. A friend of Brian's is a friend of mine. Let's get you to the hospital."

I looked at him, with a tear trailing down my face. "I can't thank you enough for your thoughtfulness."

"Anna, we will be there in a few moments, and I have alerted the staff that you are en route."

Mr. Manning was true to his word. The hospital staff met me at the car. Still in shock, I gave him a hug and was off to find Cade. He was in surgery when I arrived, and the doctors gave me a better prognosis than the original update. Still, I pleaded with the Mighty Physician throughout the night, asking for God to heal Cade.

In the waiting room that evening, Brian brought me dinner at Mel's request. He sat with me in support for a few hours. I knew I always liked him. Just as Brian was leaving, Mr. Manning appeared, with coffee in hand, to sit with me into the early morning hours. He reached over and held my hand. "Anna, Cade is going to be all right. Please let me know if you need anything, okay? Here's my number."

They kept Cade at the hospital for over three weeks. Meanwhile, Mr. Manning sent a basket filled with magazines and books to keep Cade occupied. One day, he stopped by Cade's room with an iPad full of downloaded movies, books and music to keep him entertained. Who was this man? I could observe him clearly this time. He was certainly handsome. His boyish, chestnut curls were a bit unruly, only adding to his charm. He was a visually striking man. I walked him into the hallway and stood on my tiptoes to give him a kiss on the cheek.

"I don't know how to thank you for your kindness to both Cade and me. I will be forever grateful for all you have done. Thank you, Mr. Manning."

"Anna, I'm just sorry you are going through this tough time. Please update me on Cade's progress, and remember to call if you need anything."

The day was fast approaching to leave the hospital, but Cade seemed distant. I couldn't put my finger on it. Instead, I chalked it up to knowing he had a long recovery ahead. I moved into Cade's parents' home in Pasadena to help in any way I could. He always thanked me for being there, but he was different, almost agitated, with me.

One afternoon, I got a call that changed my life forever. Brian asked if we could meet soon to talk about my job with American Airlines. Brian had to cancel our first and second meetings due to conflicts with his flight schedule, but by the third date chosen, we actually met. About an hour into the meeting, Brian stopped mid-sentence and said, "Mr. Manning's new G550 is arriving this Thursday. Anna, what I really want to know is, will you join us as his personal flight attendant? Before you say anything, the position is based in Van Nuys where we have our hangar. Mr. Manning has specifically requested you for our team."

Without much thought, I said yes.

Chapter Two

UNEXPECTED BEGINNINGS

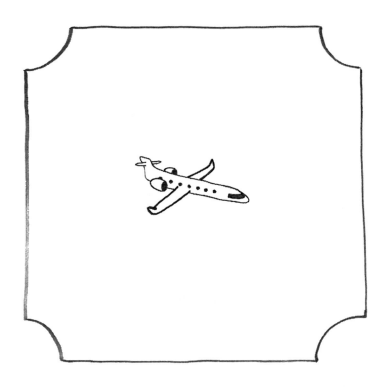

One's destination is never a place, but a new way of seeing things.
—Henry Miller

*I*n two days, my career would begin in the billion-dollar club of corporate aviation. No one could prepare me for the diversity of skills I would acquire as a corporate flight attendant, including, but not limited to, the role of bartender extraordinaire, relationship and life coach, gourmet chef, security expert, cleaning woman (yes, scrubbing toilets), interior designer, movie and music critic, geography expert, travel agent, dog handler, immigration specialist, mechanic, audio visual expert, broker, doctor, stepmother, fashion consultant, stylist, firefighter, and translator of many languages of the globe. Certainly, Brian never breathed a word of these prerequisites to me!

The signing bonus alone was more money than I made in a year at American Airlines, and the salary far exceeded the earnings of any commercial flight attendant. I worked to hide my astonishment behind a layer of calm, with a deep breath in and out and a prayer that this new job would work. Everything was happening quickly.

That evening, I googled my employer. Mr. Stuart Manning was a self-made multibillionaire by the age of twenty-three. While at Stanford, founding a successful dot-com business made him his first billions. He loved fast cars, rock and roll, yachts, motorcycles, airplanes, sports, women, and anything surrounding the world of Hollywood—not necessarily in that order. He acquired another company when he turned thirty-three, which grew into the biggest movie production company of all time. He was briefly married to the actress Morgan Sloan and the rumors had swirled of her infidelity. He owned a mega yacht and had estates all over the world, but his favorite was the estate in Cap Ferrat, France. At age thirty-seven, it seemed that anything Stuart touched turned to gold. His magnetic personality and unimaginable wealth flowed from a brilliant mind. Without question, he was among the world's most sought-after bachelors.

Mr. Manning's previous mode of travel was by Learjet, but this new aircraft promised to be on the leading edge in corporate aviation. He was excited for our maiden voyage. His Gulfstream G550 had a tail number: N23SM. The N represented a United States registry. Twenty-three was Stuart's age when he first became a multibillionaire. SM were his initials. In all, it was a personalized earmark, indicating the aircraft spared no comfort or ease the young billionaire could dream up.

Cade sat down with me while I researched. I felt a still distance settle between us that was foreign and uncomfortable. I reached over and took his hand in mine, "Cade, are you all right with my new job? I have been researching like crazy, and these jobs are quite rare, almost like a mysterious secret society."

"Anna, of course I'm happy for you. Who wouldn't jump at this amazing opportunity?"

He tried to reassure me with his words, but those vivid blue eyes told me otherwise.

I woke up early the next morning to leave a note on Cade's door. It read, "I will see you later this afternoon. How about I take you to dinner? I love you."

I had been up the night before, trying on different outfits to avoid a stereotypical flight attendant look. Yes, I was nervous. I finally settled on some black pants (my signature color) and a black, cashmere V-neck sweater that my mom had given me. Thank you, Mom! I wore my promise necklace from Cade, a gold bangle bracelet, and my diamond earrings that my grandparents had presented me upon graduation from UCLA. After a few tries, I pulled my hair up into a high ponytail for a polished, understated, and professional look. I hoped I had pulled it off.

At the hangar gate, I tried my best to look calm—just another everyday occurrence for me. Inside, I was a churning ball of nerves. I felt as if my knees would buckle at any given moment. I will never forget that morning.

My mind was a complete blur. Brian informed me that the airplane was making its inaugural arrival straight from the Gulfstream Service Center in Savannah later that afternoon. Our job was to get the airplane 'up and ready' for our trip on Tuesday to Phuket, Thailand.

My phone buzzed with an email from Linda, Mr. Manning's administrative assistant, before I could stop the car. It read like a laundry list of everything needed on board the airplane. Then my phone rang seconds later, "Oh, Anna, there you are." Linda continued, almost out of breath, "Welcome to the team. I am sending Mr. Manning's food preferences over in just a bit. You do have a passport, right? Did you get a company credit card? Can you line up hotels for the crew? You might have some extra passengers. Call if you need me and thank you."

What had I said yes to? A lovely water fountain display trickled just beyond the gate as I pressed my 'top secret code' into the box and entered this new world of privilege. I hoped I looked the part. At least I had myself convinced as I entered the main doors into the sanctity of the aviation department.

I couldn't untie the stomach knots. My head was doing a complete 360-degree spin. Surrounded by a bay of windows, I noticed a slight shake on the glass from the constant hum of aircrafts taking off and landing. This was a dream. The artwork was spectacular, the sofas looked inviting, and did I mention the airplanes? The sight of them calmed me immediately. Talk about heaven. "Hello, you must be Anna St. James. Hello?"

The pretty receptionist was trying to get my attention. "Oh, yes, hello. Yes, let me sign in."

I kept telling myself to stay calm, but it wasn't working. She greeted me with a gentle smile: "Hi, I'm Monique. It's nice to meet you. Brian is expecting you."

Monique leaned in and whispered, "Oh, by the way, in the future when you come through the gate, please make sure you pull in all the way; then stop while you wait for the gate to close. We have security cameras all over the parking areas, but for extra security measures, we always make sure to watch the gate close behind us."

Great. Cameras had already caught my nervous, first-day slip-ups! Had I stared at myself in the car mirror? Had I adjusted my clothes when I stepped out of my car? Did everyone see me do this? My adrenaline started to kick in again. Why was I so nervous?

Within moments, Brian came out to greet me, accompanied by a beautiful young woman. He gave me a warm hug and delivered the introduction. "Anna, this is Elle Patton. She's here today to help you get acquainted with the world of corporate aviation.

"Elle flies for Paramount Studios and knows this business. How about I catch up with you after Elle gives you the lay of the land?"

"Thanks, Brian, and it's really nice to meet you, Elle."

Brian added, "My office is just down the hallway. Feel free to poke your head in with any questions. Welcome onboard and, Anna, thank you. We are excited to have you on our team."

I was a fish out of water. As soon as Brian was out of earshot, Elle grabbed my elbow and said, "Is it true?"

I had no idea what she was talking about. My blank stare gave that much away.

"Anna, every flight attendant I know would kill to have this job. Mr. Manning is as rich and handsome as it gets. Do you know how lucky you are?"

She continued at great length explaining what she had heard. "What did you do, sleep with him? He requested you by name as his lead flight attendant. That's the only thing that makes sense."

I stifled my laughter and assured her that I hadn't secured the job by jumping in bed with Mr. Manning. The way I met Mr. Manning wasn't the juicy piece of gossip she was hoping for, but it was the truth. Was this a challenge to prove myself already?

She brushed it off as she led me to the kitchen for a cup of coffee before we got started. "No big deal. I have bigger things to do than be chained down to one man and his crazy schedule."

What had I stepped into?

Elle's flight background was with United Airlines. A brief affair with a Paramount Studios executive landed her an A-list job in the world of corporate flight attendants. She loved her job, the airplanes, and travel, but it was the luxuries of wealth that glittered in her eyes. Her need to find a rich man made me distance myself a bit, but she was kind to me that first day. When she placed her coffee cup down, signaling our chat had come to an end, she spoke the words I'd been waiting to hear all morning: "Let's go visit the hangar."

Most corporate airplanes have a private hangar, or the company leases space to house the aircraft. Refueling, flight department offices, maintenance and storage is necessary for any flight department. Mr. Manning owned the entire hangar just for his airplane. A handprint identification scan was the only way to access any of the buildings on the premises. Brian had given Elle a special card, granting us access until he could get my security clearance.

Now came the "hints" from Elle that proved to be crucial. "Anna, corporate aviation is a very small community. It's best to keep clear of all the drama that goes on in what everyone refers to around here as 'The Turbine Turns.'"

Check!

Elle opened the door to the hangar as I let out a loud gasp. Two airplanes were poised like snow-white fawns on a still lake. Each reflected a level of perfection I have seen in few other pieces of machinery, and there were two!

Seeing them up close was nirvana. Next, we entered a kitchen that rivaled Martha Stewart's. Commercial dishwashers were by the sinks, one for china and one for everyday dishes. Plus, there were more utensils and food supplies at our disposal than I had ever seen.

Inside the kitchen door was another passenger lounge, with places to sleep, more offices, and best of all, Nancy, the on-site catering chef. The enticing smells from her kitchen made me salivate. She was making a fresh pesto when we walked in, which we eagerly sampled on crostini; we also snatched some warm cookies that were cooling on a tray. This was nothing like American Airlines.

Brian came around the corner to announce that the new airplane was on final approach. We all hurried out through the hangar door to see the pure beauty of the G550 touch down. Everything about N23SM was breathtaking. The body of the airplane was polished white, with a black strip running down the side. Even the leading edge was shined to perfection. At a complete stop, the engines cut, and up the stairs we flew, overrun by our excitement. I had no words to describe what I was feeling—this was pure magic.

I looked at Elle to assure myself I wasn't the only wide-eyed one in the building. Her expression matched mine. "Amazing," was all she could reply.

I obviously felt the same. "It sure is. It's even better than I thought."

We touched everything on that plane. The soft, pale grey leather seats were more comfortable than anything in my home. The windows were large and round, lining the cabin without a smudge. You could see everything from those windows. No more half-drawn window shade views from the commercial airliners. Everything was different now.

TV monitors lined the cabin, with individual hidden monitors. This airplane could seat fifteen passengers, but Brian said that he generally carried one to two passengers on board. It was total luxury, equipped with satellite capability and full office equipment.

Elle grabbed my arm excitedly. "Anna, this airplane is the best. I'm so jealous that you get to work for Mr. Manning."

"But, Elle, you fly on a Boeing 767 and a Global Express with your passengers. I should be the one who's jealous."

"No, Anna, this airplane is the best there is. Look, even the wireless Internet is set up, and there's satellite TV. I love it!"

The cockpit was a pilot's dream come true, placed in front of a smaller galley with a crew lounge and lavatory, followed by the forward passenger cabin. All the seats made into beds and turned 360 degrees.

The next cabin had a credenza made of rich, Brazilian mahogany wood for storage. Linda told me to always have fresh flowers and snacks at this table. All the cabin monitors were downloaded with magazines, movies and newspapers Mr. Manning liked.

We had two dining tables in the cabin and then the galley, the site of which evoked another audible gasp from me. It was incredible. A wine cellar, sink, counter workspace and refrigerator; cabinets for china, utensils, and silverware; cutting boards and more counter-space, along with ovens, a microwave, and espresso machine. A full bar, stocked with crystal straight from Tiffany & Co. made me want to never leave this world.

In back we had closets, a pantry for all the extra supplies, pull-out drawers ready for bedding, and a beautiful, spacious lavatory. No more airline products here. These shelves were for La Mer and L'Occitane. I was instructed to fill the medicine cabinet with shavers, overnight kits (just in case), and any other imaginable request for a flight around the world. Linda had also asked me to purchase new French linens. My to-do list was growing lengthy. Whatever one might want, it would be on board.

Linda called again after emailing me the list of preferences for Mr. Manning to confirm the details. It was a long list.

Elle finally said goodnight after gushing over every detail of the airplane with me. "Okay, Anna, it's time for you to spread your wings. You are officially on your own."

"Elle, I can't thank you enough."

"Yes, you can. When you need backup, call me."

"You got it!"

I got back to Cade's home that evening, exhausted and in such a head spin I'd nearly forgotten about the dinner offer I'd extended earlier. He was ready for dinner at Shutters in Santa Monica, where our friend Scott was the new executive chef. It was nice to be together, even though I was tired. Cade seemed like his old self.

In the next few days, I was off to the races, frantically purchasing French linens for the lavatory and napkins, placemats, pillows, and throw blankets. I headed to Tiffany & Co. to get flatware; then I purchased assorted beverages and liquor to accompany Mr. Manning's *Sonoma SMS* wine. Condiments, amenities for the lavatory and cabin, flower arrangements, and the latest movie releases from the production studio needing to be downloaded to the entertainment system. You name it; for our first trip aboard N23SM, we had just about anything and everything needed.

My credit cards were maxed to the limit from all the purchases, and my head was swimming with details needed for the trip—not to mention learning the layout of the airplane and safety equipment.

Last, and best of all, Linda called to say I had an appointment with a stylist at Neiman Marcus in Beverly Hills. Mr. Manning wanted to foot the bill for my new wardrobe. His driver picked me up for the appointment, and a stylist was waiting for me at the front doors. She had a room arranged with champagne and appetizers while I tried on my new wardrobe. Yes, I could get used to this treatment in a hurry. Was this really happening? I had a new Dolce and Gabbana suit and a Max Mara suit with pants, plus skirts, blouses, and a few dresses, with sweaters to coordinate. There were also coats, scarves, and shoes to top it off. I had never owned anything like this. I felt a little like Andrea Sachs in *The Devil Wears Prada*. But this was happening to me. I had little time to spend with Cade over the weekend, and sleepless nights ensued in anticipation for my very first flight on N23SM.

Chapter Three

MY FIRST FLIGHT
ON A PRIVATE JET

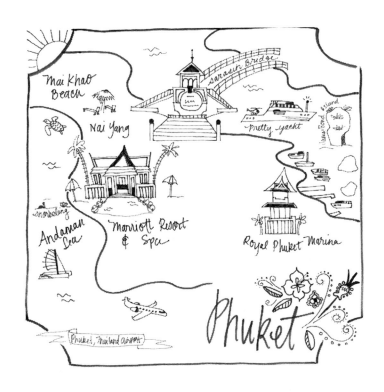

Once a year, go someplace you've never been before.
—Dalai Lama

he day had arrived for my first corporate trip to Phuket, Thailand. I drove to the hangar as rare, stormy clouds settled over the Pacific Ocean. Swells were moving in and breaking hard over those brave enough to surf in these conditions. I could not help but compare this scene to my own life. Everything predictable had turned upside down unexpectedly, like the tumultuous ocean before me.

I had left my dream job of nearly three years at American Airlines to accept this new position as a personal flight attendant to the second richest man in the world, all while nursing my boyfriend back from near death. What was I thinking? The day before our departure, I learned we would have additional guests on board. Linda had called to inform me that His Holiness the Yonten Drup and Garrett Skye would accompany us for this trip. If I wasn't nervous before, I most certainly was now.

For our inaugural flight aboard N23SM, Brian was the pilot in command (PIC) alongside a copilot filling in for Chris, our second full-time pilot who was at flight school learning the new airplane. The two of us had no idea what we were in for until Bob, our contract pilot, arrived. He was wearing a uniform complete with epaulets of four stripes, indicating his captain status. Brian was dressed in slacks with a white polo shirt—an understated move so as not to detract from Mr. Manning's celebrity while in public.

Our contract pilot quickly earned the name "Quirky Bob." From the moment he stepped onboard, I knew he would be a problem. He was flush with arrogance, short and stocky, with a face that looked like it seldom smiled

I couldn't understand the source of his pride. There was not one engaging thing about him. He was just plain odd. I instinctively knew to avoid him as much as I could. He, however, had other plans.

Bob walked out to the airplane while I was busy with last minute preparations for our passengers' arrival. He was five-foot-four inches of ego, and it showed. He puffed out his chest to approach me with a strange kind of greeting. "Hi, I'm Bob. I wanted to make sure you have everything I need before we leave. I always need at least two bottles of water at my seat in the cockpit. Make sure they are slightly chilled, but not too cold."

"Hi back, I'm Anna. I really have to get a few things done before our passengers arrive. Nice to meet you, Bob. Don't worry; I'll take care of you boys."

"Excuse me, Anna, I need to make sure you have everything ready for me. So, make sure the water is only slightly chilled, unscrew the cap, too. Also, I like to have one lemon and one lime wedge inside each bottle—not squeezed, though. Got that?"

"Bob, I really need to get moving here. I will make sure you have your water."

What an oddball! If that wasn't enough of a strange request, he added, "Anna, I can't stand my wedges squeezed inside my water. Got that? No squeezing."

He was dead serious. This was going to be one long trip. Just looking at Bob put me in a bad mood. I liked the feeling of my skin crawling better than I liked Bob. I'm so glad Brian was in charge. He was quickly becoming a good friend to me. Brian had just turned thirty-six-years-old and was the first pilot Stuart Manning ever hired. That was eight years ago, and a lot had changed since then.

Brian swore me to secrecy with his post-trip plan. When we arrived back from Phuket, he was heading straight up to San Francisco with a special proposal for Melanie. I knew I liked him. I could hardly wait to sit down with him and hear the details.

Linda called me again. "Anna, are you ready? Mr. Manning should be there in just a few minutes. Have a wonderful flight, and call if you need anything, okay?"

"Thanks, Linda. I think I have it all set to go. I'll call when we arrive in Phuket. Take care. Bye."

My phone rang again with Linda. "Anna, I almost forgot. Make sure you have all the customs forms on board. Go ahead and fill them out so all the passengers have to do is sign them. It's easy. Believe me, Anna, this is an easy trip. Just do a meal service about one hour out of Van Nuys. They will sleep after that. No problem."

That was easy for her to say. No problem, just His Holiness the Yonten Drup! No problem, just Garrett Skye. I was starting to work myself up. That dreaded phrase from Linda I soon learned was full of irony. She could have just said, "Buckle up, Anna; you are about to experience countless problems with heavy turbulence!"

Before the passengers arrived, I started getting anxious again, doubting myself. This trip was their initial impression of the beautiful new airplane and of me. Would they like the airplane? Did I have everything Mr. Manning had wanted onboard? Would they like me? How did I look? Was it too late to bail?

One could not compare corporate and commercial aviation. With commercial flights, I showed up, did a preflight, and rolled a cart down the aisle, but this was so different. Did I have all the supplies? Did I have all the food? Oh, come on, I only had three passengers on board. How hard could that be? Wait a minute, *was* there enough food for the pilots? Should I get another case of water for Quirky Bob? Lemons? Limes? Squeezed or not squeezed? Calm down, Anna!

Elle quickly popped her head in to see how I was doing and to give me a good luck hug. She looked me up and down with a seal of approval and a flicker of jealousy behind her smile. "Perfection! But, of course, you had Mr. Manning's money. There is no way either of us could afford clothes like that. You know he will want something in return."

What exactly was she insinuating? I must be imagining things. Choosing to ignore her last comment, I went on, "Thanks, yes, you're right. Mr. Manning arranged for me to go to a stylist for my work clothes. I've never worn anything like this before."

"Yes, and given with a price. Remember, Anna, I want your job and can step in anytime if you don't like it. See you when you get back. "

She left, but it felt like she was upset with me. My thoughts were interrupted by a call from Cade. "I'll miss you, babe. Good luck. See you in a few days."

Cade always ended our conversations with an "I love you," but that sign off was missing from this conversation. I was just getting ready to say it when our connection ended. Was I imagining something different, or was the abrupt ending a signal that distance was setting in? This was no time to stew over my relationship with Cade. It was time to be in work mode.

My nerves were working overtime. Did I seriously look the part? Should I quickly run to the bathroom before they arrived to make sure I looked all right?

I felt like I might burst when, in the distance, I saw the gate entry to the field open with our first guest.

Almost on cue, a Mercedes pulled up to the airplane, and out stepped a gentleman I had never met before. He had the darkest, jet-black hair I had ever seen, with a smile that made me aware I was already smiling. He came up the airstairs and introduced himself in a strong, Scottish brogue. "Hi, you must be the Anna I keep hearing so much about. I am Conor Reilly, and looking at your face makes me realize you have not heard you have an additional passenger on board today. I assure you, Brian knows me. This is just like Stuart."

"No worries, Mr. Reilly. Yes, I am Anna, and yes, you are right. Your name was not on the manifest. Please tell me you have your passport."

"Stuart just asked me to come to Phuket this morning. This seems to happen frequently, so I always carry my passports with me. I am in charge of all his financial endeavors, plus he is my best friend—or more like a brother."

"Well, Mr. Reilly, it is a pleasure to have you on board. Want a tour?"

I showed him around as he let out a loud whistle. He was a character right from the start. He gave me a Scottish and American passport, asking me to pick which one I wanted to use while the crew did the "smoke and mirrors" scramble dance to add him to the manifest.

"So, Mr. Reilly, what do you think of N23SM?"

"Anna, I love it, but I am a finance guy. Too rich for my blood. I have a Challenger 601. It's nothing like this, but it works for me. Can you please just call me Conor?"

He told me of his passion for racing and his upcoming trip to Le Mans, France. His race was in less than a year, and his wife Liz was the team manager.

"Anna, Liz will be in touch with you soon about flying Mr. Manning and his party over for the event. Sound good?"

"It sounds great. I'll look forward to hearing from Liz."

Mr. Conor Reilly was a financial genius, responsible for steering Stuart into buying his production studio. Oh, yes, I had read about him.

Conor kindly asked for a martini, settling comfortably into his leather seat as I went into bartender's mode. No one warned me about martinis. This was one of those moments when a list of prerequisite skills would have been useful for my job. That list never came.

My nerves had just settled as I placed the finishing touches on the martini when Mr. Manning's driver pulled up with Garrett Skye and His Holiness the Yonten Drup.

Never a dull moment! I introduced myself, briefing them on Mr. Manning's gorgeous new airplane. Garrett Skye was quite handsome in person, but not in the typical Hollywood way. He dressed casually, fingering his prayer beads. I could just picture him with the beautiful Cassandra Grey in one of my favorite romantic movies. This was not just anyone, but Garrett Skye, a major movie star! He was kind, but a bit aloof—or maybe it was just my fragile nerves that made me perceive him as such.

His Holiness exuded a calm spirit with his saffron-colored robe, a gold cloth above his chest, and a bare right arm. He caught me admiring his attire and turned toward me with a big smile, "Anna, what do you think of my clothing?"

"Oh, it's beautiful. The color and richness of the fabric are so unique."

"Well, let me explain why I wear the robe. See this? The saffron color signifies the earth; the gold here is to show the divine; and when I leave my right arm bare, like this, it means I am doing work."

It really was exquisite. What a presence—not to mention such a thoughtful and kind man. What an honor to be working with His Holiness the Yonten Drup and Garrett Skye on my first corporate trip. I would never forget those two, or for that matter, Conor.

Quirky Bob wiggled his way back in an attempt to be friendly with the passengers. His flattery of Garrett and His Holiness was quite embarrassing, especially considering he hardly gave Conor a second glance. He even asked to have his picture taken with them! I pulled him aside to inform him that a picture was out of the question. Okay, now I was just plain mad. He was obviously trying to make an impression of some sort, although I could not fathom what it was. I sent him back to the cockpit as he grabbed one of my arms, squeezing it while he looked over his shoulder and said, "Don't forget my water bottles, Anna."

He was squeezing my arm just like I'd squeeze that slice of lemon into his water if he didn't stay put.

The last passenger to arrive was Mr. Manning, himself. He was about fifteen minutes late, but in corporate aviation, the passengers are never late. The right time was always when Mr. Manning was ready. The schedule was just a rough timeline. He pulled up to the airplane in his customized, black Mercedes AMG convertible. Handing off his keys to the mechanic with a smile and a pat on the back, Mr. Manning came aboard.

It was like the most natural thing in the world. Before the trip, I knew Mr. Manning had first acquired his wealth when he was twenty-three years old. He purchased a small Learjet, and now he had joined the big leagues with his first Gulfstream. He was "typed" to fly the Learjet and had flown most of his trips with Brian. This was a whole new world of luxury for Stuart Manning. I couldn't believe I was a part of this world now.

Mr. Manning's eyes twinkled a greeting to his passengers. You could tell his guests liked him. Back in the galley, he extended a greeting to me. "Welcome to the team, Anna. I hope Cade is healing well."

Even among celebrities, he thought to ask about Cade, and it made me glow. His charismatic personality was irresistible, especially to women, as I was soon to find out. Like a good host, he asked his guests, "What is everyone having to drink?"

Mr. Manning requested a sweet Rob Roy. Having practiced this drink several times, I felt somewhat confident in my bartending skills—until Conor kindly asked me how I had made his martini. What could be so hard about making a martini?

"Conor, I made it with sweet vermouth and gin," I innocently told him.

He asked if I would mind making it again, but this time with dry vermouth. No problem! I put in one shot of dry vermouth and presented it again, sure of my second attempt. He clinked glasses with Mr. Manning and took a sip. Looking up at me he smiled and said, "This is the most unusual martini I have ever had. How did you make it Anna?"

I was starting to feel the panic rise. "I put one shot of dry vermouth in your drink."

He smiled and kindly said it was much better, but, "Anna, you might want to just put a splash of vermouth in it next time." A splash? Who knew? Back to the drawing board.

I could feel some movement of the airplane and knew I had a few minutes to secure the cabin before takeoff. The pilots would always wait for my signal: "All secure; four passengers, ready for takeoff."

Back to the galley, I grabbed my secret arsenal: *The Bartender's Guide to Making the Perfect Drink*. Deep panic engulfed me as I struggled to make the drink once again. Mr. Manning must have sensed the panic and took pity on me. He came back to the galley where he rolled up his sleeves to assist. I watched him intently: a dash of dry vermouth over ice, swirled around in the glass, and then poured out to add gin. Slightly embarrassed, I brought the drink up to Conor, and he took his first sip. He turned to me with a smile and said, "This is the best martini I've ever had."

Mr. Manning caught my eye with a quick wink. Next stop was the cockpit to let the guys know I was ready in back. Before I could get there, I heard the chime for takeoff and fell into the closest seat behind me in a very unladylike heap. We were off into the stormy skies over the Pacific Ocean, en route to our first stop, Honolulu. I struggled to fasten my seatbelt, feeling the weight of an entire workday in the first thirty minutes of our flight.

Once at cruising altitude, Mr. Manning requested a vodka martini, oh, and yes, a fuzzy navel for Conor. I was completely out of my element with a fuzzy navel, but he was only teasing. He caught me just before my return to the galley to say, "Anna, I am just kidding. Seriously, I'm giving you a hard time. You're doing great."

Contrary to things I had read about Mr. Stuart Manning, he was not the recluse or the impulsive wonderkid the media had painted. A little over ten years my senior, he was easy on the eyes and grounded, with a good sense of humor.

Once I had the cabin under control, I made it up to the flight deck to check on the pilots.

"Hey guys," I asked, "why did you take off without my final 'cabin secure'?" Bob ignored me, and Brian appeared confused. Once I told him what had happened, he apologized profusely. This was his first time with a flight attendant onboard. "Anna," Brian gently pleaded, "please be patient with us. Maybe together we can create a policy manual for our procedures."

We spoke the same language. In Phuket, we would map a course for in-flight briefings and procedures. He promised I would never again be caught on my feet during a takeoff.

Everything seemed to be under control after our initial launch. Next I needed to know how Mr. Manning preferred his service during flight. My first day proved he was one of the easiest men to work for. I truly liked him. On the list of his preferences, Linda wrote that he loved pizza. Nancy, the on-site chef back at the hangar was happy to oblige with his favorite pizza.

I had other options: a total vegetarian and sushi menu and a complete sandwich bar. Fruit, yes. Vegetables, yes. Dessert, yes! I was prepared for any inflight service request. For Stuart and Conor, the wine was flowing, and I kept the green tea coming for the Yonten Drup. His Holiness told me quietly that once in a while he would indulge in a glass of wine. Mr. Manning shared how he had fallen in love with Sonoma two years before this trip. Naturally, that led to his purchase of a winery there. I had a spectacular wine inventory on board to show for it. Everyone loved the wines from his SMS vineyard.

At his request, they had a light dinner, and before I knew it, they were all set up for bed. Mr. Manning complimented the French linens I had chosen. An hour later, we landed in Honolulu for the first of many times in the capable hands of Air Service Hawaii. The Hawaiians have mastered the art of hospitality. They are the best in the world. These FBOs could make or break any trip, and we compensated this service generously.

We finished refueling on the ground in Oahu before departing for Phuket. All my passengers were still soundly asleep. Now it was time to reorganize my galley and keep the pilots awake and fed.

While the passengers slept, I fed the pilots. Yes, Quirky Bob, too. Before we landed, I arranged a beautiful breakfast buffet to greet them. I also distributed the overnight kits from L'Occitane for men, filled with everything needed for a refresh, before we landed in Phuket. I placed a cold, scented mango hand cloth at each seat, along with a bottle of water and some freshly squeezed orange juice. Bob, of course, appeared just as I was perfecting my setup. He wanted one of the overnight kits. I had one left, but he was not going to get it. I told him that I had only enough kits for our passengers. The extra kit was really for Brian, who was thrilled to receive it.

About twenty minutes from landing, I quietly opened the window shades, turned on soft music with dim lights, and slowly nudged each passenger awake. Eye rubbing and stretching, each noticed how the cabin had transformed to welcome them. Mr. Manning's big smile had "thank you" all over it.

Banking ever so gently on our final approach into Phuket, we marveled at the emerald waters below. Within minutes we were on the ground being greeted by Larry, Mr. Manning's helicopter pilot for his yacht. He was all set to transport him out to the floating marvel.

We said our goodbyes, with a special thank you from His Holiness the Yonten Drup. Garrett Skye brushed my cheek with an elegant kiss of gratitude. These were intimate circles I was running in, and those I served appreciated the delicate barrier of trust I upheld between their lives and mine. He said, "I know our paths will cross soon. Thanks for everything, Anna. That was a great flight."

Everyone was in good spirits. I turned around to start cleaning up the cabin when Mr. Manning reappeared and said, "Anna, would you and Brian like to join us out on the yacht tomorrow?"

I was trying to decline politely when he questioned me with eyebrows raised: "You don't want to come out and spend the day on the yacht?"

I would not make a man of his stature ask twice. "Yes, of course, we would love to come."

"Good, I'll have Larry pick you up . . . say, around nine in the morning? It will be a lot of fun."

"Sounds like it. Thank you for inviting us."

Me, on a yacht? I couldn't imagine it.

I put the finishing touches on the airplane—closing all window shades for protection from the sun, leaving our food, bed linens, and trash with the handler. A quick walk through the cabin ensured all was in order to leave the handlers with a few hundred-dollar bills. These bills were our tickets into luxury wherever we landed. It had been a long day. I had the passports and paperwork in my hands as I went down the steps to our awaiting vehicle and my first day in Phuket. I had just survived my very first corporate trip. A nice nap would work wonders.

The JW Marriott Phuket Resort and Spa had a view of the Andaman Sea and beyond. The sea was crystal clear, and the beach was gorgeous. The air was humid with just a slight breeze, but it felt wondrous. I could get used to this in a hurry. At the hotel, Quirky Bob approached the front desk to announce that he was a captain on a private jet and a valued member of their platinum club. He insisted they put him in a suite! The outlandish requests continued, and Brian and I did our best to separate ourselves from him. They gave Bob his keys, and we waved him goodbye.

I finally found my room. A one-bedroom suite, seaside, and yes, with my own pool! I wondered if Quirky Bob had a room like this. I kicked off my shoes to relieve my now-throbbing feet. Next, the clothes came off and on went my bathing suit. It was time for a quick swim before my nap. As soon as I put my foot in the pool, my phone rang. It was our handler back at the airport, inquiring about my catering plans for our flight home in four days. I had completely forgotten. Yes, of course, I wanted to line up catering. I soon realized my swim would have to wait. I sat in my room for the next hour, planning the menu in my bathing suit.

While I was at it, I might as well call Air Service Hawaii to order fresh pizza for the final leg home. I was getting the hang of this. I hung up the phone with catering to relax finally. It had been over twenty-four hours since my head had hit the pillow.

I was anxious to tell Cade about the trip, but there was no answer when I called. What time was it back home? Never mind, I thought; I was in Phuket, and we could talk later. Today, I would relax and enjoy my lunch with a good book if my eyes could stay open. Wait. Was that the phone again? I lifted the receiver, and before I could speak I heard, "Ms. St. James?"

"Yes?" I answered impatiently.

"Well then, you have an appointment at our Mandara Spa in two hours for a facial and massage. Please enjoy with the compliments of Mr. Manning."

You have got to be kidding! But I didn't say that. I said, "Of course, thank you."

The pool, spa treatments, and dinner with Brian under the warm evening stars made me feel entirely rejuvenated. This place was heaven, and my dinner companion was quickly becoming like a brother to me.

Brian escorted me to my room afterwards. "Anna, remember Larry from the helicopter?"

I nodded affirmatively. "He called to confirm he will meet us at the hotel helipad first thing in the morning. Are you ready for a day out on the yacht?"

I just shook my head in disbelief. "Brian, who does these kind of things?"

He chuckled, shrugging his shoulders in agreement.

Back in my luxurious room for the evening, I tried again to call Cade. He answered this time. I could not wait to tell him about the flight and my plans for the next day.

"Cade, can you believe it? I am going by helicopter to spend the day on Stuart Manning's yacht!"

"That sounds like a lot of fun. While you are out yachting, think of me doing my rehab." He said it sarcastically, but I knew he meant it.

He continued, "Anna, it looks like things are coming along faster than they originally planned with my rehab. I should be able to start playing tennis within two weeks."

I was shocked at his rapid recovery, but thrilled to hear such great news.

"Seriously? That's fantastic, Cade!"

I asked if we could spend some time together when I got home.

"That would be nice."

It felt strange to be in this exotic world without Cade by my side. "I love you and can hardly wait to see you in a few days."

"I love you too, Anna."

That had sounded much more like my Cade.

Exhausted, I fell asleep to the gentle breeze of Mai Khao Beach caressing my skin; it drew me in like a lullaby—only to be abruptly awakened by a rude voice I recognized.

Out of bed with a start and pulling on my robe, I raced to the door to find Quirky Bob, wallowing on the hallway floor, drunk as a skunk and naked! That ruined my evening.

Brian had also responded to the sound, covering his eyes with an audible, "Put something on. That is disgusting!"

The hotel staff came running toward the spectacle. Doors flew open to satiate the curiosity of guests. The hotel staff covered Bob in a robe, much to our relief, and escorted him back to his room. All was quiet again, but not for long.

Quirky Bob made a breakaway from his room for a last-minute performance, still naked, and this time singing at the top of his lungs. Things with Bob just seemed to worsen. The staff was growing impatient with his belligerence. He just wouldn't stay put! I quit opening my door after the third and fourth time and learned that the staff had quite enough of him. They packed his bag and sent him to another hotel where, I am sure, he did not have a suite awaiting him. Brian got on the phone before we left the next morning to arrange for good old Bob to catch the first commercial flight home. Chris was sent directly from flight school to cover the inconvenience. Mr. Manning told Brian of his suspicions concerning Quirky Bob, even sharing his passengers' distaste for him. Lucky for me, it was the last time I ever saw Quirky Bob.

Chapter Four

IN PHUKET, ON A YACHT

That's not flying; that's just falling with style.
—**Woody**, *Toy Story*

*B*rian met me in the lobby, nerves and all. I could hardly decide what to bring on board. After a quick trip to the hotel boutique for a beach bag, I settled on my Trina Turk bathing suit, Chanel sunglasses, swimsuit cover-up, sunscreen, a book, my iPhone, and did I miss anything? Brian also had no idea what to expect either, so that made two of us. We were in it together—an entire day out at sea. What would I have done without Brian in those early days? He was a trusted companion and lifetime friend.

Looking back on that day in Phuket, I realize just how special it was. Larry was ready at the helipad to guide us by helicopter over the crystal waters of the Andaman Sea. Brian was animated, narrating how lovely the scenery was through our headsets. We were off for a spectacular day, over seas that shimmered like a mirror to the sun. I needed someone to wake me from this dream.

Through our headsets, Larry announced, "There she is! That's Mr. Manning's new, 260-foot yacht. Isn't she a beauty? He called her the *Sonoma SMS*. Clever, don't you think?" Larry expertly put the helicopter down on the stern of the yacht for our day on the sea to begin.

The yacht was moored in the harbor, just outside the Royal Phuket Marina. It was enormous! Larry said this marina was the center of the eastern seaboard of Phuket, on the doorstep of Phang Nga Bay. Sheer limestone formations could be seen vertically standing in the waters below. He pointed out James Bond Island with its signature rocky pinnacle. Right, Larry, sounds good. I needed to brush up on my geography!

It was a haven where luxury yachts floated in pristine waters and set anchor near gorgeous shores. On the deck of the *Sonoma SMS*, Mr. Manning appeared with Conor to welcome us. "You made it! Welcome aboard! Breakfast is being served out on the forward bow if you would care to join us."

Was this a normal day for the likes of Stuart Manning? "After breakfast, we will set sail to Laem Sai Beach. It is close to the airport and is said to have incredible snorkeling. Have you gone diving before?"

We both said yes, and Mr. Manning continued excitedly, "From there, we'll head to Nai Yang, hopefully finishing our day near Mai Khao Beach. It's near the entrance to the Sarasin Bridge."

He pulled out a map to show us the route. "You can see your hotel from there. Would anyone like to go anywhere else?" I shook my head, still reeling from the notion that I was on a yacht in Southeast Asia. I'd nearly forgotten to thank him for the lovely spa treatments.

His big smile said everything. "Thank you for all your hard work on the flight over. You did a fantastic job. Thank you."

I never forgot how much his thoughtful words meant to me.

The yacht was equipped with every kind of water toy, diving apparatus, and even a diving instructor. Brian and I exchanged silent grins for the unbelievable opportunity we had that day. We snorkeled; we Jet Skied; we relaxed; and we ate to our hearts' delight. Our host was gracious, and his company was nicely chosen. Conor was quick to deliver a joke, with his thick Scottish accent and a flash of blue eyes. These men shared a close friendship, a bond of brotherhood. Their loyalty ran deep in a world where it was hard to trust. They appeared as normal men to me that day, surrounded—yet somehow detached from—their inconceivable wealth.

As dusk set in, we boarded the helicopter with the purest kind of exhaustion. No words could convey our full hearts. The sunset bled into tropical colors as we moved into the night.

Our remaining days in Phuket were tranquil. I enjoyed my plunge pool and lounge area without a hint of disturbance. Sampling savory new foods and the country's rich cuisine was the highlight of every evening. There, I found sushi that I swore I could live on. My appreciation for this lifestyle was only growing. I sincerely hoped I could keep up with it!

I called Cade one night to share my excitement about the elaborate foods I'd discovered, and I noticed it again—the silence. He felt distant. I asked if everything was okay, knowing better than to believe his response. He answered me in the same way each day.

"Yes, I just miss you. That's all. Looking forward to seeing you in a few days. Bye, Anna."

Once again, no "I love you" was spoken. That was not like him at all.

Chris arrived straight from flight school being typed to fly Mr. Manning's new airplane. An immediate bond began as the three of us dined at the Andaman Grill that evening. They had steaks, which I learned was a staple among pilots. I have never met a pilot who doesn't love a good steak. Both Chris and Brian ate their fill at Andaman before our departure.

At our nightcap spot, "Out of the Blue," we sipped cocktails waterside. The lounge was nothing short of extravagant, and the entertainment almost made me forget we were headed for Honolulu the next day. Those were troubled waters I navigated between my elation for travel and my longing for home. Van Nuys was waiting. Stuart and Conor were the only passengers on board, and the best gift of all was the absence of Quirky Bob. Now I knew it with total certainty: I loved my job.

Chapter Five

GETTING TO KNOW THE REAL MAN

I travel a lot; I hate having my life disrupted by routine.
—Caskie Stinnett

T he trip home seemed extremely long. It didn't matter. I was arriving in Van Nuys soon to see Cade. I was exhausted, but felt accomplished after the inaugural flight.

Approach, final touch down, and goodbyes: this was a rhythm I could grow to love. Mr. Manning and Conor Reilly departed graciously, with many thank yous. I cleaned up, emptied the leftover catering for the mechanics to take home, washed the dishes, and finally, I was done. Glamorous! I was never so happy as when I pulled away from the hangar that evening to head home.

My phone rang just as I was pulling out from the main gate. Thinking it was Cade, I answered, "Hey, Babe, on my way!"

Instead, it was Mr. Manning. We needed to leave immediately for Teterboro. His grandfather was going in for open-heart surgery early the next morning, and I could tell by his voice that it was urgent.

"Anna, don't worry about food. Just get ready to leave in about thirty minutes. I'm on my way back to the hangar."

I never did say yes. I just turned around and went back into work mode. Where was Teterboro anyway? I breathed a sigh of relief when I entered the on-site kitchen to find Nancy, the magician, already in prep mode for our trip. Nancy had also been on her way home when she heard about our trip, and she turned around immediately to whip something up. What would I have done without her? I was relieved to find Brian and Chris, also at the ready.

Brian handed me the trip sheet with his usual composure. Our flight time would be a little over four hours and thirty minutes, with great weather conditions. I looked up and saw Mr. Manning's car at the gate. It was then I realized I had not called Cade yet! I had only seconds to dial his number frantically before Mr. Manning walked up the stairs—but all I got was Cade's voicemail. Where was he? Obviously, not at home waiting for me! I left him a message, relaying the details of Mr. Manning's family emergency. We were heading to a place called Teterboro, somewhere on the East Coast. I would call when I got in. "Cade, I'm sorry about all this. Hopefully, I'll be home in a few days. Know I love you and miss you."

Thirty minutes after Mr. Manning's impromptu phone call we departed from Van Nuys to Teterboro, New Jersey. Brian told me it was the perfect airport when coming in to New York City. Stuart's grandparents lived in Montauk out in the Hamptons, and a helicopter would await us at Teterboro to get him there quickly. During the flight, Mr. Manning seemed distracted. He was on the phone for almost the entire flight. Quietly, so as not to disturb him, I placed ice water at his place and appetizers on the credenza, along with his signature sweet Rob Roy.

When we had been in flight a little over an hour, Stuart called me over and said we needed to make a quick stop in New Haven, Connecticut, to pick up his mom and sister. "Anna, can you let the guys know we need to make a stop before going to Teterboro?"

He went on to say, "I'm sorry to make your day so long. My grandfather has always been very special to me. He practically raised me after my own father was killed in a horrible car accident when I was nine years old. All my memories of growing up include him. I hope you understand. I need to be there for him."

Understand? Wasn't this the man who flew me on his personal airplane to see Cade in the hospital? I assured him that a family emergency was no inconvenience to me. My concern was for his grandfather.

We touched down in New Haven, Connecticut. Waiting anxiously for Stuart was his darling mom, Betty, and sister, Megan. Betty Manning was one of the sweetest, most genuine women I had ever met. She was endearing, from the first big hug she gave me. She was proud of her son and loved him fiercely. His sister, Megan, resembled Stuart, but seemed shy and a little overwhelmed on his new airplane. Stuart was visibly relieved to have his mother and sister on board. After takeoff for Teterboro, I asked for their drink requests. Betty Manning responded with a wink, "Oh, yes, dear, could I bother you for a touch of Bailey's on the rocks?"

Megan asked for a glass of white wine, and Mr. Manning said, "Could I please have a B-52?"

Bailey's I could handle and white wine from *Sonoma SMS*, but a B-52? What happened to his well-practiced sweet Rob Roy? I walked up to Mr. Manning, as if his request was the most natural thing in the world. "Mr. Manning, I know you have a special way you would like your drink. How would you like me to prepare it today?"

He looked up with a hint of a smile and said, "Surprise me, Anna!"

So, the smooth, stealth-like approach wasn't working. I had absolutely no idea how to make a B-52. I admitted defeat, which got Mr. Manning up from his seat to come to my rescue in the galley. It really was quite simple. Layer Bailey's, Kahlua, and Gran Marnier over the back of a spoon, and voila, you have a beautiful, layered drink: a B-52.

Returning to his seat with drink in hand, he turned on his heels to say, "Nice try, Anna. Your 'How do you like your drink?' request was quite clever." His smile was devastatingly handsome and followed by a wink.

I realized something important about flying into and out of Teterboro that day. With the air traffic from White Plains, JFK, La Guardia, Teterboro, and Long Island airports sharing a single airspace, approach for landings and climbing for takeoffs felt more like going up or down stairs. The pilots must wait for clearance to either climb up or climb down. When reaching the altitude cleared by Air Traffic Control, the plane levels off at a different air speed to wait for the next clearance. Depending on the pilot, it can feel a bit like being on a roller coaster, making some passengers very nervous.

On our first flight into Teterboro, Betty Manning was nervous, finishing her Bailey's on the rocks in record time. Earlier, I had given Betty's drink a generous pour, filling it two-thirds full with Bailey's.

While flying at different altitudes, we could see the sky littered with airplanes doing the same thing. My training as an American Airlines flight attendant reminded me of the rule in aviation for no unnecessary talk under ten thousand feet, during takeoff, landing, or taxi and when the fasten seatbelt signs are illuminated. That rule was hard to adhere to when leveled off at three thousand feet and going in circles, with all eyes onboard glued to me. Since our first landing in Teterboro with the Manning's, I have learned to brief the passengers or to give a gentle reminder that we are preparing to tackle the stairs.

On the ground at last, with the helicopter waiting to bring the Mannings to Montauk, Betty stood up and walked to the back of the airplane. I thought she was using the lavatory, yet I noticed how the door wasn't closed. I peeked discreetly to find her attempting to leave the airplane through the cargo hold door! She would have escaped if I had not stopped her in progress. I'm afraid that the stiff drink had made Betty Manning a bit disoriented. We did get her down the main stairs safely and into the waiting helicopter. I was getting a chuckle from all the excitement when up the steps came Stuart with a big hug. He whispered just before leaving, "Thank you again, Anna. I hope you can enjoy the city. I can't thank you enough. I'll be in touch tomorrow when I know more, but in the meantime, get Brian and Chris out and about in the city."

Twenty-four hours of travel from Phuket to Honolulu to Van Nuys and now to New Jersey had caught up to us. I could see our limo waiting outside as I performed the quickest cleanup in history. It felt good to slip into the back seat and promptly fall asleep on the drive into the city.

Rudely awakened to the sights and sounds of Manhattan outside the Marriott Marquis Hotel in the heart of the city, we discovered at check-in that a noisy city was the least of our problems. The major hurdle would be the jam-packed elevator to our rooms. *Where did all these people come from?* I had to ask myself. The United Nations summit meetings were in progress, meaning enhanced security and large crowds. A sea of people stood between me and my warm, cozy bed—and room service.

I opened my door, picked up the phone to order room service, kicked off my shoes in the process, and stripped off my clothes for a quick shower. I slipped on some cozy workout clothes, realizing I was packed for Phuket, not New York City. No matter; I could shop tomorrow. In my exhaustion, I had forgotten to call Cade again. He answered on the first ring saying, "Where are you?"

I tried my best to reassure him that we would be home in three to four days.

"Cade, Mr. Manning called as I was leaving the airport, and I thought it was you. I think I even answered with 'Hi, Babe.' How embarrassing! All I could think about was how kind he had been when you had your accident."

"I get it, Anna. I was just really looking forward to seeing you finally." He said this with a slight edge in this voice.

He wasn't pleased, but there was nothing I could do. This was my job, and I would be home in a few days. It wasn't like this was the normal schedule, though I would soon realize this job was far from normal. I tried a little room service, but fell asleep after a couple bites and slept until ten the following morning. Refreshed and ready to tackle NYC in my workout clothes, I was off to Central Park for a run. I couldn't help but think, *I'm getting paid to be here.* I felt a little guilty about being away from Cade, but this was the job I had signed up for. The only difference from the commercial airlines was that my new boss was one of the richest young multi-billionaires in the world—and quite handsome.

Just as I was leaving the park, my phone rang. Thinking it was Cade, I answered, "Hey, Babe, I'm awake now!"

Mr. Manning cleared his throat and, with some humor in his voice, said, "Anna, we have got to quit having these conversations."

"Oh, my goodness! I am so sorry. I thought it was Cade again. Mr. Manning, how is your grandfather?"

"I just wanted to give you a quick update. Grandfather is recovering from his surgery, and it looks like we will be here a few more days. My plan is to stay until the end of the week to get him settled in back home with mom and Megan. Can you let Brian and Chris know?"

"Yes, I will let them know right away. Sorry again for how I answered. Let me know if there is anything I can do to help." I hung up, with my face a deep shade of crimson.

I got back to the hotel to plan my catering for the flight home. In NYC, I discovered Rudy's, the premiere catering company in corporate aviation at the time. Rudy's was a pioneer in the industry. They held my hand through my first, seven-course menu that was out of this world. The most important person I worked with at Rudy's was Sherif. We spoke many times, at all hours of the day, to coordinate the menu.

Catering done, check! Next, I called the pilots with the latest update from Mr. Manning. Brian had been busy making reservations for the three of us at the Neil Simon Theatre over on West 52nd to see Lou Diamond Phillips in *The King and I*. Now that work was done, I really needed to do some shopping! As I was preparing to leave, I got a call from the front desk. "Ms. St. James?"

"Yes?" I quickly answered.

"We have something here for you at the front desk. Can we have it delivered to your room?"

I wondered if Cade had sent flowers or something special, and before I could say yes, there was a knock on my door. As if by some magic, box after box from Saks Fifth Avenue poured into my room.

"Are you sure this is for me?" I asked, dying to know the details.

"Oh, yes, Ms. St. James, this is for you."

Once the door shut, I devoured the note attached to the biggest box. Of course, it was Mr. Manning.

The note read;

Dear Anna,

Thank you for jumping into the fire on this first trip. I really appreciate all you are doing. My mom said you would probably need clothes after Phuket. If you would like to exchange anything, call Giselle at Saks Fifth Avenue, and she will take care of you. Her card is attached. See you in a few days.

Stuart

Holy smokes! This was incredible. Box after box revealed some of the most beautiful items I had ever seen. I felt like a princess until I remembered what Elle had said. Surely Mr. Manning was just being thoughtful; that's all it could possibly be. On closer inspection, the boxes had everything I needed for a wardrobe: shoes, accessories, formal and casual clothes, and two purses. It was like being in a dream. How did he know what to pick out and my sizes? I counted over twenty boxes the front desk had delivered. There was one special item I had left to try on. It was a dress that fit like a glove, with a matching jacket and shoes. Yes! Then I saw the price tag: $1,800! That could feed a couple of villages. I could not accept this, though it was beautiful and certainly a perfect dress for the theatre. The dress won out.

I never left my room that day because I was too busy trying on all my new clothes. I sent an email to Mr. Manning, thanking him for his generosity and adding a disclaimer that I could not possibly accept his gifts.

He answered, "Anna, my mom insists you enjoy the gifts. She really wanted you to have them." Well then, if Betty insists!

I met the boys in the lobby, looking a bit more chic than usual. Their "Wow" in unison made me smile. They complimented the dress, as good gentlemen do, and we were on our way! *The King and I* was a beautiful show in an intimate theatre. We enjoyed a late dinner at Carmine's on West 44th, which was overflowing with the after-theatre crowd and rich Italian cuisine. Almost giddy, I looked over at Brian.

"Are all our trips like this?" I asked in disbelief. "If so, I'm on board." He smiled with no response but gave me a wink. I had landed my dream job—it was unthinkable, but it was true, and I never wanted to let go. All my dreams were coming true!

At our table, we schemed to create a masterful marriage proposal to help Brian sweep Melanie off her feet upon his return home. Once back, he would fly his Piper J-3 Cub up to San Jose. A limousine would bring Melanie out to the airplane so Brian could fly them both to Half Moon Bay for dinner at the Ritz Carlton. After dinner, he wanted to take her down a lantern-lit path to the beach and an awaiting violinist who would cue Brian's proposal. Champagne and music would follow, with two delightful nights at the Ritz Carlton. I loved our plan. Brian loved it even more. I was thrilled for both of them.

Our last day in NYC was jam-packed with tourist fun, starting with a classic double decker bus tour of the city. The city was vivacious, and we embraced it with our coming and going, running off to taste some new food, handle a brightly-colored handbag, or just to take in the open air from the top deck. We continued this mad dash on and off the bus all afternoon, loving every minute exploring NYC. At our late afternoon stop in Soho, we found art galleries, more shopping, and the Mercer Kitchen, which quickly became a favorite. Brian and Chris were dream companions on a day off like this one. I had tried to reach Cade for the last two days, with no answer until after dinner that night. We talked into the early morning hours, and it helped put my mind at ease. "Cade," I said, "I have got to get some sleep. I'll see you tomorrow afternoon, okay? I love you!"

He agreed, with a parting, "I love you too."

In the morning, John Celetano, the owner of Rudy's, was at the airport to meet me in person with the catering. Mr. Manning arrived two hours later for our flight back home. I was now missing Cade more than ever. Mr. Manning was relieved his grandfather was on the mend, and his renewed appetite showed it. I placed a thank you note at his seat, but no words were adequate to thank him for his thoughtfulness. The crew was in good spirits as we broke through the overcast skies above New York, headed for Van Nuys.

Stuart devoured the meal from Rudy's, prefaced by a sweet Rob Roy and an assortment of mouth-watering antipasto appetizers. He ate everything I served. After the salad was a light penne pasta marinara topped with fresh basil and shaved Italian Parmesan cheese. Each course was paired with one of his *Sonoma SMS* wines. I had a feeling I might have some leftovers that evening to share with Cade. I served Chris and Brian's meals on silver trays, which I polished myself! I cleared and cleaned the dishes before each course.

Sherif had advised me to cleanse their palettes before the main course. Naturally, I used beautiful ramekin-styled bowls I had found in the city to serve a lemon sorbet drizzled with crème de mint liqueur and a fresh mint sprig. Each bowl was licked dry when I went to clean up. Even the mint sprigs were gone!

Brian wanted more. "That was amazing, Anna. Do you have any more of that sorbet? Please?" He was practically licking his chops. Back to the galley I went for another scoop: lemon sorbet, crème de mint. STOP! Oh, my goodness! I had just served my pilots liquor while they were flying the airplane. I was mortified. Mr. Manning witnessed my usually controlled demeanor turn quickly into one of embarrassment. He sprung out of his seat to see what was up. He laughed heartily when I told him the story. I didn't see the humor in it. I had just served alcohol to pilots in flight! To make the story even more absurd, they jokingly insisted that I had pressured them into it. I could take a joke, as it was safe to say I wouldn't be reported to the FAA as the liquor-toting flight attendant!

The main entree after the crème de mint fiasco was the most delectable veal francaise. It was so tender, it literally melted in your mouth. The parade of delicacies concluded with a bounty of the most decadent desserts I had ever seen. The trays were filled with miniature delights: tiramisu, fruit tarts, five flavors of crème brulee, and chocolate-covered strawberries. Best of all was the mousse au chocolate—pure heaven. Mr. Manning agreed that it was his best meal yet.

About an hour before we landed, Brian came back to stretch his legs and say a quick hello. On his way back to the galley, he asked Stuart if he would like another sweet Rob Roy. Brian bartended while I washed dishes. He poured scotch, sweet vermouth, a dash of bitters, and a lime twist. On his way back up to the cockpit he placed the drink at Mr. Manning's seat.

Stuart said, "Thanks, Brian. Usually, a sweet Rob Roy has a lemon twist instead of a lime. I guess from now on we will have to call it a 'sweet Brian D.'" We all chuckled.

Close to landing time, Stuart asked if I had any suggestions for a restaurant near the ocean for him to try that evening.

"Funny you should ask. Cade and I were just talking about our friend Scott who is the new executive chef at the Shutters Hotel in Santa Monica. He had a good review in the local magazine, and he is an incredible chef."

Stuart picked up the phone and called the restaurant from the airplane to make a reservation. They were booked for the evening, so I got on the phone with Scott. I told him I was calling from the airplane with Mr. Manning and needed a special reservation for two. "At eight? Perfect," I said. Dinner was arranged.

Mr. Manning inquired about my connection to Scott. I shared how we had met my first year at UCLA; we'd been friends ever since. Scott trained at Spago before leaving for the Shutters Hotel. Now he even had his own radio show.

We landed in Van Nuys that afternoon and there, with a bouquet of roses, was my beautiful Cade. He was very handsome with his bleached-blonde hair and big smile. He was fairly mobile now from his injuries, but still hobbled out to greet me. I was ecstatic to see him. It had been a long, yet wonderful two weeks. He shook Mr. Manning's hand, thanking him again for his overwhelming generosity shown throughout his recovery process. He asked, "How is your grandfather doing? I was so sorry to hear he had to have surgery."

They continued their conversation for the next ten minutes while I went to work with the cleanup. I was practically floating through the airplane elated to spend time with the one I loved. His recovery was nothing but a miracle. I heard Mr. Manning mention Cade's tennis career and his nearing the top-ten most elite players in the world just before his accident. An instant smile came to my face. Cade deflected the comment modestly.

All three men did a live retelling for Cade of how I had boozed up the pilots while in flight. They had yet another good laugh, while I simply shook my head. Mr. Manning, in his usual, courteous manner, came over to thank me for the trip with a big hug. Meanwhile, Brian treated Cade to a quick tour of the airplane and the hangar. Cade was blown away. He was impressed with the operation. I was impressed with him.

Cade had a mutual friend drive him out to the airport that day. He still didn't have clearance to drive. Before we left the hangar, we said goodbye to "the boys" (Brian and Chris) and wished Brian well in his proposal. At the car, Cade saw all the boxes I had pushed on a cart along with my suitcase. "Anna, what are all those boxes for?" I told him about my hotel delivery, and he shook his head and smiled.

There was leftover catering and some, *Sonoma SMS* wine to take along with a blanket for sunset watching on the beach in Malibu. A few, faint stars began to show through the fabric of the sky, and it felt like heaven to be back home in Cade's arms. I took his hand and asked how he had arranged the homecoming surprise inside the hangar. "Anna, I have my ways," he said coyly. Linda at Mr. Manning's office helped him pull off the feat. She was always up for a challenge.

Before we left Malibu that evening, my phone rang. It was Scott calling from The Living Room at Shutters. He was in a hurry but had a quick question.

"Anna, Mr. Manning is in the restaurant bar right now with the actress Vanessa Rathman. He just ordered a drink called a sweet Brian D. No one has ever heard of it. Help! What is a sweet Brian D?"

He was totally stumped, and I sympathized with him, as much as I enjoyed Stuart's humor.

I suppressed enough laughter to reply, "Of course I know what a sweet Brian D is. Don't you?"

I told him that our bartending pilot's name was Brian D. and explained how he had made Stuart a sweet Rob Roy with his signature twist of lime.

"Scott, you should pull his leg," I added. "Serve him a true sweet Rob Roy, and then give him the sweet Brian D. at the same time. Don't let him know that we talked and watch his face."

Cade just rolled his eyes with a laugh. Yes, welcome to my new world.

The following day the doorbell rang at Cade's parents' home. The UPS man was standing there with a box for me. Inside was a beautiful pearl necklace with a gold cross and a Mother Mary charm next to the cross. It was delicate and very special. Stuart's sister had worn a similar necklace, and I had commented how beautiful it was.

Inside the box there was a note:

Dear Anna,

We are so thankful for you and the way you care for our Stuart. Thank you for making the trip out after just arriving home from Phuket. I hope that every time you wear this necklace you will know how much we appreciate you and how special you are.

Love,
Betty

I finished reading the note in tears. This family had cared for me like one of their own. Betty was exceptionally gracious from our first encounter, and I treasured her special gift.

Chapter Six

IT'S NOT HOW IT LOOKS; WHO DOES HE THINK HE'S FOOLING?

Not until we are lost do we begin to understand ourselves.
—Henry David Thoreau

Cade's entire recovery was miraculous. That, we never questioned. I knew he had to work on his physical therapy, but I wanted to spend more time together. Brian was to call me later that day to go over our schedules for any possible upcoming trips. Cade was hoping by the end of the week to get out on the court and see what it felt like to hit again. We both hoped for his limbs to show resilience after such trauma.

Elle called to say hello. "Anna, I heard the trip went great. Or should I say, trips?" she said with a chuckle. "What do you think of corporate aviation so far?"

Love was a strong word, but it was the one I chose to describe it. She was leaving for a week to Europe, but I told her I would touch base when she got home.

She left me with, "Let's do dinner when I get home. I am dying to know, Anna, did he want something in return?"

I was stunned by her boldness. She continued with, "I hope you are ready for Mr. Manning's flight schedule. Eventually, he will want more. Mark my words!"

I was quick to defend him. "Elle, that's not at all how he is. I appreciate your help, but Mr. Manning is a gentleman. I hope you have a great trip." She just laughed.

I remembered how I was brought into the Manning's inner circle on their recent trip to Teterboro. I remembered the sincerity of the hug Betty gave me. I should have sensed a storm brewing after speaking to Elle, but all I could see were blue skies. I knew I loved my job. Period. Brian called me early in the afternoon.

"Hi, Brian. Well? Are you heading up today for the proposal?"

"Hey, Anna, do you have time to go over our schedules?"

He had just spoken to Linda. Mr. Manning needed to pick up a passenger in Paris then leave immediately for meetings in Venice. It would be a quick over and back trip. We would be home for one full day before leaving for Geneva on another quick trip. "No problem," I replied, as Linda always said. Just two quick trips back to back—which was actually starting to translate into many problems with Cade.

Linda had mentioned that we might have a stop in San Francisco on our way home, but it was still tentative and probably wouldn't happen. Brian said that after this trip we would be home for about a week before our weeklong trip to Paris for the French Open. Other than that, the schedule looked light!

"Anna, I have to wait until we get back for the proposal. I wanted to go up tomorrow and stay for a few days, but with a European trip on the schedule, it will have to wait."

I felt bad because he had been excited to go and be with Mel.

Linda sent both upcoming trip itineraries over, with the list of passengers for each leg. These were business trips: fast and furious. The first trip was to pick up Stuart's business associate, Allister Cummings, in Paris, for a quick hop down to Venice. We would only be on the ground for twenty-four hours before we would come home with just Mr. Manning on board. Venice was nothing but a tease, as I spent my entire trip in the *ospetale* dealing with Mr. Cummings's mistress, Precious. Maybe someday my dream of seeing Venice would come true.

Mr. Manning gave each of us an envelope when he left the airplane in Van Nuys after the Venice trip. It was a thank you note for going above and beyond. His appreciation was a check to each of us for twenty-five thousand dollars! Holy smokes. I was already being paid more money than I could imagine, but twenty-five thousand dollars as a thank you?

The next trip was exhaustingly scheduled to leave for Geneva the next day. I said a quick hello to Cade and left. He wasn't happy, but I was jetlagged and needed to get ready. I was reeling from the twenty-five thousand dollar gift I had received. Time to snap into work mode.

All too soon, my Geneva passengers were arriving. What a group! Eddie Klein was from Colorado Springs and full of himself. Mark Spencer was fresh off his honeymoon and new to the Manning Corporation, thinking he was the most amazing man alive. I'm glad one of my favorites, Conor Reilly, was on board. He introduced me to a nice older gentleman named John McCord, who had been employed many years by him. Now we just needed Mr. Manning.

My coveted day off was more like a brief pause between two weeks of grueling travel. Nancy had jumped through culinary hoops to cater this flight. My boys were up front and ready to rock and roll. I was starting to think of Brian and

Chris as the dream team. Flight time was estimated at a little over nine hours, and Mr. Manning requested dinner before sleep. He needed to hit the ground running once in Geneva.

Next stop: Switzerland. I even made it to the cockpit this time to say, "Cabin secure, five passengers." The flight went well, but both Eddie and Mark were a handful. Mark, for one, just couldn't stop talking. No one doubted that his wife was the most beautiful woman ever or that they were head-over-heels in love. His in-laws had just lavished the happy couple with a dream honeymoon at the Jade Mountain Resort in St. Lucia. He drew the entire night's conversation into the orbit of this one topic. It was obvious that Mr. Manning and Conor had tuned him out. I wasn't so lucky. Working for Stuart was the "cherry on top" of his perfect life—or so Mark said. One could only hope he was ready to dig in and get to work.

Stuart, Conor, and John joined Eddie and Mark for dinner before retiring to their sleeping quarters in preparation for their all-day meetings the following day. Not so with Eddie and Mark. They requested drinks throughout the night. A few minutes after Eddie's return from the lavatory, I noticed water seeping out from underneath the door. The sink was overflowing because somebody had left the water on. It took me thirty minutes to clean up the sopping wet carpet. I found Eddie to ask kindly if I could give him a lesson on how to use the lavatory sink.

The lesson went like this, "Eddie, did you not notice that you left the faucet on in the lavatory? Please, in the future, understand that the sink is activated by where you place your feet on the floor. You must turn it on and off with each use. Just stepping in and seeing water start to flow does not mean it will automatically turn off by itself. I am sure when Mr. Manning wakes up he will not be happy about this—not to mention that most of our water supply onboard has been used up."

He ignored me and asked, "Anna, do you have anything more to eat? By the way, do you have plans once we get in to Geneva? You know, you and me?"

I was furious. As if I would take a second look at him! Throughout the rest of the flight, he continued to ask me to go out with him and even cornered me in the galley.

"Anna, we will be staying at the same place in Geneva. I know you want to spend some time with me."

Who was he fooling? By this time, he had consumed way too much vodka, but worst of all, he was just so full of himself. I had cut him off with the alcohol earlier in the flight, but little did I know he had taken a bottle of vodka from the galley while I was checking on the pilots up front. Yes, he drank the entire bottle!

I went straight to the cockpit to inform Brian what was going on. He immediately came back to the cabin for a little chat with Eddie. When he returned, Brian said, "Anna, if he bothers you one more time, I am going to do bodily harm to that jerk. You should not have to deal with this on our airplane. I will talk to Mr. Manning on the ground."

That didn't stop Eddie. Brian came back to intervene once more, hauled him up to the flight deck, and told him to sit down and not move for the rest of the flight. He was strapped into the jump seat up front, with two angry babysitters, and I was relieved.

About twenty minutes from touchdown into Geneva, I woke up Stuart, Conor, and John with a nice buffet breakfast. Eddie and Mark had been eating and drinking the entire flight, so I didn't bother to offer them anything. I think Eddie was still confined to the flight deck anyway. I placed their overnight kits at their seats, and Mr. Manning headed for the lavatory to shave, brush his teeth, comb his hair, put on his suit, and—viola! He opened the door and looked like a new man. He did ask me, "Anna, what are all the towels doing on the floor, and why don't we have water in the sink?"

I told him that Eddie had forgotten to turn off the faucet, leaving the water overflowing from the sink and using up all the water we had on board. Eddie, I informed him, was now sitting in the jump seat up front with Brian and Chris.

At the Genève Aéroport, the driver for Eddie and Mark was waiting. The helicopter on standby would take Mr. Manning, Conor, and John straight to their meetings. I noticed Brian and Mr. Manning in deep conversation by the main cabin door as I started the cleanup. As if on cue, the driver that had departed with both Eddie and Mark turned around on the tarmac and headed back to the airplane. As soon as the car pulled up, I saw Mr. Manning ask for Eddie to step out. They briefly exchanged words, and Eddie was escorted to the main terminal with his bags in hand. He was fired and homeward bound. Mr. Manning came back up the stairs of the airplane, looking upset.

"Anna, I'm sorry about all this. I had no idea, and I promise you, I will never let that happen to you again. Are you all right? Please join Brian, Chris, and I tonight at the Chateau for dinner. I hope you will accept my apologies. You are like family, and I will not tolerate people who mistreat you."

Brian apologized again, though I have to admit we shared a laugh. In Phuket, it was Quirky Bob, and now it was Eager Eddie. We were one down, and Mark was skating on thin ice as far as I was concerned.

The crew left the airport for our accommodations at the Château de Divonne. We brought Mr. Manning's luggage with us to ensure he was checked in, in anticipation for his arrival later that afternoon. The Château de Divonne is outside of Geneva in the French Alps, near a town called Divonne-les-Bains. I fell in love with the understated luxury of the Chateau while on this trip. We pulled up to the elegant nineteenth century Chateau, and I never wanted to leave. We had reserved the Chateau for our group—all thirty rooms.

A snow-blanketed lake was like a frozen gem on this fifty-four acre, endless landscape. The estate was framed with a breathtaking panoramic view of the Swiss Alps in winter. It was spring, but the weather was uncommonly cold for this time of year. I loved seeing the rare beauty of a Chateau that had kept many secrets over the years. If only the walls could talk. We were just a short ride by helicopter to the *aé*roport, which made things convenient for Mr. Manning.

Upon check-in, I asked the front desk to have Mr. Manning's luggage sent to the Prestide Suite. I wanted to confirm they had his welcome basket and a chilled bottle of champagne ready for his arrival. The staff gave me a puzzled look and said, "Ms. St. James, we are so sorry, but we have already checked him in about an hour ago. He said that room was reserved especially for him."

I was a bit jetlagged, but alert enough to know that something was not right. "Who is the gentleman you have checked into the Prestide Suite, please?"

"Oh, Ms. St. James, we are not to give out names. We are always discreet."

I could see the staff needed a reminder of whose room we were talking about, so I helped them remember. "Mr. Stuart Manning has personally reserved this entire Chateau. So, my dear (glancing at his nametag) Pierre, please make sure to remove whomever is in that room at once! Have it cleaned again, and make sure Mr. Manning's luggage is delivered and the amenities I have requested are in place. Please put another set of clean sheets on the bed and provide clean towels, as well."

I was getting the hang of this and learning that there were times to stay in control of the situation and be direct. He immediately said, "Oh, yes, Ms. St. James. We will remove Mr. Mark—" I didn't hear a word he said after that. Mr. Mark was immediately relocated into one of their "classic" rooms, all behind the scenes, without Mr. Manning's knowledge. The smoke and mirrors game played out to perfection.

On the way to my room, I saw Mr. Mark in the hallway, waiting for a key to his new room. I opened my door to a lake view deluxe room. Heavenly, though certainly not a classic room like Mr. Mark's.

Brian and Chris could barely keep their eyes open at dinner that evening. We had not slept on the way over at all. I had allowed myself a quick, one-hour nap, followed by a massage. I was tired, but in better shape than the boys.

Chef Eric worked his magic that evening and earned our culinary stamp of approval on everything that left his kitchen. The wine list was spectacular. Mr. Mark, however, was nowhere to be found. The six of us enjoyed our evening together. Mr. Manning once again pulled me aside to apologize about Eddie. He made me promise not to hesitate in telling him if anything happened again.

How could I ever be upset with a man who cared to fix my every discomfort? I couldn't be more thankful, and I let him know it. "I appreciate your thoughtfulness more than I can say, Mr. Manning."

He stepped forward, giving me a hug, and I was relieved when he changed the subject to a more pleasant topic: Cade.

"Is he all right with your new job?"

"I think so. There has been a lot going on in the last few months."

Mr. Manning restated how much he enjoyed having dinner at Shutters and added coyly, "You know, Anna, they make the best sweet Brian D. Hmm?"

He went on to say that he wanted Scott as his personal chef, and I wasn't surprised. He was the best, and that's what Mr. Manning had of everything. It was strange thinking about California in that moment. It seemed light-years away from the charming, European estate we were residing at. I can't say that I missed home yet, only the man waiting for me there.

By now, I'd mastered the tricks of the trade for getting good sleep. The perfect recipe for nodding off into dreamland was 1 milligram of orange, chewable melatonin, some lavender oil and a glass of wine. I woke up the next morning at eight thirty feeling brand new. I had sightseeing plans with Brian and Chris around ten, leaving just enough time to arrange for catering. I was in hot pursuit of Chef Eric. Mr. Manning, Conor, and John were having a quick rendezvous in the dining area before leaving for Geneva. Not wanting to disturb, I passed with a quick good morning. Conor turned and asked if I had seen Mark. No, in fact, I had not seen him since he had changed rooms.

They sent the bellman up to Mark's room to request his presence ASAP. No answer. Conor decided he would go and try knocking on his door. I could tell Mr. Manning was more than agitated. I had never seen him this way before. Conor came back in shock. He had knocked on Mark's door, but Mr. Mark did not answer. Instead, an attractive woman came to the door. Slightly puzzled and embarrassed, Conor started to apologize for disturbing her when another woman appeared in the background. She was wrapped in a towel and was in the arms of a very naked Mr. Mark.

Mark was using his expense account to its fullest. He flew home later that day on a commercial flight, jobless, returning to his one-month marriage and his beautiful wife. What an adventure so far! Two out of my five passengers were fired and homebound. Three trips with Mr. Manning and three employees had already been dismissed. I couldn't make it up if I tried!

What was left of the trip was a dream. We left the Chateau bright and early the next morning for our flight home, after seeing so much rugged, alpine beauty. Laden with some amazing delicacies from Chef Eric, we were off to the airport. I tried Cade a couple of times in anticipation for our reunion at the end of the day. For some reason, though, we kept missing each other.

John boarded the airplane along with Conor and Mr. Manning—except John looked grey, almost ashen in appearance. I asked him if he was feeling okay. Of course, he said he was fine, just a bit tired. I continued monitoring him during the flight. They all just wanted to watch movies and sleep.

Halfway into our flight, Stuart announced a change of plans. We were headed directly into San Francisco for a top-secret meeting with Allister Cummings. *Not that man again!* I thought. Once on the ground, Signature Flight Support would bring him out to the airplane to have a very hush-hush meeting with Stuart for no more than one hour. We were six hours into our flight home by this time, but in the spirit of Linda, I replied "Not a problem."

I was standing in the galley, preparing drinks, when I saw John approaching. His face was as grey as a ghost. He looked awful, and his skin was clammy to the touch.

"John, are you all right?" And with a "thunk" he collapsed into my arms. I leapt into medical-training mode barking out orders. Without a second to waste, I laid him on the floor, asking Stuart to grab the defibrillator while I felt for a pulse. I sent Conor up to alert Brian and Chris to call our medical service, Aircare Access. Within minutes, we had a doctor on the phone, monitoring the situation. That service was invaluable to us in the moment and available to us anywhere in the world. The doctor stayed on the phone for the entire flight into San Francisco.

John opened his eyes, denying there was a problem. "Anna, I'm fine. Just give me a few minutes." But I knew he wasn't.

We descended into the shadows of dark and gloomy skies. It seemed a premonition of what was ahead: John's trip to the hospital and the secret meeting about to take place. The paramedics were waiting on the ground to take over immediately. John had suffered a heart attack while on board. But what was more serious was that he had end-stage cancer. No one had any idea how grave the situation was. It was a night wracked with emotions and concern for John, a quiet and studious, yet kind and thoughtful man. I was so sorry this had happened to him. We were all pretty shook up.

Conor accompanied John to the hospital while Mr. Manning awaited his meeting with Allister Cummings. Mr. Cummings, as I knew from the quick Venice trip with Precious, had a reputation for being ruthless, placing an entirely new weight on an already stressful situation.

Mr. Manning came back to brief me on what to expect during their meeting. It was his intention to acquire one of the biggest media companies in the world—along with Allister Cummings and Greg Stiles. This multibillion-dollar deal, between three of the richest men in the world, was of obvious importance to Mr. Manning. I doubted otherwise he would waste any more time with Allister Cummings.

He gave me another fair warning, reminding me that Mr. Cummings could be unfeeling, while answering the question he could see forming in my mind: *Why do you continue to do business with him?* Mr. Manning explained that, unfortunately, Allister Cummings had all the right resources in place to pull the trigger on this transaction.

Mr. Manning looked distant, and I could tell he had more to say. "I'm sorry to ask this, Anna, but when we are meeting, please try to blend in. Remember what a challenge he was on the Venice trip. I know he likes green tea and biscotti. Maybe you could have that waiting at his place before he comes out?"

Then, almost pleading, he added, "Would you mind making me a mocha? Oh, and one more thing before I forget: if I make eye contact with you, that means I need something, but if there is no eye contact, all is well."

No problem; I had this covered.

Back to the galley I went to get set up while Mr. Manning reviewed last minute details with Linda over a video call. All was under control. Milk: check. Whipped cream: check. Espresso machine: ready to go! Once Mr. Manning had finished reading his notes, he went inside to escort Mr. Cummings onto the airplane. About one minute after Mr. Manning left the airplane, I had just finished making his mocha and was starting to boil water for the green tea when he popped his head back into the galley and asked, "Anna, on second thought, is there any way I could have an Irish coffee?"

Smiling, not waiting for an answer, off he went. Normally this would be easy, but not tonight. We had just arrived from Geneva after a long flight, and I had used up my liquid cream. I had poured the last of it into the canister with the CO_2 charger to make whipped cream for his mocha. I needed to figure out quickly how to salvage this situation. An Irish coffee needed liquid cream! I thought of a simple solution that might work.

Ever so gently, I released the top of the canister—just a tiny bit, trying to get some liquid from the cream. My idea made perfectly good sense to me. I had minutes to perform this magic trick. MacGyver, here I come! Brian came back to the galley to check in and see if there was anything I needed. At that exact moment, I ever so slightly turned the top of the canister, and viola, the entire thing blew up in my face—and covered every imaginable surface of the plane. Brian and I were both covered head-to-toe in whipped cream! The table, the seats, the entire galley area—not to mention the walls in the cabin—were covered. We looked like a Willy Wonka cream factory!

Brian ran back to the lavatory, leaving me in the galley to face the arrival of Mr. Manning and Mr. Cummings as they boarded the airplane for their top-secret meeting. I don't know how Mr. Manning didn't laugh at the sight. There I was, trying to greet them as if this was the most natural thing in the world, placing Mr. Cummings's green tea and biscotti at his seat. Mr. Manning looked at me, puzzled. *Yes*, I thought to myself, *I had a bit of an accident*. Mr. Cummings once again lived up to his eccentric reputation, never acknowledging the very plain fact that I was a human cloud of whipped cream.

All he said was, "I would prefer a skinny latte tonight."

Okay, make it happen, MacGyver! Some nerve that man had.

Back in the galley, I spun up a skinny latte and poured Mr. Manning a glass of his SMS wine. I was not taking any more chances with espresso drinks while they were meeting, and I tried my best to "blend in." I knew Mr. Manning would ask later where his Irish coffee was, but I thought best to leave it alone for now. *Sonoma SMS* was being served. No options. Brian popped out of the lavatory, squeaky clean. I gave him the stink eye as he passed me with a pat on the shoulder, and he was gone. Thanks a lot, Brian.

I tried my best to clean up and blend in, but just because I was keeping quiet did not mean I lacked ears. To this day, I will never forget how Mr. Cummings spoke about himself and other people. I felt nothing but disdain for his arrogance. By the time he was ready to leave, I would have given anything to have him drop-kicked down a flight of stairs. Unfortunately, it looked like we would be having a few more encounters with this egotistical nightmare.

Before they got down to business, Mr. Cummings wanted to play a round of the "bigger, better" game. "Did you say your yacht is about 260 feet, Stuart? Who's your yacht builder? You know that my latest yacht is well over 380 feet?"

Not waiting for an answer, he went on, "You know, it is the perfect size. My old one was only about 190 feet. Much too small. You know, Stuart, that I fly my own G550? I have the first serial number for the new G650 in production as we speak. Do you have your name on the list for the new Gulfstream? Yours is a GV right? Are you sure this is a G550? This seems more like the GV we use for our executives on their work flights."

I just stood there, dumbfounded at how anyone could sit at the same table with this man. He was so self-absorbed I could almost see planets orbiting around his giant ego. Was there no end to his accomplishments? Or was there anything he had owned that did not trump Stuart's tenfold? Did I mention I was still blending in?

Neither of the men ever said a word about the state of the interior of the airplane—or how I looked. They just went about their meeting as if gobs of whipped cream were not strewn about them. They reviewed some legal drafts, and I thought the meeting was over. Mr. Cummings had other thoughts. He wanted Mr. Manning to gain some of his hard-earned lessons for success. *Here we go*, I thought. I held by breath.

I knew that Mr. Cummings had made a big name for himself in the corporate arena (I think he was the fourth richest multibillionaire at the time of this first encounter). I had also heard he was feared by most people. He was quite proud of this reputation. As he was finally leaving, and might I say, not soon enough, he turned around to give Mr. Manning this unwarranted advice: "Hey, Stu, you've got to toughen up, man."

As if this was an invaluable and sought-after tip on life!

"If you have an employee park too close to your car, just fire his—!"

Mr. Cummings was really on a roll now. "If you have someone working for you and he walks past you and you don't like how he looks, fire his—!"

Who did he think he was? I was never so relieved to see someone leave as I was with that man. I could only wish we would never lay eyes on him again.

Once the meeting was over, Brian came back, looking as fresh as a daisy, to discuss what had happened with Conor and John. Brian had gone ahead and sent for the movie studio jet to fly up from Van Nuys with John's wife onboard while Stuart had his meeting. She was now en route to the hospital, and the jet could bring Conor home in a few hours. My heart ached for John and his family.

I could tell that John's prognosis had hit Mr. Manning hard. I went to his seat to check if he needed anything. He looked up sadly and said, "Anna, can you please just sit with me. Would you mind? I would really just like to talk."

He was quiet until takeoff. We were just leveling off when he turned around to look me straight in the eye. "Anna, I'm so sorry you had to hear that conversation with Allister. Did you notice a difference between the two of us?"

I dodged the question, as I wasn't comfortable with much of what I'd heard. Instead, I asked him, "Do you think you are different?"

He looked me full in the face, as if searching for something that he wasn't sure of. I saw sadness in those eyes. A lot had happened in this short time, but he did say with all sincerity, "The difference between us is simple. I have a heart, which that man plainly lacks. I really pity him. I do."

After hearing his simple statement, I was left with a profound impression. It will stay with me forever. No matter how much money you acquire or how much power you have, you must remember that every person deserves being treated with kindness. Mr. Manning never did acquire the multibillion-dollar company with Allister Cummings or Greg Stiles, but about three months later, he did it on his own. I was proud of him.

Best of all, after a quick and crazy couple of days in Geneva, with a stop in San Francisco, we were finally going home. I had been so caught up in the whipped cream fiasco that I had forgotten to call Cade once again to let him know we were running late.

I was deciding how best to tell him that I was leaving in three days for Europe, this time for a weeklong trip. So much for our three weeks at home! Our trip was to Munich first, then on to Paris for the French Open. I didn't think he would mind, but it had been a crazy month, and I felt uneasy having to tell him we were leaving so soon.

Chapter Seven

SMALL WORLD

There's more to life than being a passenger.
—**Amelia Earhart**

y arrival home was not how I had pictured it. Cade was angry. I had never seen him like this before. He said it seemed like my job was more important than he was. Why hadn't I called him to let him know we had diverted to San Francisco? What about the guy who was hitting on me and got fired?

He was really worked up, saying, "Anna, is this what you really want? Flying around with a bunch of men? I thought I was okay with this, but I'm not."

I was not only jetlagged, but also incredulous. How could he feel this way? I had been nothing but professional at work and respectful toward Cade. Our previous small disagreements were never like this. Certainly none reeked of jealousy quite like this one.

I finally had enough of his anger. "Cade, I'm sorry you feel this way, but here at your parents' home is not the place to argue like this. Why don't we talk tomorrow when we both have had a chance to cool down? I have done nothing to deserve this."

Now I was getting angry. I picked up my phone on my way out the door and called my parents. They had just arrived home after being in Panama for a month. Mom told me to come home. I had a lot of friends from UCLA I could have called, but that evening, I needed my mom and dad. I reached out to my sister and confided in her all the messy details of our first big fight. She kept reminding me that this was a transition period for our relationship and that Cade loved me very much. Why hadn't this come up when I was with American Airlines and living in San Francisco?

By the time I got to my parents' house, I was a wreck. The Colonel and mom sat up with me into the early morning hours. I couldn't shake the feeling that things with Cade were over. But why? How could this have happened after seven years together? Mom tried to reason with me, but it wasn't helping. "Anna, I know you love your job, but what about Cade? You can easily work for someone else and have a life."

I was confused on all fronts. Why leave a job that I had just started? Stuart Manning was a wonderful and fair employer. Now Cade's feelings were hurt, and I had to quit?

I woke up with puffy eyes and tried to call Cade, but no answer. I tried again later that day; still no answer. No word from Cade for the next two days. I was falling apart, but I needed to pull myself together for work the next afternoon. Finally, Cade answered his phone as I was heading to the hangar for departure.

"Anna, I just don't think I can be a part of the world you are being swept into. Let's take a break and talk when you get home. The accident and my recovery have changed me. I can't explain it, but it makes me realize what is important in life. I hope you can understand. I just wish you could put me before your job."

Responding through tears, I said I could not think of a more important thing than "us." We'd gone through so much, and now he was acting like a distant stranger. "Cade, you know me better than anyone. It's me, Anna. I have not changed, nor will I. I love you and want to spend my life with you."

He didn't respond, and after a long silence, I had to say a quick goodbye.

Downshifting my emotions, trying to concentrate on the trip, I realized we were now speeding through the air toward London. Yes, it was another change of plans. Mr. Manning had invited Vanessa Rathman to join us. She extended him an invitation to escort her to the premiere of her latest movie, *Jillian Rose,* in London. After all, his production company was backing this movie. She would be staying in London for two weeks. I liked her immediately. Not only was she drop-dead gorgeous, but also kind. She somehow broke the mold of a major movie star. She was normal. You could feel her excitement to accompany Mr. Manning on this trip. She even held his hand as we took off from Van Nuys. Both seemed very happy, and the sadness that I had seen in his eyes a few days before was completely gone.

I had the boys to help me through this time. Brian informed me that after the French Open, he was off to the Bay Area for his "big proposal." That meant he would be gone for about one week after this trip. I was happy for him, but I felt a tinge of sadness. Happy relationships seemed depressing when I faced my own situation with Cade. I needed to snap out of it quickly and get to work.

After three days in London, we would resume our itinerary for Munich. Our last stop would be Paris for three days and the French Open. Vanessa wanted to come with us, but promotional gigs for the movie bid her to stay in London.

Nancy had catered another terrific meal for the flight. I woke the passengers for breakfast shortly before touchdown in Luton. Nancy seemed to know exactly how to please our guests, who, in turn, showered me with compliments for the meal. Vanessa was exceptionally courteous and thankful for the service.

We descended into grey skies over London at Luton Airport. Saying our goodbyes to ground support, we made our way into the city and what would become another favorite hotel of mine: JW Marriott Park Lane Hotel in London. Mr. Manning had a residence in London where they were staying. Brian couldn't stop talking about going to Nobu for dinner. He even used Mr. Manning's name to get us a reservation there for nine o'clock at the Metropolitan Hotel on Old Park Lane.

Every time I am in London, I am fascinated by the English way of life. Every language is spoken, the black cabs look like they're from the set of a James Bond movie, and you never know whom you might run into while in the city. Pulling up to the JW Marriott Park Lane, I could see the famous Marble Arches straightaway to the northeast entrance of Hyde Park. I was tired and requested a massage in my room before dinner. Tomorrow would really be my day to get out and about.

I was exhausted from the travel, wanting to rest a bit before dinner at Nobu with the boys. My room was a beautiful and spacious suite, with two balconies overlooking Hyde Park. After looking out my window, I thought that maybe I should take a quick stroll before my massage. My urge to explore was strong, but fatigue won out.

I kicked off my shoes to relax my aching feet, took one look at my cozy bed, and crawled into a sea of down feathers. I was interrupted with a light knock on the door and my massage therapist. I had fallen asleep for over three hours! This was not the quick nap I had planned. She came in, set up her table, and kneaded her powerful hands into my tired muscles, bringing total relaxation. I woke up to a loud snort. Startled, I looked up and asked her if she was okay. She answered in that delightful British accent, "Ms. St. James, you fell asleep. I think you were softly snoring."

I didn't think I snored, but sure enough, there was drool escaping the side of my mouth. How very ladylike! I was certainly exhausted. Laura, the massage therapist, quickly became my new best friend in London. She gave me a massage just about every time I arrived in the city.

Once Laura left, I climbed into the bathtub for a soak before dinner. I could certainly get used to this heavenly little retreat in London. I touched base with Daniel Hulme, at On Air Dining to review an easy, tentative menu for our quick flight to Munich in a few days.

I checked the clock, and sure enough, it was almost time to meet Brian and Chris in the lobby. Nobu was a real gem. The neo-Japanese menu inspired by South American influences was the most delightful twist of the unexpected. However, finding our table proved more uncomfortable than I thought. We passed the bar and could feel the room watching us to see if we were anyone of importance. It was a little nerve wracking to watch heads turn as we passed. Heaven forbid, I might have to use the bathroom and run the gauntlet alone! This was a hot spot for celebrity sightings.

That evening there were a few celebrities sprinkled in our midst. Simon Cowell was there. Enrique Iglesias and Dustin Hoffman were spotted from where we sat too. Enrique was handsome. I admit I had no idea what the dinner cost, but it was worth every pound spent.

On our way out that evening—close to midnight—we were passing the dreaded bar. This time I heard our names being called, "Anna, Brian, Chris, over here!"

We identified the voice as Mr. Manning's, and we looked over to where he sat enjoying a cocktail with Vanessa Rathman. Would we join them for a nightcap before leaving? Of course! I thought it comical that we had used Stuart's name for a dinner reservation that evening. A steady stream of people approached the table for Vanessa's autograph that night. She was gracious and attentive to every request. I was impressed. Leaning over, she whispered to me, "I have to use the bathroom, but I hate walking through the bar area. It's like a meat market."

I had to tell her I felt the same way. She devised a plan. "Let's go together and give them something to talk about!"

She grabbed my elbow and whisked me into the women's bathroom, chatting the whole way. Back at the table, Vanessa asked, "What are you all doing tomorrow night?"

We had not made plans yet.

"Oh, good! I would love for you all to join us for the premiere tomorrow as my guests. How does that sound?"

Chris spoke for all of us when he accepted with, "We would love to."

"Well then, it's settled. Stuart will have his driver pick you up at eight o'clock tomorrow night. Where are you staying?"

Once all the details were settled, we returned to our hotel in a state of disbelief. I had to call my sister, Jesse, to tell her about the flight, the hotel, and the upcoming premiere. All she could say was, "No way, Anna. No way. What a grand adventure!"

I awoke from a luxurious night's sleep, wondering if the invitation we had all received was still real. Room service delivered a morning tray with pressed coffee, fresh-squeezed orange juice, a bowl of strawberries, croissants with assorted jams, and a toast rack. I lay in my bed, savoring the sumptuous croissants and fruit and knowing I needed to get a head start on my search for the perfect evening wear. I had no idea where to begin, but the guys were meeting me at Harrods for a late lunch and had promised to help me find a dress. Time to get moving! I reached for my running gear and heard another knock on my door. It was the bellman. "Ms. St. James, a special delivery has just arrived for you. I have four large boxes here. May I put them inside your room?"

I opened my door a little wider, filled with curiosity at the four boxes so elegantly wrapped. I was beginning to like these special deliveries. "Are you sure these are for me?" I asked.

He said, "If your name *is* Ms. Anna St. James, then yes, this is all for you."

I went to get my purse to give him a tip when he shook his head saying, "I was told not to accept any tips. It has already been taken care of."

I thanked the bellman, and he left just as quickly as he'd appeared. Upon closer inspection of the boxes, I saw a note underneath some ribbon. In my excitement, I somehow managed to open it:

Anna,

I hope you will enjoy being my guest this evening at the premiere of Jillian Rose. *I was not sure if you had anything to wear for an event like this. I took the liberty of calling my dear friend Stella, who also has done my dress for tonight. I took a stab at your size, and Stella has put together a little something for you. If the sizes are off just give her a call. She said it would be fine.*

With fondness,

Vanessa

P.S. Don't worry about the pilots. We have sent over tuxedos for them to wear this evening. Looking forward to seeing you tonight and sharing our big announcement.

Announcement? Stella? Did she mean Stella McCartney? Okay, no way this was real. No way! Quickly forgetting her mention of the announcement—that I assumed would be her next blockbuster movie—I dove into the boxes. My heart skipped a beat as I uncovered a ball gown fit for a princess, with shoes, jacket, and jewelry. Yes, yes, yes! I loved it. Moving as quickly as possible, I removed my running shoes to try on everything. I smoothed the creamy, white silk of the dress at my sides; it fit to perfection. The shimmering gold chiffon overlay accented my strappy gold sandals and matching jacket. The jewelry was just as decadent. I'd never worn anything like this. And what a surprise from the likes of Vanessa Rathman and Stella McCartney herself!

With a skip in my step and a smile that could light up all of Hyde Park, I instinctively reached for my phone to call Cade and share the news, but my fingers stopped short every time. I couldn't think of him right now. I was in London and determined to enjoy this trip.

Upon entering the park's hallowed grounds by way of the Marble Arches at the Cumberland Gate, I was immediately enraptured with the richness of its history. Maybe if I looked closely, I would see the arbiter of men's style from Regency England of days gone by, Beau Brummell, trotting by in his carriage. My new dress would certainly meet his approval. Children were everywhere. Joggers infused the park with movement. The elderly were regal, seated fixtures on benches, and life suddenly felt as if it had slowed down. I needed this.

The trees and gardens hedged a sweet-smelling pathway for me. I was heady with the perfume of fresh flowers. My map from the concierge demarcated the historical highlights, though it all seemed like a maze at first glance.

First, the concierge said, "Please remember our Hyde Park is a royal park—all 360 acres of it."

He was proud of his park, and I could see why. Quickly turning right, I followed my map toward the Albion Gate, then on to the Clarendon Gate, and on toward Victoria Gate Lodge and Buckhill Gate Lodge. Next was Queen Anne's Alcove. Thank goodness I had a map! Rounding the path by Notting Hill Gate, I felt like I might see Hugh Grant, popping out of the hedge to say, "Whoopsie Daisy!" Circling down toward Kensington Gardens, I could see a prolific display of every imaginable flower. Over at the Serpentine Bridge was the Princess of Wales Memorial Fountain. The statue was quite modern and did not match the rich history of the park, though it was a beautiful tribute to the princess.

The sun had decided to grace London with a rare appearance as I continued to stroll through the park. People were out enjoying the glorious day in record numbers. I could hear the boat paddles splashing through the water and the ping of tennis balls sent from players' rackets. My mind kept returning to Cade. I chuckled as I passed the famous Achilles, with only a fig leaf covering his naked body. Only the British could feign modesty in such a way. They do have a sense of humor.

My watch told me I needed to rendezvous with the boys for lunch at Harrods. My peaceful time in the park was over. The frenzied exchange of people and cars indicated that Buckingham Palace was up ahead—just one block to go on Brompton Road.

Harrods was an institution of British culture since the eighteenth century. Seven floors of merchandise stretched across four and a half acres of real estate. Just as I was crossing the threshold as one of their fifteen million annual visitors, the doors swung open and out came Dustin Hoffman. "Hi, Anna!" he said, as if he'd expected our chance meeting. His crooked smile was charming. He had remembered my name from Vanessa's introduction last night!

I had an hour to burn before meeting Brian and Chris. I needed to replenish our supplies for the airplane. The world-famous Harrods food court was on my radar. Was I ever in for a treat! I located the most delectable d'oie truffle foie gras for Mr. Manning. I had never been one for pate, but after tasting this foie gras, I had a newfound love. I also purchased some Russian Stolichnaya elit vodka with ossetra caviar, which I was told was one of the rarest in the world, complete with a serving set. I had to pick up a few Cuban Romeo and Juliet cigars, too. I took a liking to a handmade cribbage board with matching case that seemed perfect for the airplane. Within the hour, I had spent quite a few pounds. It was crazy, but what fun!

Lost in thought and the merchandise, I heard my phone ring while I was juggling my purchases and paying for the cribbage board. I missed it the first time, which got me agitated when it started ringing again. It was Chris trying to get a rise out of me. "Hey, Anna, I really like Russian vodka. Did you get any?" Oh, really!

My head must have spun around completely to look for him. He was really in for it now! He started to laugh, adding, "We are right behind you. Follow the breadcrumbs to Galvin Demoiselle Petit Bistro where you will find two handsome men. Hurry up; we're hungry." He hung up while he was still laughing.

I located the boys, who still thought themselves as clever as could be. I had a wonderful glass of Grand Cuvée Rose NV champagne while the boys ordered Bourgognes Pinot Noir. I had a salad nicoise a la maison while Brian had veal and Chris lamb. We were in high spirits, discussing our excitement for the upcoming premiere. I had a quick stop to make before we went back to the hotel.

"Since I was so nice to meet you for lunch, will you accompany me to Fortnum and Mason to buy their famous gift hampers and a little high tea? I promise; it's really close. It's at 181 Piccadilly. Please?"

I laid it on thick until they reluctantly agreed to join me for a traditional English high tea service. They rolled their eyes, but they still came.

Their classic male front was to scoff and act put out, yet they smiled the entire time. The fourth floor Diamond Jubilee Tea Salon should be a mandatory experience for all newcomers to the United Kingdom. We daintily savored high tea and purchased the Fortnum and Mason hampers, which their staff delivered to the hotel as a service.

I bought one extra hamper for Brian's upcoming proposal in San Francisco, adding champagne and other goodies to the basket. He had no idea. Afterward and many pounds later, we took a stroll through St. James Park as I teased the boys, "Of course we have to walk through the entire park as it was named after me."

And they fancied themselves the only clever ones! I continued, "I would be happy to walk through *any* park if it was named after either of you."

Brian and Chris hid their smiles behind smug expressions as they eyed the park's beauty. They were like brothers to me, and it was my duty to goad them every once in a while.

Walking through London that afternoon, we tossed around guesses about what the night could hold. None of us had a clue, but for certain, it would be memorable. Mr. Manning, true to his word, had sent over tuxedos that morning. The pilots expressed how rarely an occasion arose to wear a formal tuxedo. But what the heck, they couldn't think of a better excuse than an exclusive celebrity event! I went straight to my room to put on my dress, already feeling like a princess about to step foot into her awaiting carriage.

With the magic of Stella, the fairy godmother, I looked the part of a fairytale beauty. Dressed in my extravagant gown, I took the stairs at the front entrance of the hotel like in every romantic movie. I was trying to look the part while Brian and Chris stood by approvingly. They seemed even taller and more handsome dressed in tails and waiting for me. This was a moment I will always remember. All eyes fixed on me, but this time, it didn't feel like that uncomfortable moment in the bar at Nobu. I felt treasured and respected as a guest of honor to an important event. Mr. Manning's limousine was curbside and ready to whisk us away to a world that many admire but few see from the inside. We toasted with flutes of Cristal to celebrate our arrival at the Odeon Cinema at Leicester Square. The atmosphere was as effervescent as the champagne, and I was starting to feel nervous.

On the red carpet, I spotted Vanessa and Stuart posing for the photographers. From this vantage point, I felt like I had a window seat to their far-from-normal, everyday lives. We stepped out of the automobile together, just as Vanessa summoned us to join them with the photographers. She was the woman of the hour and, as always, entirely stunning. She stood back to take a good look at Stella's work and said, "You are drop-dead gorgeous, Anna."

She seemed quite pleased with the magic she had created, and I was glad for it. The cast borrowed Vanessa for more photos while we chatted with Mr. Manning. "Anna, you look exquisite. You are just lovely." He went on, "I don't mean to embarrass you, but I had to tell you."

"Mr. Manning, you look very handsome yourself. Thank you for the compliment."

Vanessa was glowing that night with the radiance of a woman well loved. It was captivating to watch her pose so effortlessly for the photographers. I felt a familiar state of admiration as I observed her, as if she were one of my beloved American Airline flight attendants from childhood. But this time, the tables had turned, and I was nearly one of this exclusive circle.

Inside the theatre, we were in for another surprise. Vanessa and Stuart requested our presence at their table. I could not believe their thoughtfulness. Stuart whispered in my ear, "Of course you are sitting with us. You are part of our family."

My mind was in a blur as the premiere got underway. Vanessa appeared on stage to thank everyone for coming out in support of *Jillian Rose*. And she had a secret to share. The press readied their cameras, with breaking headlines already scrolling in their minds. A secret to share? I studied Stuart's face and knew exactly what she'd meant. It wasn't just her beauty, but the love of Mr. Manning that set her aglow. She had just become engaged to Stuart Manning, and they were planning a wedding in about two months.

"When! Where? Tell us the story and congratulations!" I said, overcome with joy. The excitement was infectious, and we lifted our glasses to toast the happy couple during the after-party held at Mr. Manning's London residence.

In the early morning hours, we made our way back to the hotel with empty glasses and full hearts. As soon as I reached my room, it was all I could do to slip out of the dress I swore I could never take off and collapse onto my covers.

I could hear something ringing very faintly. Was it the castle bells tolling? I could only wish. What a disappointment to awaken like Cinderella to a pumpkin instead of a carriage. It was my phone ringing, with a disgruntled Cade on the other end. It was four in the morning, about an hour after I had fallen asleep. Fatigue mixed with relationship problems was a recipe for disaster. I should have known.

"Anna, our friends haven't stopped calling me. They saw you on TV. I kept telling them it was nonsense until I saw it for myself. It was you with Vanessa Rathman in a restaurant. Oh, there's more. You were on the red carpet for her movie premiere. I saw you with Stuart Manning and two other guys. One of them had his arm around you. The media keeps asking about this new mystery woman. Seriously, Anna, I am so done."

He was telling me the events of the evening as if I hadn't been there. Bracing my temples between my fingers, I felt like I'd been hit by a freight train, and after the freight train, I was hit with the emotionally charged accusations of the only man I ever loved! Blindsided, I finally let him have it.

"Cade, you are being absolutely ridiculous. Those guys are the pilots you met, Brian and Chris. Vanessa, well you already know who she is, in addition to being Mr. Manning's guest. We just happened to bump into them at dinner, and they invited us to attend the premiere for her new movie. Not that you particularly care, but they just announced their engagement at the premiere, and I, for one, am happy for them. What is your problem Cade? You have never been this way."

"Well, Anna, I am now. I can't do this anymore," he declared.

This made me even angrier than before as I dug in my heels and said, "Fine. Please thank your parents for allowing me to stay at their home. Just put my things in a box and leave them at the hangar for me. I can't believe how you have changed. You are not the man I thought I wanted to spend the rest of my life with. Please never call me again. We are done, Cade!"

I hung up good and hard, but I could not go back to sleep. Part of me was deeply hurt by Cade, but another felt almost relieved that it was over. A few months ago, I never would have believed this could happen to us. We spent over seven years sharing our innermost thoughts and dreams together, and this is how it ended? I felt sickened to think of it.

The next few days I spent quietly in my room before heading to Munich. I told Brian what had happened, and he offered his support like a good friend.

"Anna, you know this is not an easy life. We serve at Mr. Manning's beck and call, and while it's a gratifying job, I have been giving it some thought. When I propose to Melanie, I want her to approve of our flight schedule and of living in LA. She has a good job, and I don't want to force her to leave it unless she feels ready. You took this job so you could be closer to Cade. I am sorry it has ended this way for you, Anna. Maybe it was a wonderful college romance, and now it's time to move on. I don't mean to be abrupt, but you're an amazing person, and any man would be fortunate to spend his life with you. Okay, I will say this only once, but you are absolutely beautiful, inside and out."

Okay, now he had reduced me to tears, but I was touched by his thoughtfulness. Few men would verbalize what he had just shared with me. Brian's friendship was a godsend when I needed it. I couldn't restate enough my thankfulness for his and Melanie's friendship.

Chapter Eight

THE ADVENTURE CONTINUES

Off we go into the wild blue yonder, climbing high into the sun.
—"The US Air Force"

*M*r. Manning arrived early in the morning for takeoff from the UK, ready for our next stop, Munich. The skies were gloriously sunny. Maybe that meant happier times ahead. It was a short flight, but we had time to celebrate and congratulate Mr. Manning on his engagement. I thanked him for the incredible time we had at the premiere in London and presented him with an engagement gift. I had returned to Fortnum and Mason for one of their biggest picnic hampers and filled it with every kind of treat. There was even *Sonoma SMS* champagne on hand for a congratulatory toast.

Once we were up at altitude, Mr. Manning asked how I liked the dress that Vanessa had selected on my behalf. I was tongue-tied. There were no adequate words, but I was sure to say, "The dress was so lovely, I didn't want to take it off! It was a dream, really." What he said next was beyond flattering: "You were a vision, Anna. I'm so happy you could join us."

Mr. Manning's meeting left us free until our departure the next afternoon for Paris. It was over seventy degrees, and I thought a nice, long run would help release my frustrations over Cade. We checked in at the Munich Airport Marriott Hotel. We decided it was best to stay close to the airport for such a short trip.

I was off to get some fresh air and was already feeling more like myself. I made a playful pass at the boys on my way out with this line, "Well, since neither of you guys want to come, that's just fine. I'll go by myself! I'll see *you* at dinner."

I grabbed my room key and credit card but left my phone so I could do some serious thinking. The air felt great on my skin as I headed off with no map but the directions from the guy at the front desk. Stepping outside the hotel on the Aloise Steinecker Strasse, I headed toward the Wippenhauser Forst. The concierge was confident there was no way I could get lost. No problem. Oh, those famous last words!

Walking and biking paths that villagers used for travel crisscrossed the farmland. I was exhilarated. It felt so good to get out that I kept running for the next forty-five minutes. I was finally ready to head back to the hotel, but where was I? It was a small village, not unlike the many others I had passed. Here was a place to get something to drink, a cute little bakery welcoming me inside. The sky had darkened, and it looked like rain.

Thank goodness I had my credit card. I pointed to what I needed and went to pay. The lady shook her head with a clear "no," shooing me with her hand while pointing at a sign indicating they accepted only euros for currency. The wind was whipping up a sideways torrential downpour by the time I looked back outside. Where did my sunny sky go?

I showed the baker my room key, and she mimed the question, "Where?" But, I didn't know! The problem at hand was my room key did not have the name of the hotel on it. For the life of me, I could not remember the name of the hotel. For the next two hours, I was on the beaten path between villages, trying to find my way back. Sopping wet, I even hid from the rain under a barn roof for a while. I was starting to panic. Everything looked the same, and my wounds from Cade were haunting me. I did make it back, soaked to the bone and greeted by two very nervous pilots. They were pacing the lobby after having searched for me by taxi for the last few hours. "Anna, we were so worried. Are you okay? Where were you?"

I was sorry to have concerned them with what started off as a simple afternoon run. I felt silly, but the important part, they assured me, was that I was all right.

After my break up with Cade, it was nice to know someone cared. This was a big lesson learned. I would always know the name of the hotel, take a phone and some local currency (euros), and let the pilots know where I was at all times. I sure had a lot of fresh air that day—all in hopes to mend a broken heart.

Brian and Chris met me at the hotel restaurant for dinner. No more gallivanting on my part! We were having an early dinner to rest up for our stop in Amsterdam before Paris. These were new places for me, and I was eager to see them. We had just been seated for dinner when my phone rang.

"Hello, Mr. Manning. Yes, Mr. Manning, I will check on that right away."

Now what was I to do? Mr. Manning's staff had dropped the ball on getting tickets to the French Open. The event was in two days, but he figured Cade might have a connection. I was reluctant, but none too prideful to ask for his help. While it was one of the most difficult calls I have ever had to make, I had little choice. Surprisingly, he answered my call.

"Cade, I'm sorry to call. Mr. Manning doesn't know we broke up. We are in Munich right now, but headed to Paris tomorrow night. Mr. Manning just called and asked if you could get us tickets for the French Open. I'm sorry to ask for a favor, but he said his office dropped the ball, and he knew you could help. Can you?"

He was quiet for a moment and then said, "I can call my sponsors and see what they can do. Do you want them for the tennis matches in two days?"

"Yes, in two days if you don't mind. That would be great. I'm sorry to bother you."

I felt an aching sadness while speaking to him. We had never been apart like this. He called back in thirty minutes with four tickets to the French Open secured. He had pulled through for me—if not for me, at least for Mr. Manning. He said we would be seated with Chandler and Lisa Powell. They owned the largest sportswear company in the world and sponsored him. They had a box seat and would love to host Mr. Manning and his guests.

"Cade," I said, "thank you so much. I am truly sorry about our horrible conversation the other day. I'm trying to weigh all that has happened between us, and that evening was a total surprise to me."

I continued, "I'm still that girl you met on the tennis court at UCLA, and that will never change. I will always love you, but after our conversation, I agree that we should go our separate ways. I want you to have an amazing life and get your tennis back on track. You deserve that. I will always care deeply for you, Cade."

I was in a state of melancholy for the rest of the evening. Back and forth, I counterbalanced the conflicting thoughts that only love brings. Could our relationship be salvaged? By morning, I knew the answer was no, though it hurt to admit. Enough of this! It was time to see amazing places and put my heartbreak to rest. Cade would always hold a special piece of my heart, but I needed to let him go.

Brian gave me a long, hard look at breakfast and then broke out shortly into a smile. "Way to go, Anna! You look great!"

"Is it that obvious?"

I was on the mend and moving on.

The catering for our short flight to Amsterdam left much to be desired. It was a far cry from gourmet; in fact, it was more like commercial airline food from a pre-packaged container. Frustrated, I walked out to the airplane with my head filled with too many details. How could I spin my next miracle and turn this mush into something spectacular? Two men in black t-shirts and distressed jeans were walking parallel to me toward a BAC 111. It looked like a giant slug alongside our sleek G550.

I expected they would deviate on their own path, but instead they fell in step with my path and asked, "Is that your Gulfstream over there?"

I looked to where they pointed. "The G550? No, no, I'm the flight attendant."

"Oh, well, do you want to come check out our airplane?"

My catering was a disaster, but curiosity killed the cat. You needn't twist my arm. I introduced myself to the men and turned to have a better look at them. It was Steven Tyler and Joey Kramer from Aerosmith! Steven wasn't as tall as I expected, but his style and those lips were one of a kind.

They certainly fit the bill in black, cut-off tees, ornate jewelry, feathers, and tattoos—in stark contrast to my cashmere sweater, black skirt, and black pumps. I liked their free-spirited nature. Steven Tyler introduced me to the band, a couple of girlfriends, managers, and agents.

Their chartered airplane was more like a tour bus in need of refurbishing. Musical instruments were scattered around the cabin, and everyone seemed okay with it. I extended them an invitation to tour the Gulfstream. As suspected, they tried to negotiate a swap after seeing the inside. I chuckled, "No thanks, guys! I think I see my passenger arriving early. We'll be taking off soon." Before they left, though, Steven pulled me aside and asked, "Would you like to meet us in Boston next month for a concert we're doing?"

I tried to decline the invitation gracefully—I knew I'd probably be working. Mr. Manning pulled up just as they were leaving, so I introduced him to my new friends. They knew exactly who he was. Stuart could make friends out of thin air, and before I knew it, we had plans to reconvene in LA in a few weeks.

I called Brian and Chris, who were still inside with the handler, to make them aware of Mr. Manning's early arrival and my chance run-in with Steven Tyler. "Well, why didn't you say so earlier?" they exclaimed. "Dream On" was stuck in my head for the rest of the flight to Amsterdam. I think I even sang it to Mr. Manning, who just chuckled and shook his head.

The catering, well, let's just say I was thankful it was a short flight. I would run into Steven Tyler many times throughout the years. What a character he was! And filled with amazing talent.

We touched down in the land of dikes and windmills. Mr. Manning was off to his meetings, and I was hungry for exploration. "Hey, Brian, Chris! We need to see Amsterdam. It's my first time here. Please? Just humor me, okay? Let's take the short canal tour. At least that way we'll see some of the city."

They hadn't forgiven me for the Aerosmith slight yet. They had the car ride to the canal to warm up to the idea.

The weather was perfect for touring, and what better way to see Amsterdam than on its many waterways? The driver dropped us off and pointed us in the right direction, promising to return in three hours. Welcome to Amsterdam! We had the boat to ourselves, so we stretched out like royalty.

There are only two wooden homes left in all of Amsterdam—who knew? The gorgeous historical homes along the canal had beautiful, gabled facades. We saw the oldest home, the narrowest home, the widest home (Tripp House), the home adorned with the most stone-carved heads, and the one I was waiting for: Anne Frank's childhood home. Our guide was happy to see my enthusiasm. Anne Frank's home is the most popular tourist attraction in all of Amsterdam.

The city was dreamlike as we slipped through the canals, though I don't remember much after Anne Frank's home. The motion of the boat lulled me to sleep. I was nudged awake in what seemed like minutes. Chris could not contain himself. "Anna, the tour is over now. Glad you enjoyed it. You really saw a lot of Amsterdam!" Very funny, Chris!

He held out his camera with the unfortunate evidence of me sleeping (drooling, no doubt), with my face down on a table inside the boat. I tried to grab the camera to get rid of the nasty evidence, but it turned into a game of keep-away, and I gave up. In between gasps from laughing, Brian sputtered, "Wait until Mr. Manning sees this! This is what you get for not telling us you had Steven Tyler onboard." Real cute, boys.

Chapter Nine

TAKEN BY SURPRISE
UNDER THE SKIES OF PARIS

Paris is always a good idea.

—**Audrey Hepburn**

verything was in place for takeoff. We were going to Paris. Mr. Manning studied me intently as I placed a sweet Brian D. and some light appetizers before him. "Anna, something has changed. You look refreshed and happy."

"Why, thank you," I responded, mulling over what he'd said, not wanting to share my breakup with Cade just yet. This flight, however, was quick and easy. How incredible to land in an entirely new city in less than an hour. Air travel still was a bit of a miracle to me. It seemed minutes before Le Bourget airport welcomed us to the City of Love.

Mr. Manning usually stayed at the George V while in Paris, but his meetings were closer to the Hotel Concorde Montparnasse on this trip. He wanted to take us to a little bistro off the beaten path where they served the best Irish coffees in the world. He added with a wink, "They also add whipped crème on top that doesn't explode!" I thought he had forgotten our San Francisco trip. Obviously, he hadn't. We meandered through the charming streets of Quartier Latin, Saint-Germain-des-Prés, and then toward the Rive Gauche for what seemed like hours until we arrived at Le Petit Zinc on the rue Benoit. It was heavenly, but how he had found this little bistro is still a mystery to me.

Cade's brother Reynie and his wife lived in Paris. They had a charming home I had visited many times in the southeast area of Paris, the twelfth arrondissement, in St. Maurice. Reynie's wife, Monique, was French and had lived in Paris her entire life. Cade told them that I was in Paris, and they asked to meet me for dinner. Mr. Manning overheard my conversation with Monique and insisted they join us for dinner. He still didn't know about Cade. The more the merrier?

Cade had not told Reynie we had parted ways, but now didn't seem like the time to say anything either. Mr. Manning was right. The Irish coffees were out of this world. We must have toasted to his engagement a dozen times over dinner. Before we left the bistro, Mr. Manning addressed Reynie and Monique, "I hope to see you a lot in the future as family of Cade and our Anna. Thanks for joining us this evening."

Reynie told Stuart over dinner that Cade's accident happened just before he would have been a seeded player for the French Open tournament this year. This was news to me, and I wondered why Cade had never told me. *Oh, Anna*, I thought to myself, *let it go*. It was harder than I thought after so many years together.

The goodbye to Reynie and Monique was bittersweet. We exchanged hugs and kisses on cheeks. They couldn't wait to see me again at the family's summer home in Normandy. I just smiled and said how special those times had always been. They were family to me, but I had a new life now, and I couldn't change the past.

The City of Lights, or as the French said, *La Ville Lumière,* glistened on every street corner. The walk back was long, and my feet started to notice. Chris and Mr. Manning even came to my assistance, linking elbows alongside me with big, goofy smiles. All three men had become quite special to me.

Past the bar on our way to the elevators, a very handsome man caught my eye. His face lit up in instant recognition, calling out to Mr. Manning in a delightful French accent, "Ah, Stuart, *Bonsoir.*"

Mr. Manning introduced us in French to the attaché to the Ambassador of Mauritius. The country was formerly a French colony, and Monsieur Jean Michel Durand had met Stuart a couple of years ago while vacationing in Mauritius and later in LA while on business. Jean Michel greeted me with a very elegant, "*Enchante.*" I thought, *Who says things like that in this day and age?*

Stuart quickly brought Jean Michel up to speed on his recent engagement. "I am surprised you have not seen it in the tabloids."

Jean Michel cleared his throat. "Stuart, you know I don't pay attention to those things. My congratulations to you both. May I invite you all to join me for dinner tomorrow at the embassy to celebrate? My driver could pick you up here, say, at nine tomorrow evening, *oui?*"

Saying goodnight after Stuart accepted his dinner invitation, he stepped toward me and kissed me ever so slightly on each cheek and left the room with,

"Ce sera un plaisir de vous voir demain soir," translated to, "It will be a pleasure to see you tomorrow night."

Oh, my, was he handsome! And smooth as ever. Brian and Chris seemed unimpressed and by now could read my thoughts. "Really, Anna?" I ignored their cynicism.

We parted ways to our rooms to rest up for a big morning. First the French Open at Roland Garros, followed by dinner at the residence of the Ambassador to Mauritius.

In the morning, there was a slight knock on my door. In the short amount of time I had worked for Mr. Stuart Manning, many surprise gifts had taken my breath away. What else could there be? A breathtaking bouquet of flowers awaited me. Perhaps after my dinner with Reynie and Monique, this was an apology from Cade? My heart skipped a beat at the thought.

I dove into the flower arrangement, looking for a card with Cade's apology. The flowers were gorgeous, and all I wanted to do was step back and admire them. Maybe Monique had helped Cade. With a big smile, I found the card. It was a hand written note:

Dear Ms. St. James,

It was such a pleasure to meet you last night. I look forward to our dinner this evening and ask that you allow me the privilege of taking you to dinner again tomorrow evening.

Until tonight,
Jean Michel

Oh, my, he was not only devastatingly handsome, but charming as well. I was in trouble and very attracted to him!

Quickly downshifting, I needed to get ready to leave for Roland Garros in a few minutes. What a way to start my first full day in Paris! Mr. Manning pulled me aside on our way out and said, "Anna, I had a call from Jean Michel this morning about you. I told him you were in a serious relationship with Cade, but he wanted to invite you to dinner tomorrow evening. He was a perfect gentleman about it. I have always been impressed with him. I just thought you should know before he asks. By the way, Anna, can you please just call me by my first name, Stuart? I am much too young to be 'Mr. Manning.'"

"Mr., errrr, I mean, Stuart, thanks for letting me know about Jean Michel. I did receive flowers this morning, with an invitation to dinner tomorrow night."

I apologized for calling him Mr. Manning and promised to do my best with just Stuart in the future. He smiled and said, "That's my girl."

Mr. Manning asked Brian that morning what he thought about flying to Mauritius. He was going to suggest it to Vanessa as the perfect place for a wedding. After all, the wedding was in two months' time! We would discuss it later, he said, as we approached the prestigious gates of Roland Garros.

I have always loved the formality of a tennis match. This was a true gentleman's sport. Escorted to our seats where our kind hosts awaited, we were made to feel right at home with Chandler and Lisa Powell. I thanked them incessantly for accommodating us on such short notice. Lisa waved the concern away with the back of her hand and said, "It's nothing at all. We were thrilled when Cade called. Please come and sit down with me, Anna. It's nice to have you here. This is my favorite tournament in the world."

Chandler took my arm endearingly and said, "Anna, your Cade is going places. He's become like a son to me. How's his recovery coming along?"

During the match, Cade's friends came out in droves to greet me. Brian leaned over and added, "I didn't know Cade was such a big deal in the world of tennis."

I couldn't deny it. As I tried to march forward each day without him, it felt more impossible after so many years. I missed our companionship, but not the struggle of the last few months. Chandler asked me to get Cade on the phone. To my surprise, he answered. It took all I had to keep my voice bright with enthusiasm as I passed along a hello from everyone shouting in my ear.

Chandler got the phone first, followed by Stuart. Everyone wanted to speak to Cade. Once I was back on the phone, Cade replied, "So, I heard about your dinner with Reynie and Monique last night. Monique said she spoke to you this morning and you are dining tonight at the embassy to Mauritius. Did you know that my mother's great, great grandfather was the governor to Mauritius?"

"Wow, Cade, I had no idea. Do you want me to mention it?"

"Sure, you can let them know. Might be interesting, and my mom sure is pleased to hear about it," he said.

"Hey, Cade?" I paused. "Thanks again for lining up tickets for today's matches. Stuart is thrilled, and guess what?"

He laughed, "What, Anna?"

"Chandler and Lisa invited us back again tomorrow. Oh, before I forget, your tennis buddies keep coming over to say hello. They really miss you."

"Anna?" Cade's voice changed. "What's with calling Mr. Manning *Stuart*?"

I hesitated, stepping out of the box. "Cade, it's a long story, but he asked me to start calling him Stuart. He said he is too young to be a 'Mr. Manning.' I said I would try." Changing subjects quickly, I finished our conversation, "Hey, thanks again. Bye, Cade."

My heart felt like it was splitting in two. He was still angry.

The ambassador's residence was on rue de Tocqueville. Beneath waving flags overhead, we stepped out of the cars at the grand entrance like diplomats. We were escorted to the top floor and greeted by a panorama of Paris. After the formalities, the ambassador announced, "Tonight is quite special. I have been told that you, Ms. St. James, have a connection to our humble island."

He continued, "I had a call this afternoon from a cousin of a Mrs. Williams, who has a beautiful family estate in Normandy. She told me of your many visits and how she expects Mrs. Williams to be your mother-in-law soon. Mrs. Williams's great, great grandfather was the governor of our island long ago. We searched our archives and found his name was Governor de la Chaisse. In years past, he governed when the French were in power."

"Yes, I just heard about the connection today. Everyone has told me that Mauritius is quite beautiful."

Jean Michel quickly added, "I am hoping we can arrange for all of you to visit our island soon. Its beauty and mystique is like no other. In fact, Stuart, it's a great place for a wedding."

Stuart and the ambassador called Vanessa after dinner. They asked what she thought about the idea of getting married in Mauritius. She quickly gave Mauritius a hearty thumbs-up for a destination wedding. I knew she'd be up for it!

Jean Michel, seated next to me, whispered, "Anna, can I meet you back at the hotel this evening? Perhaps we can go out for a late *aperitif* together?"

Why not? I was due for a little fun after the last few emotional weeks.

He did not disappoint. He met me at the hotel bar fifteen minutes after I'd arrived. Almost immediately, I was under his spell. "Anna, thank you for meeting me. I would like to get to know you, though I have a feeling you won't be in Paris much longer."

He explained everything in that devastatingly beautiful French accent. He had a driver out front, and off we went. To where, I didn't care. We drove toward the Champs Elysees with its broad streets and past the Arc de Triomphe. La Tour Eiffel was lit up as we passed. It was an invitation to romance and one that I accepted. City of Love, City of Lights—they both were alive that evening. We pulled up in front of a small club that was located close to the Sorbonne, within steps of the Pantheon.

Inside, Jean Michel swept me into his arms, and we danced into the night. His eyes absorbed me in such a moving way. These were all new sensations to me. Later, we strolled from the club to the Jardin Luxenbourg, the beautiful gardens where royalty had lived hundreds of years ago. We lingered in conversation while he draped his jacket across my shoulders. With the sun breaking on the horizon, I knew it was morning, and the magic had just begun.

Could my heart be feeling this way so shortly after ending things with Cade? Once back at the hotel, I could sort out my feelings, but for now, I held onto the promise of another evening with Jean Michel. He escorted me back to the hotel and pulled me in for a kiss that nearly lifted me off my feet. It felt like the first real kiss I'd ever had! Pulling his lips from mine, my handsome escort professed, "I felt such a pull to you last night, or was that two nights ago now? You are beautiful, Anna. I feel like I have known you forever. Please tell me if it's over with Cade. I will not interfere if he still has your heart. Can you begin to give me your heart?"

He kissed me again, and I remained speechless. "I'll pick you up early around eight this evening, *oui, mon Cherie*? Have fun at the matches."

I was quickly falling for him! Cade was the last thing on my mind as I flew up the elevator to my room. Was it possible I had forgotten him so quickly?

Next up, Roland Garros. Did I look like I had been up all night? I told Stuart I was only staying until early afternoon. I wanted to get some rest. Before he heard it from anyone else, I told him I had accepted the dinner invitation from Jean Michel.

"Anna, Jean Michel is a great guy. Last night he seemed a bit reserved, but I think he was just nervous around you. I know he likes you, but what about Cade?"

I finally delivered the news. "Cade has not been happy with my work schedule. Something has changed since his accident, and I think my flying is just too much for him. Obviously, he is not a guy I can marry if my job affects him in this way. I never saw it coming, but we broke up last week."

Stuart replied tenderly, "I'm sorry to hear that. I never thought to ask. Well, I'm glad you've accepted Jean Michel's invitation. Knowing the two of you, I have a feeling you two are meant for each other." He added with a wink, "Yes, I saw how he looked at you."

At the French Open, Stuart was not his usual, composed self. For starters, he left most of his clothing options at his London residence. The only shoes he had brought on this trip were a brand new pair of Bruno Maglis and his Sperry Top-Siders. The Brunos had given him blisters from our walk to the bistro, so he switched them out for the Top-Siders.

A recent Harley Davidson ride in the South of France had melted the soles of his boat shoes, which he wore reluctantly to the tennis match. Chandler encouraged him to swing by the hospitality suite and pick up a pair of shoes.

To make matters worse, one of his contact lenses was chipped. He wanted to wait until we got home to replace it, so he donned a pair of his glasses with thick, coke-bottle lenses to watch the tennis matches. Thank goodness Vanessa didn't have to see him like this! Though he still was handsome, he looked less a multibillionaire by the minute. He could see me laughing at him from the corner of his eye. I had stopped trying to hide it. It was impossible now with Chris and Brian in on it. I even got him to crack a smile over his unfashionable appearance. I offered to get new shoes for him, which he proudly declined, "No, thank you. I'm fine. I like my glasses and my melted shoes." Now he was just making a statement.

About midway through the event, Stuart asked if we could go for some lunch. Chandler and Lisa offered to order food for the box, but Stuart wanted to stretch his legs. He wanted to try the restaurant bar Terrasse Les Jardins. After our search to find the restaurant, we arrived to find an enormous line. I was desperate to find a seat for our little group, and to make matters worse, I had lost Stuart in the process. This was, after all, a multibillionaire I was responsible for! Still searching for a place to sit, I found him after a quick scan of the line. He looked quite happy with his croque-monsieur and a trashcan as his tabletop. This man always surprised me.

After that unforgettable luncheon, we went back to our seats, and I thanked Chandler and Lisa for their generosity. I promised I would convey their well wishes to Cade. I left the boys to taxi back to the hotel. First things first: I needed posters and a few shirts to bring home as gifts. My trusty old Rolex watch that my grandmother gave me indicated it was time to catch a taxi at Avenue Gordon-Bennett on the Boulogne side of the stadium. The line seemed eternal. The wait was at least an hour long. Plan B was the Metro, or I'd be late for my date.

I clung to my map in the swarm of people, hoping I was headed in the right direction. Should I have switched from the orange line to the purple line for Montmartre? Trusting my keen sense of direction and with hands full of paraphernalia, I hopped off the Metro in a mad dash. I was feeling quite the Renaissance woman—traipsing across subway stations in foreign countries like it was no big—oh, no! In the middle of a busy Metro station, I lost my grip on the souvenirs. Poster tubes and bags went flying. How incredibly far those containers can roll! Scrambling to gather my things, a kind man stooped down to help me collect all my strewn purchases. It was Stuart—thick spectacles, melted shoes, and all.

My knee-jerk reaction was, of course, what any professional would say to her boss, "I thought I ditched you back at the tennis match!"

Stuart gently reached for my elbow to lead me to the next Metro to Montmartre. So much for being a Renaissance woman. I was mortified at the words that had escaped my mouth, while he thought it hilarious. We decided to stop at a little café next to the hotel for a *café au lait* and a few moments on the streets of Paris.

Back in my room, I was dressing for my anticipated evening with Jean Michel when my phone rang. It was Stuart. "Anna, I'm sorry to bother you, but I just got word from my production studio that I need to get back to Van Nuys for some important meetings in the morning. I'm sorry. I know you had a big night planned. Can you get hold of Brian and Chris so we can plan to leave together from the hotel in about two hours?"

We left the hotel at seven thirty. Beforehand, I contacted our catering staff out at Le Bourget, terribly sorry for the late notice and in need of a food delivery in less than two hours. After a quick change of clothes, my flight bag was packed, and I was ready to go. I had almost forgotten about my dinner with Jean Michel! Feeling horrible, with no way to contact him, I left a note with the bellman and the front desk staff to ensure the message was delivered:

> *Dear Jean Michel,*
>
> *I am so sorry I cannot make it for our dinner tonight. Stuart needed to leave immediately for Los Angeles, and I had no other way to get in touch with you. Please accept my apology and know that I was looking forward to our evening. Last night was wonderful, and I enjoyed getting to know you. I, too, feel like I have known you for a long time. I hope to see you in Mauritius for the wedding.*
>
> *Anna*

Before we left Le Bourget, Stuart had received a gift delivered right to the airplane. He looked pleased to find it was from Vanessa.

Everything was secure and ready for takeoff. The boys and Stuart were wearing new baseball caps from the French Open I had purchased for them. We were next in the lineup for takeoff when Stuart said, "Anna, you've got to come see this."

"Stuart, we're just about to take off. I'll come up and see it once we are in the air."

He wouldn't let it rest. "Stuart, I will be there once we launch, okay?"

Unfastening his seatbelt, he was headed back with the package when I warned him one last time. "Stuart, please sit down or you could get—"

The thrust from takeoff made his head hit the ceiling. He suddenly got quiet and went back to his seat. "Stuart," I said, "are you all right?"

No answer. "Stuart?"

A soft voice whispered, "Yes, Anna."

We launched into the beautiful skies above Paris as evening set in. At about seven thousand feet, Stuart got up a second time and headed for my seat. He handed me his new hat. I could not for the life of me figure out what was going on. As I took the hat out of his hand, he leaned over so I could see the top of his head. My breath caught in my throat. There on top of his beautiful head was a hole, about the size of a quarter, with raw skin exposed. Stuck to the metal button inside the hat was his skin with the hair still attached! Alarmed, I went to grab the Neosporin for his head. I could only wonder if his hair would ever grow back in this new, two-inch crater?

Poor Stuart! Coke bottle lenses, melted shoes, and now this? I felt horribly for him. Looking across at me he said, "I wanted to show you this."

He opened the most exquisite black box, and there inside were two watches. Not just any watches—these were the same watches that James Bond wore. Both had custom 007 faces and "James Bond" inscribed inside what looked like a gold bullet. One was a James Bond 007 Omega Aqua Terra watch with a blue dial, and the other was my favorite, a James Bond 007 Seamaster Ocean Limited Edition Omega watch. What an amazing gift.

Stuart picked up his phone, and I could hear him from the galley, "Vanessa, I love my watches. Where did you find them?" Then silence followed with, "Yes, yes, Anna did too. We are going to watch your movie here in just a bit—"

He fell asleep before I could even start the movie. The cabin was quiet, and the time passed surprisingly fast. As we neared Van Nuys, the onboard phone started ringing. Stuart answered, spoke for a while, and then handed me the phone with a smile. Who could possibly be calling me at work?

To my surprise it was Jean Michel! He had found a way to contact me. "Anna, I could not find you anywhere. I asked for you at the hotel reception desk, and they gave me your note. Thank goodness, because I was so worried."

"I'm really sorry. Stuart had a last minute meeting back home, and we were off! I wanted to see you again. I hope you understand."

"I'm sorry too, and yes, I understand, but either in Mauritius or sooner, I owe you a dinner, okay?"

"I would love that. I'll hold you to it."

"Anna, would you mind if I called you at home tonight?"

"Yes, please."

When I hung up, Stuart was relentless for details, which I did not give. His persistence was admirable, though.

One of my best friends from college would pick me up from the airport. I had arranged to stay with her when I returned. I was excited to see Karen, her husband, Bob, and their adorable little girl, Tara. They had been high school sweethearts from a small town north of Seattle, Washington. Back at UCLA, Bobby had a full ride basketball scholarship.

Karen was my best friend at UCLA. I loved to tease her about growing up on a dairy farm and earning the esteemed "dairy princess" title one year. She was a dear friend and a voice of reason I could trust. I couldn't wait for some good cuddling time with little Tara, too.

We were home! On the ground, Stuart met Karen just before getting into his customized AMG Mercedes convertible. He thanked me with a hug, saying he would be in touch soon, and off he went. Karen was giddy to see the airplane and even helped me with the cleanup. "Anna, this is incredible. I wish we could fly around the world like this!"

I gave Brian a good-luck hug before leaving wishing him success with his surprise proposal the next day at Half Moon Bay. I hopped inside Karen's Toyota minivan, and off we went!

Once in the car, she looked over at me. "Anna, you look amazing. I still can't believe you and Cade broke up. Are you doing all right? You have got to fill me in on everything—"

She stopped mid-sentence. We were both trying to see what was happening on the right side of the road in front of us. Stuart's customized convertible was on the shoulder, and there was Stuart, trying to change a flat tire with his phone to his ear. There was a problem: his custom car wasn't compatible with his tire jack. He was on the phone with AAA. Being Memorial Day weekend, AAA was busy and could not come out for at least two hours.

We pulled over and got out of the minivan. Karen took one look at the problem, went back to her minivan, grabbed her Toyota tire jack, and jacked up his car. Together we rolled his spare tire around the side of the car and changed it, free of charge! He looked over at us sheepishly after it was done. A minivan had rescued the Mercedes! It was one for the headlines. Karen, the dairy princess, stood back with her hands on her hips, assessing his car. "You know, Stuart," she began, "all of your tires look bald. It's a wonder they didn't all blow out on you."

They were bald all right. Poor Stuart. As if the bald spot on his head wasn't embarrassing enough! "What's the matter?" she continued. "Can't afford new tires?"

At this, we all burst out laughing. It was good to be back on the ground for some much-needed girl time. If only Jean Michel could see me now! Cleaning toilets, changing tires, and oh, so very sophisticated. We followed Stuart to his estate where he insisted we come in for a bit. We had a glass of wine by the pool before saying our goodbyes and leaving him to his meeting. He promised to call if he ever needed Karen's help again. On our way out, Karen demanded the details. "Okay, Anna, spill the beans. I want to hear about your trip, Cade, this new guy . . . and what's the deal with Stuart Manning?"

Off we went.

Chapter Ten

OFF TO LE MANS, MORE SECRETS, AND THE BIG RACE

Le Mans, France

The world is a book, and those who do not travel read only one page.
—**St. Augustine**

efore the Mauritius wedding, Stuart had a few trips planned. Jean Michel called every day. It quickly felt like he had always been there. Our brief meeting in Paris had changed everything.

I was pouting on the eve of our trip to Le Mans, not having spoken to Jean Michel all day. My phone practically rang on cue for our regular, late night chat. Outside under the warm glow of the evening stars, I poured out my heart as his warm accent held me captive. My heart was beating to a new pulse.

"Anna, do you even remember what I look like?"

"Are you kidding? You caught my eye the first time I saw you at the hotel in Paris. You're tall, dark featured, and if I recall, extremely handsome—but that could have been my imagination," I finished playfully.

"Really? I'm sure I made a complete fool of myself when I saw you with Stuart. I thought you were a movie star. You took my breath away."

I was smiling at his witty remarks, until I saw his face on the screen of my phone. He wanted to video chat. Oh, no! I had already washed my makeup off and was sitting out on the back deck at Bob and Karen's—not at all my best look. I pushed the button to accept the call just as I heard, "*Oh, combine tu es belle, Anna. Je n'ai jamais senti comme ca avant.*" It meant, "Oh, how beautiful you are, Anna. I have never felt this way before."

"You really know how to sweep a girl off her feet after one evening in Paris. I'm sure this is normal for you. You turn on the *je ne sais quoi,* and all the girls swoon, right?"

He scoffed at the idea, naturally. His words were music to my ears. The intensity of my feelings was surprisingly deep. I had once thought this about Cade. We had grown together in love over the years. This was different; but how could a long distance relationship work?

During our time home, Brian flew up to San Francisco, as planned, for the proposal on the beach below the Ritz Carlton. Of course, Mel said yes, in utter astonishment and surprise.

My sister, Jesse, had gone ahead to stage the setting for the special night and take pictures. It was a gorgeous evening for a very happy couple. They planned for a wedding in less than six months at the Four Seasons in Wailea. Of course we would go! Stuart asked me to be his date, as Vanessa would be filming her sequel to *Jillian Rose*. I was flattered, really, but for now, enough wedding talk. I needed Brian to focus on our upcoming trip to Le Mans.

Jean Michel was among Stuart's guests at the race, along with the ambassador and his wife. We would meet again, but would we feel the same? I could hardly wait to find out.

The 24 Hour Le Mans race was sponsored by the Automobile Club de l'Ouest at the Circuit de la Sarthe. I put my interior decorating skills to work with banners, flags, glasses, and table linens onboard to match the logo for Conor Reilly's team. His passion for racing was shared by his wife, Liz, who managed the team he owned and a few racetracks in the United States.

Conor was the financial genius behind CR Global Investments in the Bay Area. He had helped Stuart with his assets and proved to have the golden touch with his investments. Conor was a seasoned risk-taker, as is true of the personality type of most investors. How fitting it was to learn he was also a car-racing enthusiast.

It was not enough that Conor was a financial wizard. He was also considered one of the world's top Formula One racecar drivers. The plane was stocked with jackets, shirts, and hats from our HHG Porsche Kremer Racing team to wear in support. His team and racecar were on the ground in France, awaiting his arrival. The team was driving a Porsche 962CK6.

Conor and Liz were excitedly awaiting the arrival of our other guests. Stuart had requested an evening departure from the West Coast to ensure an arrival into Le Mans by midmorning the next day. Both the Reilly's were thrilled with the racing paraphernalia onboard, thanking me for the special attention to detail.

"Conor," I said, "we are so proud of you. I can hardly wait to watch you race. I've heard you are quite the driver. Stuart has made it clear that you are to sleep on the flight over and drink water until you practically burst! I put two whole cases of it at your bedside."

They both laughed. Conor and Liz would only accompany us on the flight over to Le Mans. His Challenger 601 would fly over a few days after the race to bring them back home.

We could see Stuart and Vanessa pulling up to the airplane. They looked happy. I could hear Stuart's "Wow!" as he stepped onboard. We had two more guests due in from San Francisco, and once they arrived, we would take off. I don't think that Stuart was accustomed to waiting for guests.

All we knew was, Allister Cummings and his plus one were the tardy guests. We were not told who the plus one was, though I could only imagine. The first time we'd met was the Venice trip with Precious onboard. The second time I was covered head to toe in whipped cream from the explosion and was not at all impressed with him. This should be interesting, as they were running late.

Allister Cummings was the kind of man who would dismiss a subordinate for sharing the same oxygen as him. The tower called with news of his airplane's approach. I couldn't say I was relieved—just ready to begin the trip. Stuart, Vanessa, Conor, and Liz let out a big cheer. A Learjet landed and we were all surprised that Allister had not arrived in his prized G550.

The airplane taxied over, and the door opened. Things seemed strange. If Allister had been on board, he would have been the first one off. Something was wrong. The pilot finally came down the stairs toward us. He spoke without a greeting, just a statement: "Our passengers will be coming shortly. We came ahead with their luggage."

Now I got it; he was only the messenger with their luggage. Very like Allister to send a plane ahead of him with just his things. Looking directly at me, he went on, "These hatboxes need to be transferred directly on to your airplane. They want them onboard with you—not in with the cargo. Please make sure that nothing is set on top of them."

Oh, I sure will . . . not, I thought as I chuckled to myself. Heaven forbid if one of those prized hatboxes is placed beneath someone else's personal luggage! What did they think this was, a C-5 cargo airplane? This trip was a grand total of six days. What could a person possibly need with all these hatboxes?

Stuart was visibly impatient, shaking his head and rolling his eyes when I told him what Allister's pilot had said. Our poor ground crew was working overtime to offload mounds of luggage from the Learjet. I counted a total of thirteen large and five medium suitcases, four full garment bags, and five big hatboxes. They practically filled the entire cargo hold.

Fifteen minutes later, the tower got another call. A second plane was approaching out of San Francisco. "It had better not be Mr. Cummings's shoe collection onboard," I said under my breath. It landed and taxied next to us, just like the first, except this pilot was a hint friendlier.

"Hi, I'm Mr. Cummings's pilot. His guest is onboard. She will need to go straight to your airplane, with no fanfare, but first, could you please pull down all the window shades and dim the lights?" Come again? I asked him to repeat his outlandish request. He must know this was quite ridiculous, but something told me he was used to this kind of thing.

Stuart wanted to know where the missing "man of the hour" was so that we could be on our merry way. The pilot assured him that Allister would show up soon. Hopefully. He pleaded, "Just let me know when everyone is here, and the drama is done, please."

"Yes, sir," I answered.

Meanwhile, I closed all the shades to signal Allister's pilot to bring the mystery passenger onboard. What a ridiculous procedure! Out of the Learjet stepped a pale, waif-like woman with jet-black hair. She walked up the stairs and right on past me, like she owned the airplane, taking her place near the back. Not one to shy away from a challenge, I went over to welcome her and introduce myself. I wondered what had happened to Precious.

"Hi, I'm Anna St. James, Mr. Manning's flight attendant. I need a few things from you before we leave for Le Mans. First, your passport, home address, and some details for our manifest before we can leave for France." She introduced herself as Mr. Cummings's assistant and gave me her information. How many admins did Mr. Cummings have? "Ms. St. James, where did you put my hatboxes?"

Was that all she could think about? Here we were, celebrating a trip to one of the most famous car races in the world, and she is worried about her silly hatboxes? I told her they were in a special compartment just for her and that her boxes had nothing placed on top of them. *Once in flight,* I thought, *who knows what might land on top of those boxes?* There was no thank you, no emotion, and no smile—just this pale, fragile woman. I pitied her for some odd reason. "Ms. St. James, you can expect Allister to arrive shortly."

Yes, Madame! What was all the secrecy about? This woman was not what I would call attractive. Maybe if she could muster a smile it would have helped. True to her word, we had another call that Allister's airplane was approaching on final.

The airplane landed on a runway that was lit up like a Christmas tree. It turned off the active runway toward our parked airplane. Brian went to share with the others that Allister had landed at last. What were these people thinking? Three airplanes were required to get two people from San Francisco to Van Nuys? Stuart told me later that our dear friend Allister was smack dab in the middle of a divorce. His wife was going for billions in the settlement after catching him in the act with his administrative assistant. That wasn't all—he was also trying to frame his ex-wife as the cheater, though others knew differently. He didn't want cameras to catch him with his administrative assistant onboard, as they were on a work trip, naturally. What a bizarre man.

Stuart's guests made their way back toward the airplane to greet Allister. Everyone seemed to be in great spirits—except the administrative assistant. Stuart had made it a point to remind me again that Conor needed to rest. "Anna, make sure he gets constant water so he will be hydrated for the race. It's very important."

He pulled me aside again, asking, "What do you think of the secretive guest?" I rolled my eyes, and he grinned.

"Hang in there with Allister and his guest. I promise we will never again have them onboard. This trip was planned a long time ago."

I dimmed the cabin lights as we left Van Nuys in a darkened sky, filled with twinkling stars. Next stop, Le Mans, in a little over nine hours.

I served a light meal at Vanessa's request, with appetizers and drinks right after takeoff. We had every kind of food onboard: snacks, drinks, desserts, and breakfast—really just about anything you could possibly want. After our meal,

Liz sat at the dining table reading a book. I really liked her. She looked cozy wrapped up in a warm cashmere blanket with a matching pillow propped up at her side.

"Liz, I made some lavender chamomile tea, and here are some cashmere slippers to keep you warm."

She was happy, relaxed, and appreciative. Stuart and Vanessa had already retired for a good night of rest. Allister and his plus one must have gone to sleep, too. I hadn't noticed.

Two hours inflight with everything cleaned up and put away, I left out a few trays of evening snacks: a beautiful tray of fruit, vegetables, an antipasto assortment, and cookies—just in case anyone woke up wanting something to nibble on. I had to get up to the flight deck to check on the boys, too. We really were quite the team and had fallen into an easy working relationship. I considered them a part of my family now. I tried hard to take good care of them, and tonight was no exception.

On these longer trips, I did everything I could think of to keep Brian and Chris awake. Even being bossy enough to make them stand up and stretch every hour. Yes, they also had to drink lots of water, no soda and no coffee until morning. I always had two full water bottles at their seats. One bottle had water, and the other was a concoction of Airborne with Emergen-C powder to keep them healthy and alert. I was learning the ropes quickly.

I was heading up the main aisle toward the cockpit when I stopped dead in my tracks. Two pairs of feet were sticking out from underneath the table where Liz was reading her book. I looked up at Liz, and she confirmed my suspicion. She nodded her head and put her finger up to her mouth like she was gagging. I just could not believe this!

No way was I climbing over those two. I went straight back to the galley, calling the boys up front. Brian picked up. They were hungry and in need of refills. "Brian, I know you guys are hungry, but there is no way I am heading up there right now. We've got a situation on our hands, and you will not believe what kind."

I quickly told Brian what I had seen. "Brian, I am not going to try and climb over two pairs of feet to make a run for the cockpit."

Brian gasped, "Anna, no way, there is no way. Hold on, I'm coming back."

"No Brian, no—" He was already on his way back toward the galley, shaking his head.

He got to the dining table with the protruding feet and straddled the big captain's seats to pass, with his jaw on the floor. Had he not believed me? Yes, there on the floor was one of the world's richest men having sex with his administrative assistant out in the open. We were all disgusted. Absolutely incredulous, Brian came back to the galley. I gave him some food and water bottles to tide him over. "Anna, I think I have just lost my appetite."

Liz came back shortly. "Okay, I'm totally grossed out!"

Allister and his plus one finally went to their private quarters after sufficiently traumatizing everyone still awake in the cabin. Poor Liz looked relieved to see them disappear. I already knew that Allister Cummings was thoughtless and mean, but this tactless stunt was nothing short of disgusting. What could any self-respecting woman possibly see in a man like Allister? Money was the only thing that came to mind. I felt bad for Liz and incessantly apologized for the couple's indecent exposure.

Meanwhile, I had run out of storage room. I got some form of pleasure from piling things on top of those silly hatboxes, and yes, I think they might have received a dent or two—likely smashed from the shifting of items in flight, of course.

Brian tried to distract me with a chance to see the Northern Lights from the flight deck. Good move. I asked Liz if she would like to join us. The shape shifting of hues across the sky was magical and entrancing. That moment lifted me out of my immediate surroundings to understand the awe and beauty of God's creation; it nearly took my breath away.

Everyone was finally asleep as we blazed a trail to Le Mans. I would see Jean Michel very soon! Would sparks fly again? One could only hope. Our descent took much longer after flying at an altitude of forty-nine thousand feet.

Throughout the main cabin, I opened the window shades when we were about twenty minutes from touchdown and put out the L'Occitane overnight kits for the passengers, each customized with its own toothbrush, toothpaste, comb, brush, and skincare products. At each seat I placed a glass of fresh-squeezed orange juice, a bottle of water, and a refreshing, scented hand towel. The buffet was set up with a continental breakfast before touchdown. Never fear, the boys up front had already had their breakfast. I went through the cabin and put out race team backpacks embroidered with each passenger's name. Each was filled with a t-shirt, polo shirt, jacket, blanket, sweater, hat, water bottle, and a team poster. I also included a booklet about the race. Each piece was a special gift to commemorate the race. I had backpacks made for Brian, Chris, Jean Michel, the ambassador, and his wife as a surprise, hoping they would also feel a part of the celebration. Stuart thought it was great.

My passengers were slowly starting to rub the sleep from their eyes. Stuart was up first and happy to see my arrangements. He came back to the galley and said, "Good morning, dear Anna. Thank you for all your efforts in making this, once again, such a special trip."

He asked how the flight had gone. I winked and said to ask Liz in private when he had the chance. Oh, no, I was not going to comment on Allister's behavior with his plus one! Stuart would not approve, but it did make for one crazy story. I apologized to Liz again for their inappropriate behavior. She brushed it off, saying she would keep her distance well enough in Le Mans while working with Conor and his team. We shared a laugh and a big hug.

Everyone was awake except Allister and his guest. I woke them after breakfast, just as we were about to land. They actually sat up as we were landing. The runway at Le Mans Arnage Airport is very short: 4,626 feet long. I had briefed everyone that, with this shorter runway, a change in weather might cause us to divert to another airport. The weather was holding out for us that day, however, at about seventy-five degrees and sunny.

Brian nailed a great landing with an abrupt stop, as expected. A few items shifted about the cabin. Classically unprepared, Allister's wonderful guest tumbled out of her seat and onto the floor. It was a joint effort to suppress our laughter at the incident, and let me say, it was hard. Once at a complete stop, we turned around on the active runway to taxi toward the terminal. People were lined up on top of the building to watch the arrivals and departures, hoping to see someone of interest. Our beautiful airplane garnered special attention as we came to a stop and cut the engines.

A little café had bistro tables dotting the rooftop of the terminal, with spectators beneath colorful Perrier and Carlsberg beer umbrellas. The terminal in Le Mans is small, making it difficult for a group like ours to enter discreetly. You could see people watching us through binoculars. Vanessa, of course, would be the most recognized of our little group. She was always very intentional where her fans were concerned, signing the many autographs and thanking each person. I don't know how she did it, but it was lovely to watch. Sans makeup, with a high ponytail and large sunglasses, she looked every inch the movie star that she was. Her tight, straight-legged jeans fit to perfection with a casual, white t-shirt, Chanel flats, and her new racing jacket.

I was thrilled to step into the bright morning sunshine of France. I opened the stairs for our passengers and watched them head for the terminal. We sent Conor off with our best wishes; he was very hydrated, I might add!

Vanessa stepped off the airplane, and the crowd cheered. Allister was next and could hardly stand being upstaged. Knowing he was now in a foreign country, he left caution to the wind, no longer concerned with secrecy. With a flair for drama, he scooped his rail-thin lover into his arms and whisked her off toward the terminal like some treasured prize. If only the world knew what was on the other side of Allister's flimsy public veneer.

What to make of the closed window shades and dimmed lights in Van Nuys I will never know. The man was a lunatic, if you asked me. He was just about to step inside the terminal when he turned to the group and asked, "Isn't she the most beautiful woman in the world?" If that wasn't the loaded question of the year! In fact, no one responded at all.

Stuart and Vanessa looked happy holding hands while walking inside. My gaze caught at the terminal door where Jean Michel stood. He looked as amazing as I remembered. He shook hands with Stuart, gave Vanessa a hug, and introduced himself to Conor and Liz. I started down the stairs at the same time he came out to greet me. I threw myself into his arms, not noticing anyone but him. That night in Paris seemed so long ago when we watched the breaking of dawn together. He slipped his arm around my waist as we walked. It felt like he had been doing that for a lifetime. Yes, this felt good!

The entire section of onlookers above the terminal broke out into loud cheers and whistles. They thought we were celebrities. It's no wonder; I was with an incredible looking man. He couldn't resist flattering me with the notion that they were cheering for me. In Le Mans, I was in the arms of Jean Michel, and it felt amazing. Would we finally get the dinner we had missed in Paris?

First, I had to tidy the airplane and touch base with ground services for our departure on Sunday morning. I got all my contact information and told them I would be in touch the following morning. I had arranged with Chef Christophe Renou at the Chateau to cater the return trip. The menus were done, and we had confirmed the entire order before I had left the United States. I had smoothed out all the details beforehand to leave more time with Jean Michel. There was a method to my madness!

Jean Michel had driven to Le Mans to bring me, along with Brian and Chris, to the Chateau where we were staying while here. We were all giddy with laughter, probably from our lack of sleep, but it didn't matter. We had arrived. Jean Michel thought it cute to caricature our group with family roles. Brian was the big brother; Chris was the baby brother; and I was the princess, naturally. The boys thought they were clever, ganging up on me like that. I pretended to be upset with them for sport.

We traveled through a beautiful town called Alençon, with cobbled streets, quaint shops, and outdoor markets. Jean Michel pulled up at Rive Droite at 31 rue du Pont Neuf for a gran café. He announced that we looked in need of a little caffeine. He took hold of my hand and led us to a charming café with outdoor bistro tables to enjoy the early summer weather. I was under his spell. Brian and Chris took full advantage of every opportunity to tease me while I sat in the spring air, spellbound. We enjoyed the warm café along with fresh, melt-in-your-mouth croissants. Could life get any better?

Our drive through the French countryside to the five-hundred-year-old Chateau de Saint Paterne was spectacular. It was about forty minutes from Le Mans, providing some privacy for Conor and Liz during the race. We had two helicopters at our disposal to shuttle everyone back and forth and two cars with drivers on standby to take us wherever we needed to go. We would all meet at the Chateau for dinner to celebrate Conor, but for now, I was basking in the glow of newfound love. Jean Michel turned off the beaten path and onto a charming lane leading to the Chateau and into another world.

Its grounds were maintained to perfection. The Chateau had ten rooms and six suites. Stuart and Vanessa were in a self-contained suite on the property called L'Orangerie Suite. Liz and Conor, Allister and his lover, and the ambassador and his wife had suites, too. I was given a suite down the hall from Jean Michel's. Both Brian and Chris had smaller, but equally luxurious, rooms. It was perfect in every way. Charles Henry and Segolene de Valbray greeted us warmly at the front door. They made each person who stayed at the Chateau feel right at home.

The café had given me a needed jolt to stay awake for at least a couple of hours. But once I stepped into the room with my handsome escort, the caffeine seemed to wear off. I just wanted to hop into my cozy, four-post bed for a quick rest. Jean Michel said he would hold me in his arms until I fell asleep. It was heavenly. Just one hour. I snuggled deeper into his arms, thinking that after a hot bath I'd be as good as new. I don't remember much except waking up about three hours later to him standing over me in workout clothes as he softly whispered into my ear. He had left me to rest while he went for a run.

He came bearing a tray with some lunch the chef had prepared. I must have looked a sight. He was still at my side, after seeing me at my worst. All he could say was, "Anna, you are so beautiful."

Oh, my! After our lunch out on my small terrace overlooking the grounds, he said he would return in about thirty minutes, to give me time to get ready. "Dress casually. I want to go and explore a little village close by with you. We don't need to be back to the Chateau until eight this evening. *Bon Son, ma Princesse?*"

"Jean Michel, it sounds perfect, but could you give me forty-five minutes? I want to hop in the bathtub for a few moments."

He responded, "I will meet you downstairs in one hour. I hope you don't mind. I'm just happy to see you finally."

He leaned over with a kiss that practically made me speechless. "You have become so special to me, Anna. *J'espere que vous savez que* . . . I hope you know that."

Not wanting to miss any time together, I made it downstairs in forty-five minutes, even before Jean Michel. I left messages for Brian and Chris to let them know I would catch up with them that evening. They were probably taking naps after our long day of flying.

Within minutes, a very handsome man headed toward me in the hallway. He took my breath away every time. It wasn't just his good looks; he was the whole package: intelligent, romantic, a family man—he was a gentleman in every sense of the word. We had shared our lives over the phone for what seemed like a lifetime, and now here he was in front of me. It felt like God had perfectly orchestrated how we met. The only thing now that stood in the way was a country and an ocean.

He hadn't seen me watching him until he got a bit closer; his face lit up. I was rewarded with a kiss that could steal any girl's heart. No, not a cheek-to-cheek kiss, but the kind that swept me off my feet. He grabbed my hand as we headed for the village of Bagnoles-de-L'Orne.

We pulled up in front of a beautiful lake surrounded by well-kept gardens. Bagnoles-de-L'Orne was a healing place cradled by natural thermal baths and spas. Hand in hand, we found a perfect place close to the lake to put a blanket down on the early summer grass. A hint of fresh flowers floated through the air as Jean Michel opened a picnic basket, popping the cork on some wonderful, chilled champagne with fresh fruit, a baguette, and assorted cheeses. I knew I must be in heaven. We sat there, reveling in one another's company. He kissed me again and again. This was better than any dinner in Paris.

Back at the Chateau, around seven that evening, we had just enough time to change for dinner. Jean Michel knocked on my door to escort me to the dining room and our celebratory dinner. We walked into the dining room, with only the light of candlesticks in silver holders to guide us. This felt a lot like love. Could I possibly have fallen in love so quickly? Shadows danced off the walls, and Jean Michel held on tightly to me. *Please never let go*, I thought. Brian and Chris had just arrived, still a bit groggy, giving Stuart the ammunition to give them a hard time. "What did you guys do this afternoon, sleep?"

The dining room was an enclave of romance. Slowly, our group arrived by couple. The ambassador and his wife were happy to see us again and to meet

Vanessa. It was clear they loved Jean Michel like a son. They were excited to hear about the upcoming wedding in Mauritius. Conor and Liz came down having rested all afternoon. Rest was crucial for the next day's race. Allister and his plus one didn't join us that evening, which made the dinner even more delightful.

In a dining room surrounded by friends, I could only feel gratitude to Mr. Manning for seeing something in me all those months ago. I had heard the stories of different flight departments—some good and others just plain crazy. I knew one flight attendant who was not allowed to speak to her main passenger. She had to first speak to the personal assistant, even while the passenger was sitting in plain sight! Another popular TV personality never let anyone speak to him directly. Staff couldn't even ask for his drink preference. They had to ask the personal assistant. If a person ever tried, they were fired on the spot.

With Stuart Manning, I worked long, hard hours with a demanding schedule, but he was the real deal. I knew he would go the distance to help any of his friends. He had done it for me with Cade. We were family, and I felt it on this trip.

Jean Michel's job for the Ambassador of Mauritius was similar, with a demanding schedule. They were like father and son. The Durand family and the ambassador's family were extremely close. They had a daughter who had grown up following JM all over the island, like a little sister to him. Jean Michel traveled the world and loved spreading goodwill on behalf of his small, island nation. The ambassador told me that my JM was being groomed to take over for him someday.

Charles Henry made a crackling fire for us to enjoy our nightcaps in the main room. The night was perfect. Stuart lightly tapped on his glass to make a toast. "I would like to thank you all for making this trip so special. First, though, my best wishes to my friend Conor, who is more like a brother to me. We are proud of your accomplishments and expect you to take Le Mans by storm this week with a win. Secondly, I want to thank the amazing woman next to me for saying yes. I am the happiest man in the world, besides Brian these days, and excited for the beginning of our lives together." He leaned over and gave Vanessa a long kiss, which she in kind returned. Our world was a happy place.

He continued, "Also, congratulations are in order to Brian on his recent engagement to Melanie. Vanessa and I would like to give you the gift of your wedding in Maui. Please accept this gift with our congratulations. And if it wasn't for Melanie, I dare say this next toast wouldn't be possible. Thank you, Anna, for joining this crazy family of ours. You have made it better just with your presence. We are also happy to see you and Jean Michel together." He paused for the hum of laughter around him and cleared his throat as I felt Jean Michel's arm tighten around my shoulder. "You two are some of my favorite people in the world. I love you guys. Last, but certainly not least, to Chris. We will keep our eyes opened for you to find the perfect woman. More importantly, welcome to the family. Thank you all for being here."

The evening was a dream with Jean Michel by my side. Almost as good was seeing Stuart and Vanessa so much in love and Brian still with his head in the clouds from his recent engagement.

Jean Michel took me on a moonlit walk through the Chateau grounds that evening. I was fading fast from my lack of sleep, and he knew it. He led me to my room by the hand and waited while I got ready for bed. As I stepped back into my cozy room, warmed by the fire, Jean Michel pulled me into his arms and carried me to bed. I was exhausted, but my heart was beating wildly. I was nervous, too. Laying me down ever so gently, he kissed me goodnight. "Anna, do you mind if I lie down next to you for a bit before heading to my room? I cannot seem to say goodnight." He kissed me again, pulling away to look into my eyes while I caught my breath, "*Doux reves.*"

I woke up from my wonderful dreams of Jean Michel to a room flooded in bright sunshine. My phone said it was still early, six thirty, but I felt rested for the first time in a while and ready to start my day. Before going on a run, I had things to do. I tiptoed quietly down the ancient stairs for a tray of café, croissants, and fruit as a wake up surprise for Jean Michel.

Trying to balance the breakfast tray and turn the espagnolette-style lock on his massive French doors was a major feat at this time of morning. Once inside, I found him still peacefully asleep. He must have been tired from taking care of me the day before. Though he worked a full-time job, he always seemed to put me first. Sneaking around the side of the bed, I kicked off my shoes and climbed into the warmth of Jean Michel, gently giving him a wakeup kiss. He rolled over to draw me in close, "*Bonjour, mon amour.*" I gave him another kiss. "I come bearing breakfast. I think this could become a habit."

He chuckled and nuzzled my neck. "Yes, Anna, let's make it a permanent habit."

My heart skipped a beat.

We ate breakfast, followed by a run through the twenty-five acres surrounding the Chateau. Brian joined us to make my morning complete. I was in heaven, running alongside two of my favorite men in the glorious French countryside under summer skies. Oh, *oui*!

Back at the Chateau, we had the entire day to explore and play. We spent time relaxing at the pool in the glow of each other's company. We played croquet, followed by ping-pong, and I won! Poolside massages were the perfect treat in the early afternoon. Brian and Chris asked us to join them on a bike ride through the countryside, followed by a café stop in the nearby village. I will never forget that afternoon. Riding the short distance through the verdant, rolling hills, surrounded in heavy summer blooms, I found the view breathtaking; it was a spectacular display and provided the perfect enticement to slip a kayak through the placid waters of the nearby lake.

The evening was just as good. Our small group boarded a helicopter to Angers for dinner at La Favre d'Anne, with another astounding view of the Chateau d'Angers on the river Le Maine. I remembered being in Angers with Cade's family one summer. His godmother had a beautiful Chateau on the outskirts of Angers, with English formal gardens that I had fallen in love with. It was a beautiful city, also famed for its slate. This city had been very special to me, but somehow with Jean Michel by my side it was like a dream that I never wanted to wake up from. How beautiful it was strolling through the Angers Jardin des Plantes surrounded in the rich botanical gardens—the city seemed alive in a new way through the enchantment of a summer's night.

We left Angers close to midnight, with a big day of race festivities ahead. I asked our group if anyone had seen Allister. "No," Stuart replied. "I think they are staying at a castle close by. They wanted to be on their own, and I, for one, couldn't be happier. I let him know we would be staying another day after the race, and that was it. He's sent for his airplane to fly them home once the race is completed."

I couldn't keep the look of joy from my face. Stuart noticed and just winked at me. He pulled Jean Michel aside in deep discussion. Vanessa looked over at me with a big smile. "I hope you don't mind, but Stuart thought it would be nice to invite Jean Michel back to Van Nuys with us Sunday morning. Stuart loves him and couldn't be happier for the two of you. Is that all right?"

I gave her a big hug and said once again, "Thank you for always being so thoughtful. It means so much to me."

That evening, Jean Michel and I could not seem to say good night. He told me about Stuart's offer to come to Los Angeles, asking if I would mind. I reminded him that he would have to behave himself on the flight home and responded with a laugh, "Yes, I would love for you to come to California and meet my family. I've been soaking up our last days together, hating the thought of saying goodbye. I am pretty crazy about you."

He really wanted to meet my parents and Jesse, too. He said, "Anna, I do not take 'us' lightly. I have fallen in love with you. Yes, I know it's been such a short time, but I knew it the first time I met you. When I think of you, I cannot see anyone else in my life, ever."

I could not believe it! My entire world was changing.

"Is it all right with the ambassador for you to come out to the West Coast?"

"Stuart and I actually have a few projects we're working on, and the ambassador sends me with his blessings."

Curled up in front of his fireplace, we fell asleep in each other's arms.

The only thing that woke me was the sunshine peeking through the window. Today, fifty-six cars and one hundred and sixty eight drivers would register in the city center of Le Mans. The entire town would show up for an autograph, a picture, or just to celebrate. Next was "Test Day," or practice and prequalifying. Jean Michel took all of us to the famous Ferris wheel at the Ford Curves. The view from the top made it worthwhile. We went into the restaurants at the Mulsanne straight. Arnage was just plain crazy. Everyone was celebrating, and the race had not even begun. Friday is called "Mad Friday," and the name is well suited. It is one crazy and mad day! And finally, race day.

The Le Mans race is one of the most grueling in the world. It began in 1923, and the tradition lives on. It is six times longer than the Indianapolis 500. Just before the race begins, jets do a flyover, emitting a trail of blue, white, and red smoke, adding to the drama during the second week of June. Remember, this is tradition. Once the smoke clears, the race begins with the waving of the French *Le Tricolore.*

It starts in the afternoon and ends twenty-four hours later. There are all kinds of rules, but what is different at Le Mans is how the race continues off the main track and into the streets that have been closed for this special day. The surface can get rough, which only adds to the drama. Each car has no less than three drivers.

With the early summer weather like we had that day, the cars would get hot inside. Now I understood why Stuart was so insistent that Conor drink water like a fish! Stuart was going to help with the team for half the day. We all showed up in our race gear in support of Conor. We had passes for our box, the Pitwalk, T34 Stands, the Village, the Mulsanne and Arnage Corners, a concert, the Grandstand, the Butte Spectator, and the Paddock. I had no idea there was this much to take in. It was hot, and it was loud, and I said a prayer for Conor and his team to be safe.

The race began with hairpin turns, tight eases, and short straights, but my favorite was the long Dunlop Curve. We saw the Dunlop Bridge and La Chapelle. It was total craziness! My insides shook from the vibrations of the cars flying by. It was incredibly loud. We were given radio hats to hear what was going on minute by minute. As evening approached, the cars passed through the Tertre Rouge. The brakes on the cars glowed, and the numbers on the sides of the cars were like spotlights in fluorescent colors. Headlights seemed to fly by with the scream of the engines. Speeds can top out around 202 miles per hour. Fireworks and a concert were beginning, and the party was just kicking into high gear. It was a blast, but also a chaotic scene. Conor and his team were well within the top five spots at all times. My voice was hoarse from all the cheering. Jean Michel kept looking over at me as I rooted for Conor; my cheeks were flushed from all the excitement. Soon he was screaming as loudly as I was. "Jean Michel, you should've been part of our cheer squad back at UCLA!"

He just shook his head and chuckled. "Anna, I love to watch how you embrace each moment of your life. Soon, you'll have me carrying pompoms." He smiled and planted a kiss on top of my head.

I stepped away from our group to use the restroom—or WC as they call it in Europe. From out of nowhere, a man came up and told me, in a strong accent, that Mr. Manning asked for me to follow him. He grabbed my elbow so hard it felt like my arm was breaking. The man's eyes were dark, almost black and seemed to bore holes into my soul. I will never forget those eyes. They were piercing and angry, and the hair on my arms stood up at the sight of him. Thankfully, Jean Michel had watched me walk away and saw the man grab my elbow. He made a quick run toward me, yelling at the top of his lungs, "Anna, I'm here. Help! Over here! *Arretez*! Let go of her." As quickly as the man had grabbed my elbow, he vanished into thin air. All eyes were trained on me as Jean Michel wrapped my shaking body into his arms. Was it my imagination? My elbow didn't feel that way.

Jean Michel was upset and worried for my safety. He asked Stuart's security to look into it, but I tried to downplay it. Surely I must have misunderstood what had happened. Why would anyone want to harm me? From that point on at the event, I had a shadow watching over me at all times until we were to leave on Sunday. We went back to the Chateau late that evening to rest up for a few hours before the final at Le Mans early the next morning. The race was spectacular. We stayed for the end to watch Conor cross the finish line in second place! I was so proud of him. He had placed well in an incredibly tough race.

The podium ceremony was next, and Conor invited us to go up with his team. It was a wonderful celebration, topped off with the soaking in champagne. I tried to forget the dark cloud that had left a mark on my elbow and enjoy sharing the honor of this special moment with Conor and Liz.

We left the Chateau early Sunday morning for the airport in Le Mans and our flight to Van Nuys. On board, I had Stuart, Vanessa, and Jean Michel and life seemed perfect. The catering from the Chateau looked spectacular. Chef Christophe had prepared breakfast fit for a king—or at least a wealthy billionaire. He made the fluffiest quiche, along with his signature pastries. He also prepared our dinner to serve later inflight.

My Menu:
Gaspaccio Trios
Duck Breast Topped with a Balsamic and Honey Sauce
Assorted French Cheeses with a Salade Vert
Apricot Tart with Rosemary Sorbet and a Poires au Pommeau

It was spectacular! I also needed ice and our clean dishes from our handler. He came out to the airplane with twelve of the tiniest ice cubes I've ever seen. I looked at them, thinking he was trying to be funny, and started to laugh. He was dead serious. He looked at me and said, "*Ce n'est pas possible!*"

With our banter over ice cubes, Jean Michel stepped in to ask how he could help. Ah, my diplomat! The handler told us we could go to the bar inside the airport to buy our ice. So we did. The ice was in sheets of twelve tiny cubes, fifteen euros per pack. I bought all the packs they had, which was twenty. That was three hundred euros for the tiniest ice cubes on earth. They didn't even fill up one third of my ice drawer, but I had ice!

Jet setting with Jean Michel on board? What a dream. Next stop, home! Stuart and Vanessa wanted to review wedding details with me during the flight, followed by a relaxing movie. They loved our food from Chef Christophe too. This was *la bonne vie*!

Chapter Eleven

OFF TO THE BIG EVENT, WITH A FEW STOPS FIRST

We all dream of far away.

—Anonymous

he day was so close I could almost taste the wedding cake. Melanie had taken time off from work to join Brian, Chris, and I in Mauritius for the big event. I was flying with my A-team once again. I had even put an offer on a cute, little bungalow in Santa Monica that Jean Michel had helped me find while he was visiting. It was one block from the beach, adorable, and perfect for me. We had spent an amazing time together in California. I showed him around, and he had my parents eating out of his hand before long. Jesse just said, "Anna, I get it. This guy is your perfect match. You hang on to him. I mean it! He loves you, but don't spend too much time away from him. Oh, and yes, he's hot!"

My heart felt like it would explode. Everyone was under the Jean Michel spell. I was crazy about him too, but also realistic. How could we make this work with the distance of continents between us?

Jean Michel left for Paris much too soon. The ambassador had been generous to loan him out for a week, even if he had been working with Stuart in LA. He called every day, at least once. He even offered to come back to Los Angeles to help me move after the wedding, but I knew we would be headed straight to Bora Bora for Stuart and Vanessa's honeymoon. He would meet me for at least one of our days in the South of France with a surprise in store. "Remember, Anna, we will have more time together once we are in Mauritius."

That thought made my heart skip a beat.

The wedding left countless details to arrange before our departure, so I busied myself with all the prep work. I stayed near the phone, when I could, to take his calls. I loved hearing his voice.

Stuart and Vanessa had asked me to have baskets filled with gifts in each room at the resort in Mauritius when the guests arrived. They suggested I go to Saks Fifth Avenue in Beverly Hills and have them create something special to send ahead of us. Both Stuart and Vanessa told me to do anything I thought would be special as a thank you gift for their intimate group of guests. "Anna," Stuart said, "please don't worry about the budget. Just use my credit card, and do what you think is best. Make it beautiful as you always do. We appreciate all of your help with this."

I dragged Chris and poor Karen along on my shopping ventures after some convincing. Chris was whining about not being a shopper. My response to him was, "Then you can be my bag boy and carry all the purchases. For your reward, I promise to buy you a meal wherever you want."

He liked that idea. I knew he would take full advantage of the meal. He called from Saks to make reservations, on the spot, for Melisse on Wilshire Boulevard that evening. This was going to cost me.

We walked into Saks Fifth Avenue and went straight for the specialty area. It seemed like the perfect place to start. I spotted these handmade baskets from a tribe in Uganda. They were the perfect size to fill with lots of wonderful gifts. I was asked to get forty gifts, customizable for both men and women. This was going to be fun. Chris wasn't too thrilled, but Karen and I were up for it. We waited patiently for the woman who was working in the department to help us. She ignored us. After waiting patiently, I approached her to ask if she could help us. She looked over at me, through her half-moon glasses attached about her neck with an eyeglass chain, and said, "I will get to you when I can, but I have other customers who have been waiting. I need to take care of them first."

Really? When we had arrived, there was only one other customer in front of us—who was long gone by now. She had walked right past us to help the four other customers who came in after us. We'd had enough of the waiting game. I grabbed Chris and Karen's arms, dragging them into the next department. We found a nice sales clerk named Joan who was only too happy to help. She came with us to the specialty department as I pointed to the baskets. "We would like forty of those Ugandan baskets, please. Also, I would like to fill them with different items and have them wrapped and shipped overseas. Can you arrange that, please?"

She said it would be her pleasure. Just then, the first saleswoman got wind of our conversation and tried to dismiss the helpful sales clerk, "Joan, I was helping these kids earlier. I'll take it from here."

Without giving her a chance to respond, I made it clear that we would like Joan to help us. Off we went, handing Joan our list of what to put in the baskets:

Le Maison du Chocolat gift box, Petrossian royal ossetra caviar with serving set, Squirrel assorted nuts, a Canon camera, binoculars, men's and women's Prada totes, customized luggage tags, cashmere slippers and throw, Missoni beach towels, adapters for international travel, Mont Blanc pen sets, headsets, and last, a Jo Malone gift set. The only thing missing was the book of activities planned for the week of the wedding and two bottles of Sonoma SMS.

I would place the booklets and wine in the baskets once we arrived. I wanted one of these amazing gifts. Each basket was valued at over five thousand dollars. To me, they were extravagant, but very special. We thanked Joan, gave her the address of the hotel in Mauritius, and asked her to have the baskets delivered by the early part of the following week. It's amazing what one can do without a budget and with the credit card of one of the richest men in the world. We spent over two hundred thousand dollars in less than two hours. It was a lot of fun, too. It took everything I had not to walk over to the first saleswoman, like Julia Roberts in *Pretty Woman*, and say, "Big Mistake!"

Our first destination on the wedding adventure was to Nice, in the South of France. After the South of France, we would be overnighting in Cairo to see the pyramids. From Cairo, we were off to the Royal Malewane Safari Lodge by way of our final destination—the wedding in Mauritius. Vanessa and Stuart were my only passengers on the flight to Nice. It was obvious how much they loved one another, and their excitement for the wedding was intoxicating.

In Nice, they would stay at his estate in Cap Ferrat. Let the joyous celebration begin. I offered *Sonoma SMS Champagne* for the occasion, which Stuart was happy to receive, but Vanessa declined. That seemed unusual, but I thought little of it. We left at about four o'clock in the afternoon and arrived in the morning to crystal clear skies and temperatures in the mid-eighties at the Aeroport Nice, Cote d'Azur. Our good friends at Landmark Aviation (LFMN) took care of us on the ground. All was well. We said our goodbyes to Stuart and Vanessa and wished them a wonderful time in Cap Ferrat. We were just a call away if they needed anything.

Our hotel was in Cannes. The JW Marriott Cannes was right on the Croisette Promenade, officially called the Boulevard de la Croisette. When we stepped foot into the hotel, there stood Jean Michel to greet me. I must have been a sight for sore eyes after working a long flight, but it didn't matter, I was very happy to see him. Brian said, with a wink, "I guess we won't be seeing much of you while we are here."

Jean Michel had already checked me in and invited Brian and Chris to join us at the Chateau Eze for dinner. They both thanked him, but declined the invitation to give us time together. I loved that he thought to include them. I told both of the boys that I would be in touch.

We had dinner plans for the following night. Jean Michel gave me a funny smile and said, "Don't forget, Anna, I have a special day planned for you tomorrow."

He didn't have to twist my arm!

Up to my suite with my handsome escort, I stepped back before entering the room to have a look at him. "I have never seen you so casual, even in Le Mans and California. Here you are, wearing boat shoes and shorts. I like this look, Jean Michel."

The suite was filled with flowers. Before I could turn to him and say, "I missed you too," he pulled me into his arms and kissed me. We stepped out together onto the terrace overlooking the magic of the Mediterranean Sea. I never did hear the sounds of the ocean below as he showered me again with a repeat of his kisses. We sat out on the terrace and enjoyed a wonderful breakfast as he asked to show me around the Cote d'Azur that afternoon. Did he really have to ask?

Jean Michel said he would meet me in an hour to do some sightseeing. Sure enough, he was outside at the front of the hotel, holding a helmet for me to put on. I stared at it and just laughed, letting him know it would mess up my hair. "Seriously, Jean Michel?"

He looked at me and said, "Yes, Anna, but you could never look bad. You have my heart with who you are, as well as with your beauty. Now, your hair…?" He added with a wink.

Oh, my! Who says this kind of stuff? I did give his arm a punch for the hair remark. He put on his helmet and said, "*Viola, allons!*"

He took me to Nice where I discovered my favorite store, just off the rue d'Antibes, called Oliviers and Co., originating out of nearby Provence. They sell the most fantastic olive oils.

I fell in love with an olive tapenade we sampled there, and ordered a case to be shipped home to California. We stepped into Place Gambetta for some picnic supplies and then over to Happy Flowers on Chabard. I liked the flowers so much I ordered a delivery out to Landmark for our flight to Cairo.

We headed inland toward the village of Grasse. We stopped to enjoy our picnic along the way before he bought me some incredible perfume that was my new signature fragrance. It was heavenly.

Over our picnic lunch, he told me how he had come to work for the ambassador. Their families were close. He had lived between Mauritius and Paris his entire life. His parents split their time between the two places, as well as outside of Cap d'Ail. They were in Mauritius now. I would meet them in a few short days. His parents both came from old, aristocratic families that had been in the textile trade for generations.

His father owned one of the largest textile mills on the island. Jean Michel went to the Sorbonne for his university education and continued with a law degree and internship with the ambassador before finishing his schooling. Once he was done at the Sorbonne, the ambassador asked him to be his right-hand man. He had worked for him for about three years now, not including his internship, and loved it. He said that he thought the ambassador and his wife secretly had hoped he would marry their daughter, but he had always just thought of her as a little sister, nothing more.

Off we went toward a little town called La Turbie to have an afternoon glass of wine out on the *tarrasse,* with a view of the entire coastline. The footpaths once used by the Romans were still visible in little dotted lines leading up the sides of the coast to the medieval town. Jean Michel pointed to the *tete de chien*, head of a dog, etched into the mountainside rock. It was magic.

The couple who owned the restaurant, La Tarasse, had met my parents' friends from California. They had put La Tarasse on the map in their latest travel book, which made us instant friends. Our hearts were full, leaving La Turbie that afternoon with new friends and lifetime memories. The couple said farewell with big smiles. "You come back, *oui*?"

Oui, we would come back.

Jean Michel delivered me back to the hotel late that afternoon, with an hour's notice before dinner. I raced up to my room in a daze, thinking of Jean Michel and nothing else. I threw on a dress I bought as a bit of a splurge before coming on this trip. It was a Louis Vuitton dress that I had somehow scored on sale in Beverly Hills. It wasn't the Stella, but it was close.

I stepped out of the elevator that evening to my handsome date. He gave me another one of those unbelievable kisses. Coming up for air, he stepped back, let out his breath in awe, and said, "Are you ready, my Anna?"

With his arm draped around my shoulders, he led me through the door to a Mercedes speedster parked outside. He was staying at his family's home in Monaco, and this little number was his father's pride and joy. What else did he have up his sleeve?

I had been in love with Cade before, but Jean Michel really knew how to romance me. He made me feel like I was the only woman in the world. I could not help but notice that wherever we went, people would stop and take a second look. We did make quite a striking pair—if I say so myself!

High above Monte Carlo, the gentle breeze cooled us after a warm day. Up, up the famous Moyenne Corniche's steep and windy road we drove, with nightfall giving us perfect guidance by means of a path of stars hovering above the medieval village. The magic of Eze was another world. We were enchanted with each step through the gate and into the tranquility of the village's narrow, cobblestone streets toward the Chateau. I was holding onto the arm of a man who I knew was the love of my life. UCLA and the world back home was nothing but a distant memory. Tonight was the beginning of truly letting go and moving forward.

I should have known by now that tonight was special. Jean Michel had a table out on their private balcony, overlooking the lights thirteen hundred feet below. It was the magic of the Cote d'Azur. This is where the last slopes of the Alps took their dramatic and final plunge into the Mediterranean Ocean below.

If this was a dream, I never wanted to be awakened. The chef at Chateau Eze, Alex Wagner, was expecting us. He came out to say he had prepared an eight-course meal for us, paired expertly with wines from the region. To this day, I cannot pronounce what we ate that evening. It was after one in the morning before we reluctantly left.

Jean Michel slowed the car down on the Moyenne Corniche, pulling over to the side of the road. We sat overlooking the French Riviera. He spread out a blanket as we lay on the front of his car. It reminded me of how my father, sister, and I would lay down, watching the airplanes take off and land back at Andrews Air Force Base. "Jean Michel, my parents loved you. Thank you for coming to LA. Jesse even gave us her seal of approval."

"Anna, I loved your family. I knew I really liked Jesse. It's very important to me that we know each other's families. I know you will love living in Mauritius. You are the most important part of my life. I cannot imagine sharing it with anyone else. Not only do I want you to meet my parents, but the ambassador's wife and daughter, too."

I brushed off the thought of living in Mauritius while under the spell of the evening, but a seed had been planted in the back of my mind. I loved working for Stuart, and I loved living in Los Angeles. I also loved this man beside me. I didn't want to think about making a decision now.

I told him a little more of my upbringing: the constant moves, the new schools, and never ending changes. He understood in a way no one else ever had. I was falling deeply in love. But why had I not told him yet? Was it because of my past relationship with Cade which inevitably surfaced? I told Jean Michel that what Cade and I shared was special, but now it was my past.

I thought to ask if he had been serious with anyone before. He told me he had reconnected with a childhood friend while at the Sorbonne. They had dated in his last two years there. When he began his internship with the ambassador before accepting a permanent position, she had suddenly announced her engagement to another man. She had not wanted to move to Mauritius. He admitted it was more about his bruised ego and the rejection than anything else. It was then that he threw himself into his work.

His eyes met mine with an intensity I was growing to love. "Anna, I have never felt this way before. I am head over heels in love with you. I have never been this bold in my life, but I knew if I didn't do something, you would be gone."

The feelings I shared for Jean Michel were equally intense.

He returned me to my hotel with the promise of tomorrow, yet it had already come. He said a car would pick me up at nine, please bring a bathing suit and dress casually for the day. That's it! Now what was he up to? I opened the door to my room, taking the time to look at my phone. I had over fifteen messages. It was Karen, and she just kept saying, "Call me, Anna; call me now."

I quickly dialed her number, and she picked up on the first ring.

"Karen, is everything okay?"

"Oh, Anna," she explained, "I am so sorry, but I thought you should know before you hear it from someone else. Cade is engaged!"

Yes, I was shocked, not to mention a bit hurt, but why? Nothing had changed about my love for Jean Michel, but the news was so odd, so sudden. How could Cade have become engaged to someone within a few months? My pride took hold of me.

Karen asked, "Anna, are you okay? Seriously, we had no idea about this. I hear he met her while he was at PT. She is a physical therapist."

I told Karen the truth about my wounded pride and confided in her the details of my magical evening with Jean Michel.

"Karen, he is amazing, and I swear I have never felt this way about anyone."

She said, "Anna, we all loved him when he was here. He seems like the perfect guy, but you need him to move to LA. Don't let him go."

I thanked her for letting me know about Cade. "Karen, you're my best friend, through and through. I love you. Say hi to Bob and Tara, and I'll call you in a few days."

Before going to bed that night, I thought to call Cade. He picked up right away. "Cade, I just spoke to Karen, and she wanted to make sure I heard before the rumors flew that you are engaged."

"Anna, I'm sorry. It happened pretty fast. I didn't want to hurt you."

"Cade, I want you to be happy. She must be very special to be engaged to you. You will always hold a special place in my heart. I wish you all the happiness in the world."

He said, "Anna, I will always love you, too, but I also know things had changed between us. I heard that you met someone as well. I'm really happy for you."

That evening I felt a bit of sadness for what could have been, but it made the feelings Jean Michel had stirred inside of me seem even more right.

I awoke a few hours later to warm sunshine flooding my suite with the promises of the day still ahead. I agreed to meet Brian and Chris for breakfast.

"Remember, guys," I said over my shoulder, "tonight we are having dinner together, and I was hoping to ask Jean Michel to join us if you don't mind."

I flew up to my room, grabbed my bag, and hopped into the car that was waiting for me downstairs.

Was I ever in for an adventure! The car drove to the Vieus Port Marina (Cannes Old Port), and the driver directed me to a skip that was waiting for me below at the dock. This was going to be fun. I was thinking it would be like enjoying a day out on the water at home. I boarded the skip, asking the man at the helm where Jean Michel was. He pointed to a yacht floating a distance away from the marina. Oh, come on!

True enough, we were headed towards a yacht. As we neared it, I noticed how it was scrubbed to perfection. The sparkling white cast a glowing reflection off the crystal blue seas. This was wonderful. The *Bleu Azur* matched its name to perfection.

As we came astern the *Bleu Azur*, I could see Jean Michel standing above us. He was like a schoolboy with that infectious smile. He swept me into those now-familiar arms with a kiss. I could never get enough of him, and for that matter, he always gave me butterflies. What was happening to me? He broke away and held me at arm's length to look into my eyes. "Anna, are you surprised?" I could only respond with a giggle and no words.

He told me his father's best friend owned the yacht. In fact, as his godfather, he was only happy to make arrangements for us to enjoy a day on the Cote d'Azur. "He did make me promise that next time we are in the South of France together to come by so you can meet him, *oui?*"

"*Oui*," I replied. "I would love to."

It was called an islander. The yacht was, to my estimate, about the same size as Stuart's in Phuket. It was 192 feet long, with five cabins, and it was entirely ours for the day! I was still speechless. The onboard chef would keep us well-fed and the Veuve Clicquot champagne flowing. I was quickly developing a taste for champagne.

"Jean Michel, is this how your life has always been?"

He looked over at me with a wink and said, "Of course, Anna! No, I just wanted to make this special. Your parents took me to Catalina Island while in California, and your friends opened up their homes to me. It meant a lot. So to answer your question, I have never taken anyone to dinner at Chateau Eze, or for that matter, out on my godfather's yacht. This is most definitely a first for me, too."

I was smiling.

We set sail for the Iles de Lerins. It didn't take us long to arrive and head ashore. Starting on the island of Sainte-Marguerite, we strolled hand in hand toward Fort Royal where the real Man in the Iron Mask was held. It was dark and musty and felt like stepping into a dungeon. We both just wanted to get outside.

We laughed our way to a "quick exit." The glorious day welcomed us to take the island's walking paths. The smell of pine and eucalyptus from the gentle breeze was intoxicating. Forever more, the heady scent of pine and eucalyptus will remind me of that day. Those scents must have magic powers as Jean Michel had most certainly cast his spell on me.

We looked across the Mediterranean Sea at the stunning coastline freckled with buildings as far as the eye could see. The Grand Hotel du Cap Ferrat was stark white against the blue sea. You could make out Stuart's estate near the hotel. No wonder the Cote d'Azur is called the "Coast of the Blue."

I shared with Jean Michel how Karen had left multiple messages for me the night before. I told him about Cade's recent and unexpected engagement prompting my call to Cade wishing him my best. Parting on good terms felt like a wonderful release. I actually felt relieved and happy for Cade.

He pulled me closer and said, "Good. I want to spend the rest of my life with you. I know it's crazy after such a short time, but Anna, I love you. So, what do you think of Mauritius? Could you live there?"

"Jean Michel, I never thought I would be standing here in your arms, but here I am, completely in love with you. The first night in Paris when you greeted Stuart, I wanted to assume you were just a typical French guy. I wanted to protect my heart from falling for you."

He replied, "Anna, the first time I saw you, I knew I needed an introduction, but I am not that kind of guy. My parents always called me shy."

Suppressing playful laughter, I said, "Sure, that's what I thought. I did find you extremely handsome. It was kind of impulsive for me, too."

We sealed our confessions with a kiss and continued our exploration to Ile Saint-Honorat. Ile St. Honorat was suspended in a world and time all our own. Could time stand still? If we closed our eyes, we could enter into that place of old with the Cisterian Abbey and the Abbey of Lerins dating back to 405 AD. In present day, the abbeys are still active. In our flip-flops and beach clothes, we sampled Syrah and a liqueur called Lerina made at the abbey. Jean Michel bought me a few bottles to remember our special day.

Between the islands, there is a protected passage called the Plateau de Mileu. There we jumped into the crystal-clear water, laughing and swimming toward the passage. It was actually quite shallow. We could walk between the islands if we wanted.

Together in our Mediterranean playground, we were touched by the charm of years gone by and welcomed the quiet escape from the hustle and bustle of Cannes. We laughed; we played on the yacht's Jet Skis; and we even had a splash war he thought he had won by dunking me into the water headfirst. It was an effortless flow of rest and play.

Glancing back, he nuzzled my neck and turned my head back toward the majestic cities lining the shore. Squinting, we could make out the winding roads leading higher and higher into the hills. There, sitting on its dramatic perch, was our beautiful Chateau Eze, overlooking the sweeping panorama of life below. It was breathtaking scenery, but so was my Jean Michel.

Jean Michel had secretly arranged for Brian and Chris to join us on the yacht for dinner. He wanted to surprise me once again.

He asked, as they were boarding, if I would mind. "Do I mind? Of course not!" I had promised the boys dinner, and this was even more perfect.

The chef had prepared for us a mouth-watering selection of food from the yacht's galley. We dined on the Mediterranean Sea under a starry sky. Brian and Chris were just headed back to the hotel when Brian pulled me aside. "Anna, I wasn't sure about Jean Michel when we first met him in Paris, but I can tell he clearly loves you. You know how much both Melanie and I love you. We have never seen you so happy. He really is a great guy."

I accepted his approval with a hug.

The sun was just peeking up into the sky when Jean Michel brought me back to the hotel. I had some work to do before our early departure for Cairo the next morning. We needed extra supplies, catering, and all the paperwork ready for our passengers. With one day remaining, Jean Michel had promised he would come back in about three hours to show me his family home. He also let it slip that the home was actually a small villa. Yes, for just the two of us! Into the elevator I went in my dreamlike state.

Someone grabbed onto my arm. I looked into the now-familiar eyes of the man who had approached me in Le Mans. There was no mistaking those piercing black eyes. I had not even noticed him standing next to me in the elevator. I was too busy daydreaming about my day on the water to have noticed anything else that morning. "Wait, Mademoiselle St. James—" he tightened his grip and the way he said my name sent a shudder down my spine. "The man I work for demands—"

The elevator door was nearly closed when a hand reached in to stop the closure. It was Brian. He was going for a run when he noticed the man and reached in to prevent me from being trapped.

Brian asked, "Anna, what's going on?" He grabbed for his phone to call hotel security and Stuart's security detail. He stood there, just hugging me. I was a mess. The only description I had of him was his intense eyes and the darkness of his skin. I knew it was the same man from Le Mans. He had an accent reminiscent of an African dialect, but I could not place from where. This was not my imagination, but what could he possibly want with me, and who was the man he worked for?

Brian gently reminded me of Stuart's vast wealth. "I know Stuart seems like a regular guy, Anna. Unfortunately, the reality is that his affluence puts a target on his back—and on all of those who are seen with him regularly. You need to always have someone with you until we get back home, okay? For your safety, Stuart will want a shadow with you at all times. In Mauritius you will be fine, but until then, we must be careful."

Jean Michel came back three hours later, as planned. I could hear voices outside my door. Someone had stopped him, demanding his identification. "Excuse me; can you please show me some photo identification? I am Ms. St. James's bodyguard. We need to make sure we know everyone who is around Ms. St. James."

Brian had not been kidding about the shadow! His name was Mark. I popped my head out the door as Jean Michel showed his identification. I tried to assure my new friend and protector that Jean Michel was with me, but there were no shortcuts. He was dead serious about his job. Mark was a former Navy Seal, so I knew I was in good hands.

I explained to Jean Michel what had unfolded in the few short hours since he had left. He felt horrible about not escorting me up to my room that morning. I kept telling him it was fine as I pushed the uneasy feeling deep into the pit of my stomach. How had the man learned my name and employer?

Mark accompanied Jean Michel and me to his family's villa. He tried his hardest to give us the privacy we both wanted that afternoon, but things were not as planned. We now had a friend sharing the rest of our time together, but in light of recent events, we were thankful to have Mark.

At the Durand Villa was another unexpected surprise. I had not expected anything so beautiful. The villa sat just below the walking promenade on the west side of Cap D'Ail. From the outside terrace, I could see Cap Ferrat in the distance, surrounded in blue sea below. I relaxed and snuggled into Jean Michel arms, asking rhetorically, "Who are you, really?"

We spent the day planning our next few months. It was hard for me to plan anything when my schedule mirrored Stuart Manning's. It did, however, seem hopeful that after Mauritius we could be together again at Brian's wedding in Maui. I was already starting to miss him. I leaned in for a kiss on the outdoor lounger we shared above the sea. With his arms wrapped tightly around me, I felt safe. "Jean Michel, I wish you'd come with us on our safari after Cairo. I know; I know you have to work, but someday, okay?"

I would see him on his island in less than a week. Until then, he walked me up to my room and stepped inside for a quick goodnight kiss. Oh, yes, I was deeply in love with Jean Michel. "Anna, please make sure Mark is with you at all times. Promise to be careful, okay? I love you, my sweet Anna."

Peeking out my door as he was leaving, I saw Mark watching down the hall after me. I tiptoed over to give him a hug for protecting me so faithfully. I was in safe hands.

Chapter Twelve

STARRY NIGHTS

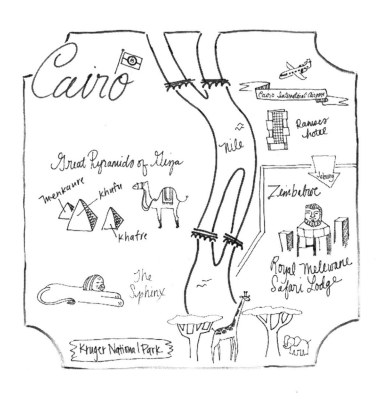

Travel is more than seeing the sights; it is a change that goes on, deep and permanent, in the ideas of living.
—Miriam Beard

$\mathcal{I}$ left the hotel with Brian, Chris, and my new friend Mark at six in the morning—just a few short hours after saying goodbye to Jean Michel. I needed to quit dreaming of my last few days and start concentrating on our flight to Cairo. Stuart and Vanessa had invited some guests for this pre-wedding celebration trip. We were excited, but I was leaving a piece of my heart in the Cote d'Azur.

Stuart and Vanessa had a bronzed glow from their time in the sun. It was nice to see Stuart so happy. I don't know how they did it with paparazzi trailing them straight up to the security gate. Telephoto lenses dotted the security fence to get any shot of the high profile couple. Yes, the media knew of our trip, but all they knew was that we were leaving Nice. Stuart and Vanessa practically leapt into the airplane to escape the watchful lenses. They had wanted to keep the wedding an intimate and private affair. Only forty guests were invited and each had to sign a confidentiality agreement upon his or her attendance.

Conor and Liz had already arrived, looking well rested from the big event in Le Mans. I marveled at their history together as childhood sweethearts and listened to their singsong accents with delight. Everything about them was endearing. I wondered what it could look like to spend a lifetime with Jean Michel by my side. Would I ever learn to speak with his flawless French accent? Never mind that; it was back to work!

Vanessa's agent was also onboard with his girlfriend. The cabin was filled with celebration and merriment as we took off over the Cote d'Azur for the city of Cairo, with the promise of a tour at the Great Pyramid in Giza. Conor, the comedian, wrapped a scarf around his head, saying, "Arabian nights, here we come!"

On our final approach into the city of Arabian nights, all we could see below was a sea of brown desert dust and people scattered everywhere. This was a far cry from the warm Mediterranean Sea. Welcome to Egypt, the ancient land of adventure!

Smart Aviation was on the ground to ensure we had a smooth entry. Brian went with our passengers to customs and sent them via limousine to the hotel. Stuart had insisted on the Ramses Hilton on the Nile. We were to follow shortly with the passengers' baggage. In two hours, our tour of the pyramids would begin.

With all the excitement, the airplane was a mess. From romantic highs in the South of France to scrubbing airplane toilets within the same day, my job had a way of leveling the playing field. An Egyptian ground handler came up the stairs to see if I needed any assistance. What he really wanted was a doll for his daughter. I listened to the story of how his poor daughter never had a doll. The only way to buy the doll was on the black market. Uncertain of his story, I still gave him some of our candy and money so we could both be on our way.

Everything was done here with the motive of money. We handed it out by the fistful, and people knew it. I felt like a sucker, but I couldn't say no. I had a few moments to myself after he left to step outside the airplane and look around. I was in Egypt for the first time! This solitary moment was worthy of a picture or two. It's not every day a girl goes to Cairo. I could see some Egyptian military airplanes and the commercial area at the terminal within the brown desert that engulfed us. We were parked a good distance away that required a ride in our handler's van to the terminal. Chris and I were awaiting their return. No problem, right? I had my doubts.

Inside the airport security and customs office, our handler repeated the dreaded words, "no problem." Relinquishing my passport and security papers to the angry officer pointing at me, our handler whispered into my ear not to worry and that everything was fine. Everything didn't seem fine. The problem was with my phone. The officer practically ripped it out of my hands and grabbed my already bruised arm to shove me into a private room where a woman was standing with her hands on her hips. I could hear Mark's protests from the room. She searched me head to toe treating me like some sort of terrorist. I had no idea what was going on, but this certainly wasn't a "no problem" situation.

I was finally released from the humid interrogation room, feeling disheveled and violated. When I appeared, a wave of relief crossed the faces of Brian, Chris, and Mark, who were being held by armed guards. With a gold-toothed grin, our handler gave back my passport. Two pages were scribbled and stamped with Egyptian writing all over. I have no idea what it said, but it was probably better that way. I asked for my phone back. "It's no problem, Ms. St. James. We will have it here at the airport tomorrow when you leave."

Growing impatient, I practically yelled, "Maybe you don't understand, I need that phone for work. Where is my phone?"

I got my phone back after much quiet chatter amongst the officials with all my new pictures deleted. Yes, no problems!

Two men beside us pushed all the luggage piled high on top of carts to our awaiting limousine. Once outside, a wave of dry, hot air welcomed us to the desert. Our open-air 'limousine' in Cairo was an old, 1970 Mercedes 240D sedan. I looked over at Brian, shaking my head. There was no way we could all fit in one car with over fifteen pieces of luggage in tow. Our handler, of course, didn't see the problem as he nervously ushered us toward the car.

I kept looking at him, shaking my head and pointing to all the luggage we had sitting on the curb. People and rifle-bearing guards were everywhere. I wasn't feeling good about the luggage sitting curbside with so many people pushing and shoving past us. Our handler pointed to three men who started loading the luggage onto the roof racks. How they got fifteen pieces of luggage onto the roof of one car is still a mystery to me. We looked like a Jenga tower on wheels. Our handler leaned back, with hands on his hips in satisfaction. "See, no problem." *Sure*, I thought. He tapped the roof of the car, and we were off. Next stop, Ramses Hilton.

Away from the airport, we stuck out like a sore thumb in our limo. Entire families were riding on the back of a single motorcycle or scooter. The motorcycles had at least one child sitting over the handlebars, two more children in front of the driver, and the rest of the family stacked like sardines behind the driver. A couple of scooters flew by with nine family members on board. This was insanity!

The Egyptians do not use lanes, either. Why bother? Just drive. It was a mad scramble of horns blaring from cars, motorcycles, and scooters; bikes and people were jockeying to navigate the dusty streets. On each street corner stood armed guards with AK-47 assault rifles, with bayonets protruding from the ends. This was not the city of "no problems"!

We watched our baggage being unloaded in front of the hotel. We had two more security checkpoints to clear just to get inside. Finally, I felt relief inside the air-conditioned lobby, but not for long. We had to push and shove just to get to the front of the line for check-in, but we did it. One could not help but wonder how all these people got through the two security checkpoints.

The bellman promised to deliver our passengers' luggage to their rooms. Key in hand, I opted to hang on to my bag. The smiles, with repeated "no problems" from the staff had me leery. I wasn't sure about anything in this crazy and crowded den of humanity. Mark followed me to my room, just in case. We were in adjacent suites overlooking the Nile. I had envisioned Elizabeth Taylor in the movie *Cleopatra*, overlooking the mysterious Nile. On closer inspection, there was nothing that looked remotely like the Hollywood set from that movie.

Inside were two bedrooms and a sitting area with two balconies. Mark insisted that I keep my balcony doors closed at all times for security. I felt bad, but I snuck outside on the balcony for a view. Below me, the Nile River flowed like a wide, brown snake. Horns were still blaring in the background; this was nothing like I had envisioned.

I promised Jean Michel I would call him once we arrived safely. He picked up his phone right away, wanting to know how the trip had gone. I described the events so far, and we both laughed over my naïve misconceptions of Cairo. "By the way, did I tell you I miss you?"

He laughed, saying he was just departing for Mauritius and would call when he arrived. I could hear a female voice in the background. "Jean Michel, who is with you?"

"It's just Bridgitte, the ambassador's daughter. She's on the flight with me."

"Say hello from me. I hope I will meet her soon. Call when you get in."

It was time for me to get ready for the pyramids.

Mark's room shared an adjoining door with mine. Glancing again at my bruised arm from the elevator incident in Cannes, I was happy to know he was only a knock away. The four of us went to the lobby together to meet the rest of our party for the pyramids tour.

With one billionaire and one famous Hollywood actress soon-to-be wed, the entourage headed off to one of the world's Seven Wonders. It was quite a scene. We all wore pants and shirts to dress according to cultural norms and detract from any media attention. We had just gathered in the lobby when a man approached Stuart and gestured for us to follow him. He had two limousines waiting to take us to the pyramids. The man introduced himself. "I am Kahma. I am here to be your driver, Mr. Manning. I will take you in our nice limousines to the great pyramids. Yes? You are in very good hands. No problem. Please, right this way."

Two Honda Civics was their idea of a limousine. I guess when you see nine family members on one scooter, their definition of a limousine starts to make sense. It was six people per car, including the driver. To make matters more interesting, the weather was, shall I say, sweaty. Vanessa opted to sit on Stuart's lap and made light of the situation instead of complaining. She was no prima donna, and I loved her for it. She was fun, thoughtful, and surprisingly normal for a woman of her celebrity status. There was not a single Allister Cummings among us as we all piled into the Hondas, thank goodness!

Vanessa looked beautiful with or without makeup. No wonder she had captured Stuart's heart! They were a cozy pair in the front seat of the Honda Civic, and what a sight! We gave them a hard time, capturing pictures of them, with tears running down our checks in laughter. Conor, Liz, and Mark sat in the back of their limousine. In ours, I sat on Brian's lap so that Vanessa's agent, his girlfriend, and Chris could all fit in the back seat. Both cars were a pile of arms and legs. We were together all right!

Thirty minutes later, we approached a little mud shack with hanging carpets and an array of colorful beads at the entrance. On the side of the building, our camels were less than thrilled about our arrival. They were sitting on the ground, looking somewhat bored with the situation. With acrobatic maneuvers, we made it onto our camels' backs, and they stood up in preparation for our desert journey. They knew what to do—even if we didn't have a clue! Our drivers waved goodbye, indicating they would return to pick us up. Both drivers honked their horns and flew out into the street, disappearing in a cloud of dust.

In the distance, a man on horseback was approaching with what appeared to be a little boy running on foot alongside him. It was our tour guide. I could tell that the entire scene made Mark nervous, but he was trying to keep his cool. As a former secret service agent and Navy Seal, he knew this was a difficult setting in which to assess and control threats.

The little boy continued running next to us; for what purpose, we didn't know. We mindlessly followed in the direction he led us. If anyone knew the path to the pyramids, it was the camels. We were "along for the ride" in every sense of the term! We stopped unexpectedly. An imposing gate stood before us and behind it, the pyramids. I have to admit, they are something to behold. I was waiting for James Bond to step out from behind one like he did in the movie, *The Spy Who Loved Me*. I felt like Cleopatra perched high on a camel, marveling at the regal Sphinx.

Our illustrious leader doubled back on his horse, explaining that the pyramids were closed for the day. It was only two o'clock in the afternoon. How could this be? Stuart picked up on it right away. This was a rouse to conjure up more money from our party for a "private tour" of the pyramids. Stuart handed him two hundred dollars, which he took into a building near the gate. The adorable little boy who had followed us all this way stood by, smiling with the cutest, chocolate-drop eyes I had ever seen. The scene was almost comical.

Minutes later, the cloud of dust returned. Our leader stopped on a dime in front of us as we choked back the desert dust. The gates magically opened. The horseman turned around in his saddle to speak with us as the sun glinted off the gold teeth in his mouth. A full smile would nearly blind us. I was seeing a lot of gold in Cairo. "I had to work very hard with the officials to negotiate the opening of this gate. Yes? The gods are smiling on us today in your favor. The gates don't open for everyone. You, my friends, are lucky. Allah has smiled on us."

The pyramids were worth every haphazard means it took to get us there. Our smelly, grunting camels took a bow so that we could hop off. We started up the outside of the Grandfather Pyramid first. No words can capture this wonder adequately. Each step is about waist high. How these pyramids were built entirely off slave labor was something I could not wrap my head around. I turned around to look back at the Sphinx, with the body of a lion and the head of a king. Some ego that Pharaoh must have had to make the head of the Sphinx in his image! He must have felt like a god.

Standing at the first pyramid with breathtaking panoramic views, we noticed a man lingering near our group. After a quick greeting, he began to reveal his knowledge about the pyramids, as if on cue. He told us in his strong Egyptian accent, but in excellent English, how the three Pyramids of Menkaure, Khufu, and Khafre are perfectly aligned with the constellation of Orion. He was referring to the Father Pyramid, the Grandfather Pyramid, and the son, Khuful, of the fourth dynasty Egyptian Pharaoh. We stood there soaking up the history lesson. What a stroke of luck to have run across this knowledgeable man by chance!

He kindly offered to take our pictures. Oh, yes, please! We were thrilled to have him take our pictures and asked if he would like to pose in a shot with us. After finishing our photo shoot, he turned to the men and said, "That will be twenty dollars for the first tour, twenty dollars for the second tour, and twenty dollars for each picture. You owe me two hundred dollars." Two hundred dollars seemed to be the going rate in Cairo. We just stared at him for a while, in shock. He was not going to leave unless we paid him, so we parted with another two hundred bucks.

Not surprisingly, he vanished into thin air about as quickly as he had appeared. We spent the next few hours exploring the majestic beauty of the pyramids, without being heckled for money. Our leader mounted his horse with a whistle, indicating it was time to go. The little Egyptian boy reappeared to run back with us to the mud shack. We trudged back home on the weary camels and were eager to part ways with them when it came time. We were invited inside the mud hut while we waited for our limousines. We first declined, but they were insistent. "No" means "yes" in Cairo. Huddled inside the cool, dark den, we sat on carpets, awaiting our rides. "Don't worry, friends, your drivers will be here soon," said our tour guide. "Please accept some refreshments."

Mark surveyed the perimeter of the hut with his eyes before he settled in. Each of us unknowingly had tipped the little boy one hundred dollars. Little Chocolate-Drop Eyes had just earned one thousand dollars for his jog to the pyramids. We also took care of our tour guide, to the tune of over fifteen hundred dollars.

The mud shack experience was an authentic taste of Egyptian culture. A woman brought us jasmine tea as we reclined. I was waiting for Aladdin to appear with his magic lamp. Stuart ribbed Conor over and over again, saying, "Arabian nights here we come!" We leaned against cushions on the many carpets beneath us. Another man brought out different perfumes for us to smell as we sipped our tea in the Egyptian den. It soon became apparent that our limousines would never arrive unless we bought some perfume. We each bought a bottle of perfume and poof! Our limousines arrived as if we'd rubbed a magic lamp.

The heady oils we'd purchased mingled with the smell of sweat and dirt. We were dusty and dirty and ready to get back to the hotel. Both drivers, however, had other plans for the group as we pulled up to the front entrance of the Egyptian Museum. We shook our heads, saying we wanted to go back to the hotel, thank you very much. Neither driver liked that answer. They were not taking no for an answer. "No, no, you need to see the museum while you are here in our beautiful country," one of the drivers said.

The pieces of the puzzle were all coming together now. The tourism circles were intimately connected in Cairo. The drivers, the little boy, the guide on the horse, the mysterious man at the pyramid, the gatekeeper, the woman serving tea, the man selling perfume, and the guy running the museum all had a profit to make. The drivers orchestrated each destination to ensure we visited all the "right" locations. Stuart knew how to play this game. He leaned over with Vanessa on his lap to hand the driver another two hundred dollar tip. "Take us back to the hotel," he said.

Like magic carpets, our limousines transported us straight back to the hotel. We shuffled through the crack squad security checkpoints, and at last, we were in! We had a few hours before evening cocktails and dinner by the pool at the Citadel Grill. First, I needed to dust off.

Slipping into the poolside crowd unnoticed proved yet another feat. People from many cultures gathered outside, and some covered in modest, traditional dress. I felt self-conscious in my Western wear, fielding looks of disapproval from strange men. I knew it was not my imagination, though I wished it had been. I was not covered in an abaya or a burka, and somehow, I felt naked. Vanessa and Liz were garnering similar, scornful looks.

Vanessa was walking by the pool when a man recognized her and spat on the ground before her in disgust. Mark was working overtime tonight. I stayed close by, not taking any chances after my encounters with the stalker from Le Mans. I started to relax after the toasts began. I noticed how Vanessa hadn't touched a drop of champagne again, opting for sparkling water instead. She had loved her champagne while we were in London. I asked her if she would like me to have something else on board.

Connecting the dots in my mind, my eyes locked with Vanessa's, and I knew. She was pregnant! This explained her slightly baggier clothing since we left Le Mans. Most people would never have noticed because she looked amazing. She smiled and pulled me aside. "Anna," she said, "please keep this our secret. Stuart and I are expecting our first child in about three months. We are having a girl. Can you believe it? A little girl! We even have a name picked out: Sabrina. I'm so excited I could burst. It's so good to share the news with someone else besides Stuart."

This was, indeed, wonderful news. I threw my arms around her in congratulations. "I'm so happy for both of you, Vanessa. Of course, I never would have known, but for the champagne clue. You certainly don't look pregnant at all, Vanessa. In fact, you look radiant. Congratulations! And yes, your secret's safe with me. Sabrina? What a beautiful name. I love it."

When the dancing began, I was swept up into the fun. It was a natural way to express my excitement for the changes ahead. I had lots of good dance partners: Chris, Brian, and yes, even Mark, followed by a turn with Stuart. Marveling at this happy news and spinning around on the dance floor, I thought for a moment I saw a man who fit the description of my stalker. Upon second glance, I noticed how just about every man around me fit his description in some form. It really did look like him, but maybe it was just my imagination after a glass or two of champagne.

Mark walked me to my room after dinner, and I thanked him for taking such good care of me. "Anna, it is my job. I am here for you twenty-four seven. Call if you need me for anything, okay?"

"Yes, Mark." He stepped into my room to make sure everything was safe. My balcony door was slightly ajar. Mark looked over at me and asked if I had opened the door. "Well, yes. I'm sorry. I know how you told me not to, but I just wanted to look."

"Anna, if you want to look, knock on my door, and I will look with you, okay? That's what I'm here for."

Mark gave the all clear, said goodnight, and reminded me to knock if I needed him. I saw that I had missed Jean Michel's call. Quickly abandoning my promise to Mark, I sat out on my balcony to call Jean Michel. By night, the Nile had an air of mystery that had been drowned out earlier by the blaring of car horns. So much for my romantic vision of Cairo!

Jean Michel answered, out of breath. He had just arrived in Mauritius a short time ago and recounted his day to me. "So, Anna, what do you think of Cairo and the Great Pyramids?"

"The pyramids really are a sight to behold, but the dusty, crowded den of people doesn't do a thing for me."

We both laughed for hours into the night. I told him how I had sat on Brian's lap in our "limo" for lack of space and about the celebration we had over dinner. The pregnancy, of course, was still a well-kept secret. I didn't want to go, but I needed sleep. Just before hanging up, I said, "I thought I saw a man who looked just like the man in the elevator in Cannes. It had to be my imagination—all the men here look so similar."

"Anna, I don't know what to think, but you should stay close to Mark. Promise me. Anything that could seem suspicious, just tell Mark. I think if I saw the guy, I could identify him. Please just hurry and come meet me in Mauritius."

He added, "Promise you will be careful. I love you, *mon Cherie*. Never forget that."

"I won't!"

Mark showed up at my room the next morning for checkout and our next stop: Royal Malewane Luxury Safari Lodge. I had seen enough of Cairo and was one step closer to seeing Jean Michel. Mark pulled me aside that morning for a chat.

"In the future, Anna, please let me know if you see anything that alarms you. It could help me protect you." I could only assume that Jean Michel had spoken to him late last night after our conversation. "I was sure it was my imagination, Mark. I didn't want to alarm you."

We took off from Cairo without a hitch. The Royal Malewane, in the heart of South Africa, had promised sightings of the big five: lions, elephants, café buffalo, leopards, and rhinoceros at the Greater Kruger National Park. Thankfully, I had my phone in hand to take pictures. Three more nights, and we would be in Mauritius. I could hardly contain my excitement.

Johannesburg was a piece of cake after Cairo. Stuart, Vanessa, and their guests went ahead of us in the Royal Malewane SUV. Just as they were packed and ready to leave, Vanessa jumped out from the back seat to catch up with me. She wanted to know if I would join her for spa treatments at the resort in preparation for the wedding. She did not have to twist my arm. Yes, please! She was thankful to have me on this trip, and this was her way of showing it.

Off they went while I finished cleaning the airplane for our departure in three days. I had called the lodge weeks ago to make arrangements for our catering on the final leg of our trip to Mauritius. Those orders were confirmed. With an easy customs and security experience, the pilots and I breezed our way out of Johannesburg, with Mark close behind. I admit that when I am tired, I have a tendency to get a bit giggly. That day was no exception to the rule. At first Brian and Chris would tolerate me, but nothing more. Mark put his sunglasses on, trying to maintain composure. At some point, however, everyone lost it, and the laughter was so infectious that even our driver joined in.

I was enchanted with the dramatic landscape from the moment we left the airport to our arrival at the lodge. It took us forty minutes to get there, and it didn't feel long enough. How could I possibly describe this place? The staff was expecting us when we arrived, and the bellmen were ready to escort each of us to our rooms. Brian called me as soon as he stepped foot into his room. "Anna, I know we have seen some pretty spectacular places, but this is one of the best! Do you think Melanie would like it for our honeymoon? Before you answer, I know it's far from Maui, but look at this place!"

"Brian, I like how you think, and I know she'd love it. Have I told you just how happy I am for the two of you? You are, after all, two of my favorite people in the world. I say, go for it! Maybe a few days after the wedding in Maui, you could head west to Africa for a few weeks."

My room was an oasis I never wanted to leave. I looked out from my beautifully polished wooden deck straight into the bush. Yes, the bush! My view from the deck stretched as far as the eye could see. It was beyond words. I felt like I had stepped into another era, yet with every kind of modern luxury. I had a beautiful gazebo with an infinity pool and an inside fireplace in front of my canopied bed. I would surely put to use the large bathroom with a Victorian-styled bathtub. It was so private, I think the only creature that could possibly see me was the wildlife beckoning at my back door.

There was only one thing missing: Jean Michel. I picked up my phone to call him. He answered on the first ring, like he had been timing it. "Anna, I was trying to figure out a way to surprise you there, but I have too much work to do before you arrive. I promise. Some day we will go there together. *Oui, mon Cherie?*"

It was good to hear his voice. I told him what Brian had said about a honeymoon here. I added, "Hopefully, one day my Mauritian prince will meet me here too. It's fantastic!"

Our schedule was full for the next few days, but he encouraged me to rest. Once I arrived in Mauritius, I was all his. "I have spoken to the ambassador about the next few weeks. He has given me a holiday for the entire two weeks you are here. He's invited to most of the same wedding events as us, anyway. So rest up! I want to spend every possible moment with you. Got that?"

"Yes, sir!" I promised to call him before I went to bed. I smiled at the thought of him. He was now part of my crazy life.

The sun had begun its final descent over the bush. A gentle evening breeze refreshed my soul. My heart felt like it would burst as I followed the daintily lit footpath to meet the group for dinner. The chef was preparing a feast for us to enjoy under the stars at what they called the "Watering Hole."

Over our shared meal, I reflected on all the unforeseen changes of the past few months. I was working hard, but enjoying every moment of this new world. I loved my job, the airplanes, and the travel. I loved the people too. My pilots were a dream and so was Jean Michel. Life had drastically changed for me, yet I could not picture it being any different. Life was wonderful, and this was my new "norm." There was no going back for me. It gave me goose bumps just to think about it.

A feast under the stars could only be matched with dessert and dancing by the fire pit. This was a group that loved to dance. Oh, we most certainly danced! A lifetime of memories included this special night. Brian and Chris were great dance partners, and Mark took a turn on the floor with me again. We were one big "Manning clan," as Stuart liked to say.

Stuart came over for a dance. "Vanessa and I don't know how to thank you for being such a wonderful part of our lives. You are special to both of us, Anna, and she told me you know about little Sabrina. Can you believe it? Me, a father?"

"Yes, I can, Stuart. You will make a great father, and if she looks anything like her mama, watch out!"

"Please promise you will always be there for us. We value your friendship and loyalty more than we can say, but more important, promise me you will be careful."

He drew my arm out to look at the bruises, softly running his hand over the swollen skin. "I'm trying to get to the bottom of this to figure out who is behind these attempts on you. It feels like someone is going after you to get to me. Everything I have is at your disposal. Never forget that. And Mark is one of the best in the business. He won't let anything happen to you."

He continued, "The world I live in is cutthroat. I can take care of myself, but when it hurts those I love, I draw the line. We will find out who did this, I promise."

In the excitement, I realized I missed my friends, especially my big sis, Jesse. Before calling Jean Michel that evening, I updated Melanie on some of our adventures. She thanked me for being a good friend to Brian. "Mel, Brian is a good man who loves you very much. It makes me happy to hear him talk about you. Safe travels tomorrow, and see you in a couple days. Love you."

Next I needed to hear Jesse's voice. I wanted to know how she was doing. She was the sister everyone wanted, the supportive best friend. People had often thought we were twins growing up. I told her about the Cote d'Azure and the surprise yacht trip. "Jesse, can you believe it?"

"No way. Jean Michel took you out on a yacht? What a catch! Turner will be so jealous to know you were out at sea!"

My sister had been married for five years to a great guy. They met at a small, private college and got engaged in the last half of their senior year. He had a job in securities in San Francisco, and they lived on their sailboat in Tiburon. Jesse was still based in San Francisco for American Airlines, and I was happy for her.

After talking to Melanie and Jesse, I also called Karen. I knew she would want an update. I told her all about the trip, but she really wanted me to cut to the chase about Jean Michel. We ended our conversation shortly after she told me she had run into Cade. She said he seemed happy, but also sad in a way she hadn't noticed before. My heart hurt to think of him, yet how could I be sad? I ended my night with the voice that was like my other half, my Jean Michel.

Stuart and Vanessa invited everyone out the following morning for a tour of the bush in open-air vehicles. Our guides and trackers brought us thrillingly close to "the big five." We saw them all that day. I don't know how they managed it, but after our time in the bush, another adventure awaited us. Watching the sunset over the African wilderness from a hot air balloon was the kind of vantage point I'll never forget.

Day two was my day with Vanessa and Liz at the spa. I was buffed, polished, and relaxed in a way I had not been in months. Each day at the Royal Malewane passed quickly for others, but to me, it felt like an eternity. At the end of each day, I would lay out on my lounge chair to share the day's adventures with Jean Michel.

On my last night at the lodge, I shared our group's plan to visit an orphanage the next day. I could hear the excitement bubbling over in Jean Michel's voice. He told me that his parents had a special love and concern for orphans. "Anna, I have spent my vacations as a child visiting orphanages all over the world. My parents wanted to change the world by starting with one child at a time. That's why Stuart and I have been working together so much. With the ambassador and my parents' help, we will get a foundation up and running that will spotlight this need all over the world."

Once again, he surprised me in new and profound ways. Struggling to hang up the phone, our parting words were in unison: "I love you."

Chapter Thirteen

OFF TO THE WEDDING AND THE MYSTERIES OF MAURITIUS

I am not the same having seen the moon shine on the other side of the world.
—Mary Anne Radmacher

*I*t was time to depart for Joburg and our final leg of the journey to Mauritius. The arms of Jean Michel awaited me there. At dinner the night before, Stuart and Vanessa had asked everyone if we could make one stop before leaving for Mauritius. The plan was to leave The Royal Malewane together flying up to Harare, Zimbabwe to have lunch, prepared by the chef from the lodge, with the orphans at "Hands of Hope." We would leave the orphanage in the late afternoon, driving back to the airport to ensure our scheduled arrival into Mauritius that evening.

Nothing prepared us for the kids at "Hands of Hope" in Harare. I felt love for each and every little one, hoping I would return soon for a future visit. Stuart and Vanessa sat on the ground to play in the dirt with a little girl who kept climbing onto their laps for hugs. It was hard to say goodbye to their little friend that day. None of these kids knew or cared about Stuart's wealth or Vanessa's fame. They loved without merit based on performance or reputation. It was the pure, unconditional kind of love.

Brian, Chris, and Mark led the boys in a makeshift game of baseball. Laughter resounded at such a simple thing as a game with wooden sticks. The children were enthralled with our white skin, putting their brown arms up to ours and laughing at the contrast. Equally mesmerizing were Mark's tattoos. It was raw and heartwarming. With heavy hearts, we got ready to leave the children and felt the burden to help each precious, little face. Stuart and Vanessa went off on a private walk in deep discussion.

Before we left, they agreed on the best wedding gift they could possibly give each other: a check for one million dollars to the orphanage. They said it was just the beginning of building a decent home for the kids. It also meant schooling, food, and a safe place to teach them skills to pay it forward to others. The lump in my throat and tears streaming down my face were a natural outpouring of joy and heartbreak. It was all so bittersweet. I addressed both Stuart and Vanessa and said, "You have given those children a gift that is priceless. I hope we can come back someday and see them again."

Stuart had tears, too. "Anna, this is just the beginning. This is part of what we have been working tirelessly for with Jean Michel and the ambassador."

Just before takeoff, the celebration was kicking into high gear. The chef at the lodge had outdone himself with the catering for our passengers. We toasted over the blue waters of the Indian Ocean, a mere two thousand kilometers from the continent of Africa. A hush filled the cabin on our final descent. The island was a dull outline after sunset, illuminated by the glowing white reflection of the moon on ocean waves. It looked like a sprinkling of lights extending us a warm greeting.

As each of us got off the plane, we marveled at the moon's rays in a darkened sky. Yes, this was magic. The island embraced us in its beauty. We were finally in Mauritius—the homeland of Jean Michel.

From the Mauritius Seewoongasar Ramgoolam International Airport, we headed to the town of Flacq, toward the resort, Le Touessrok. Stuart and Vanessa wanted the wedding kept under wraps, so they rented the entire resort for our stay—yes, just for our little group of forty guests. A band was flying in from California a few days before the wedding. Stuart knew the band well and wanted them to play at the wedding reception. Who rents an entire resort? Who flies in people from the West Coast of the United States to play at a wedding reception in Mauritius?

Vanessa and Stuart had two weeks' worth of fun events in store for their guests before the big day. Each room had a list of the planned activities, and the baskets from Saks were awaiting their special placement. Before leaving the plane, Stuart said, "Anna, I'm so glad you're here to celebrate with us. Thanks for all your hard work to make it special."

I knew I loved working for this man.

We put the airplane to bed for the next two weeks. Every part of me expected to see Jean Michel at the airport, but he was nowhere to be found. He usually made such a special effort to surprise me. He was probably held up with last minute work before we arrived. Still, I could not help but feel a bit disappointed.

Brian, Chris, and I hopped into our open-air SUV bound for Le Touessrok; it felt odd to be on the left side of the road. Mark had gone ahead, believing that I was safe here on the island. We passed the capital city of Port Louis about twenty kilometers from the airport, continuing the thirty kilometers to the resort. Our necks craned to see the evening lights dancing off the ocean's surface. The perfume of tropical flowers was overwhelming. Jean Michel had asked if I could live here. It was far away, but . . .

At the resort, the staff was expecting us. Appetizers were served the moment we stepped into paradise, paired with an iced citronella drink. It was delicious. I kept expecting Jean Michel to appear around the corner, but he wasn't there. Brian read the look of disappointment all over my face, offering a sly wink, "Seriously Anna? I'm sure he's coming soon."

Wow, thanks Brian. But Melanie was there! She had arrived earlier and was grinning ear-to-ear at Brian's side. They were adorable. She was a natural part of the Manning clan, too. It was a little over six months ago that she was my supervisor at American Airlines. What a crazy thought! She looked fresh-faced and vivacious after visiting the spa, and I told her so. She noticed a look about me that was different too. "Anna, something has changed, and I like it. You look amazing." She winked and gave me one of her warm, inviting hugs before heading off to her room. I could hardly believe that we were all in Mauritius—and with plenty of time to catch up.

The bellman escorted me to my oceanfront suite with a twenty-four-hour butler and every imaginable amenity. The room was exquisite, like walking straight into an extravagant Robinson Crusoe adventure. I had a greeting basket brimming with tropical fruit and a vase with Trochetia boutoniana and red anthurium flowers. Simply gorgeous! Scents of jasmine flowed gently through the air around me. The fruit basket reminded me about the special gifts from Saks. I needed to disperse those to the guest rooms soon.

First, I had to see the rest of the room! Out on my oceanfront terrace was a chilled bottle of champagne. Wandering barefoot to the shower with champagne flute in hand, I heard a light knock at my door. It must be my baskets from the bellman! To my surprise, it was my best gift yet. Jean Michel greeted me with his wonderful smile. I jumped into his arms, and he held me before voicing the sincerest apology. "Anna, I'm sorry I couldn't be at the airport. The ambassador needed me to complete some work, and I thought it would be best to meet you here. I hope you don't mind."

Mind? It didn't matter now.

Stuart and Vanessa had booked one of the guest rooms for Jean Michel. I could not believe it! We were guests to one of the most glamorous weddings of our lifetimes—and in no other place than Mauritius!

We skipped dinner with the group that first evening, as did Brian and Mel. Chris said he didn't mind either, so I left Stuart and Vanessa a message saying we would touch base in the morning. I called the bellman to deliver the Saks baskets to each guest room with the added *Sonoma SMS* wine as a personal touch from Stuart and Vanessa. Check! My work was complete.

Jean Michel ordered dinner out on my terrace. We sat in the lounge chairs, basking in the warmth of just being together. Could I fall any harder for this wonderful man whose companionship was a constant surprise to me? We did finally part ways in the early morning hours as he said, "I'll be back in twenty minutes, okay?" Then, he disappeared. I reclined outside, still drinking in the view of the darkened ocean, when he peaked his handsome head around the neighboring terrace with a mischievous laugh. His suite was right next to mine!

Curled up in his arms that morning, I savored every moment. Jean Michel had ordered a breakfast tray with fresh-grown local coffee served in a coffee press. Tropical fruits, freshly squeezed juices, and French pastries filled the tray. We were both so hungry that I think we devoured every last morsel on our plates. Once finished, it was time to explore!

We walked hand in hand through the resort, followed by a run. The island almost felt deserted as we gazed out into the tranquil bay of Trou D'Eau Douce and the Indian Ocean. We had not seen another soul! There were signs of life closer inland. Near the resort, we passed the staff, speaking in hints of Creole and French. It sounded like a melodious song to my ears.

Jean Michel would look over at me and smile in an attempt to sell me on the benefits of island living. It was working. Mauritius was incredible, but it was continents away from home. We had come a long way since that first meeting in Paris, yet it was important to Jean Michel that I also fall in love with this island nation, as he so clearly was.

He taught me everything he knew about the geography of Mauritius. "The island is surrounded by clear lagoons that are protected by coral barrier reefs. Isn't it one of the most beautiful places you have ever seen?"

"Yes, I have to admit; it's incredible. The water is so clear, too."

The island meant everything to him. How could I not fall under its spell?

We had a small tennis tournament that afternoon with the others, but first we swam. My first time in the Indian Ocean was such perfect refreshment from the warm air. We had lunch at a little cabana on the beach before reluctantly heading to change into our tennis clothes. We both insisted they put us on the same team. I actually told Vanessa that if we weren't a team, I wouldn't play. She just laughed at my seriousness. She had already put us together.

I was actually a decent opponent from the times I had played back home. While I was not worthy of the UCLA girls' team, I was still good. Jean Michel surprised me, too. He was really good. Laughing, I said, "Where did you learn to play like this?"

He grinned. "Anna, on this island growing up, I had a good friend who is now playing out on the tour." He winked and said, "I was his drilling partner."

This man was full of unearthed talent. We easily won the tournament. Stuart was not one to take his loss sitting down. "This tournament is totally rigged and unfair. I insist we change it up and play again."

I just laughed. "Stuart, I brought a ringer, and I want my trophy!"

Jean Michel added, "Hey, Stuart, I brought a ringer, too."

Stuart just rolled his eyes.

Chris played with a friend of Vanessa's who had just arrived in Mauritius against Brian and Melanie. I loved the vigor in the air from a little friendly competition.

After the tournament, Jean Michel lined up a couples massage at the Givenchy Spa before dinner. We arrived at a little thatched roof cabana with the ocean as our music. A breeze flowed around us, carrying the light scent of jasmine. Before long, I had drifted off to the land of dreams. I felt a gentle shake as the massage therapist woke me up. Jean Michel was fast asleep too. I put my finger to my mouth to let his massage therapist sneak out the back. We were left alone to wake up our languid bodies with glasses of iced citronella.

I was only away from him long enough to get dressed for dinner. About thirty minutes later, he knocked on my door. When I opened it, he just stood there with the most wonderful smile. There was a gift for me too. "Anna, would you mind opening it before dinner? You might want to wear it."

A chill of excitement ran down my spine as I looked at the exquisite box. Inside was one of the most beautiful diamond necklaces I had ever seen. It was elegant, yet simple. I was speechless. He looked suddenly concerned by my lack of speech and said, "Anna, I am not trying to rush you. I just wanted you to know how much you mean to me. Mauritius is an island known for its diamonds, and this necklace will forever remind us of our love for one another, *oui?*"

I threw my arms around him with the assurance that there would never be anyone else for me, but him. He had swept me off my feet in such a short time. Securing the necklace behind me, his lips grazed the back of my neck. I turned around slowly to melt into his embrace. "I guess this means you like the necklace, my Anna?"

I felt like a million dollars at that evening's celebration dinner. Stuart and Vanessa had already arrived, looking content in the presence of their closest friends. With Stuart still nursing his tennis loss, I teased that he was the one responsible for introducing us.

The resort's Barlen Restaurant served mouth-watering seafood caught fresh that morning. Island music surrounded us, just like our wonderful friends. Stuart's mother, Betty, and his sister, Megan, would arrive the day of the car rally. They didn't want to miss this part of the wedding activities. So far, there were thirty-eight guests in all.

After dinner, the celebratory toasts began in the Sega Bar, with live jazz music and dancing by the pool. One of the guests who had arrived that day was a nice woman named Olivia. She was a close friend of Vanessa's from the UK. On hiatus from her work as a wardrobe designer to the stars, she was enjoying every moment of this island vacation. Olivia was involved in the making of costumes for a recent Star Wars movie. She was also a close family friend of the former 007, Sean Connery; she knew him better as "Uncle Sean," a constant part of her family. Her father was actually his golfing buddy. He insisted that she do his wardrobe whenever he was in a movie.

Chris was instantly smitten with Olivia, asking her to dance. We all followed his lead. It reminded me of our first evening in Paris together, dancing near the Sorbonne. Jean Michel whispered in my ear, "*Ma Cherie, vous souvenez-vous de notre premiere danse ensemble?* My love, do you remember our first dance together?"

Every time he spoke to me in French, my feet lifted off the ground. Before we knew it, Stuart interrupted with his crazy conga line changing the mood instantly, pulling us apart to dance ourselves into the early morning hours. Olivia became instant friends with both Mel and me. In fact, everyone seemed to bring a collective harmony to this beautiful celebration.

Jean Michel and I made it back to our rooms in the early morning hours. We decided to open the connecting door to our rooms to curl up together for a few hours of rest. Not wanting to leave him, I fell asleep in his arms. Jean Michel had been kind not to pressure me about sleeping with him. I needed time after Cade and knew I was saving myself for the man I would marry, but this was getting difficult. I knew he was struggling too.

We woke up together with the entire day free until dinner. It was another celebration for Stuart and Vanessa, but today, we had celebrations of our own. Rubbing my eyes, I rolled over to Jean Michel, who was surprisingly awake, staring intently at me with those eyes. "Jean Michel," I said, "what do you want to do today? Do you just want to spend the day at the beach? You know I love to waterski or wakeboard. Do you want to try waterskiing?"

Jean Michel looked more deeply at me and said, "Anna, this is our only free day. My parents would love to meet you. They asked if we could stop by for a visit. They have heard me talk about you, and it's time they meet the woman who has captivated me. Would you mind?"

"I know they are very special, and I know you're their only son. Are you sure they'll like me?"

He looked at me with an indescribable passion. "*Mon amour*, you know what you mean to me. And they will also know. No one has made me this happy before. They will love you, as I love you. *Ils vous aimeront.*"

We finished our leisurely breakfast on his terrace, drinking in the sounds of the ocean. I didn't want to move an inch. "Could we just stay here forever?"

Jean Michel smiled down at me and said, "Yes! That is exactly what I was hoping you would say."

He was anxious for me to meet his parents and broke our morning spell with the imperative to get dressed. Back in my room, I put on a new sundress from Fred Segal in Santa Monica with a pair of sandals for our visit. Jean Michel appeared behind me, whistling in admiration as he wrapped me in his arms. I whistled back.

I called Brian and Chris to let them know I would be gone for the day. Chris was going sailing with Olivia, and Brian was taking Melanie sightseeing around the island. He whispered into the phone, "Anna, I am going to buy her some diamond earrings. What do you think?"

I told him Melanie would be thrilled, of course! It was such a great idea. Off we went for our day with the Durand's. I brought some of Stuart's *Sonoma SMS* wine along as the perfect gift to share: one bottle of the Private Reserve and one bottle of his specialty sparkling wine.

At the main entrance of the resort, a parked car awaited us. Again, he surprised me, as this was no ordinary car. "Jean Michel," I said inquisitively, "this is quite the car. What is it?" He answered casually, "Oh, my parents gave this to me when I graduated from the Sorbonne. It's a vintage 1960 Ferrari. Actually, it's a 250 GT SWB California."

Well, whatever it was, it was awesome. Who gets a gift like this for graduation? I got diamond earrings. No complaints there, but a 1960 Ferrari? He started the engine, and it roared to life as we headed toward the northeast Roches Noires area of the island. We stopped at a quaint flower stand to purchase a bouquet for his mother, to accompany the wine. Before Jean Michel pulled up to the gated entrance, he explained how they actually had a little island of their own. In the past they could only access their home by boat, but his parents put in a small causeway so we could now drive right up. His family surely kept the warmth of the island alive at their beautiful island in the Indian Ocean. Who was this family with estates in Mauritius, Cap d'Ail, and Paris?

His parents were outside waving when we pulled up. I fell in love with them at first sight. Mousier and Madame Durand had a deep love for their son that I also shared. They were a handsome couple, dressed in casual yet understated elegance. This is where Jean Michel got his charm! The two had carved out quite a wonderful life in Mauritius.

They had wealth, but somehow stayed grounded.

"Please, Anna, call us Patrick and Francoise. We hope you don't mind."

We spent the day getting acquainted. They wanted to hear about my family and the early days of military life. "Anna, we have never been out to the West Coast. Perhaps we should come out for a visit someday." Patrick said this as he reached over and held my hands. They had only been to the East Coast, but had always wanted to visit California.

"Please, come out soon for a visit. You are always welcome, and I know my parents would love meeting you. After all, your son did help me find my little bungalow in Santa Monica while he was visiting. Please say yes."

The invitation to them was open, of course. I meant every word of it, and they said they would gladly accept. After a day out on their terrace overlooking the ocean, I knew how easily the Durand's could be family.

I recounted to them about all my recent travels before Mauritius, remembering to compliment them on their stunning villa in the South of France. I shared my thoughts about Cairo and the Royal Malewane and tried to convey how much the orphanage in Harare affected me. I showed them pictures from my phone of the kids playing with us. Best of all, I told them about the gift from Stuart and Vanessa. I saw a tear trailing down the side of Francoise's beautiful face. She reached out to stroke the screen of my phone displaying a little boy's face.

As we were saying our goodbyes that afternoon, Patrick pulled me aside. "Anna, please know that you are always welcome here. We love our Mich very much. How special you are to have captured his heart. You have also captured ours. *Merci pour passer la journee avec nous. Ciela signifie beaucoup pour nous, cher Anna. Thank you for spending the day with us. It means so much to us. Dear Anna.*" We would see them again at dinner that evening, and I was already making plans to spend more time with them before I left. How wonderful! Kissing their cheeks in gratitude, I also did the American thing and reached around to embrace them. They giggled and kissed my cheeks again. They waved us many farewells as we drove off together. With a coy smile, Jean Michel pulled the car over when we were just out of sight to steal a few kisses. When I came up for air, he said, "Thank you, *mon amour*. They loved you."

The feeling was mutual, of course, but I needed another one of those kisses! I drew him closer with my fingertips and said, "Mich, huh?"

The week's events passed quickly, and we couldn't get enough of celebrating Stuart and Vanessa—or one another. One of the days, Mich and I went out to the Ile aux Certs. We boarded the hotel boat bound for the island. Palm trees swayed in the breeze with a welcomed relief from the heat of the day. Banana boat and tube rides were just getting under way. It was a private oasis just for the staff and our forty guests. I could get shipwrecked here easily! A hut in the lagoon was set up for water skiing and wake boarding. Oh, this was too perfect! Canoes and kayaks were already in use, and the Hobie cats and pedal boats were lined up too. There was snorkeling, scuba diving, and fishing, but the first order of business was to waterski. "Oh, Mich, do you mind? I love to waterski!"

We both had long turns skiing and wakeboarding. I was in heaven.

When Chris and Olivia arrived, we swept them up for a ride on the banana boat. It was just as silly as it sounds. They couldn't resist the humor of being jostled about on the giant banana. I could hardly breathe from laughing!

Brian, Melanie, Conor, and Liz heartily joined a duel challenge on the tubes. Whoever fell off first lost! It was a battle of the sexes, and the winners got bragging rights. The girls didn't win, but we were having too much fun to care.

We took a lunch break at the Paul & Virginie Restaurant in the wooden huts overlooking the beach, famished from a day of play in the water and sun. Stuart and Vanessa soon joined us. The huts were lined with palm trees and live music playing just for us. There was dancing on the beach, of course, at the Sand Bar. Mich and I spent the afternoon sailing through crystal waters. Was there anything he could not do? We skipped the golf tournament just to relax.

He smiled and told me to be the lazy wench. Lazy wench? I dangled one foot over the edge in pure enjoyment of the ride. Jean Michel came over and lay down beside me as we drifted through the water. He reached over and held my hand. No words, just a love that transcended everything. This was the first place I had felt totally safe in a long time.

Mich and I stayed in for dinner and met the group later at the Sega Bar. Under the crystal stars, we swayed to the island music into the early hours of the morning and left around two o'clock. He held tightly to my hand as we walked back to our rooms. Each night, we feel asleep in each other's arms. Tonight was no exception. How could I imagine life without him? His strong and steady arms wrapped around me.

A gentle knock at my door signaled another sumptuous breakfast tray, and it was almost time for the car rally. Mark preferred that I stay at the resort where he could keep me safe from potential threats, but I was determined to go. The two-person teams received their first clue at the reception desk of the resort. Jean Michel, who knew the lay of the land, gave us an immediate advantage. Stuart let us know it too. Oh, not this again!

Stuart and Vanessa arranged to have special convertible cars for each team. It was like every kid's dream come to life! We were giddy with excitement to grab our keys and make a run for it when Stuart approached us in the lobby for one final competitive dig: "You two are going to lose this one. Just watch."

We leapt into the seats of Mich's car and sped off, with Stuart and Vanessa hot in pursuit. Stuart thought he had a chance. Did they really want to challenge us? This was the perfect way to see the island I could call home someday. The thought rode with me in the front seat as we flew down the road. We took pictures with our phones at each stop to document our progress. Without picture evidence, our team would be disqualified. This was serious business!

Our first clue was near the Floreal shopping area. We were shopping for textiles and diamonds. Mich took the back roads, but we noticed how Stuart stayed on our tail to follow Jean Michel's shortcuts. He certainly was eager to win! Our first stop at the Boutique at Barkley Wharf in the Plaines Wilhems district contained a clue. It read, "Purchase a Ralph Lauren polo shirt for ten dollars from the boutique. Now, how many textile companies are on the island? How many Mauritians are employed in the business? Name ten textile companies. Pay for the polo shirt with Mauritian rupees."

We felt like detectives pursuing a case. We learned that Mauritius has over 285 textile houses and employs over eighty thousand people. Ralph Lauren, The

Gap, Galleries Lafayette, Selfridges, Harrods, Eddie Bauer, Hugo Boss, Max Mara, Victoria's Secret, and The Limited are just a few. Check!

The second clue read, "Go to ATVA Gems Ltd at the ATVA Duty Free shop at 32 Mon Desir Bonne Terra Vacoa in Vacoas and document that you have found a four carat diamond." Check! Could I keep it?

Third clue: "Find the Veranda Grand Baie Hotel and Spa Mauritius in Grand Baie. There you will receive your next clue." I noticed that Stuart was still right on our tail. He was taking that tennis loss harder than I thought. While we took in the sights around us, we were sure to give him a run for his money!

Mich looked over at me, grinning. "Anna, I had no idea how competitive you are. Stuart, too."

"Well then, hurry up and lose them!"

Our fourth clue read, "Find the Balaclava Ruins near the Baie aux Tortues on the northwest coast of the island. Find the Maritime Hotel. At the Maritime Hotel, find the original sea wall the French built." Check! The scenery was spectacular. A butler came out and served us lunch on white china with crystal glasses and French linens. It was heavenly. We were the first to arrive, with Stuart and Vanessa close behind.

Our fifth clue read, "Find the oldest settlement built by the Dutch in Mauritius. Your next clue is waiting at the Vieux Grand Port."

Jean Michel knew exactly where to go and told Stuart and Vanessa they could follow us, or else they might get lost. I don't think they appreciated our humor, but we found it in no time!

Next, the sixth clue: "Go to the Martello Towers built by the British to defend themselves against the French. Find La Preneuse, and then go to La Mariposa. There you will find a quaint resort to view the Black River Range and LeMorne Brabant. Ask at the front desk for your next clue." We enjoyed taking pictures together and set out on the move!

The seventh clue read, "Find Triolet Shivala. Shivala is the longest village on the island in the Pamplemousse district. Find the Hindu Shrine constructed in 1819 in the village of Triolet." Check!

Clue eight: "Go to the Labourdonnais Orchards. Find the gardens at the Chateau de Labourdonnais, and look for the Aldabra tortoises lounging in the sunshine among the vegetation." Wow, those were cool! We quickly grabbed the next clue.

On to clue nine: "Head toward the Rhumerie des Mascarignes at the chateau built in 1858 by the Wiehe family. Inside the distillery, watch the art of rum making."

Out of nowhere we heard, "Oh, Mich, over here."

This beautiful young woman came over, kissing JM full on the lips. Coming up for air, she looked over at the rest of us in mockery.

"Will you stop that, Bridgitte?"

He pushed her away before introducing us to this little spitfire. "I want you to meet Stuart and Vanessa and my beautiful Anna. This is Bridgitte, the ambassador's daughter."

She glanced at us with a quick greeting and left as suddenly as she had appeared. I could tell Jean Michel was clearly upset, apologizing over Bridgette's display. This would be a subject for later, but for now, we were in a race and needed to continue our adventure, so off we went to the tasting bar, trying their two estate rums called Rhumeur and La Bourdonnais. Done! Vanessa got a pass on sampling the estate rums.

Clue ten, the final clue! "Find your way back to Le Tousserok and the finish line." This felt like an episode of *The Amazing Race*. It was the perfect way to see the island and learn some of its rich history. We pulled over near the end to let Stuart and Vanessa lead the way back to the entrance of the resort. They came fittingly in first place. They were, after all, the couple we came to celebrate! We were both at least two good hours ahead of the others. Evening had set in before everyone made it back to the finish line. Once they returned, the party began. Mauritius had quickly become my favorite place in the entire world.

Dinner and dancing was the prelude to Conor's presentation of the trophy ceremony. He made it look like Le Mans all over again with the spraying of champagne. Each team received a trophy and a Ralph Lauren polo shirt embroidered with "The Manning Clan Car Rally, Mauritius." Each team member won a three-carat diamond inside their trophy. I couldn't believe it! The top three teams won four-carat diamonds from clue number two.

Between Jean Michel and me, we had eight carats! What a dazzling gift. It was Stuart and Vanessa's way of thanking their guests for coming to celebrate their marriage. I felt like they already had. As we were dancing, there stood Bridgitte. Now what did she want? "Anna, I just wanted to apologize for earlier. You see, I think our families always thought Jean Michel and I would marry someday, but I know that he has always thought of me as a little sister. Watch out, though. I still haven't given up on him."

Jean Michel rolled his eyes just as Stuart pulled me to the side. With a wink he said, "Anna, you sure know how to pick them."

"You introduced us."

He laughed as I looked closely at him; "Seriously, I know we talked the other day about you becoming a father. I couldn't be happier for you and Vanessa. When I saw Vanessa refuse a glass of champagne in Cairo, I knew she was pregnant. I can't begin to tell you how excited I am to see you both in love and expecting your first child. Congratulations, Stuart. You deserve all the happiness in the world."

He leaned in and gave me a big kiss on the lips! I hardly had time to react, but made light of it. He was caught up in all the celebration.

Stuart's mom, Betty, had arrived that morning with his sister, Megan, on a flight he chartered for them. It was good to see them again. Stuart told Brian that Melanie could also fly home with them after the wedding—another generous offer. Betty and Megan were the last ones to cross the finish line, and we welcomed them with hugs of celebration. It was good to see them here in Mauritius.

The band arrived from Los Angeles for the wedding reception. One of my first days working for Stuart, I had a pirated black market CD of Jackson Love's first album just before he made it big. I played it onboard, and Stuart asked about his music. A couple days later, the two met up and became surfing buddies. Stuart loved his music and asked him to fly over for the wedding. Jackson got his band of six together, and the magic began.

The ceremony would commence on the resort's main beach, with a reception to follow, featuring Jackson and his band. I went down early to ensure everything was set up exactly how Vanessa had wanted it. We rendezvoused on the beach in the late afternoon soon to be followed by the setting sun. Stuart looked handsome standing next to the ambassador, who would officiate the wedding. Patrick and Francoise joined us for the event. Mich's mom sat next to me and held my hand during the ceremony. Betty and Megan sat in the front row. Betty was one proud mama, grinning from ear to ear, with tears of joy in her eyes. The island flowers were arranged to perfection. This was a fairytale wedding.

Jackson started to sing "Marry Me" followed by "All of Me" as Vanessa walked onto the beach, escorted by Conor. Her eyes were fixed on Stuart as she floated gracefully past the guests, every inch of her a real princess. Jean Michel grasped my other hand with a squeeze. They had written vows to each other. In tears, I listened to their words so thoughtfully shared. It was a joy-filled celebration for the two of them. Jean Michel leaned in reassuringly and gave me a kiss. "Anna, our day will come soon."

I hoped it would. I was so in love with him. His mother was on my left, squeezing my other hand. I looked behind me to find Brian and Melanie, also teary-eyed. Soon we would be in Maui celebrating them. Love was undeniably in the air. I glanced over at Chris standing by Olivia. Were they an item, too? The following evening, I would accompany Stuart and Vanessa, along with the boys, to Bora Bora on their honeymoon. Where had the time gone?

A display of fireworks ignited in perfect unison as the ambassador introduced Mr. and Mrs. Stuart Manning for the first time. The twinkling lights illuminated the resort in every direction. It looked like a set from a tropical kingdom. The guests stayed up into the early morning hours, caught up in the magic of this dream celebration. Stuart and Vanessa were beaming in happiness!

During our last night on the island, I savored each moment with Jean Michel, and our lovemaking reached a new level. We would see each other soon; we just weren't sure when. My heart was full of joy for the happily married couple, but was also breaking at the thought of leaving my love behind on this island in the Indian Ocean.

There was talk of going to the island of Jersey soon. It was off the coast of Normandy, France, in the English Channel. Vanessa's parents lived there, and she wanted to visit before the baby was due. Her father's health prevented them from attending the wedding, but I could tell she wanted Stuart to meet them personally. If we went, Jean Michel could hopefully meet us there.

We spent a quiet time together the next morning and afternoon. "Anna, I love you so very much. Please never forget how much you mean to me. We just need to get through this short period of time before our lives together can begin, *oui*?"

All I could say was, "I don't know how long I can keep doing this. You have my heart in every way. I do love you, Jean Michel, my Mich, but saying goodbye is killing me."

He took my hand and dropped to one knee to place a diamond ring on my finger. "Anna, I am in love with you. I fell in love with you that first time I saw you in Paris. I never want to let you go. Will you do me the honor of spending the rest of your life with me by saying yes, *mon amour*?"

Stunned, the only words I could speak were, "Yes, yes, yes!" He sealed his proposal with a kiss that I never wanted to end.

Please save me! I was drowning in our love together. Must I leave his arms ever again?

My father had given his seal of approval heartily during Jean Michel's visit to LA. I took a moment to look at my ring. It fit perfectly. It was a family heirloom, a three-carat diamond surrounded by emeralds that he said matched my eyes. It was exquisite. His mother insisted he use this ring to propose to me. I treasured it above anything else I owned.

After all the excitement, we were quiet driving to the airport. These were our last moments together for a while. I met Brian and Chris onboard. They took one look at me and whistled at my ring. They shook Jean Michel's hand and slapped him on the back in congratulations, as men do. I asked them not to tell Stuart and Vanessa yet. I would share the news with them after their honeymoon.

I said one last goodbye to this incredible man, even while it was tearing me apart. He gave me the kind of kiss that always left me breathless, professed his love, and pulled away with, "Remember, Anna, now we are engaged! Please keep Mark close, and be careful. You are the love of my life."

Off he went into the swirl of activity that was Mauritius. I needed to pull myself together for the long flight ahead and focus on my arriving passengers.

Chapter Fourteen

BORA BORA AND THE HONEYMOON

Everyone gets to decide how happy they want to be because everyone gets to decide how grateful they are willing to be.

—Ann Voskamp

The newlyweds arrived, and we took off into the skies above the magical island of Mauritius. Somewhere in that beautiful view below was my Jean Michel, who I was leaving behind. I was happy to see Stuart and Vanessa, but it was more difficult each time Mich and I parted. They wanted to know if I enjoyed the wedding. "It was truly spectacular," I said. "These last few weeks, I've had the time of my life. What a celebration! No words can begin to convey how special it was." They just smiled.

They were exhausted from the wedding, with no more than a couple hours of sleep each night. Our flight was stopping in Auckland for a refuel and then heading to Tahiti where Larry was on the ground to pick us up in the yacht helicopter. First, he would take Stuart and Vanessa out to the *Sonoma SMS*.

The chef at Le Tousserok was delighted to cater the honeymoon couple's flight, and he certainly did not disappoint. He had outdone himself with a mouthwatering array of food. Neither Stuart nor Vanessa had much of an appetite after two weeks of celebrating, so I set out light seafood appetizers and the most enticing island fruit. Later on, I would serve the baked goodies from the resort's patisserie. They just wanted to cuddle up and watch a movie together. Who could blame them? Vanessa had never seen *Jillian Rose* in its entirety, so they watched it. What a treat! I caught a few of the scenes while I was working. I had to admit, Vanessa was a fantastic actress. The film had exceeded box office projections, and Vanessa was scheduled to begin the sequel in a little over one month after her due date. "Anna, how am I ever going to get in shape for filming?"

"Vanessa, I can't even tell you're pregnant now," I reassured. "I promise, once Sabrina comes, I will personally help you lose any baby weight. I have a feeling it won't be much."

She was mindful to continue training and to eat healthy foods during her pregnancy, making it easier to stay in great shape for the upcoming sequel. She hardly looked pregnant at almost seven months.

I continued to check on Brian and Chris. They were a little quiet up front. Brian was grateful for his time spent with Melanie, yet he wished she could have joined us in Bora Bora. She loved her new jewelry: a set of diamond earrings and the diamond from the rally they made into a necklace. Chris was hoping for a trip to England soon to see Olivia. She was in LA for the next couple of months, but with our schedule, who knew if we'd be home? The three of us looked at each other and burst out laughing. When had we turned into such romantics?

We had a long flight ahead of us to Tahiti. The runway at Bora Bora was too short for landing, which meant we would land in a little under eighteen hours at Papeete, Tahiti at Faa'a International Airport. Larry would be waiting on the ground to take the Manning's out to their yacht, then he would double back to take us to Bora Bora. We were staying at the Four Seasons Resort on the island of Motu. Stuart and Vanessa wanted an intimate honeymoon after the flurry of events surrounding the wedding. They invited us out to the yacht near the end of our stay to dive and Jet Ski, and they planned to join us for dinner at the Four Seasons for an evening dinner. With our plans settled, I made up their beds and closed the shades to let them get some sleep.

We were on our way to French Polynesia, with our first stop to fuel in Auckland. Next stop, Tahiti! I gave Stuart and Vanessa big hugs, assuring them we would fulfill any of their requests at a moment's notice. "Don't forget, Mr. and Mrs. Manning, this is your honeymoon. Now, go relax, and enjoy every moment. You two deserve it."

Larry whisked them over the brilliant ocean above Papeete to the awaiting *Sonoma SMS*. Vanessa had only been aboard once before, and I could tell she was looking forward to some privacy. No schedule, no cameras, no fans on the lookout—just husband and wife.

We closed up the airplane for our six days in Bora Bora. This meant closing all the window shades, cleaning the interior top to bottom, and ensuring anything perishable was put inside our FBO, TASC (Tahiti Air Service and Concierge). Once finished with our tasks, we saw Larry touch down in the helicopter, as if on cue. We boarded the helicopter, fatigued but enthusiastic for Motu. Flying over the island of Bora Bora was spectacular. The lush, emerald vegetation below was like a gemstone couched in aquamarine waters. It reminded me of the beautiful ring Jean Michel had slipped on my finger less than two days ago. I sighed at the thought of him. The sun was up and shining now, illuminating white, sandy beaches touched by calm currents. It was idyllic.

Our helicopter landed on the private motu of the Bora Bora Four Seasons Resort. We thanked Larry as he delivered us to the attentive staff at the hotel. They served us chilled towels with an icy-cold, coconut-mango drink for refreshment. Our greeters showed us to the lobby for check in and had our luggage delivered to our bungalows. The customer service was over the top world class.

Bora Bora is called the "Pearl of the Pacific" as the famed British explorer James Cook once dubbed it. The island was overflowing with a leafy beauty. Dormant volcanoes rose up in the center of this lush tropical paradise. The native tongue was a lovely mix of French and Tahitian I could listen to all day. We had heard the statement, "Aita pea p," quite frequently since landing. Larry told us it meant, "Not to worry." Of course the phrase "no problem" had transcended every culture!

Our rooms were the water bungalows so often featured on the Travel Channel. Like a small village suspended over aquamarine waters, each one was constructed in true Polynesian style, with bathtub shutters opening into fresh air over the lagoon and behind the hotel the jagged peaks of Mount Otemanu and Mount Pahia. Exhausted from the long flight, I just wanted to sleep for the next twenty-four hours. I wished sincerely that Jean Michel could share this paradise with me.

I immediately sent my work clothes to the dry cleaners after wearing them for over twenty hours. I dug my swimsuit out of my suitcase for a quick dip into the water. I had arranged before we arrived to have a Polynesian massage that first evening. It was two hours of complete bliss. I ordered dinner out on my deck from the Sunset Restaurant and Bar for a taste of their magnificent sushi.

Brian and Chris came over to lounge for a while. By the water with a glass of wine, we watched stars dot the sky against a brilliant sunset. I took a moment to examine my engagement ring again. It was a promise from Jean Michel of our future and his love for me. It was a stunning ring, and I could not stop looking at it. I knew that sleep would come soon, but first I needed to hear his voice.

I was anxious to talk. He picked up the phone, "Anna, did you make it safely? I watched as you took off from the island yesterday and thought my heart would split in two. I already miss you. Did I tell you that I love you?"

He caused my heart to flutter rapidly. I could only say the same. "I'm really happy for Stuart and Vanessa, but it broke my heart to leave you this time, too. I love you, Mich."

I went on, "I keep admiring this beautiful ring on my finger. Did I imagine that you asked me to marry you?"

I could hear his laugh as if he was right next to me.

"Mich, if I did imagine it, don't wake me up, okay? Oh, I wish you were here with me."

"Me, too. Do you really like the ring?" he asked.

"Seriously? It is the most beautiful ring I have ever seen. How did you know it would fit perfectly?"

He had recruited Jesse while he was visiting in LA to send him my ring measurements. So, my sister was in on this too! I needed to call my family soon and let them know I was engaged. Tomorrow. I still had not said anything to Stuart and Vanessa about our engagement. I didn't want to infringe on their honeymoon. I could tell them on the way home to LA.

"Mich, I can barely keep my eyes open, but I just needed to hear your voice. How are we going to do this long distance relationship?"

He soothed me by saying that it wouldn't be forever. We both had to finish our obligations. We could get married within two to three years at the very most. That seemed like an eternity to me, as I sat there under the stars of Bora Bora. Still, I knew we could make it work. I feel asleep with thoughts of my handsome fiancé, who had captured my whole heart.

Our time on the island went quickly. We spent one day at sea on the *Sonoma SMS* with Stuart and Vanessa. We indulged in the best sushi the island offered— all except Vanessa, who could not eat raw fish. The boys were impressed by her restraint, thinking it was part of her regiment in preparation for her next movie. It was hard to hold the happy secret for much longer.

The three of us hiked up to Mt. Otemanu one morning and stopped in the quaint town of Vaitape to spend the last of our French Pacific francs before leaving the island. I bought a little island treasure for my family and a colorful wooden tiki poll for Jean Michel. Bora Bora is easy to navigate. The island is two and a half miles wide. That's nothing more than a morning jog! The taste of sushi still brings back memories of the island's specialty: poisson cru. This was raw fish cured in lime and coconut juices until it's melt-in-your-mouth tender. Once again, I wished for Jean Michel to see it all with me.

We spoke at least twice a day and were still hoping to meet in Jersey if Vanessa could make the trip. Stuart also indicated that we could be heading to Paris soon. The decision would be made once we were back in Van Nuys. Mich was leaving for Paris with the ambassador in the morning. They had some important meetings to attend with the President of France, and Jean Michel was speaking at the event in a few days. I was excited to hear about his trip. "Anna, have a safe flight home. I am with you every step of the way. Never forget that. I love you."

My heart swelled with pride for his accomplishments and character. Our love for each other was as evident as the beautiful engagement ring on my finger. I stared at it while waiting for Larry to pick us up for Papeete. This time we were his first stop as we needed to prepare the airplane ahead of Stuart and Vanessa.

In no time, we were due east over the vast waters of the Pacific Ocean, heading for home. Home seemed like the most foreign place. I had been away long enough for my entire world to turn upside down. We were bringing Stuart back as a happily married man. And they finally learned of my engagement. Vanessa couldn't get over the ring. Stuart said that he had given Jean Michel his approval before we arrived in Mauritius. So he was in on it too! Stuart looked intently at me and then broke out into a smile. "Well, that certainly didn't take you long."

"Remember, Stuart, you introduced us. Need I say more?"

In flight both Stuart and Vanessa confirmed we would visit her childhood home on the island of Jersey to see her parents. Part of the Channel Islands off the coast of Normandy, France, it was her favorite place in the entire world. When I was in college, Cade and I had gone on the Manche Ils ferry from a resort town called Barneville Carteret to the island of Guernsey. From there we went to Jersey, arriving in St. Helier for a day. I had fallen in love with Jersey and always thought it a great place for a honeymoon. Vanessa was surprised I had been there before.

Her father's heart attack two weeks before the ceremony prevented Vanessa's parents from attending the wedding. Vanessa wanted to see them before Sabrina arrived and give Stuart a chance to get acquainted. You still could hardly tell she was pregnant. She looked radiant.

Vanessa asked, "Anna, I know we have been gone a while, but would you mind terribly if we did another trip in three days?"

I responded a little too eagerly, "Of course not, Vanessa."

I would see Jean Michel again soon, and we would work out this long distance plan to perfection. Chris was thrilled and quickly made plans with Olivia. Jean Michel was beside himself, knowing our time together was so near. He would meet us on Friday and stay through Monday. We arrived in LA on Monday and were leaving again Thursday afternoon. I would be exhausted, but I didn't care. I needed to unpack, then repack, or maybe go shopping; but first, I needed to see my parents.

Chapter Fifteen

A RARE VISIT TO JERSEY

I would gladly live out of a suitcase if it meant I could see the world.
—Anonymous

Thank goodness Brian and Mel had two lovely weeks together in Mauritius, but now it was crunch time in preparation for their wedding. What a rollercoaster of events! I wanted to do an onboard baby shower for Stuart and Vanessa's upcoming trip to Jersey now that they had finally announced her pregnancy. I decorated the cabin in pale pinks and stashed gifts and goodies throughout the interior. The big gift was the stroller that Chris helped me buy in our brief time home. The stroller was like a jet! It had cost over three thousand dollars, but it was worth every penny.

We had fun picking out cute baby girl outfits by Jacadi, my favorite children's clothing from France. It was hard to resist buying the entire store—and hard to remember that the three of us were actually paying the bill. Nancy made special red velvet cupcakes with pink frosting and the most incredible menu for this trip. She was a magician in her kitchen at the hangar.

My parents were elated to hear about my travels and my engagement to Jean Michel. It was important to us that our parents meet and get acquainted soon. I knew they would love each other instantly. My mom sent the Durand's an invitation, asking them to visit soon.

On a brief shopping trip to Fred Segal, my mom helped me pick out a couple of new outfits and a new bathing suit for my trip to Jersey. I hadn't heard from Elle in ages, but she breathlessly called earlier that day, saying she heard I was in town and wanted to see me for at least a few minutes. She met my mother and me for coffee after our shopping trip. It started off well until she felt the need to remind me how I was never home and basically living out of a suitcase. Thank you very much. It felt like she was placing doubts in my mind about work. She turned almost as green as the emeralds around my diamond ring when she asked incredulously, "When were you going to tell me?"

"Elle, I just got engaged and have made no formal announcements. This is all new and exciting to me. I really appreciate all the help you offered me months ago when I was getting started, but I haven't seen you in months."

She brushed off what I had said to share how she was dating a guy from the Bay Area with his own airplane. If things went as planned, she would never have to work again. I left that conversation feeling uneasy. My mom was the first to observe what I had wondered about Elle. "Anna, I have never met her before, but she's angry at you, or she wouldn't say those kinds of things. Stay clear of her, but also be there when she finally realizes she needs a friend."

My mom was the voice of reason. I tried to brush it off, but I sensed the latent jealousy Elle had toward me finally bubbling to the surface.

No time to stew. By Thursday afternoon, we were headed for Jersey. Stuart and Vanessa were overwhelmed by the display of baby gifts we had arranged onboard. Stuart kept handling the cute little items and even read one of the baby books. "Anna, Brian, and Chris," he said, "you guys are amazing! When did you have time to put this together?"

"Well," I responded, "Chris helped with the stroller; Brian picked out the books; and the rest—I just couldn't resist with my mom by my side." They thanked us with eyes full of tears at this lovely gesture.

Stuart came back to the galley during the flight, still a bit emotional from earlier. He was going to be a good dad—I just knew it. "Anna, no one ever does this kind of stuff for us. From the bottom of my heart, thank you."

Now I was the one tearing up! Both Stuart and Vanessa had become my family, too. How could I find words to convey how I felt? I just loved them and would do anything for them.

We arrived in Jersey in record time, descending into a beautiful and cloudless sky. Pro Air Aviation Limited was on the ground to take care of all our needs. They brought out a passenger in their company van to meet us at the airplane. It was Jean Michel, and I could not wait to get my arms around him. First he greeted Stuart and Vanessa before they left for the Royal Bay of Grouville. Her parent's home had a view of the sea that stretched infinitely into the horizon line. This trip meant a lot to her.

Jean Michel wrapped me in a long-awaited embrace. He gave me a kiss, then stood back and looked at me with a big smile on his face. "Anna," he said, "you look amazing. How did I get engaged to such a beautiful woman?"

All I could say with a big smile was, "You got lucky!"

It was wonderful to see him. While it had only been a little over a week, that was too long as far as I was concerned!

"How did your speech go with the president? I want to hear all about it."

"Oh, you know, *mon Cherie*, it was the normal, everyday kind of thing."

Laughing, I said, "So, you have turned in to a wise guy, huh?"

Both Brian and Chris came over to greet Jean Michel. With a slap on the shoulder, Brian added, "So, you just can't stay away, eh? Does this mean we will be seeing a lot of you, JM?"

JM? Now Chris started in on the banter. JM retorted, "*Bien sur. Vous pouvez compter sur elle.*"

We quickly closed up the airplane for the next few days and hopped in the van to reach the car Jean Michel had rented. We were off with JM, driving correctly on the wrong side of the road in a Land Rover Defender 90. We wound our way through the narrow streets with stonewalls. The Atlantic Hotel was close in St. Brelades. The hotel had dramatic views of the Atlantic Ocean and St. Ouen's Bay. We all had oceanfront suites. Jean Michel had just reserved one room for the two of us because we never seemed to be able to leave each other.

"Anna, do you mind that I made that assumption?"

All I could say was, "You have always been a perfect gentleman, JM. I always fall asleep in your arms anyway. Can you please hurry up and get over here?"

He looked relieved as he swept me into his arms and loved me like never before. I came up breathless, wanting even more of him. I did take a peek at our room. It was done in a refurbished 1930s seaside marine architecture style. The views were heavenly from our terrace overlooking the tennis courts to the ocean below. I loved it.

I don't think I had ever had a less than perfect time with this man, and our trip to Jersey was no exception. The hotel had filmed a segment for BBC's *The Apprentice* a few years back, and it was their claim to fame. An equal mix of both French and English was spoken throughout the hotel. It was romantic and wonderful to be there. We went out a little later to explore around the hotel. JM had never been to Jersey, and we thought to grab the boys for a hike along the rugged cliff paths that dotted the entire island coastline.

The landscape was unspoiled and quite striking just before sunset. The sand below reflected a golden hue from the sun that caused me to squint. The air was warm with a slight breeze, and at that moment, I could not think of any place I would rather be.

That evening, we ate at the Ocean Restaurant in the hotel. It lived up to its reputation as one of the best restaurants on the island. They opened the dining doors to serve us out on the patio above the sea. Olivia joined us for dinner that evening, having just arrived from London. It was great to see her again with Chris, who was looking very pleased. Jean Michel toyed with my engagement ring all throughout the evening. I never wanted him to let go of my hand.

Back up to our room, he spoke to me in French as we lay in one another's arms. He knew how to romance me with the language of love. He said he loved my accent. What accent? That first night in Jersey, we feel asleep with the terrace door open and the stars illuminating a path to our room. If it were humanly possible, we were growing even closer together and more in love. He was playful yet deep, and he was serious about his love for me. Even his touch made my skin tingle with new sensations. What more could I ever want?

We woke up to a few cloud puffs drifting in the sky, with sunshine streaming through our terrace door. I opened my eyes, and there was Mich, staring at me.

"Anna, I love you. Sometimes it hurts to say how much."

I wouldn't mind waking up to that confession for the rest of my life! "You are so beautiful when you sleep, and you are so beautiful when you wake up. I love you, *mon Cherie*."

Was I just at UCLA four years ago? Now here I was with this sophisticated French Mauritian lover by my side. "I love you, too, my handsome and amazing Jean Michel."

We had a delightful breakfast delivered to the room and then decided to go for an ocean swim.

"JM, Anna, wait up!" It could only be Brian.

He was headed down for a swim, too. The currents through the Channel Islands keep the water temperature comfortable. I think the water was warmer here than what I was used to in Southern California. It was a perfect dip in the sea as we chatted, laughed, and listened to Brian and Mel's wedding plans for

Maui. On our way back to the hotel, we stopped downstairs for a café presse and sat outside in the warm sunshine by the pool to dry off. I pulled Brian aside and said, "I'm happy for you and Mel, but can I ask you a question?"

He nodded, and I continued. "I am kind of scared because I'm so happy with JM. Have you ever felt that way?"

He gave me a big-brother hug and told me it was clear how much John Michel and I loved each other.

"Anna, it is so obvious; the two of you were made for each other. Be happy and thankful you found each other. It is no mistake that God put you in each other's lives. I have a feeling He is going to use the two of you for something very special."

I was over processing. This was a time to relax and enjoy, not overanalyze my happiness! That's when Jean Michel grabbed my hand and declared, "Enough pool time. Let's go have a look around the island!"

We walked the Le Grand Etacquerel to the path at Devil's Hole along the spectacular coastline. We stopped by the Jersey Lavender Farm so Brian could buy some gifts for Melanie and we could have lunch with a spot of tea. We went by the Mont Orgueil Castle, built in 1204, where we stopped for fresh shrimp and beer. It was a perfect afternoon. We were alone that evening, with Brian off to relax and Chris and Olivia still touring the island. I had Mich all to myself, and I wasn't complaining.

Stuart called later that night to ask if we would join them at Vanessa's parents for dinner the following evening.

"Anna, why don't you all come earlier, and we can swim, then play some tennis and relax outside before dinner on the terrace?"

"Thank you, Stuart. That sounds wonderful. Should I bring my ringer?"

"This time, Anna, you're my partner."

We weren't really hungry that evening, so I asked the hotel to pack a light picnic dinner with a bottle of wine for us to take down to the beach and watch the sunset. We sat together in the sand, waiting for the brilliant, blood-orange sun to drop off the edge of the earth as the sky turned red, then pink, then violet, and finally became full darkness around us. My strong and amazing Mich had me in his arms, and I was lost for good. He took hold of my hand as his finger played with my now-familiar engagement ring. It reminded him that we would always be together. His face lit up just at the thought that we were about to make a lasting promise to each other.

Our time on yet another island passed much too quickly. I opened my eyes every morning to his beautiful face staring at me with such love and adoration. We knew each moment was golden. I was hoping to return to Europe soon, but with the due date of Stuart and Vanessa's baby quickly approaching, I didn't know when.

We spent a wonderful day at Vanessa's childhood home. Her parents thought Stuart was pretty special too. They could hardly wait to meet their new granddaughter. They were adorable, and I could see why Vanessa was such a lovely woman. In the comfort of her childhood home, she was just Vanessa Rathman, the daughter of two delightful people. When the paparazzi caught up with her, she could turn on the charm of a Hollywood star, but today, she didn't have to. It was beautiful watching her exist without the added pressures of the outside world bearing down on her.

We were not leaving until Monday afternoon. I was back in Stuart's good graces by helping him win the tennis match the day before, and he happily suggested that Jean Michel join us on the flight home to Van Nuys. Mich called the ambassador on the spot. He was taking the month off for his family to go on summer vacation and suggested Jean Michel do the same. Are you kidding? We were going back to LA together for a whole month! I was beside myself with happiness. It seemed that every time I was struggling with the thought of saying good-bye, our plans changed with another open door. I was grateful to Stuart and Vanessa and thanked them both before we left that evening.

Once back at the hotel, Mich took my hand and led me on the path to the beach below. We practically skipped our way down to the sandy shore. I was giddy with happiness just to be together. One kiss led to another, and then he stopped and looked at me very seriously, "Anna, do you mind if I come to California for a month with you?"

I put my finger up to the side of my face, as if mid-thought, and replied, "Hmm . . . let me think about that." Then, I leaned over and kissed him with my whole heart. I think the answer was yes!

Chapter Sixteen

GROUNDED

Travel does the heart good.

—Anonymous

*W*e were home! Vanessa started to go into premature labor shortly after we got home, and Stuart announced that we would be grounded until after Sabrina was born. He was getting into the spirit of her arrival, and you could tell he was concerned for Vanessa. This was the side most people did not see. This is why I cared so much about the Mannings.

My parents were beside themselves in happiness that I was coming home with Jean Michel in tow. My mom picked up the phone to call Mich's parents and ask them to come stay with them to celebrate our engagement. They heartily accepted and were coming in a week. Jean Michel and I fell into an easy and comfortable life rhythm together. We just understood each other. I never wanted him to leave.

Brian went up to see Melanie for two weeks before she came down for our engagement party. It was a special time. Olivia was in LA, too. I don't think I had ever seen Chris happier. We had many barbecues at my darling new bungalow, with time on the beach in the warm glow of the setting sun. We were all very happy anxiously awaiting the birth of the Manning's little girl. Stuart and Vanessa joined us on many of those nights, also returning the favor by hosting us at their estate. Yes, I worked for them, but they were my friends before anything else. Jesse and Turner were visiting, too. My heart was full!

Karen, Bob, and Tara spent every minute they could with us. Karen even announced that she was pregnant again. Mich enjoyed watching Karen and I together. He said he had never seen two people laugh at the worst jokes. "Anna, no one else understands what's funny about those jokes."

Life was wonderful, and we were celebrating. Jean Michel loved my friends and family, and the feeling was mutual.

One afternoon we were strolling hand in hand through the shops on Montana Avenue, savoring our time together. Mich looked over at me with a smirk about some silly statue he noticed as I rolled my eyes at him. "Seriously, Anna, did you see how much you Americans pay for that kind of art—if that is truly art?"

It was over ten thousand dollars, and yes, it was ridiculous. He added, "After your time at the orphanage, can you imagine how many kids we could feed for that amount of money?"

I agreed and was so proud of him. His family had wealth, but supported so many wonderful organizations all over the world. It was touching. I leaned over and kissed him, and yes, it was—as always—one of those kisses. Just as I opened my eyes, there, as plain as day, stood Cade. He looked great, but I was a bit embarrassed to be caught in a passionate kiss in front of my ex-boyfriend. Clearing my throat, I made introductions. Cade asked if we could join him for coffee to catch up just like old friends. Jean Michel was impressed at how nice he was. I have a feeling Cade thought the same. Was I the only uncomfortable one?

It was so strange sitting there with Cade and thinking about our college years gone by. Back then, I had every reason to believe I would be married to him by now. Seeing him with only feelings of friendship was strange, but also a relief. He would always hold a very special place in my heart. I asked about his tennis, his fiancé, and family. Jean Michel and Cade broke into French very naturally. Cade knew Jean Michel's childhood friend who was out on the tour. Preparing to leave after our nice encounter, I said, "Cade, I'm really happy for you. Congratulations on your engagement, and please know how glad I am to see you healthy and back out on the tour."

He shook Jean Michel's hand and gave me a big hug. "Anna, I am so glad I got to meet Jean Michel. I understand he's a great guy, and I can tell he makes you happy. Congratulations on your engagement, too. I wish you all the happiness in the world."

We parted ways, and when we rounded the corner, Mich took me into those warm arms of his and kissed me. "Anna, I am so glad we ran into Cade. He's a great guy, of course, but I am the one who is fortunate. You are going to spend the rest of your life with me."

At that, he looked quite pleased with himself as he playfully grabbed me around the waist and lifted me up in the air while spinning around and around. Ever so gently, he lowered me back down, while possessively wrapping his arm around my shoulders for our walk back to my bungalow.

I kept stealing glances over at him. He just smiled that devastatingly handsome smile. I could not resist him. "Mich, you are truly the love of my life. Thank you for that first night in Paris, for begging an introduction. Or was that groveling?"

He nudged me at that, but I continued. "I think I knew then how there would never be anyone else for me."

Ah, *amour*!

We had a wonderful month together. Our engagement party was a great success, and what made us the happiest was seeing our family and friends together. It was like a little preview of our wedding day. My parents were planning to meet the Durand's at their villa in Cap d'Ail at the end of the year. They had already become fast friends. Vanessa and Stuart welcomed the arrival of sweet Sabrina earlier than expected, but the doctors felt that Vanessa was actually further along in her pregnancy than they originally thought.

Vanessa was a champ during the labor. Seeing her shortly after Sabrina's delivery made me wonder if she even broke a sweat! One would never have known she had just delivered a baby. How did she do it? Natural beauty was her best-kept secret. Little Sabrina had all of Vanessa's most enviable features. Stuart was one very proud daddy, and Jean Michel and I were totally enamored by little "Brina."

Our time was coming to an end, and my heart was breaking at the thought. Stuart pulled me aside reassuringly. "Anna, I have to be back in Paris and Geneva within the month. Don't worry, you will see Jean Michel soon."

He and Vanessa asked us if we would like to be Sabrina's godparents. We both accepted with honor. Vanessa was scheduled to begin filming her sequel in a little over a two months, and we were only a couple months away from the wedding in Maui. Life did not seem to slow down, but continued to get better and better—or so I thought.

Chapter Seventeen

TRAVEL BEGINS AGAIN

I have left my heart in so many places.

—Anonymous

We were on our way to Paris to my utter delight. Stuart was to meet with the President of France on the afternoon of our arrival. This time we were all staying at the Hotel Meurice, situated between Place de la Concorde and the Louvre. Artist Salvador Dalí made regular appearances there during his life, and other patrons of the Paris art scene still frequent the hotel.

It was a wonderful place, filled with old-world charm. I couldn't wait to see Jean Michel that evening after his meeting with Stuart and the ambassador. The President of France wanted to partner with their dream of having orphanages on every continent around the world for children to receive good care, love, food, education, and a safe place to live. The president was affected by the story of the orphanage north of Joburg. He requested that the ambassador arrange a meeting with Stuart to see how they could further the cause together. I had never been so proud to be part of the Manning clan.

Stuart immediately accepted the offer, and there we were on a late summer morning at Le Bourget. Jean Michel was there to surprise me with a big smile in greeting. He looked devilishly handsome dressed in a suit, tie, and—oh my, I needed to focus! Stuart started waving his hands in front of my face to break the spell. "Anna, I think he feels the same way. What am I going to do with you two?"

Mich had lined up a car and driver to take us to the hotel. What I had not known was that he would be on the ground to meet us on arrival. What a wonderful surprise! Stuart said he would go inside Signature Flight Support to meet with Jean Michel while we put the airplane to bed. That way we could depart to the hotel together. Jean Michel peeked his head onboard before going inside, and I pulled him tightly to me, threatening not to let go. Had it only been a couple days? Paris stirred up memories of that first night with Mich.

Stuart quickly pulled me back to reality by asking if I would like to join their meeting with the president. What? Seriously? Well, yes, but what should I wear to meet a president? They both just looked at me and said not to worry. Not to worry? Of course I was worrying! Unknown to me Vanessa had already arranged an outfit for me to wear to the meeting. She called her stylist, who called the Louis Vuitton store off the Champs Elysees. In my hotel room awaiting me was a beautiful outfit with a purse and shoes to match for our meeting with the President of France. This was truly generous! Stuart had arranged for Vanessa to take care of it before leaving the United States. She worked her magic once again. Of course, Stuart didn't share any of this with me. He just left me to worry the entire car ride to the hotel until I opened the door to my room and there lying on my bed was the ensemble.

I opened my closet to hang up my clothes that I had packed from home. There inside was yet another surprise! Vanessa decided to add a couple more pieces. I had an entire wardrobe from Louis Vuitton, with a couple more purses and some sandals and boots.

I only had an hour to shower and change, but I wanted Jean Michel first. He stepped into the room, professing his love with a kiss, offering up a café, and leaving me quickly so he could meet with Stuart and the ambassador in the lobby to prepare for the meeting. A little under an hour later, I was making my way down the main staircase when something felt wrong. I tried to look around without being too obvious. Yes, there he was. There was no mistaking him this time; the same man who grabbed my arm in Cannes, the same man who tried to get me to leave with him in Le Mans, was beside me. I was shook up, with every alarm bell ringing in my mind. All I could think to do was reach for the bannister. He was too quick for me. He caught my hand in a vice-like grip, pulling me away in a lightning-swift move. I could feel his hot breath on my skin as he said, in that strangely familiar accent, "Ms. St. James, you need to come with me now. You will never get away from us."

Oh, yes, I would! I screamed loudly, just like Mark had taught me. Stuart rushed up the stairs and was by my side with his arms around me within seconds. Hotel security followed Jean Michel quickly up the stairs, but Stuart had seen the man approach me first and immediately came running. Everyone was in a panic. I tried once again to shake it off so we could get to our meeting with the president, but this incident had left me unsettled. When had I become the source of all this drama? Jean Michel was beside himself and wanted answers. Mark was at home watching over Vanessa and Sabrina. Stuart thought we would be fine coming in at the last minute—under the radar, so to speak. I could not stop shaking. What did these people want with me?

The ambassador called the president to convey what had just happened, asking if we could delay our meeting by an hour, at least. The president felt awful and sent over the best of his security team to accompany us for the rest of the trip. I pulled Stuart aside and said, "I really want to be at the meeting. At the same time, I don't want to detract any attention from the purpose of the meeting. If you think this incident will be a distraction, I will stay here. Remember, both Brian and Chris will be here, too."

Stuart placed his arm around me with concern. "Anna, I think you will be safer at the palace than here. You and Jean Michel play a big part in what we are trying to achieve. We are not going to take any more chances, okay? Do you think you can sit through the meeting after this incident?"

I would go to the meeting feeling abundantly loved and protected by these men. Jean Michel was clearly not going to let me out of his sight, and I was okay with that.

We left the Hotel Le Meurice with a security detail at the ready. We were escorted to 55 rue du Faubourg Saint-Honore. The walls looked impregnable with armed guards everywhere. We arrived at the Palais de l'Elysee in the eighth arrondissement, or as the French called it, "The Palace." It had been the residence of the French President since 1873.

The fortified gates opened up to ceremonial gardens. We walked into the main entrance of the *palais* toward the Vestibule d'Honneur Elysee, where the president greets his guests. Was I really walking into the French President's *palais*? What would my parents say? Our meeting was one I will never forget. The president was passionate about the foundation that Stuart and Vanessa had started. Intrigued by the orphanage in South Africa, he wanted to know more about what he could do to help.

A few of the targeted areas for orphanage construction were heavily influenced by the French colonies. I felt like I was sitting in a meeting with my dad, not the French President. He was warm and inviting and loved the United States. He had worked one summer as a soda jerk in a drugstore while visiting. I asked where, and his answer surprised me. "Well, Anna, I went to California and worked at the old South Pasadena Pharmacy. I had Route 66 on my mind that year from the old song but found myself spending a fun summer in Southern California instead."

Jean Michel chimed in. "Anna's parents live in Pasadena."

"You don't say." The president looked genuinely pleased. "Do you by any chance know if the pharmacy is still there?"

I explained how it had been renamed to The Fair Oaks Pharmacy & Soda Fountain.

I went on, "I have gone many times with my dad, who loves a good root beer float."

At that, the president's eyes seemed to light up. "Anna, I would love to come and visit. Perhaps, someday . . ." He had the faraway look of a happy memory.

Stuart told him his estate was close to Pasadena and extended an invitation to visit anytime.

The President said, "Watch out, Stuart. I just might take you up on that offer."

He invited us on a tour of the Elysee apartments. The apartments were his private residence. His staff looked shocked that he was bringing guests into such intimate quarters, but he opened the doors to grant us full access.

About two hours later, we said *au revoir* with cheek-to-cheek kisses. The president beckoned me for a hug. "Come on, I want to give you a hug like you do in the United States. It has been a pleasure to spend the afternoon with all of you." I hugged the President of France, hardly believing it had happened at all. He continued, "Congratulations on your recent engagement, Anna, and also to you, Stuart for getting married and having your first daughter. My wife has a gift for you to take home to little Sabrina. Unfortunately, she is at our home in Bordeaux enjoying the grandchildren. Please do me the honor of coming back to visit anytime. Promise?"

Walking us back to the main entrance, he patted Jean Michel on the back. "Your speech the other day was excellent. Thank you. By the way, this is only the beginning. We are going to help these children."

Back in the car, en route to the hotel, we all just looked at each other and smiled. Words were not adequate.

As we left, I made some calls from the car to have a root beer float, with refills sent to the *palais* as a thank you. The president called Jean Michel later that evening to offer his thanks. He was genuinely touched.

Back at the wonderful Hotel Le Meurice, I had time to see the true beauty of this first palace of Paris. Believe me, I was surrounded by security wherever I went. It was built in 1835 and decorated in a Louis XVI style. Time was suspended inside the walls of this hotel. This was Parisian luxury at its finest. The most wonderful aspect of the Hotel Le Meurice is the location. It is in the first arrondissement, right across from the Tuileries Garden. If I was allowed, I could quickly run over to the Place de la Madeleine and on to Fauchon to pick up their famous macarons.

The Place Vendome, the Louvre, the Place de la Concorde, the Opera, the Palais Royal, the Musee d'Orsay, my beloved Place des Vosages, and Notre Dame were before me in every direction. How could one possibly choose? The Eiffel Tower was the backdrop in the distance. This city was familiar to me, but with Jean Michel by my side, it was home. Unfortunately, the security made it difficult to step outside and explore together, but it was necessary. Stuart suggested we meet in the dining room for dinner that evening. I called Brian and Chris to see if they could join us around nine o'clock.

Brian said, "Anna, do we ever have a story for you. I will save it for dinner. Just enjoy your time with Jean Michel, and we will see you in a couple of hours."

Up in our room, I fell into Jean Michel's arms for a little nap. We lay there holding hands, reminiscing about all the places we had been. He reminded me that this is what most people see in an entire lifetime, if that! Fingers interlaced, he brought my hand up to his lips for a kiss. He followed with a kiss on the neck, then a kiss on the lips, and well—when he was like this, I just melted.

From playful to serious in an instant, he leaned over me and said, "Anna, please promise me that you will always be careful. These men have targeted you for a reason that we do not yet know. Both the president and the ambassador are looking further into it, as well as Stuart. Please promise to be careful, *mon amour*. I never want to lose you. We have a lifetime ahead of us."

I promised him that I would be careful. We came down to dinner a little later than the others. Brian was beside himself with a story about what had happened in front of the hotel that afternoon.

According to Brian, he and Chris were going for a walk when they noticed bodyguards talking agitatedly into their headsets in front of the hotel. Both of the boys decided to stick around for whatever was happening. They acted like they were waiting for someone to pick them up. One of the security guards asked them to step aside. Each was heavily armed and appeared of African descent. A man in robes stepped outside, whom they were told was the king of African nation.

Once outside, the bodyguards rushed him back inside the hotel. The boys overheard the security receiving a call from the president's staff at the Palais de l'Elysee, telling them their meeting was cancelled until the following day. The president had run late with one of his appointments and had to delay their visit. So the president canceled a meeting just to spend more time with us!

Our departure was set for early evening the following night. That gave me the rest of the evening and the following day with Jean Michel. Call me an addict. We had a month in LA, and I still wanted more. The more we had time together, the more my heart needed him. Without him, it felt like I would suffocate. It was likely we wouldn't see each other until Maui. That was way too long. "Jean Michel, my Mich, I promise I will be careful. I love you with all my heart. Please never forget that."

I continued, "Please know I will look at this ring and remember our promise every day. I love you."

He just cradled me gently in his arms, delicately laying me on the bed. I was ready to quit my job right now if it meant we could be together forever.

Chapter Eighteen

IS THIS NORMAL?

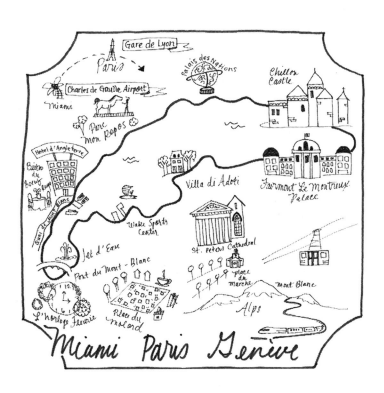

How do you spell love? You don't spell it—you feel it.

—Pooh

hen we touched down in Van Nuys, Stuart wanted to stay home for a few weeks with Vanessa before the filming for her sequel started. Just as he was getting off the airplane, he said, "Anna, I need to send Conor down to Florida for some important meetings in two days. I know we just got home, but is there any way you could work the flight?"

"Stuart, you know I will help in any way I can. You never have to ask."

"Good, I'll have Linda send over the trip sheets. I can't thank you enough, Anna. I know Conor will be happy to hear it. Thank you."

Back home that afternoon, my cute little bungalow felt empty without Jean Michel. I was overcome with sadness at the distance between us. Yes, I had seen a lot of him recently, but how could we make this work with our commitment to our jobs?

Preoccupied in self-pity, I was startled when the doorbell rang. It was a courier dropping off a letter. This should be interesting. Inside was a check for twenty-five thousand dollars, with a simple note enclosed.

Thank you for all you do, Anna. This is a little gift for going over and above for us. We love you.

—Vanessa and Stuart

Again? I couldn't accept this, but now wasn't the time to think about it. I would take this up with them in person. Designer wardrobes, a fantastic salary, a lifetime friendship, a beautiful goddaughter, and an introduction to my fiancé— yes, this was far too much.

Mich and I spoke every night and multiple times throughout the day. I missed him with such an indescribable yearning. This kind of love was a totally new emotion. *Oh, Anna, get a grip*, I thought to myself. The trip with Conor came as a welcome distraction, and besides, I hadn't been to Miami in years. Yes, this was the perfect remedy to soothe my emotions.

The flight down to Miami was rather uneventful. On the ground in the oppressive humidity, we made our way over to SW 27th Avenue to the Ritz Carlton in the Grove. Every time I stepped outside, my sunglasses immediately fogged up. Damp was the only word to describe it. We checked in at the hotel with a few hours before dinner. With Stuart's express permission, we headed over to the Grove Harbour Marina to take the Jet Skis on his yacht for rides around the bay. The water was a refreshing escape from the soaring humidity.

That evening, we went to George's in the Grove for dinner. Brian had the week off for wedding planning with Melanie. He sent his friend John to work our trip to Miami. John wasn't my Brian, but he got along fine with my two old favorites: Chris and Conor. Conor was in rare form at dinner, and as always, I was the object of his humor. Walking back to the hotel in laughter the whole way, we stopped in the lobby bar for a nightcap before turning in for the evening. At the table next to us was a very nice man, his beautiful young wife, and as he told us, his yacht broker, another attractive woman in her forties. He was laden in gold jewelry, and his young wife wore diamonds. They struck up a conversation with us naturally. "Hey, we saw y'all at the marina today heading out toward a yacht. Well, anyone with a yacht like that needs a round of drinks. Waiter, please get a round of drinks for my new friends."

He went on to make introductions. "I'm Michael, and this is my wife, Peyton. This is our broker, Miranda. That was some yacht you were out on today."

We introduced ourselves, without telling him any associations we had with Stuart. Michael looked at us closely. "You have got to be here with Stuart Manning. Conor . . . Conor Reilly?"

Conor made an affirmative nod with his head, reluctant to encourage Michael to continue. "We were on our yacht in the South of France when the Le Mans race was happening. We decided to see for ourselves what all the hype was about. We popped in on a charter, and might I add, you were absolutely brilliant, Conor."

Conor smiled and tried to deflect the attention while the wealthy couple assumed the role of our new best friends. Poor Conor, Michael peppered him with questions about how to invest his money. I could tell Conor was uncomfortable with the whole scenario, while John seemed intrigued by our new friends. He was single and a bit naïve where the intentions of this couple were concerned. John excused himself from the table to use the restroom, followed shortly by Peyton.

Meanwhile, Michael and Miranda regaled the rest of us with their tales of adventure, even offering a second round of drinks. It took about two seconds after the second round of drinks for the light bulb to go off. I leaned over and whispered into Chris's ear to go and check on John.

Feigning enthrallment by Michael's tales, I discreetly shoved a hand-written note on my napkin into Conor's hands. He glanced down to read it with his eyes growing as big as saucers. Conor and I waited in stunned silence until Chris appeared with John in the hotel lobby with the signal to get out of there. Conor politely interrupted Michael with our ticket out of there. "Anna, I need to do a quick review with you. Michael, can you excuse us for a bit?"

"Don't go too far!" he warned suggestively. "We want to spend the evening with y'all. You guys are great. Hurry back. We'll be waiting."

In the elevator, we all breathed a collective sigh of relief. "Well, that was close one!" The wealthy married couple was seeking a ménage a trois! Who were these people? When John had left for the men's restroom, Peyton took advantage of the alone time to ask if he would like to join her with her husband that evening in their room. She approached him right there in the men's restroom with a bag of cocaine, asking if he was ready for the time of his life. She kissed him, then snorted a line of the white powder right in front of him and reached out for his hand to follow suit. He was totally out of his element. Thankfully, Chris interrupted—with perfect timing. He swiftly pulled John out the door, leaving a sorry Peyton all to herself.

Closing the door to my room and still reeling from what had just happened in this crazy night in the Grove, I had to call Jean Michel to relay the story. Who would ever believe this? He picked up on the first ring, and my heart was flooded with tenderness for him.

"Anna, I'm glad you will be leaving tomorrow for home. What really concerns me is that they made the connection to Stuart through Conor. Who knows what else they could want? Please promise you will be careful, okay?"

Inhaling quickly, he continued, "By the way, it's your birthday tomorrow, right? What are you going to do when you get home?"

Though it sounded crazy to admit it, my birthday had really crept up on me. "I will probably stop by my parents' house to get spoiled and hear about how wonderful you are."

"They know me well," he said, with a bit of a chuckle in his voice.

A loud knock sounded at my door, and I knew immediately who it was. I looked through the peephole to confirm it was Michael, our new best friend. No way was I going to open that door! How did he even get my room number? Creepy. I continued whispering to Mich until Michael was gone, and I could relax.

"Anna, if he knocks again, please let me know. Stuart would be upset if he knew about this after everything that has happened recently."

We talked for another hour or so before I finally turned in to get some rest. Before we hung up, he said, "Guess what? Now it's officially your birthday. Happy Birthday, *mon Cherie! Vous etes l'amour de ma vie.*"

"*Comme tu es a moi,*" I replied.

His voice was the last thing I heard before I slipped into a deep and wonderful sleep. I woke up bright and early for a run that morning. Chris was my running partner, and it was hard to keep pace with him. On our way back, he surprised me with a stop in the Grove at a little bakery for a birthday cupcake. On our way out of the bakery, we were just passing a bookstore when Peyton and Michael appeared on the sidewalk up ahead. Chris grabbed my hand before they noticed us and rushed me through the door of the bookstore. Like secret agents, we ducked low, peeking our heads up to make sure they were gone. We crawled down the aisle on our hands and knees to make our escape. We saw our escape and made a dash for the door. I'm sure no one noticed! Once outside, we both broke down in hysterics at how silly we must have looked. What a close call that was! Regaining my breath, I linked elbows in camaraderie with Chris when two very familiar faces caught my eye. It was Allister Cummings and Elle, locked in an embrace. What a sore sight. I felt sick to my stomach. This place was full of bad vibes! We had to escape for good.

This time I grabbed Chris by the hand for a quick exit. We were not taking any chances. This place was crawling with couples of ill repute. Get me to the airport and fast! Conor laughed until I told him about Allister's appearance in the Grove with Elle. He looked up and said, "How did he know we were here? He was not supposed to know anything about this until the deal was secured. I'm glad we signed the papers today. This could not be a coincidence with Allister."

I was worried about Elle on the flight home. What a bad man to get mixed up with. I was tired from the flight. My little bungalow welcomed me home at last. It was good to be back. I unlocked my door, and there stood the best present of all, Jean Michel! So much for being tired. He wrapped me in his arms, saying, "Happy Birthday."

Yes, it certainly was. My fatigue melted into joy.

"Jean Michel, please never let me go."

He could only stay for a few days, and it was more than I could ask. "Anna, I was not going to miss your birthday."

The ambassador and the President of France asked him to meet with Stuart about the newly formed foundation, which meant a quick trip to LA and my birthday surprise. I just wanted to savor each precious moment with him. We sat on my deck that evening and watched the sunset. My heart was full.

We both went up the following day to the Manning estate for his meeting with Stuart. It was the perfect excuse to see our goddaughter, Sabrina. She was precious in every way. Stuart and Vanessa were proud and doting parents. Stuart sat down with Jean Michel in a serious discussion. When we got back to my bungalow that evening, Mich shared that Stuart had asked him to become the director of the foundation.

"That's wonderful, Jean Michel. What an honor."

I sensed hesitation in his voice. "Anna, I am not sure what to do. I would love to do it. Yet I feel I have made a commitment to the ambassador. What do you think?"

We stayed up that night discussing his job offer. A breeze skimmed over the darkened Pacific Ocean and brushed past our skin. It felt natural to be on the deck, discussing his career. Many important conversations had happened between us out in the open air. He held my hand as we sat united in prayer over where his future would lead us. It was a turning point, and I continued to marvel at the heart he had for others.

Mich was leaving for Paris the next evening on a red eye, and an idea had formed in my mind. I called Stuart and asked if he had anything planned for the next couple of weeks. He knew immediately what I was thinking. "Anna, the three of us are going on a road trip to Lake Powell to review the shooting locations before production begins on Vanessa's next movie."

"Stuart, would you mind—?"

"Anna, go back with Jean Michel for a week. I am sending Mark to watch over you. You won't even know he's there. Please do this for me."

"Stuart, thank you again and again. You and Vanessa have been so generous."

"Let's surprise Jean Michel. I can drive you to the airport. It's settled then."

One thing I always appreciated about Stuart Manning was his love for surprises.

Mich was quiet the next day, and I could tell he did not want to leave. I had Linda reserve the seat next to his on the airplane. The plot thickened! I snuck my suitcase outside when he wasn't looking. Stuart showed up as our ride to the airport, slapping Jean Michel on the back with a sorrowful look. He was laying it on thick!

He said goodbye to Jean Michel, giving us some time outside the car to say our goodbyes. He pulled out my suitcase and brought it around to where we were standing. Mich looked up at me suspiciously as he started to put two and two together.

"You're not the only one who can pull off a surprise," I quipped.

I hugged Stuart and gave him a kiss on the cheek. I liked him as my partner in crime.

"Please give Vanessa my love, and give Brina a kiss from both of us. And, Stuart, thank you."

I interlocked fingers with Jean Michel, and off we went to the international terminal. I had not flown commercially in quite some time. He was touched that I had arranged to have the first class seat next to him. Thank you, Linda! We could cuddle, sleep, and wake up together in Paris. I was staying at the embassy where Jean Michel had a beautiful flat. His mood was certainly lifted by my company. He looked over at me with delight. "This is the best present ever."

It was! We were together, and that was a gift.

During our flight, Jean Michel got an email from the ambassador, asking him to attend some meetings in Geneva. He showed me the email with a crestfallen face. "Anna, I am so sorry, but I have to be in Geneva in less than two days." I reached over for his hand and lifted it to my lips for a kiss.

"I am here to be with you. I want to go wherever you are, okay?"

He leaned over closely and said, "Yes, Anna, I would like that very much."

When he looked at me that way, I would go anywhere in the world with him.

We landed in Paris and would travel to Geneva by train. Mich had emailed the embassy in flight, requesting their driver meet us at Charles de Gaulle to take us directly to Paris Gare de Lyon to catch our train. It was a beautiful trip on the TGV Lyria into Geneva, with spectacular scenery. My heart was beating wildly as I looked over at my fiancé. This never got old.

We curled up together on the train, watching majestic landscapes go by our window. It took a little over three hours to get there. I think it was faster than waiting for a flight. We arrived in Geneva before nightfall. Mich took hold of my hand and whispered, "Anna, have I told you how much I love you? I'm so grateful to have you on this trip with me."

This trip was so different from my last stay at the Chateau de Divonne. I was fresh at my job and had not met Jean Michel when I was here last. How quickly both our lives had changed. I could not imagine my life any other way.

Geneva is known for its dramatic landscapes, most notably the Swiss Alps. It was also a mecca for fantastic food, excellent shopping, and a treasure trove of history. Geneva had a cosmopolitan feel without losing its old-world charm. It was also the hub of European commerce. Mich had made reservations at the Hotel d'Angleterre on the shore of Lake Geneva. It was a stunning location. We had a beautiful Luxe Panorama Suite with a balcony overlooking Lake Geneva and the Jet d'Eau in front of us. Our backdrop was the majestic, snow-capped peak of Mont Blanc glistening in the distance. I was in Geneva with my fiancé for the next five days. What a dream! We were tired, but wanted to stay awake to combat the jetlag. We jumped into bed for a quick power nap, or so I thought. The nap was three hours long. I woke up in the loving gaze of Jean Michel's eyes. I could not get enough of our time together.

We decided to go for a walk. On our way out, we saw two gifts on our entry table. We must have missed them when we arrived earlier. Who could possibly be sending us gifts in Geneva? Opening the card attached to both gifts, we stood there speechless, staring at the letterhead of the President of France:

Please accept this as a small token of my appreciation for your efforts. Jean Michel, your work has just begun in saving children throughout the world. Thank you for speaking at the United Nations on behalf of everyone involved in the foundation. My sincere gratitude always.

—Bernard

My heart could burst with pride. Jean Michel opened his box to reveal a Rolex Yachtmaster edition. Mine was a Rolex Datejust Lady. The gifts were terrific and even more valuable was the note.

We walked out on the Quai de Mont Blanc, overlooking the shimmering waters of Lake Geneva. Our walk continued to Old Town. Quaint streets and alleyways framed the city's picturesque squares. Geneva's two thousand years of history came alive to us. The Place du Bourg-Four was the heart of Old Town since the time of the Romans. We stopped at the Hotel de Ville where sixteen countries had signed the first peace treaty back in 1864. Place du Molard was on the left bank, with the octagonal fountain surrounded by department stores. Jean Michel was the perfect tour guide, but really, I was just happy to be with him anywhere.

We went to Saint Peter's Cathedral on top of the hill, which dated back to 1160 with the history of the Protestant defiance during the Reformation. I finally looked at Jean Michel and said, "I'm fading fast. Can I just have room service and you?"

Say no more!

The morning sunshine poured through our balcony doors. Jean Michel was already up practicing his speech for the United Nations. I was thrilled at the invitation to witness this important event. First, though, a quick run through the park sounded perfect. We were on the western side of the lake, with Jean Michel expertly leading the way toward the Mon Repos Park. He educated me on the rich history of the park. Even Casanova spent some time here in the eighteenth century. I could see why. It was like stepping back in time with the Mediterranean gardens, botanical beauty, and nature trails. How did he know all this information?

"So, you are kind of like Casanova?" I jokingly asked.

My mind conjured up images of the past as we made our way through the dense vegetation to stop at Perle du Lac café on our way back to the hotel. We just sat there, holding hands in the shadow of the noble Mont Blanc looming above, with the water at our feet. It was heavenly, but now it was time to get back and prepare for the United Nations.

The Palais des Nations is the crown jewel in the City of Peace. The monumental white building looked the size of Versailles in Paris. It was constructed for the League of Nations in the late 1920s. Our instructions told us to go straight to the Pregny Gate to pick up our identification badges through the secretariat of our conference. Walking inside with Jean Michel at my side was an experience I could never forget. I put my lips near his ear to say something in confidence. "You, my handsome fiancé, will change the world today. I love you."

I tried my best to commit each moment to memory. The ceiling was a rapturous mural by abstract artist Miguel Barcelo in the "Human Rights and Alliance for Civilization Room." The splash of vibrant colors almost threatened to drip from the ceiling. The artist used one hundred tons of paint to complete it, and the painting was valued at over twenty-three million dollars.

Jean Michel was representing France, Mauritius, and the newly formed Manning Foundation before the Human Rights Council. He was an outstanding public speaker. I put Stuart on speakerphone so he could hear once Jean Michel started. The speech was translated into six different languages. Once Jean Michel had completed his speech, a group of people eagerly formed around him to hear more. The foundation was now a reality. Stuart was beyond thrilled.

Stuart asked, "Anna, how did our boy do?"

"Stuart, he was fantastic. You would be proud. I can't believe I'm here at the United Nations with him. Thank you for allowing me to come. Now, when do you and Vanessa leave for your road trip?"

He laughed, "We are in the car as we speak. We can all hear you, including Sabrina."

Vanessa chimed in. "Hi, Anna! Our love to you and Jean Michel."

"Vanessa," I said, "good luck with the beginning of production. You will be awesome in the sequel. My love to all of you."

Back at the hotel, we went to the Leopard Bar for a celebratory champagne toast before our invitation to dinner. A very influential investor had invited us to join him for dinner at the Bistrot du Boeuf Rouge. Neither of us had heard about the restaurant, but it was only a few blocks from the hotel on 17 rue Dr. Alfred-Vincent. It was an unbelievable event.

The owner and chef, Paul Bocuse, escorted us downstairs to a private wine cellar where we met our group of investors. They called the cuisine Lyonaise bouchon. All I know is that it was fantastic. We had chatuaubriand and a quenelle du brochet paired with wonderful wines. By the end of dinner, we had secured over one hundred million dollars for the Manning Foundation, with promises of more to come. We were just getting started. We called Stuart and Vanessa on our way home to share the good news. They were in total disbelief at the amount of support we had raised. What could I say? I'd brought my ringer to Geneva!

The next few days were all our own. We took the tram to the Carouge neighborhood to visit the Place du Marche marketplace. We laughed and enjoyed the sights, sounds, and smells of the Marche. We also went to Cologny. It is the Beverly Hills of Geneva and only five kilometers from the city. We stumbled upon the Villa Diadoti, where the poet and writer Lord Byron often stayed. The coach house was visible, with stonewalls tracing the property. The home overlooked what the locals call Lac Leman. This is where Mary Shelley wrote *Frankenstein* after a violent storm. I could picture Frankenstein inside the walls of the property as Mich began to walk with his arms frozen out in front of him like a zombie.

"Anna, come to me and be my prisoner. Up in the home with the green shutters, I will watch over you for all time."

Out in front of the property, the gates opened as if Frankenstein had heard us taunting him. It was really just a friendly gentleman who asked if we would like a tour. Caught in our play-acting, we pushed past our slight embarrassment and gladly accepted a ticket into the world of Mary Shelley. I had the best kind of man. Suit and tie at the United Nations one moment, and the next, he was gallivanting in the countryside with me.

Back at the hotel, Jean Michel made secret arrangements to take me wakeboarding at Wake Sports Center. Wakeboarding on Lake Geneva? Fabulous! The cool water was a balm to my skin and soothed my travel-weary muscles. The water was my love language, and he knew this well.

That evening we did the tourist thing and strolled to the Edelweiss Restaurant for cheese and chocolate fondue. We listened to famous yodeling and laughed our way out the door for a walk toward the Flower Clock across from Pont du Mont Blanc. We kissed standing in front of the clock. I felt like Cinderella, without the concern of the clock striking twelve. I had my prince, and he was charming.

We decided to walk out on the pier to see the Jet d'Eau to end our evening. Everyone told us it was the best vantage point to see the fountain lights in the dark. The noise from the fountain was unmistakable, with water rocketing up to 140 meters in the air. The name actually translates to "water jet," and after standing on the pier, I could understand why. The descending water made a deafening crash and even seemed to generate its own wind. It didn't take long for us to get drenched. Mich held me tightly in his arms as I laughed.

Our time was wonderful, but as always, seemed to evaporate into thin air. We took the train the following day to Montreux past steeply terraced vineyards. Breathtaking. The vineyards stretched all the way down to the blue waters of Lake Geneva. Above the vineyards rose the snow covered Chablais Alps. It was called the Vaud Riviera in the Lavaux region for its exceptional weather. The air was warm and the sun was shining brightly above as we arrived in Montreux in the sheltered Lake Geneva Bay.

Mich held my hand, watching my expression with a smile on his face the entire time. We had breakfast at the Fairmont Le Montreux Palace before strolling along the promenade among palm trees and exotic plants toward the

Chillon Castle. The Chillon Castle is a sentinel above the rocky shores, with fortified walls and prisons inside. The prison held the famed Bonivard, Lord Byron's inspiration for his famous poem "The Prisoners of Chillon." Jean Michel recited a few lines from memory to me:

Lake Leman lies by Chillon's walls:
A thousand feet in depth below
Its massy waters meet and flow
Thus much the fathom-line was sent
From Chillon's snow-white battlement

Giggling, I asked, "Jean Michel, is this how you get all the girls?"

I could hear the train whistles in the distance as we walked along the shores back toward the Fairmont Le Montreux Palace. We had dinner out on the Terrasse du Petit Palais as the sun set before returning to Geneva. I wrapped Jean Michel in a thankful embrace for taking me on this trip.

Our time sadly had come to an end as we boarded the TGV train back to Paris. What an unexpected week in Geneva. We both loved it. We stayed in his flat at the embassy. It was a charming space. He had our picture in Mauritius on his desk. I was flying home the next morning and starting to miss him already.

Stuart called to let me know we had another quick trip in three days. Our parting in Paris was the hardest yet. We would rendezvous in a few weeks in Maui at Brian and Mel's wedding. I was already counting the days. As we said goodbye the following morning, he left me with, "*Je t'aime de tout mon couer.*" I felt the same way.

Chapter Nineteen

TIME'S MAN OF THE YEAR

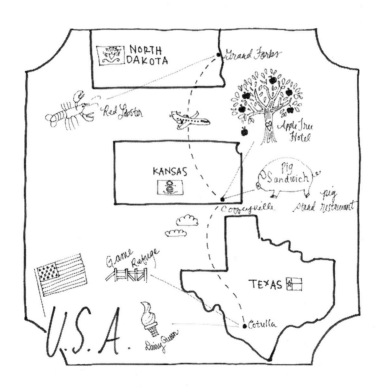

Only those who will risk going too far can possibly find out how far one can go.

—T.S. Eliot

W hen I got back to Santa Monica, I was in for a surprise. Stuart had received the coveted *Time* magazine's Man of the Year award. We were leaving on a two-week trip with the editorial staff. They were covering Stuart's life from his childhood on to his first success and his climb to multibillionaire status. Stuart insisted that Brian spend time with Melanie before the wedding. This meant my crew was Chris and our friend John. No trip was the same without Brian, but at least I had my other little brother. This was well-deserved recognition for Stuart, but he hoped it would draw attention to their foundation and help bring relief to so many children around the world.

Our first stop was Grand Forks, South Dakota. Yes, from Geneva to Grand Forks I went! Grand Forks housed one of the enormous service centers for Stuart Manning's website. I had no idea just how big until we arrived at the airport. At the gate of the airport was a big tour bus with signs advertising SM dot com. In front of the bus, at least one hundred people held banners in support of Stuart's arrival. This was just the beginning of the road-trip fanfare. Stuart and the *Time* crew boarded the bus for a tour of the service center. We could hear the fans all the way down the road, with music blaring and banners waving.

Vanessa called to thank me for working the trip on such short notice. She was looking forward to seeing us soon. "Anna," she said, "it means a lot to me, knowing you are looking out for him. He's been tired lately. Must be our little Sabrina waking up at all hours. Call me if you need me. Will you promise?"

Chris called ahead to the FBO to make sure we had a crew car reserved. We were in for a long day and needed to get some lunch. The handler told us to go to 32nd Avenue where we would find the Red Lobster. He handed us keys that said, "burgundy automobile," on the key chain and nothing more. What royal treatment. We walked out to the parking lot, and sure enough, there was only one burgundy automobile. This wasn't like any crew car we had ever used. Chris was heading back inside to see if we were in the wrong place when I decided to try the key in the lock. I turned the key, and the door opened.

Chris reluctantly turned around to hop in the driver's seat of the 1980 Oldsmobile Cutlass. Over eighty percent of the front windshield was shattered, making it difficult to drive. The car was filthy, inside and out, with dents all over the outside, holes in the dashboard, and rips in the upholstery. The Cutlass roared to life, in desperate need of a new muffler, notifying everyone for miles around that we were coming. We careened down the road toward 32nd Avenue, pulling into the Red Lobster parking lot in much relief. Chris turned the ignition key off, but the car kept running. A couple minutes later, it coughed out two big clouds of smoke then died with three loud "bang, bang, bangs!" There was no mistaking; we were at the Red Lobster.

My friends back home thought my job was glamorous. If only they could see me now! Chris and I sent Brian, JM, and Olivia a picture of us standing at Red Lobster by the car. We ordered lunch, knowing that Stuart probably would arrive back to the airport earlier than planned. My phone was ringing the entire time with calls from our handler in Coffeyville, Kansas. He said catering for the next day would be "no problem." I shuddered at the phrase. I never did get to enjoy my Red Lobster lunch with my phone ringing the whole time. Back to the burgundy automobile we went with a loud blast. Not only was it loud, but it also emitted a trail of black smoke as we made our final run for the airport. I now knew what was causing the global warming phenomena—it was this car.

We practically threw the keys back at the handler, who said, "Thank you, I have another gentleman here in need of the car." He walked over to the lobby area, giving the keys to a man as if it were a Lamborghini. It was Rush Limbaugh. I went over to say hello and discreetly give him the 411 on the burgundy dream-mobile. We both laughed and, being a good sport, he went out to the parking lot to fire up the Cutlass. I could not only see the car, but I could also hear it—all the way down the street.

The bus made its way back to the airport, and we left Grand Forks for a quick stop in Omaha, then down to our final stop in Coffeyville, Kansas. All day long I had been trying to line up catering for the following morning's departure. I called the place that our handler told me would gladly help. Stuart requested some good, authentic Kansas BBQ. I was told that a place called The Pig Stand would help. The woman at the restaurant said, "No problem; just stop by when you arrive and pick up the food." Famous last words! Our handler also added that we could always use the local grocery store or Kentucky Fried Chicken as a backup plan.

Chris had also communicated with our handler that we would not land unless we had ground personnel to meet us with lights on for landing our aircraft safely. Yes, aircraft to ground communication. That too was "no problem." We arrived at 2015 hours (8:15 p.m.) that evening, with our handler on the ground to meet us. We secured a Chevy passenger van out of Wichita, Kansas, to drive our passengers to the hotel and dinner that evening. Stuart came back to the galley before leaving to say thank you, and "Anna, please don't forget the BBQ for tomorrow."

You bet; no problem! Yes, I was learning exactly what no problem meant.

I did a clean sweep of the airplane to bring out our leftover catering for the handler. He had literally disappeared into the night. Perfect. Were we to assume that the car parked outside with the keys in the ignition was for our use? It might be the handler's car. Who knew? We moved the catering to the wings of the airplane, with the background noise of howling coyotes drawing closer. They probably smelled the food. Welcome to a darkened Coffeyville, Kansas.

Chris motioned me toward the lovely car. It far outshined the burgundy dream-mobile in Grand Forks, which wasn't saying much. This deluxe beauty was a Chevy Impala station wagon, with wood-grain paneling down the side. I felt like we were headlining a junkyard car show or about to embark on a road trip with the Griswold family.

We couldn't even make out the color of this clunker from years of fading. The back doors didn't close, and the car had dents and scrapes everywhere. It looked like squirrels had made a home in the upholstery. At least the earlier burgundy dream-mobile eventually turned off. This one was even better; it just kept running and running and running. This was worthy of another picture. We followed the GPS on my phone toward a few lights in the distance. Our hotel was the Apple Tree Hotel of Coffeyville. Stuart and the group from *Time* were staying there too. The rooms cost fifty-two dollars a night!

Had I just been in Geneva a few nights ago? I could hardly wait to tell Jean Michel about this! It was eight thirty that evening, and I had a bad feeling about my catering in the morning. Takeoff was at ten o'clock. When I spoke to the woman at The Pig Stand earlier, she again reassured me, "No problem. Just come by when you arrive tonight, honey." We asked the young man at the hotel where The Pig Stand was. He gave us a blank look and said, "I really don't know because I don't live around here." Where could he possibly live and not know about The Pig Stand? We whipped out our GPS and went off in search of some down-home BBQ.

We walked into the restaurant at 8:55 p.m., with a hungry Chris leading the charge. It stunk inside. The Pig Stand—or whatever it was called—had a few tables of people eating from plates overflowing with meat slathered in BBQ sauce. Presumably, it was dinnertime for the staff. As we stepped in, a woman looked up at us and said, "We're closed." I quickly introduced myself, letting her know we had spoken several times before. Yes, she remembered, but said matter-of-factly, "Sugar, that was earlier, but we don't have enough time to do an order like that."

I even offered to pay extra with generous compensation for the inconvenience. They just shook their heads and went back to plowing through their plates. They could have used the money I'd offered to buy an air-freshener or two.

"Honey," she said, "you won't find anything else in town. Everything closes at nine o'clock."

We left hungry with clothes that smelled greasy and a bad taste in our mouths. We stopped at the only other place that was open in town. It was the grocery store. Driving through town, we noticed signs everywhere welcoming SM dot com, but we weren't feeling the hospitality here in Coffeyville, Kansas. The grocery store had a few items, but snacks aside, we had struck out again. I was starting to panic.

I called up the FBO in Wichita, Kansas that I used to line up Stuart's transportation earlier explaining my desperate situation. They gave me the name of a catering group they used. Did they ever know BBQ! I had no idea how far away Wichita was, but it was our only option. He said he could make it work, but I would have to pay for a driver for the delivery to Coffeyville. By one in the morning, we had a driver who could leave Wichita by three with the catering. He arrived at the hotel at five in the morning. I had been up for most of the night, but for an extra fifteen hundred dollars in his pocket, the driver handed over the catering for our departure in the morning.

I called Mich before trying to catch a quick hour of sleep. It was afternoon in Paris. He was leaving the following day for Mauritius and, in a little over a week, on to Maui for the wedding. He kept laughing about The Pig Stand and the coyotes. I'm glad someone found it funny. Yes, how I loved him!

I had just shut my eyes when the phone rang. It was Stuart, headed out for a morning run. Rubbing my eyes and looking at the clock, I realized I had just hung up with Mich. I knew I wouldn't be able to sleep, so off I went through the streets of Coffeyville with Stuart Manning. It was already muggy, and I just wanted to sleep. I got back and changed for our next stop: Cotulla, Texas. If this wasn't a tour of the most nondescript locations in the Southwest, then I don't know what was! Stuart was taking the group out to a big game ranch and refuge he owned. Once on board the airplane the smell of mouth-watering BBQ permeated the cabin. You could almost hear a pin drop, which assured me they loved it! I never did tell Stuart about the drama his BBQ request stirred up, but it was reward enough to see him enjoying the food.

While Stuart and the *Time* crew went out to the ranch, I stayed back to clean out the airplane. I also got acquainted with the family who owned the airport. They had bought the airport the year before, finding out it was a hotspot for unscheduled landings throughout the night meaning—it had been a major drug-running airport. I worried for their safety, but they said it was a rare occurrence lately as they had cracked down on the drug operations. Their daughter came home from school before we left. She was adorable and sat down to snack on some hummus I had brought over from the plane. She decided it was okay. Her dog seemed to like it, too. I will never forget that brave, hardworking family in Cotulla, Texas. I told Stuart about my concern for the family. He sent in a team shortly after our trip to put in security measures for the family's safety.

Stuart had the chef at the ranch prepare another meal for the next leg of our journey with a quick stop at the local Dairy Queen to pick up Blizzards before arriving at the airport. The pictures that *Time* captured of Stuart that day were priceless. The crew also took a picture of me with the family at the airport that I will always treasure.

The trip continued for the next ten days with stop after stop. We were on our way home from Boston when one of the cameramen let out an unnerving scream. Somehow he had wedged his finger into the bottom of his seat and practically severed the whole thing off! We had to do an emergency landing. Off to the hospital I went with Mark and the cameraman, hoping to save his finger with stitches. This wasn't a Precious in Venice scenario, but I was ready to get home.

After five hours of waiting, Stuart and the rest of the passengers headed into the city to find dinner and a hotel. What I didn't know was how Mich had a change of plans. He was in Santa Monica for two days to surprise me at the end of our trip. He was at the airport waiting for us to arrive and thought he should give me a call to make the surprise complete. His voice changed when I told him what had happened with our emergency landing in Chicago. He let the cat out of the bag, making matters worse now that I knew where he actually was.

My heart sunk, knowing how difficult it was to arrange time together. He was leaving on the redeye the next evening, which gave us only a few, precious hours. He wanted to take me to breakfast the following morning. "Mich, stay at my place. You have a key and know where everything is. My car is at the hangar with the keys inside. All you have to do is pick me up when we get home, okay? I love you."

We arrived home, with Jean Michel waiting at the hangar. Stuart jumped off the airplane to say hello, with the *Time* crew trailing behind. They added to Stuart's story the partnership with Jean Michel and his recent work at the United Nations. Once they learned he was my fiancé, the cameras were rolling. I just wanted to be alone with him and out of the spotlight.

We headed back to Santa Monica through heavy traffic. "Jean Michel, I would swear you have lived in this city forever. You drive like you know your way around LA."

His face spread into an easy smile, followed by a wink. When we got back to my bungalow, he scooped me into his arms, and I had everything I ever needed.

"Anna, it seems like it's been forever. Two weeks is way too long without seeing you. I couldn't wait any longer."

We walked hand in hand to the Dogtown Café for a late breakfast. He thought it hilarious what Americans do to coffee.

"Anna, this is a sea salt caramel latte? What happened to a good grand café au lait?"

"They have café au laits, but these are really good. Just try one for me, okay?"

He agreed, and he actually liked it! I had to kiss him for that. We decided to ride bikes all the way down to Manhattan Beach. The day was perfect, but I wasn't ready to see him leave that evening. Our schedules were crazy. Couldn't he just stay and never leave?

Chapter Twenty

THE MAGIC OF MAUI

That's sort of like halfway between Earth and Heaven. It's the halfway point.
It gives you a little taste of Heaven.

—**Alice Cooper**, on waking up in Maui

We quickly flew Stuart down for a few days to see Vanessa while she was filming at Lake Powell. They invited us out on set to watch the production. Vanessa was spectacular. Best of all, I got to hold my goddaughter during filming, even though I had to fight off Stuart for the privilege. Sabrina was the cutest little girl, and each of us was falling for her charm. They had at least a good month left of filming at Lake Powell before heading down to Guanajuato, Mexico for the final wrap. Stuart would go from Lake Powell to Maui for the wedding, claiming there was no way he could possibly miss the event.

I said sadly to Vanessa, "We're going to miss you at the wedding. It will not be the same without you."

She could not get away during the middle of filming without costing the studio millions of dollars. After a warm hug of friendship, she suggested, "Anna, please make sure to take good care of my Stuart. I am a little concerned with his health lately, but maybe it's the long trip you guys just did. I know Jean Michel will be there, but please look out for him. This is the longest we have been away from each other. I already miss him."

The plan was to return to LA after the wedding before flying down a few days later to Lake Powell for the US wrap. Afterwards, we would fly down to Guanajuato for the end of filming before bringing Vanessa back to LA for the final wrap party with the cast and crew. It would be a celebration! Stuart had something special planned for her arrival in LA to celebrate further, but I was held to secrecy.

Vanessa was a pro to watch in action. She was the entire package. Beautiful in almost an ethereal way, she was also able to come across as tough on screen. I could see why she was chosen as one of the most beautiful women in the world—she truly was. She was also kind beyond imagination, fun to be around, and very much in love with both Stuart and Sabrina. They were a couple that just looked like they belonged together, and they made a wonderful team. I felt privileged to know her and call her my friend. She made me feel like an important part of her life. Yes, they were pretty wonderful.

It was finally time for Melanie and Brian to join hands in marriage at the Four Seasons Resort in Wailea. The resort is on the sunny and dry side of the island. Stuart was the best man, and Melanie had asked me to be her maid of honor. I accepted joyfully a few months back.

We arrived at the Kahului Maui Airport in the capable hands of Ginger at Air Service Hawaii. Ginger, Josh, and Lynn always knew how to extend the true spirit of an Aloha greeting. When the airplane came to a complete stop, we could see their smiling faces ready to welcome us on the ground. Stuart and Melanie were the first off the airplane to receive the traditional lei greeting, accompanied by an expertly made mai tai. The soul of the island came alive in the warm, tropical sun, tempered from the light breezes of the trade winds. Stuart said he would wait inside so we could all head to the hotel as a group, which really meant he wanted to enjoy one more mai tai while the crew finished up. Yes, I knew all the hidden intentions of Mr. Stuart Manning. We were all anxious to head to Wailea as soon as possible.

Stuart decided to surprise us with a helicopter ride over to Wailea. We waved goodbye to Ginger and our Air Service family in anticipation for the wedding celebration. The majestic Mount Haleakala, the dormant towering volcano, loomed in front of us with a slight cloud cover at the very tippy top. Scattered sugar cane fields stretched out in a path toward the mountain, with the beautiful beaches below. In the distance we viewed the islands off the shores of Maui: Lanai, Kahoolawe, Molokai, and the crescent shaped Molokini. It was exciting to be here.

The Four Seasons was ready for our little group and those arriving separately. My room looked out onto the beach below, and the water was beckoning me. First, though, I had to call Mich and let him know we had arrived.

"Anna, did you all make it over to Maui?"

"Yes, we are here, and I can hardly wait for you to arrive. Three more days, but can't you just come now? I miss you. Please? You are going to miss all the sights of Maui by arriving on the morning of the ceremony."

With sadness, he said, "I know, but I can't leave the meetings. I will be there soon. Anna, I am thinking of you each minute we are apart. Never forget."

My heart ached, but this was no time for wishful thinking. We had some celebrating to do. Stuart knocked on my door and said, "Let's go!"

I was not sure to where, but I followed suit. We were joined shortly by Chris, then Melanie and Brian, for an afternoon of stand-up paddleboarding off Wailea Beach. Melanie and I had spa dates later that afternoon for a facial and a massage. Who was I kidding? I was totally used to this lifestyle now!

On our first evening, we met downstairs at Ferraro's to dine above the shores of the Pacific Ocean. Torches were lit and Don V. Lax was playing the violin, accompanied by his guitarists, Vance Koenig and Ricardo Dioso. The music filled the air with hints of love and romance. Their music had underlying notes of passion that brought the soul to life. Don was playing the music for the wedding, and after hearing him on that first evening, I knew he was perfect for Brian and Melanie. The stars were enchanting that evening as we gathered under the open-air design of the restaurant. In the distance, the beginning of a luau was faintly heard. It was the perfect way to start our trip. Blueberry mojitos and mango martinis accompanied polenta-fried calamari. The night was perfect in every way, with one exception: Mich had not arrived.

Stuart and I took a stroll after dinner to dip our feet in the ocean. He shared more of his vision for the orphanages, his love for Vanessa, and being totally spellbound by little Brina.

He turned to look me in the eye. "Anna, I know we are forever grateful to you. I can't imagine anyone else being a part of our crazy family. This world I live in is one where it's hard to trust. Promise you will never leave me, or my family. My world is not easy, but knowing you are here makes it bearable."

There was a hint of desperation in his voice. "Stuart, I love working for you. Honestly, there's no place I'd rather be. You, Vanessa, and little Brina are all part of my world now."

He gave me a funny look and continued, "How about Jean Michel? Can you marry him and still keep working? Do you think he will take over as director of the foundation? We have always hoped he would take the position, but now I have ulterior motives knowing it would bring him closer to you." He continued walking again, this time linking his arm in mine.

"Stuart, I know Jean Michel wants to come and work for the foundation, but he also made a commitment to the ambassador. I think if you allow him the time to complete his work and unite the countries in support of the foundation, he will come on board."

Stuart gave me a hug and said, "Thank you for sharing that with me. I know he is a man of his word. I also know his heart. He has compassion for our mission. Please just assure me you will always be part of our lives."

"Of course I will, Stuart. Remember, Sabrina is my goddaughter!"

Up in my room that evening, a funny feeling had washed over me. I could not place it, but it was real. I called Mich to say goodnight and hear the words I needed from him to sleep: "Anna, I love you, *mon Cherie.*"

We all woke up before the sun rose to begin our downhill bike ride from the top of Mount Haleakala. The sun was rising as we approached the sleepy town of Makawao on Baldwin Avenue. The rustic charm of upcountry Paniolo County embraced the heart of the Maui cowboy. We passed the K. Matsue store building and the art shops and jewelry stores surrounded by sugar cane fields overlooking the blue below. We finished our morning dropping into the hippie chic town of Paia.

We were told to stop at Anthony's for a good cup of coffee. Anthony settled in this town years ago from the Pacific Northwest. The coffee was fantastic, as promised. Anthony had catered to many locals, tourists, and celebrities through the years. He was a true character. While we were enjoying our caffeine break, one of the Olsen twins walked in the door. She spotted Stuart and came over to say hello. She was adorable. A little later, Laird Hamilton pulled up in his Toyota Tundra. I had never seen so many surfboards on a truck, and I lived in Santa Monica. Stuart made introductions as we sipped our morning coffee with Laird Hamilton, the king of surf.

Stuart and I dined oceanfront at the famous Spago restaurant at the Four Seasons for dinner. My love for sushi met its match with the famous spicy ahi tuna "poke" in sesame miso cones and island ceviche. It was fantastic. Brian and Melanie went on a quiet evening cruise to enjoy some alone time before the family arrived. Chris left to pick up Olivia, who had just arrived, so I hung out with Stuart. This man was much more than an employer to me. I valued his friendship above all else. He'd taken to the nickname "Annabelle" for me, thinking it was very clever. The entire group quickly caught on too. Once back in my room, my phone rang, and it was Jean Michel. He would be in Maui in two days. I could hardly wait. I told him about our bike ride, celebrity sightings, and then dinner.

He asked, "It was just you and Stuart for dinner?"

"Yes, everyone had other plans, but somehow, we made do by eating at Spago. The food was to die for. They are catering the reception, so you will get to try it. Are you sure you can't get on an earlier flight?"

I went to sleep dreaming of the arrival of my Mich to this island paradise.

By morning, we departed for an island sailing adventure. Captain Chris led our small party of eleven on the *Akii Nuu*. Brian and Melanie's parents arrived the night before, along with my sister, Jesse, and her husband, Turner. Stuart reserved the boat for the entire day. We could dive; we could snorkel; or we could just lounge all day long. Captain Chris asked, "Where do you want to set sail for first?" Off we sailed toward Lanai, enjoying breakfast on board.

It was a spectacular day on the ocean and surrounding islands. Spinner dolphins rode the wake off the bow, and whales breached close to the boat.

First we snorkeled at Lanai. The ocean was a transparent window to view turtles and fish of every color below. This was another world, existing below the *Akii Nuu*. Back on board, Captain Chris and his crew served another meal, shortly pulling up anchor to set sail for Molokai. We made a last minute turn toward Lahaina so Brian, Chris, Stuart, and I could dive at Shell Station. The Hawaiian sea turtles there are fiercely protected by the State of Hawaii as an endangered species. We were to look, but not to touch! It was fascinating to watch the fish dive down to clean their shells before the next turtle pulled up. We swam up as close as we could get for a better view.

Our last dive was in Makena, just before sunset. Chris and his crew served us another meal. We ate well that day! The best part of the evening was when they started playing music aboard the *Akii Nuu*. We danced and sang and toasted to

Brian and Melanie over the Pacific. I was happy enough to live my life without ever touching land again.

The third morning in Maui, the men went to play golf in Kapalua at The Plantation Golf Course. That left us girls to a day of pampering before the rehearsal dinner and a bridal luncheon at Sarento's on the Beach in Kihei. The rehearsal dinner was on the lawn by the Hotel Wailea Resort and catered by Capische Restaurant. It was staged like a fairytale for an Arabian princess. I made sure it looked perfect before leaving for our luncheon. The pampering began after the luncheon. Vanessa reserved the entire spa just for the wedding party as a gift to Melanie. Even in her absence, she was thinking of others. What a woman!

The rehearsal dinner went off without a hitch. Even Captain Chris and his band came and played for us! The sky turned a deep crimson as the sun sank below the horizon line and stars peppered the nighttime canopy. This really was the halfway point between heaven and earth.

Back to my room for my nightly routine, I tried to call Jean Michel and could not get through. He must be on the red eye by now. I could hardly wait for him to arrive. I had instructed him to sleep on the flight so he would be awake for the wedding the next day. I fell asleep, realizing this was the first time I could remember not saying goodnight to Jean Michel.

My dreams were abruptly disturbed by the ringing of my phone.

"Hullo," I answered sleepily.

"Anna, sorry to wake you, *ma Cherie*. I don't know how to say this, but I cannot make it to the wedding. Our meeting ran late, and I missed the flight out of Paris. There are no other flights that would get me there in time. *Oh, Cherie, pouvez-vous pardoner moi?*"

"*Oui*, Jean Michel. *Je vous pardonne, mais mon coeur est triste.* Yes, I forgive you, but my heart is sad."

"Anna, my love, I will call tomorrow. I really tried to do everything I could to get there. I'm so sorry. I love you, my Anna."

"I understand, Mich. I was just dreaming of your arrival. I love that you tried, but I am still sad. I love you, too."

I woke up hours later with the tropical sun warming my skin and a gentle breeze drifting over me. It felt heavenly. It wasn't a dream last night. Jean Michel was not coming. I needed to pull it together to celebrate my amazing friends today. My room was the go-to spot for Melanie and the women who wanted hair or makeup done. Melanie looked absolutely radiant in white. Brian was one very lucky guy!

Mel's parents came up to my suite to escort her down to the Oceanfront Lawn for the ceremony. White chairs were set up in neat rows, and you could hear the violin music beginning to play. Down the stairs, we could see both Brian and Stuart standing at the ocean's edge, waiting for the arrival of Melanie. Both men looked extremely handsome. I walked down the aisle first, followed by the bride escorted by her parents. I shed some happy tears over the beautiful union about to take place. The couple repeated their vows to love, honor, and cherish each other always, with Christ at the center of their union. My heart could explode in happiness for the two of them. Yes, they were now officially Mr. and Mrs. Brian Morgan.

The Oceanfront Lawn quickly transformed into an intimate wedding reception. Twenty-nine guests were in attendance, and it was done perfectly. Music was flowing, and the happy couple took a turn on the dance floor. Melanie's dad stepped in as they entertained us on the lawn with eight different dances they had practiced. Everyone was clapping as the merriment rose to a higher decibel. Stuart reached over and took my hand for a spin on the dance floor before sitting down to dinner. Everything was perfect. When Stuart walked me over to our table, my place card read, "Annabelle, the Buffer!"

Stuart had once asked me to join him at a dinner to act as his buffer so he could escape the affair. My dance partner was a real jokester, or so he thought. Stuart and Chris were enjoying this way too much. All I could say was, "Very funny, guys."

The evening was perfect, except for missing Jean Michel.

Two more days in paradise before it was finally time to head home and get back to work. I missed Jean Michel desperately and hadn't the slightest idea when we would see each other again. I wanted to see him every waking hour of the day, and now I would have to wait.

When we arrived back in Van Nuys, Brian and Melanie would take off for their two-week honeymoon at the Royal Malewane Lodge. I always missed Brian when he was gone. It just wasn't the same.

Nothing prepared me for what was about to happen. The press had somehow captured a picture of Stuart dancing with me in Maui. Pitched with a seductive, headline-grabbing angle, they churned up the rumor mill to infer something juicy about Stuart's "faltering" marriage.

Mortified, I picked up the phone to call Vanessa. "Vanessa, I just saw the tabloids. I hope you don't think that anything has happened between the two of us. It was just a dance."

Vanessa just laughed it off. "Anna, trust me; this is something I know a lot about. The media is always trying to get a story, even when there isn't a story to get. They will try all kinds of things to invent one. I'm just sorry you have to experience this."

Stuart called me shortly after, saying, "Anna, you know how much I love you. Of course the media picked up on that! Please excuse their wrong assumptions about our relationship."

Now I had to explain this next to Jean Michel, who did not think it so funny. He thought the world of Stuart, but still felt uneasy. "Anna, I know Stuart is amazing and very much in love with Vanessa, but I have a feeling if she were not in the picture he would be pursuing you. Maybe it's just my mind going crazy in the time we've been apart. I'm sorry for thinking that."

"Jean Michel, there is no one else, and there will never be anyone else but you. Never forget how much I love you."

Chapter Twenty-One

A LAND OF BEAUTY, MEXICO

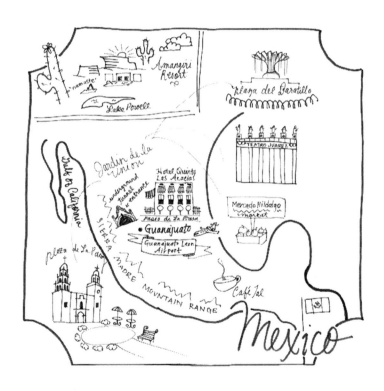

We live in a wonderful world that is full of beauty, charm, and adventure.
There is no end to the adventures we can have if only we seek them with our
eyes open.

—**Jawaharial Nehru**

*I*t was finally time for us to pick up Vanessa and Sabrina at Lake Powell. I had never seen Stuart this excited. He was like a school kid, filled with anticipation. Not able to contain himself any longer, Stuart jumped off the airplane to run toward Vanessa and Brina. It was heartwarming to watch the happy reunion. Make no mistake: Stuart had missed his girls. Brina had grown before our eyes. Each time Stuart even attempted to put her down, she would cry at the top of her lungs. She was in his arms almost the entire time, and he was totally enamored with his little girl.

We spent one night in Lake Powell for the US wrap party before our departure to Mexico. The entire cast and crew was there at the Amangiri Resort. Amangiri actually means "peaceful mountain," but the resort was in full party mode that evening.

We were only a fifteen-minute drive from the airport. The team had just wrapped up filming earlier that day, and spirits were high for the final push in Mexico. Under the exotic pastels of the desert sun, the spectrum of colors was equal to none. This was the perfect backdrop for a movie. Ending the day's performance was the gift of a true Southwestern sunset. Deep burnt orange hues layered the dusky blue darkness. High in the atmosphere, a shooting star was visible, its flames streaking the sky.

Vanessa and her leading man, the famous and dashing Bode Taylor, were giving a toast when a seemingly invisible outdoor screen dropped from the midnight sky to show the first half of the movie. Bode turned to Vanessa and planted a kiss right on her lips. Stuart bore the expression of a dark cloud before a storm. All had seemed right until this. I moved a little closer to Stuart and asked, "Are you okay?"

I could tell this had upset him deeply. "Anna, you thought having our pictures splashed in the media was rough? Well, how would it feel to watch someone kiss Jean Michel right in front of you like this jerk just did with my wife?"

I reached over to squeeze his hand and whisper into his ear. "Stuart, you know how much Vanessa loves you. That kiss meant nothing to her."

I looked over to where Vanessa and Bode were standing, he with his arm casually, yet possessively, around her shoulder. She looked up and locked eyes with me as if to plead her case.

Restlessness washed over my heart. I longed for Jean Michel like never before. How long could we keep love alive across continents?

Jean Michel must have known my thoughts. The party was kicking into high gear when he called, but I couldn't answer. I couldn't leave Stuart's side after watching how upset the interaction between Vanessa and Bode made him. Jean Michel was part of my soul, but my heart ached for the hurt Stuart felt. Vanessa loved Stuart, without a doubt, but celebrity life encompassed a few grey areas that are hard on a marriage. Here we were in a place most people only dream about, yet all I saw was heartache. I hadn't seen Jean Michel in over three weeks, and this evening placed doubts in my mind.

I finally got up to my room to call Jean Michel. He asked where I had been. I told him about the party and what had happened. Lowering my voice, I softly said, "Mich, we leave for Leon, Mexico, in the morning. Please tell me we will see each other soon. Is there any way you can come to Leon? I just miss you tonight and every night. I felt bad not wanting to leave Stuart there at the party—"

I was rattling on when his voice broke through my separation anxiety. "Anna, we can do this. Only one more year, okay? That means late next summer we will be married for the rest of our lives. *Oui?* I cannot wait until the day you become Madam Durand. Never forget how much I love you, *ma belle princesse.*"

I desperately needed to hear those words. I fell asleep, knowing sunrise was near.

I woke up earlier than the rest of our group to embrace the enchanting sunrise. My gaze drifted over the desert's brilliant display of violets and reds, hues beyond my wildest dreams. After my conversation with Jean Michel, I felt renewed. Yes, we could make it work. From my terrace, I could see a few clouds forming like cotton candy puffs. We were leaving for Mexico.

Stuart, Vanessa, and Brina arrived for our flight in much better spirits than the night before. Before takeoff, Vanessa pulled me aside. "Anna, Stuart and I talked late into the night about Bode. It is not at all what it looked like. Unfortunately, I still have a few weeks left of filming with him. Our chemistry onscreen is great, but off, let's just say he's a jerk. Can you understand why I didn't react when the media was hounding you and Stuart in Maui?"

"Vanessa, I have never doubted how much you love each other, but thank you for sharing. I don't know how you make it look so easy in this crazy industry."

We climbed high over Lake Powell with little Sabrina in my lap. I was not going to share this little cherub today. Stuart and Vanessa held hands, rekindling their romance. I gave them some space and enjoyed time with my goddaughter, sitting up front with Chris and John.

We flew in over the Sierra Madre Mountain Range. Leon is in the state of Guanajuato in the northern central part of Mexico. We were off to Guanajuato where *The Return of Jillian Rose* was being filmed. The Festival Internacional Cervantino ran parallel to our trip, attracting artists from all over the world. People were everywhere, and somehow word had leaked that Vanessa Manning was in town. We sent the Manning family ahead of us, couched in security, hoping the media would simmer down. Mark was my constant companion wherever we went, always prepared to act in a split second. I was starting to feel like it was safe again, until I remembered how my assailant knew me by name and left bruises to show for the encounter.

We left the airport in Leon on Mexico Highway 45. The roads were treacherous and steep into the mountains. We endlessly climbed up higher onto Mexico Highway 110D, but the view was the reward. An hour later, we dropped into a valley at the Hotel Quinto Las Acacias on the Paseo de La Presa in Guanajuato. I had to take a second look. A French style mansion in Mexico?

The reception at the hotel was warm and inviting. The entire staff welcomed us, including Rocio, the concierge. In my nineteenth century-style suite, French doors opened to a little terrace with inviting chairs. A few stairs led to an infinity pool overlooking the lush valley. The stairs above my room led to a secret garden with rich aromas of lemons and native flowers. I could hear the sound of the nearby Guanajuato River flowing. The river followed the Belaunzaran, the main street, into the heart of Guanajuato. The road winds through town for about three kilometers of unique and mysterious underground tunnels.

Guanajuanto is a city of deep enchantment. Its rich, hilly terrain held me captive at first sight. Mansions, churches, and small plazas abound. Each day the staff refreshed each room with colorful paper flowers and fresh fruits plucked right off the garden trees. Chris walked with me every day to the center of town to delight in the old-world charm. We ate outside in the plaza, with the sun at our backs. At night, musicians serenaded us and lights were strung from every corner to illuminate the colorful fruits and spicy peppers lavished on each dish. The festival was still in full swing, dotting sidewalks in artistic impressions of the rich culture.

One day we walked to the Mercado Hidalgo on the Avenida Juarez, near the Alhondiga. The main plaza, called the Jardin de la Union, was filled with vendors selling antojitos, or "little whims," such as tamales, quesadillas, burritos, and enchiladas. The main restaurant at the plaza served enchiladas mineras. They are stuffed with cheese, potatoes, corn, salsa, and just about everything but the kitchen sink. The locals embraced us with a mutual warmth and love. They laughed as we ate tunas de xonocostle for the first time. It's a native fruit from the area's prickly cacti. How could cacti be so delicious?

We followed dinner with a stroll to the Teatro Juarez to see the original *Jillian Rose* movie. The action-packed film featured Vanessa looking as beautiful as ever. After the movie, we strolled to the Plaza del Baratillo and the Plaza de la Paz. Chris and I were fighting over who would hold Brina while Stuart and Vanessa laughed at our playful banter.

Each morning, with a faint knock on my door, a breakfast tray was delivered with pastries and fresh fruit. After my sumptuous breakfast, I went for a run to Café Tal for a cup of steaming coffee. It was Mexican coffee at its finest.

The Spaniards first discovered Guanajuato. The mountains were once rich in gold and silver, sourcing about two thirds of the world's silver. The influx of money spurred construction in the 1540s, resulting in the town's rich culture and its university. It was the perfect place to film an action movie.

Rocio lined up a little horseback excursion into the mountains. I can still smell the fresh sage that delighted me each time I filled my lungs. Guanajuato was a hidden gem deep in the heart of Mexico, one I would return to again for sheer enjoyment in years to come.

Stuart had a surprise brewing for Vanessa and wanted to go over the details again. He met me one morning for my run to the café in town. His plan was to leave Guanajuato early the next morning for Van Nuys to pick up Brian. Melanie was coming too. A few hours later, we would fly direct into Bologna, Italy, to visit the Ferrari factory where a special, custom-built surprise was in the works for Stuart to present to Vanessa at her wrap party in LA. The man loved surprises, and this was a big one!

Our last evening in Guanajuato, both Chris and I offered to take Sabrina for a few hours so Stuart and Vanessa could enjoy the evening together. Little Brina fell fast asleep in Chris's arms. He was a sucker for her, as we all were! Rocio worked wonders to serve us dinner outside on my terrace. It gave me time to spend with Chris, too. He and Brian were my brothers in the truest sense of the word. He and Olivia were in a happy relationship, but work was getting in the way. I knew something about that.

Stuart and Vanessa came to collect a very sleepy Brina. She curled into Stuart's chest as we handed her over. Vanessa gave us both a big hug and whispered, "You two are the best! Thank you for babysitting tonight. I will see you here in less than two weeks."

For some reason, I gave her an extra hug that evening. "Vanessa, thank you for your friendship. I love you, dear friend. I promise I will watch out for Stuart."

She returned the sentiment wholeheartedly.

At the airport in Leon the next morning, I was preparing things for departure. Stuart was to follow by helicopter so he could get more time with Vanessa and little Brina before leaving. I opted to walk across the tarmac for some fresh air before we left. A tall, distinguished-looking gentleman dressed in jeans fell in step next to me. I had seen him inside the FBO earlier. He looked familiar. He said hello, indicating that his airplane was parked next to ours.

"I personally like to walk out to our airplane instead of getting a ride in the van. How about you?" he asked in flawless English.

"Oh, yes. I'm always embarrassed to get a ride when it's such a short walk, and I must admit, I love the smell of jet fuel."

He asked if I was the owner of the G550.

I chuckled in response. "I wish. I'm the flight attendant."

He was professional, educated, and kind, but where had I seen him before? We introduced ourselves by our first names, and he showed significant knowledge of the G550. I asked if he would like to take a look inside. After his brief tour, I stepped outside to shake his hand while shading my eyes from the sun with the other. Out of the corner of my eye, I noticed snipers perched on the FBO building where we had come from. I was startled to see the assault weapons fixed on us.

"Don't look, but there are men with guns watching us!" I said in a state of alarm.

I looked over at my new friend as a smile emanated from the corner of his lips. "Anna, please allow me to introduce myself officially. I am Manuel Herrera, the President of Mexico."

Chris came running when he saw what was happening. With the flick of his wrist, President Herrera dismissed his security personnel. Stuart was just leaving his helicopter when I asked President Herrera if he would like to meet the owner of my airplane.

Manuel shook Stuart's hand. "I hear congratulations are in order on your marriage to the beautiful Vanessa Rathman."

Stuart swelled with pride. "Thank you. Yes, Vanessa is finishing production, as we speak, in Guanajuanto, and our daughter, little Sabrina is staying with her. We will be back in a couple weeks for the production wrap-up. I must say we have been very impressed with Guanajuanto and the people there."

President Herrera looked pleased. "Fantastico. It's an honor for all of us here in Mexico. By the way, I recently heard a wonderful young man speak at the United Nations about the vision of your new foundation. Please know I will help in any way I can."

Stuart let him know that my fiancé was that wonderful young man and expressed how honored he would be to have President Herrera's involvement.

Once onboard, Stuart gave me a funny look. "Okay, just how did you two meet?"

I just laughed and gave him a wink. We stopped briefly in Van Nuys for Stuart's meeting at the hangar. Brian was there, looking bronzed and glowing from his honeymoon. Even better, I got to see Melanie. She looked very happy, wanting to catch up on everything. The A-Team was back together again. Next stop: Bologna, Italy!

Chapter Twenty-Two

THE WORLD OF WEALTH

239

You can fail at what you don't want, so you might as well take a chance on doing what you love."

—Jim Carrey

*O*n flight, Stuart pulled out all sorts of pictures to show me his gift for Vanessa. He was excited about his surprise. Between Melanie and me, we had a lesson in the building of a Ferrari. He had ordered a California T convertible with a hard-top. Yes, she would be thrilled. He qualified it with, "Well, she does have the Range Rover for Sabrina, but this is customized just for her."

His excitement was masked by a look of exhaustion. I set up his bedding so he could rest before our arrival. Mel went to sleep for a bit, too. We arrived in Bologna in the early morning hours, just as the sun was rising. It was another beautiful day in the ancient city. TAG, Bologna, FBO had everything lined up for us. We were staying at the Grand Hotel Majestic "Gia Baglioni" in the oldest part of Bologna. Our English-speaking driver rattled off some historical facts about the Via Indipendenza, close to Piazza Maggiore and Due Torri and built on ancient Roman roads. I had no idea what he was talking about. I just wanted to fall asleep.

The hotel was another historic beauty. Brian and Mel, Chris, and I had junior suites while Stuart had the Art Deco Terrace Suite. He asked if I could arrange dinner that evening for the five of us out on his terrace. I called the concierge, who took over from there. Stuart was rested from the flight and headed to the Ferrari factory while the rest of us got some sleep. First, I had my massage. We would visit the factory the next day. I heard a light knock at my door, but was too tired to answer and went back to sleep. Then my hotel phone rang, and I silenced it. My cell phone rang, and I finally answered it sleepily. Jean Michel was asking me to open my door. Surprise! There he stood at my door with that smile. Yes, it was a wonderful surprise!

Jean Michel just kept looking at me as he said, "*Il a ete trop longue. Vous, ma belle princesse, sont plus belles que jamais.* It has been too long. You, beautiful princess, are more beautiful than ever." I could not have imagined a better welcome.

We enjoyed dinner that evening on Stuart's terrace. The next morning we saw Vanessa's finished Ferrari. The color was Blu Scozia, a midnight-navy hue. It was a beauty! We had unfettered access to the production assembly on the ground floor where they built all the V-8 models. Later in the afternoon, we were invited to the Fiorano Circuit, Ferrari's privately owned racetrack for testing their Formula One and GT cars.

The Morandi wine cellar was reserved for the six of us that evening. Emilia-Romagna-style cuisine was served with some of the best wines in the world. It was a memorable, candlelit dining experience in Bologna. Stuart wanted time to meet with Jean Michel about the UN conference, asking if he could fly back with us to LA. That was a definite yes! He shared how he met President Manuel Herrera through my introduction in Mexico. "Jean Michel, he was impressed with your speech at the United Nations. Did you have a chance that day to meet him personally?"

"Actually, yes, I briefly spoke to him while we were at the United Nations. He seemed very interested in the foundation."

That evening we sat out on my terrace, viewing the city lights of Bologna in the comfort of each other's arms. "I am so in love with you, Mich. Please never lose faith in us, and trust me always."

I added, "Since you would miss me too much anyway!" He laughed as he pulled me closer."

He suddenly got serious. I thought something was terribly wrong. "Anna, I want you to know I'm a bit concerned about Stuart. I have not seen him in a while, and he looked worn out."

"I know. Vanessa asked me to keep an eye on him. She was worried, too, but we thought it was from all the sleepless nights with Brina. You really think he looked that exhausted?"

"I am sure he just has a lot on his plate lately, but I have never seen him look so tired."

"He made me promise in Maui that I would always be there for him. I know; I know it sounds strange, but you have to understand how much they have done for me. Remember, if it wasn't for Stuart, I would never have met you."

"Anna, I understand, but every once in a while I just get an uneasy feeling. I know it's probably my imagination. You do know how much I love you, right?"

We left early the next morning with Jean Michel in tow. His plan was to leave LA the next evening on the red eye for Paris, but for now, he was here. He and Stuart planned the next steps for the foundation almost the entire flight. They had a one-year plan in motion for Jean Michel to take over as director with the ambassador's pre-approval.

Mich left with Stuart, and I would meet up with them back at the estate after putting the airplane to bed. My heart was warmed as I walked in to see these two powerful men so animated, deep in council. We left Stuart in the early evening for our treasured alone time together. JM pulled me into his arms with a rare look of concern.

"Anna, I have known Stuart for a few years now. I cannot put my finger on it, but something is off with him. I know it's not my imagination. Please keep a good eye on him, okay."

I countered, feeling sad, "I thought the same thing. I just wanted to wait until you had time with him before I spoke to Vanessa again. I don't want to alarm her further, but will bring it up again when she gets back to LA."

We both agreed this was the best course of action.

Mich left on the red eye the following evening. I hated to say goodbye. This was crazy with the back and forth international travel, but it was only temporary.

Vanessa's new car had arrived by cargo airplane and was sitting in their driveway with a big bow on top. It was a beauty. Stuart was bursting with excitement for Vanessa and Sabrina's homecoming. I had not seen that kind of energy from him in weeks! It was time to head down to Leon to bring Stuart's girls home for good. Brian and Chris fired up the engines to head south. Unfortunately, a red warning light flashed in the cockpit. Our mechanic called Gulfstream to discuss what could be done. We needed some parts that would not arrive for at least two days. We were grounded.

The red light was a take-off warning indicator that could result in a pump failure or a rupture of the hydraulic line, meaning loss of control. Stuart was growing anxious and made a quick call to his movie studio to see if their airplane could bring the girls home. The airplane was ready within the hour. Stuart sent me to Leon while he, Brian, and Chris waited in Van Nuys for our arrival later that day. We launched for Leon within the hour. It was great to be reunited with Vanessa and Sabrina. Little Brina had grown in the last few weeks and rewarded me with a giggle. Vanessa asked about Stuart and was beaming at the thought of finally going home to her husband.

Brian kept in contact with the studio airplane all the way down, and once on the ground, he checked in with me to ensure everything went smoothly. I called him just as we took off and gave the phone to Vanessa for a quick hello to Stuart.

Shortly after take-off, with Sabrina in my arms, I went up front to close the door and check in with the pilots. I knew something was up as soon as I stepped into the flight deck. We had lost all radio contact! The pilots assured me not to worry. "We both agree we are experiencing a system failure, with no cause for alarm. We'll try resetting the circuit breakers, and we'll keep you posted during flight."

"Thanks for keeping me in the loop. Is there anything I can do to help?"

"No, we'll touch base with our mechanic on the ground back home after we test the circuit breakers; we'll see what he says."

I remember walking back to Vanessa and cooing over Brina in my arms. Then, without warning, the airplane pitched with such force that it took all I had to hang onto Brina with a supernatural grip. The last thing I heard was Vanessa's scream before blackness covered me.

I woke up to the whirling of what sounded like helicopter blades and hands maneuvering me. Little Sabrina was still in my arms as I came to consciousness hearing her soft whimper. Thank you, dear Lord, for keeping us safe. I must have passed out again. I woke up again, but this time with Jean Michel's voice close to my ear. Slowly opening my eyes to focus on my surroundings, I was blinded by bright lights above me. Where was I?

"Anna, can you hear me? I'm here. You're going to be all right, my love."

"What happened?"

"Shhh, be still and rest. There's plenty of time to talk later. Just rest. I'm here."

"But . . . Sabrina? Vanessa? The pilots? Where am I?"

"Stuart is with Sabrina in the next room. Be still and rest."

I fell back into my world of blackness. I could hear soft voices lulling me deeper into sleep. I awoke again to a massive headache and a horrible pain in my leg. Tuning in on my surroundings, both Stuart and Jean Michel were speaking to a man. Both of them looked very sad and exhausted. "Are you all right?" I asked in a whisper.

All three men rushed to my side to examine me further. "We are better now that you're awake."

"Where's Sabrina and Vanessa?"

"Anna, Sabrina has been moved in with you. See? She's right here."

I looked over to see her sweet smile. She was fine.

"Vanessa . . . ?"

Jean Michel came closer, lifting my hand to his mouth while my eyes darted to Stuart, beseeching him for an answer. Tears were filling his eyes, and I knew. Oh, no, this could not be happening! It was a horrible nightmare that would not go away. My heart broke in half at our great loss. How could Vanessa be taken so quickly from us? I tried to get up, but my leg prevented it. Somehow, Brina and I had survived with only a few cuts and bruises, but Vanessa and our pilots had not been so fortunate. How could we be the only survivors?

Stuart struggled to explain, through his grief and tears, what had happened five days ago when we took off from Leon. My heart was shattered. Brian had a call from our ground handler back in Leon. He had lost radio contact with the studio plane but assured Brian he would keep him posted. They assumed it was a system failure. Brian conveyed how he had just spoken to Vanessa and me just minutes before. Shortly after they hung up, ground control in Leon had a mayday alert from the crew and lost all contact with the plane.

A search team was dispatched immediately. Brian and Chris contacted Jean Michel, who took the first flight into Leon to help with the search. Chris, Brian, and Stuart had already arrived. All of them were desperate to deploy more search parties. During that time, BBC somehow caught wind of the situation.

News release from the International Wire Service:

An airplane thought to be taking off for the United States disappeared shortly after takeoff from Leon, Mexico. No word as to how many passengers were onboard. Stay tuned to our broadcast for the latest updates posted by the minute.

Breaking news update:

This just in, speculation from our sources on the ground say the airplane was a Gulfstream from a major movie studio. There is no confirmation as of yet. Last contact from the crew was said to be a mayday call shortly after takeoff. Mexican officials are organizing search crews in hopes of finding the airplane.

Correction, this just in, authorities are responding to the reported crash of a Gulfstream GV business jet that disappeared after takeoff from the Leon International Airport in Mexico. The initial search area is focused on the Sierra Madre Mountain Range northwest of the city, and as of yet, no wreckage has been found. We have a ground source confirming that one of the passengers onboard is the famous actress Vanessa Rathman Manning. We will continue with live updates.

I was released a week later from the hospital. I stayed in my darkened world another three days before I found out all the details of what happened. I wish they had never awakened me. Stuart and John Michel insisted I stay at the estate during this time of healing. My mom came and cared for both little Brina and me. My heart was shattered.

The final report came weeks later after all of the wreckage was found miles away from the last point of communication. An electrical fire started shortly after takeoff and had worked its way through the airplane when the mayday call was issued. The pilots had somehow found a clearing to bring the airplane down before being consumed in flames.

I don't remember anything, but was told I must have first gotten Vanessa out the window near the back of the airplane then climbed out with Sabrina in my arms. We were found about a quarter of a mile from the wreckage. Vanessa's body was next to mine. They say I must have helped the three of us escape a safe distance away before passing out. The pilots had been trapped in the charred wreckage, but had heroically landed the airplane in the mountainous terrain. By some miracle, both Sabrina and I had survived. My heart ached for each person we lost that awful day.

The next three months were like a nightmare playing out. We were devastated, but none more than Stuart who lost the love of his life so suddenly. We were grounded in this time of darkness and overwhelming sadness. Adding insult to this horrible situation was the call from Vanessa's doctor confirming that she was pregnant and scheduled for an appointment shortly after she arrived home. I don't know how much more Stuart could handle, but it helped to know he had Sabrina to love. She could even make him smile at times. I spent every waking moment I could with Sabrina. We were consumed in grief.

A few months after the crash, Stuart asked if I could arrange a quiet memorial for Vanessa. He wanted her ashes scattered over the ocean below their home. He was determined to carry out their common vision of rescuing orphans throughout the world. The memorial was touching. We had a beautiful celebration of Vanessa's life on board the *Sonoma SMS,* moored just below the estate with invited guests only. Stuart somehow found the strength to speak, as did Jean Michel and Vanessa's parents. It was heartfelt and beautiful—just like Vanessa. I was still mentally recovering, but I would do everything in my power to support a grief-stricken Stuart and my precious goddaughter, Sabrina. Had she somehow foreseen this tragedy when she asked me to watch over Stuart?

Jean Michel was concerned to leave me, but had to get back to work. He called each day to check on me.

For over three months, Stuart continued to hibernate from the world. I knew none of us would ever forget Vanessa. How could we? She had left us better for knowing her. I knew she would not want Stuart to give up hope or continue to grieve like this. He needed to live and live fully for Sabrina and the work of the foundation. I woke up one morning and threw open the doors and windows to let the healing California sunshine permeate the darkness of our grief. I walked to Stuart's bedroom and knocked on the door before stepping inside.

"Okay, Mr. Stuart Manning, today is the day. We are going surfing and then we are going to bring Sabrina outside for a play day."

I was prepared for his excuses, but I had it covered. The boards were ready, and the nanny had arrived to help with Brina while we surfed. It was time to start living. The two of us paddled out where Brian and Chris met us on the waves. It was a beautiful day, and a perfect swell had just rolled in. The ocean's healing powers took us the rest of the way. I always loved the water for this.

After our session, Stuart thanked me. "There are no words to say what this means to me, Anna. I know I will never marry again. I will never love like that again, but I can start to live."

I looked over at him as a tear escaped the corner of his eye. There was nothing I could say. We would get through this somehow.

Since that day out on the ocean over two years ago, Stuart turned a corner. It wasn't quite what I had in mind; it's more like a pendulum swing to living life on the edge with renewed energy. He bought another airplane. Yes, there were women in his life, but you could tell it was just for companionship. Commitment threatened to make him forget Vanessa, and he never would.

I knew Stuart and could see the look of emptiness behind his eyes. The only ones who kept him grounded were Brina and me. Yes, Conor, Jean Michel, Brian and Chris were there, too. We were his tight-knit family and everything he seemed to treasure. There was one woman, Mystique, who seemed to come around more than any of the others, but I knew Stuart was not in love with her. She was a famous professional tennis player, and she did intrigue him. I think she liked his wealth and all that came with it. Stuart didn't allow her to meet Sabrina. That was always off limits.

Jean Michel had been patient with me. We had postponed our wedding after the accident. I knew that I could not leave Stuart right now. The promise I made to him in Maui weighed heavily on me. I also knew that our wedding would remind him of Vanessa. That left Jean Michel with a very hard question: "When will it be right for us to get married?"

It seemed like our time together was getting harder to find. He was working more on the foundation, but had promised the ambassador he would stay on with him for another two years. He was basically working two jobs, while I was in overtime with Stuart and Sabrina. These days, it was a rare day we weren't flying. Our crazy flight schedule took us all over the world, with Venice and the

South of France as regular stops. What I noticed more than anything was that my Mich was getting impatient with me. I knew he was the man I wanted to spend my life with, but after Vanessa, all our lives were in a spiral of grief from which we couldn't seem to escape.

We were flying into Paris one evening, much later than expected. In the morning we would depart for Nice. Mich had plans to meet me in Paris. I was really missing him and looking forward to this trip. Once in Nice, Stuart was staying at his home in Cap Ferrat, while we had reservations at the famed Hotel de Paris.

Jean Michel had meticulously planned a romantic dinner that was canceled because of our late arrival. He was clearly upset. I could see it in his eyes; they were filled with something I had never seen—anger. There was nothing I could do about being late, but something told me it wasn't just about our schedule. That evening, in the city where it all began with Jean Michel, my life came to a crashing halt. I never thought I would hear him give up on us, but here he was in front of me, breaking my heart.

"Anna, you are the love of my life, but I cannot keep doing this. I care about Stuart; he is like a brother to me, but we need to live our lives, too. Things can't keep up with the three of us like this. No one will ever capture my heart as you have, but I cannot do this anymore. I need to come first in your life. I want to be here when you decide, but for now, I can't keep this up. I know I will always love you as long as I live, but Anna, I just can't keep waiting."

I was filled with panic at his reaction. "We said we could wait a few years to get married. Please, Mich, I want to marry you, but right now, I just can't leave Stuart. He made me promise. I just can't."

I was in tears as we said goodbye that evening. Walking away from him, I ran straight into Bridgitte, who looked quite pleased to see me upset. A part of me had just died as I left, but I could not walk away from the promise I'd made to Stuart almost three years ago in Maui. I felt I owed it to him. If I was truly honest, I felt guilty I was even alive while Vanessa had died. It just wasn't fair. I couldn't admit it out loud, though. I couldn't find the words to explain this to Jean Michel. The accident had left me with a deep, profound doubt of why I was even alive. I was heartbroken as never before. Yes, I loved Jean Michel in a way I could never love another, but a promise was a promise.

I cried tears of devastation over what I was losing—seemingly everything. First, Vanessa and now my one true love. I could not tell Stuart, or he would feel responsible, but I knew the boys would take one look at me and know. I was downstairs early in the morning, with red-rimmed eyes. Brian just came over and hugged me in support. No questions asked. Chris followed suit. I fought off a sense of despair all the way to the airport. Stuart arrived, this time with Mystique in tow. I was glad he was preoccupied as I was barely holding it together. The trip was quick, and thank goodness, Stuart didn't suspect anything. Before leaving the plane, he came over to say goodbye.

"Annabelle, thank you for sticking by my side. I could not do this without you. If it weren't for Jean Michel, I would change my thinking and ask you right here and now to marry me. These women since Vanessa mean nothing to me. You are the only woman besides Vanessa I have cared for. You know I love you. I always have. I probably shouldn't have said anything to you. Will you accept my apology? When Jean Michel arrives, why don't you come over for dinner? Bring the boys too."

I was speechless listening to Stuart. He took a second look at me.

"Anna, is everything all right?"

"Yes, yes, I'm fine."

Relief washed over his face as he hugged me before leaving.

I'd anticipated my stay at the Hotel de Paris almost every time I had come to Monte Carlo. But this wasn't like every other time. I barely took note of my surroundings as I headed up to my room overlooking the ocean. The water only reminded me of Jean Michel, so I drew the curtains.

In the evening, the boys hounded me, not taking no for an answer. They arranged a quiet dinner at the Café de Paris next door, close to the casino. We could watch the glittering nightlife of Monte Carlo around us while catching the sunset at the same time. All of this made me choke-up in grief. I needed to get out of here before I totally lost it. I was about to excuse myself when my phone rang. It was Stuart.

"Annabelle, I thought you were coming for dinner? Tomorrow? I need to ask a big favor. Can you call Cade and ask if he knows what kind of ball machine Mystique would prefer? Can you also ask if there is any way we could have my other airplane pick it up in LA tonight to bring it to the estate by morning?"

"Seriously, Stuart?"

"I know, Anna; it's crazy, but she is getting ready for a tournament and wants to have a ball machine set up."

"Stuart, I will try my best. It will be awkward, as you know, but I will call. If he has the machine, do you want it flown over on N23SM? "

"Yes, that would be great. I really owe you big time if you pull this off."

"You sure do." I actually smiled at that.

I hung up with Stuart then called Cade from the Café de Paris. To my surprise, he answered right away.

"Anna, is that you? How are you? I wanted to call many times, but didn't know what to say. I am so sorry for your loss."

I almost lost it there, but I had a job to do, and it had been over three years since we had last spoken.

Feigning cheerfulness, I said, "Yes Cade, I'm better. I'm actually sitting here in Monte Carlo and just had an interesting call from Stuart. He wanted me to find out if you have any idea what kind of ball machine Mystique would prefer. If so, do you know how we could have one delivered ASAP to Van Nuys for his airplane to bring it over here by tomorrow?"

Cade laughed, but about ten minutes later, he called back to confirm that the ball machine was en route to the airport.

"Cade, how can I thank you?"

We spoke for a while, getting caught up. He was happy to be in the ranks of the top-ten tennis players in the world. Yes, my Cade! I was impressed, congratulating him on his success. He said again how sorry he was to hear about Vanessa and asked how Stuart was doing. All I could say was, it had been a tough few years.

"Hey, Anna, I'm coming to Monte Carlo for a tournament in about a week. Let's try to have dinner, okay? Will you be there?"

My voice was barely audible as I said, "Yes, Cade, that would be special. Give me a call when you arrive."

I hung up with Cade to arrange for Stuart's airplane to overnight Mystique's ball machine, naturally.

Stuart called bright and early the next morning. I reluctantly answered. "Anna, you won't believe what just happened. The ball machine arrived, and my groundskeeper plugged it into the electrical outlet. He forgot to use an adapter to change the voltage, and it just blew up!"

Rolling my eyes, with an incredulous tone I said, "Seriously? Only you could have a story like this."

"Very funny, Annabelle."

I had to call Cade to thank him for his efforts and to tell him what had happened with the ball machine. He said I should see about having the machine refurbished. But why? He was preparing for an upcoming auction, and it would be the perfect item to help raise some money. My instructions were to have Mystique autograph it, and he would take care of the rest. I heartily agreed, and what a story for the highest bidder!

"Anna, I'll call in a week, and let's make sure we have that dinner."

It couldn't hurt to catch up with an old friend at a time like this. I was looking forward to it.

I kept reaching for my phone to see if Jean Michel had called. It was silent. I wanted him to call and say it had all been a terrible mistake, but I knew he was serious. I also knew I wanted to spend the rest of my life with him. How had my world become so complicated?

Brian knocked on my door to join me for breakfast. I told him what had happened with the ball machine, and he shot me a look of disbelief. Yes, this was a story we'd never forget.

My ringing phone interrupted our peaceful moment out on the balcony. I thought it had to be Stuart, but instead I heard Elle on the other end. "Anna, I haven't spoken to you in ages. Where are you?"

It had only been six months since we last spoke, and I had never considered us close. Yet I did remember her kindness to me my first day on the job. "Hi, Elle. Good to hear from you. How are you these days?"

"I'm great and still dating my billionaire up in the Bay Area. I haven't flown for him in over a year and a half. I expect a proposal any day now."

"That's great, Elle. I'm so glad to hear your good news."

"Anna, where are you?"

"I'm in Monte Carlo for a while. I'm sitting here on my balcony with Brian having breakfast."

"That sounds wonderful. Well, I won't keep you, but let's get a coffee date in when you get home. Okay?"

We hung up in record time for an Elle call. Brian said, "Okay, sis, it's time to hit the ground running. Both Chris and I have a day planned for you!"

I wanted to disappear into a cabana on the beach to sulk, but Brian would not hear of it. Taking me by the hand, he led me to the front entrance of the hotel. Brian and Chris thought a motorcycle ride through the South of France would help me clear my head.

I couldn't suppress my smile. This activity was just their style, and I was more than happy to come along.

"Okay, boys, there is no way I am holding on to either of you for a full day," I threatened.

Chris looked pleased. "Anna, that's what this is for."

He pointed out the grab bars on each side of the seat and handed me a helmet to wear. Chris and Brian were my personal bodyguards for the day to give Mark a long overdue day off. A smile pulled at the corners of my mouth as I pictured Mark trying to follow us on motorcycles. The Harleys roared to life, and off we went: next stop, Cannes! I took turns hopping on the back of Chris and Brian's bikes. These boys were the best medicine for a broken heart. The day's excitement happened when we got lost on our way back to Monte Carlo in the late afternoon. Brian and I were ahead of Chris as we pulled into the tollbooth.

"Anna, do you have coins for the toll?"

"Chris has all the money in the fanny pack he's wearing."

There was no turning back in the sea of cars around us. He yelled, "Hang on!"

I did! We piggybacked off the toll from the car in front of us. The lights and sirens went off as Brian put the bike into high gear. We raced high above the

Mediterranean. Chris caught up to us eventually, saying he had dropped every coin he had in the toll, hoping it would keep us all out of jail. I was breathless from laughter. This was just the kind of day I needed.

Back at the hotel, the sun had already set. Our plan was to change clothes then hop on the bikes to head over to Italy for dinner. Before going inside, I wanted one more picture of us standing with the Harleys in front of the gardens between the hotel, casino, and the café. The lighting was perfect. A man in front of us had just stepped out of his car. I grabbed Chris's brand new camera as fast as I could and ran it over to ask the gentleman if he would mind taking our picture.

"It would be my pleasure, mademoiselle."

In my peripheral vision, I noticed that he wasn't alone. Before I could give it further thought, someone grabbed me, and I was pulled into the car. I could hear Brian and Chris yelling in the background for a few seconds before all was silent.

I woke up in absolute darkness, with no idea where I was. There was a cover over my head, and my hands were tightly bound behind my back. I thought I could taste dried blood on my parched tongue. That was the least of my worries. Where was I? I knew I was in some sort of automobile, but going where?

I could hear the sound of water falling. It sounded like the thundering of a very large waterfall. I could hear the distant sound of a train just as the motion of the car stopped. The air seemed cooler than in Monte Carlo. I was frightened and coming to full wakefulness. Voices outside were speaking in a language I couldn't understand. It sounded like some sort of Swahili or African dialect. Hands picked me up like a rag doll and carried me into a room. I was shoved onto a bed, and then I lost consciousness again.

I dreamed that I was running after Jean Michel, but he wouldn't turn around. I screamed his name over and over, but he just kept going. Then I heard a gunshot and woke up. The cover had been lifted off my head. Clothes were laid out for me to wear, with a tray of food next to my bed. Where was this prison? What did these people want? I stood up on wobbly legs to walk to the door. The door was locked. I called out, but there was no answer. I was famished and inspected the food on my tray. Should I eat? It was best to keep my strength. I ate everything on the tray. There was toast, fruit, water, and a cup of strong, black coffee. Before I finished my last bite, a wave of dizziness swept over me, and it was darkness once again.

I had no sense of time. How long had I been in this room? My body was weak, and I always felt groggy. Inspecting my body, I found needle marks on my arms. I started to panic. What would happen to me, or worse, what could they have already done to me? I had no memory of being awake. I was never this scared before, but I tried to gain control over my fear. Oh, my Father God, please protect me. Please give me strength to get through this. Instantly, a peace washed over me, and somehow I felt safe. I could still hear distant water falling and, at times, the sound of moving trains.

One day my door finally opened. Two men stood on either side of the door while another man stepped inside. They looked as I suspected, dark-skinned from somewhere in Africa and dressed in business suits. That explained the voices I heard outside. I was informed that the man who clearly looked to be in charge was their leader, King Al Ahmed Bedel. He was evil, with a look of hatred emanating from his eyes. I recognized his bodyguard. I could never forget those eyes. It was the man who had tried to abduct me in Cannes and then in Le Mans and Paris. I was told to listen carefully, or I would die. They wanted over three billion dollars from Stuart and the immediate closing of the Manning Foundation. If Stuart did not comply with their demands, they would kill me. They pulled out a phone and asked me to read a script written on a small piece of paper.

"*My name is Anna St. James. I am being held prisoner. Please do as they ask, or I will be killed.*"

I knew that time was running out. I learned that I had been with them for three weeks. The days were a slow hell, and I could tell they were getting impatient. One evening they angrily broke open my door to transport me somewhere. I tried to fight them off as they stuck me with yet another needle. Once again, into the rabbit hole of darkness I fell.

I don't know how long I was in that horrible state, but I awoke to Stuart's voice, like music to my ears. He was pleading with me.

"Anna, my sweet Anna, please wake up. She's not waking up. Do something!"

My eyelids broke open to a panicked Stuart holding me. "Anna, this will never happen again. I'm so sorry. Stay with me. Don't close your eyes. I'm here, and I love you, my Anna."

Though I could see Stuart, my mind was slow to comprehend what it meant. They had found me. For now, all that mattered was my safety. There was time for answers later. I must have blacked out again. I woke up in a helicopter with Stuart's arms around me, accompanied by two very worried men. Brian and Chris broke down in tears when they saw me open my eyes, and that's the last thing I remember.

A slight breeze tickled my skin. The curtains floated ethereally in the breeze. Warm sunshine streamed through an open window and made a path on the floor. Fully alert to my senses, I had not felt this way in weeks. Stuart was by my bedside, holding my hand. He was drained from worry; I could read it on his face. When I looked up at him, his expression changed. I think he even kissed me full on the lips! "Anna, you're awake." He said in relief.

I would take it easy for a few weeks. Doctor's orders! I had to meet with a therapist each day to debrief from the trauma. My body was also in detox after repeated injections with sedatives. I stayed at Stuart's estate in Cap Ferrat for almost a month before I was cleared for travel. Brian had flown in Melanie to join Stuart, Chris, and Olivia. My parents called every day, along with Jesse and Karen. One good thing happened. During my time of recovery, Chris and Olivia quietly got married at Stuart's estate becoming Mr. and Mrs. Cooper.

Fresh air was my new drug. I couldn't get enough of it. It was a healing balm for me, almost like the water. Cade came to visit me one day, and we sat out by the pool. It felt like old times again. I was proud of the comeback he'd made from the accident. He was solid and still seemed like the man I used to know. His travel had gotten in the way, breaking up his engagement. Yes, a part of me would always love him.

He stopped in every day for the next week to check on me. I knew deep within my soul that we would always be friends. One day, he reached over for my hand and looked at me with those blue eyes. "Is there any way we could make it work again, Anna? I have never stopped loving you."

I responded in the only way I honestly could. "Cade, I'm honored. You're amazing, and any girl would be lucky to marry you. I wish I could say yes, but . . . I am still in love with Jean Michel. I don't want to hurt you, but I cannot seem to get over him. It hurts so much thinking about it. I'm so sorry."

"Anna, I will always be here for you. I could see how much in love you were when I saw you in Santa Monica. I guess I was just hoping you could look at me that way again. I'm sure he still loves you, and I have a feeling your story is not done. I just needed to tell you how I felt."

"You are a good man, Cade Williams."

Cade continued to visit, and one evening, he took me out for dinner. I even got to watch him win the tournament in Monte Carlo. I was so proud of him. Yes, he held a very special place in my heart—if only I could get over Jean Michel and recapture the love I once had for Cade.

I finally had answers for what happened that dreadful night. On that evening in front of the Hotel de Paris, I had approached my captors to take our picture. I practically walked right into their hands. The men who abducted me had hoped not only to stop the work of the foundation, but to get at Stuart's money. They knew the only way to Stuart was through me. Their country was oil rich, but they used child labor to fight their wars and maximize their profit. To them, orphans were cheap and expendable. They disgusted me so much that I could spit on them. Their form of business was the undercurrent of unrest in many of the African nations. After multiple unsuccessful attempts to abduct me, they had finally succeeded with a little help from me.

There was more. Allister Cummings was funding their efforts and turning a profit through the sale of weapons. It took Stuart a while to investigate, but with the help of other nations, he unveiled who was financially backing the group. Allister Cummings was a snake. The business deal that Stuart had closed without Allister cost the evil monster billions and made Stuart the owner of the largest communications enterprise in the world. Allister wanted revenge any way he could get it.

Stuart said, "Anna, this goes back to that meeting on the airplane in San Francisco. He felt threatened by me and knew if he hit me where it hurt most, I would do anything. We are still investigating the plane crash further, but there could be a link to Allister there."

I was rendered speechless. Who could possibly be this ruthless? Allister was out to destroy Stuart for his own money, pride, and power. This is why Elle had called me in Monte Carlo. She set me up to aid Allister's revenge plot. He had promised her wealth beyond her imagination and a ring on her finger. I pictured my hands slowly closing in around her neck. I was so mad.

"Allister is in jail now, facing a slew of charges for plotting the abduction and the illegal weapons sales—not to mention what he may answer for if we believe he had anything to do with Vanessa's death. Elle is also being held without bail for aiding and abetting these crimes. No amount of money will be able to save them, Anna. That awful warlord and his thugs are awaiting trial in their country. I cannot imagine what their dreadful fate will be."

My head was spinning with this news, but I was beyond thankful to hear it.

"Stuart, I'm safe now, and it's time to get home to little Sabrina. My heart will always ache over time lost with Vanessa and that precious life inside of her, but we can honor her passion with the work of the foundation. Together we will turn this tragedy into triumph."

I had one more burning question. "Just how did you find me, Stuart?" I was strong enough now to hear the details surrounding my near-death experience without bursting into tears.

Stuart had tried every connection he could think of, but kept running into dead ends. He even recruited the help of the Ambassador of Mauritius and the Presidents of France, Mexico, and the United States, and he begged for their assistance. Jean Michel was frantically trying to locate me as well. He never called, but Stuart assured me that if he hadn't stepped in, who knows what would have happened.

Jean Michel had insisted they use a mercenary group that specialized in covert extraction missions. Within a week, the group had located my whereabouts and waited for the right opportunity to move. The night of my relocation was their chance. My captors were holding me in a villa just outside of Geneva. The sounds seemed familiar because it was near the train Jean Michel and I had taken to Montreux and the Jet d'Eau. They had plans to move me to their country on the night the mercenaries stepped in. I could not stop thinking about Jean Michel and what if they had not found me. I wanted to call him, but something stopped me whenever I tried. I loved him more than ever, but he had made it clear: he could not be in my life anymore.

I was grateful for the time to mend, but I was ready to go home to my parents and Jesse. I wanted to see my beautiful goddaughter Sabrina and hold her in my arms. Yes, a good dose of Brina would be the perfect medicine.

Chapter Twenty-Three

THE HEALING POWERS OF VENICE

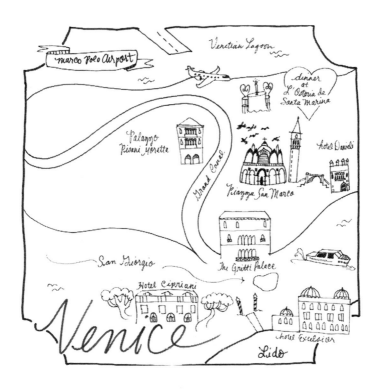

Smile and be happy. You are in Venice.
　　—**Ruth Edenbaum** and **Shannon Essa's** book, *Chow! Venice*

*S*tuart was hosting a masquerade ball in Venice. This was my first work trip since that awful day. Over two hundred guests were being flown in for the event on chartered airplanes. The production studio was using N23SM, and we were flying Stuart over on N29VM. Each airplane was stocked to the hilt to make this trip outstanding in every way. I was getting back into the swing of things.

A glass of chilled prosecco awaited each arriving passenger. Each guest had a gift basket with items selected for his or her specific interests. The invitation to the ball was a custom wooden box, delivered months before to each guest. Once opened, the box contained the most exquisite mask, nestled in rich, velvety satin. The mask's intricate details were one-of-a-kind and the only way to gain access into the ball.

As we descended into Venice, I knew this trip would mark a new beginning. I wanted to rid myself of the memories that haunted my dreams. Below me was the spectacular floating city. If we looked closely, we could see its famous water highways. We reserved the Hotel Danieli on Riva degli Schiavoni around the corner from Piazza San Marco for the main event. We had also reserved the Gritti Palace, the Hotel Cipriani, and Hotel Excelsior on the island of Lido. Water taxis were lined up in a small fleet to whisk our guests through the waterways of Venice.

I watched the faces of our guests with delight as they stepped into their water taxis. Yes, I was back in Venice! Venice always had a "first time" effect on me. Romance filled the air here, and intrigue was around every corner. This was a trip for new beginnings. My skin tingled at the thought. Colors of every hue enveloped me in a rich bouquet of greetings. My face lit up as I inhaled the magnificence of Venice.

From the moment we landed at the Venice Marco Polo Airport, this event looked like a scene straight out of Hollywood or the Cannes Film Festival. Movie stars, musicians, and producers descended in droves. The press was everywhere, clamoring for their attention. It was like watching a page out of the tabloids.

The boys and I arrived at the Hotel Excelsior exhausted and wind-blown but infused with excitement. Our welcoming committee was Melanie and Olivia, standing at the dock. The hotel was pure bliss, and it was good to be back in this city without Precious and her baggage, but in the style we had become accustomed to for the last few years. In front of us, the waters of the Adriatic sparkled. Had it truly been just months since I was last here? The staff knew us well after our many trips. At the reception desk, I could see my darling Roberto coming around to greet me with three air kisses: cheek-to-cheek-to-cheek.

"Welcome back! Your rooms are ready. Ms. St. James, you have your special room. Francesco is bringing your bags up straight away. Please, do not hesitate to voice any special requests. As always, we are at your service."

Handing me an ornate, old-fashioned key with green tassels dangling from the ends, he added with a wink, "It is always a great pleasure to have you as our guest."

I endured the jabs from Brian and Chris for my special treatment, while Melanie and Olivia just rolled their eyes at the boys. Brian just couldn't resist. "Anna, you know that Roberto has the biggest crush on you?"

I ignored his teasing. "Yeah, I love you, too! I'll meet up with you guys in about an hour at the beach, okay?

"Sounds perfect."

"Mel and Olivia, we'll need catch up, too."

On my way up to my room, I ran into a very grown up Heath Grey. In that delightful British accent, he said warmly, "Anna, I had a feeling you would be here. How are you doing after—?"

He caught himself midsentence, but it was too late. "Anna, you look smashing. I cannot say how relieved I am to see you."

I tried to put him at ease as I turned the conversation around. "Well, hello to you too, Heath. You're looking quite handsome and grown up these days. When did that happen?"

He grinned.

"It's great to see you here for Stuart's party. I know he will be pleased to see you. How did filming go?"

He was enjoying a little downtime from his latest movie, which was on track to be the next blockbuster. He was an overnight sensation in the industry from his breakout role in a film released a few years back. He seemed like a genuine person, and I greatly enjoyed his company.

Seeing Heath was a testament to Stuart Manning's close friendships. Being thrust into this opulent world of privilege, I had seen many people destroyed by a love of money and lack of concern for others. This lifestyle had a seductive way of driving people toward greed. I had been by Stuart's side for quite a few years now and knew his story better than most. His heart was bigger than Mt. Everest. His trust was hard to earn, but once earned, it was forever kept.

I had seen him cry tears of joy when he married Vanessa and at Sabrina's birth and first steps. I had seen him weep and grieve for the loss of his best friend and love of his life, yet he resiliently moved forward to give back to others. Stuart was much more than a friend to me. He had touched my heart.

Up in my suite, the French doors were opened, showcasing the ocean below with the sun at its highest point. I felt a bit like Grace Kelly in her palace. Lost in thought about Stuart, I couldn't help but worry about how tired he looked, again. I hadn't seen him look this way in quite a while. When I broached the subject, he always dismissed the question, saying he was fine. He couldn't fool me, though. Something was wrong, and I would get to the bottom of it after this trip. At the pace he kept, who wouldn't be exhausted?

Working for Stuart Manning was an indescribable adventure and a badge of honor. I had traveled most of the world with the Manning clan. My schedule was not my own for years, but I was proud to have the job—not to mention its many perks! Very few people in Stuart's life had gained his full, unfettered trust, and that meant the world to me.

I met my group downstairs at La Terrazza before heading to the beach. It was great to be together. Chris and Olivia were thriving, as were Mel and Brian. The Hotel Excelsior's well-known beach club bordered the Adriatic Sea. We had reserved the private cabanas that dotted the perfectly groomed sandy beach. The stark white cabanas sharply contrasted the aqua blue seas. Everything in Venice was a visual delight. Many a film director flocked to this location for its allure. The Moorish-style palace held a certain fascination among the rich and famous personalities who frequented this location. Glamour was alive and well here, and I could see why.

We relieved our jet lag with the coastal air. Brian and Chris were still a bit nervous about my first trip out since the kidnapping. I felt, at times, like a porcelain doll, but it was time to feel normal again. So I started a water fight! Brian and Chris picked me up and made a run straight for the sea, dunking me into the waves with a toss. Olivia and Mel were drawn into the antics. It felt so good to laugh again.

We boarded the water taxis, feeling sundrenched and relaxed. Stuart was on the dock, waiting for us to arrive and rounding off our little dinner party at the L'Osteria de Santa Marina. The food was sumptuous and from the piazza we heard classical music drifting through the night from San Marco Square. A stroll after dinner was followed by a gondola ride through the mysterious canals of Venice. Stuart was quiet, sitting next to me and pulling me up close with a blanket over my shoulders. It was nice to be cared for in such a way; I was falling under the city's musical spell that followed us everywhere. The magic and mystery was tangible.

Back in my room that evening, I was caught up in reflection. I could not shake the fear that someone was still out there in the shadows watching me. A chill ran down my arms to think of it. Would these feelings ever go away? Sometimes I felt like I was suffocating, yet I knew I was safe now.

I had not broached the subject with Stuart, but it was strange how not a single member of the Manning clan was invited to the ball. I had planned the entire event, and this was the first time I had not received an invitation to one of his parties. It made no sense. Was Stuart trying to protect me? Nothing was going to stop the five of us from attending the masquerade ball— even Stuart.

Breakfast was served downstairs at the Sala Stucchi for all our guests. I ran downstairs to join the legendary Antonio Lunas and his band for breakfast. They were the entertainment for the masquerade ball. Antonio made me promise to save him a dance. I smiled and accepted, without saying we weren't invited. Next on my agenda was a run. Brian wouldn't let me go alone, suggesting that he and Mel join me. We saw the island of Lido in a new light and stopped at a local café before getting in some beach time. It was the perfect way to start a fresh, new day.

We spent most of the day in the warm sunshine. We discussed the ball and our plans for an early dinner beforehand at the Hotel Danieli. Without the prized special invitation masks, we would have to get creative. The plan was to arrive early at the Palazzo, before the guests arrived, and blend in. How I loved a good intrigue!

I stopped to think about Jean Michel. Where was he? Did he miss me? I desperately missed him. Would that ache ever go away? Had Bridgitte finally gotten her wish? My friends and family had encouraged me to move on.

In my finest black Prada dress, I made my way down toward the lagoon and the Hotel Excelsior's dock. Brian and Mel were in the water taxi waiting. Brian playfully whistled to get my attention. How could I miss it? He broke into song: "Have you seen the most beautiful girl in the world? I mean, the second most beautiful girl in the world—next to my Mel!"

Mel just rolled her eyes, smiling. Holding the intricate black and white post to step aboard, I turned around to look back at the Hotel Excelsior. In the early evening sky, it took on a golden light, with Chris and Olivia illuminated in the glow, making their way down to the dock. They looked happy and in love.

The celebration kicked off as we crossed the Venetian Lagoon for a night of celebration. Not even Stuart could stop us! Each one of these special friends proved how much they cared when my life had spiraled out of control. They were true friends. Both couples were beautiful, inside and out. Before Olivia, women were drawn to Chris's rugged good looks, but now he had Olivia.

The breeze was a welcome relief as we sped through the waters with the Island of Lido at our backs. We could just make out St. Mark's Square looming in the foreground and the Bridge of Sighs up ahead. Our driver expertly pulled into the dock at the Riva degli Schiavoni with the ease of a lifetime of practice. Next stop: Hotel Danieli.

Somehow the hotel caught wind of our arrival. The fanfare greeting at the dock was no coincidence. They placed glasses of chilled prosecco in our hands as we stepped off the water taxi. The paparazzi descended in a sea of camera flashes, hoping to land a money shot. Now I really felt like Grace Kelly! Hotel guests were craning their necks to see if we were celebrities. I kept hearing them say, "Is that Anna St. James?"

I had been in the news during the search. Even our friends at *Time* ran the story.

The bellman led us to our table overlooking the Grand Canal. For Venetian standards, this was an early dinner, but tonight was not really about dinner. We were, of course, there to gain entry into the star-studded masquerade ball starting in just a few short hours. First, we would soak in the stunning panoramic view, assailing us from every direction.

Our hearts were as effervescent as the bubbles in our Murano champagne flutes. Chris led the toast with a bottle of Veuve Clicquot Ponsardin La Grande Dame. He looked straight into Olivia's eyes as he gave the toast. "Here's to the start of our evening and many more to come in Venice. Salut."

Our glasses resounded from the toast, with our anticipation soaring into the night. Our waiter arrived to start the courses of food. With many excited hand gestures, he introduced a mouth-watering bigoli pasta. It was from the medieval town northwest of Venice called Bassano del Grappa. "You are about to taste the world's most outstanding pasta."

Almost out of breath, he added, "Please enjoy what chef has chosen for you this evening. I will also be serving a wild mushroom truffle from the Molise region, accompanied by a lobster risotto. Bon appetite!"

The flavors were savory, and each new food brought out a layer of taste I had never before experienced. I was set on trying everything. In my signature black Prada dress, I felt I had some room. The dress usually fit like a glove, but I had lost a lot of weight from my abduction. Tonight was for pure enjoyment, and I would indulge in every delectable morsel.

I wore my elegant Prada purse that Stuart gave me as a birthday gift. It matched my Jimmy Choos perfectly. The special diamond necklace that Jean Michel gave me in Mauritius was about my neck. I rarely took it off. All were extravagant, but each piece was meaningful. I felt sexy and sophisticated and very much in my own skin. I treasured these extravagant adornments.

The culinary delights kept coming. Cheese followed the meticulously paired wines for each delectable entrée. The pièce de résistance arrived: a cappuccino tiramisu complete with a steamed café presse and a glass of port that melted as it trickled down my throat. It was pure pleasure! The chef came to our table to soak up our praises. He made us promise to come back to Venice. I was determined to never leave!

I stepped away from the group for a brief, reflective moment to look over the lagoon. It was a rare moment for me. I was usually the life of the party, doubled over in laughter at some kind of ridiculous story Brian was telling. Unexpectedly, I was overcome with feelings of homesickness. This was not like me at all. Just moments before, I was drinking in the beauty and excitement, yet here I was wondering if I could ever go back to my old life.

Maybe the wine was making me sentimental. I looked over at the two couples lost in one another—as lost as I had been with Jean Michel. Mel came over to check on me. I tried to fake a smile. She knew me better. She asked, "Do you want to talk?"

I shook my head resolutely. The feeling would pass; wouldn't it? I had lived with the yearning to travel all these years, and now, finally, I was homesick. Something about it made me feel human again. Jean Michel was still an ache in my heart every day that passed. Our story was like a perfect movie script. How could it ever end? I missed Vanessa too and tried hard to swallow the lump in my throat.

I had seen many exotic places, and the comforts of this lifestyle were alluring. Yet, I barely had time to enjoy my darling little bungalow back home in Santa Monica. I was always too busy to enjoy it. Oh, my, I needed to shake off these deep thoughts! I had a party to sneak into, and I wanted to savor this view of the city before we left for the Palazzo.

Mel grabbed my hand as we took in the view together. My spirits lifted as the sky before us transformed into a brilliant, glowing ember of rich pink before surrendering in its descent to a magnificent, blazing orange. Venice donned her evening mask for the masquerade ball, and we were about to follow suit.

The island of San Giorgio awakened in a show of light as water taxis, vaparettos, and gondolas aglow with lanterns flowed in from the Grand Canal to the basin known as Saint Mark's. The two of us stood there a little longer, glazed over in awe. Mel gave my hand a loving squeeze and said thoughtfully, "Anna, you're going to be all right, you know? Your life is just beginning."

We looked at each other, with tears in our eyes. "Mel, you've been such a wonderful friend. It all began when you put me on that flight with Stuart on the day of Cade's accident. I'm grateful to you, my friend."

As if to shake off the mood, she added, "Do you really think we will get into the ball?"

"Of course! We will see the fruits of our labor. I have a sneaking suspicion that Stuart thinks he is protecting us by keeping us away from the spotlight. But he also knows me well enough to expect a harebrained scheme to crash the party. It will be like Fort Knox in there, but if we arrive early enough, it will be just fine. Anyway, it's time for some fun and a little craziness, right?"

"Yes. Come on; let's go and make it a night to remember!"

Off the dock of the Hotel Danieli and into the water-taxi, we set our course toward the Palazzo beneath the promising blanket of stars. The cool waters ushered us into the San Polo District for our secretive mission, like a bunch of sly, mischievous kids. As always, Brian was the ringleader.

Under the veil of darkness, the Palazzo Pisani Moretta was a beacon of twinkling lights. The ink-blue water mirrored its perfect reflection to the stars. My evening dress was ideal for a night in Venice, but would we look out of place?

At the dock, I cautiously stepped onto the floating wooden platform. I had my eyes on the palace door. My stomach was tied up in knots at the thought of being turned away. I knew almost all of the guests who were arriving in a little over an hour, and what if one saw us being turned away? I would die of embarrassment! Mel and Olivia linked elbows on either side of me. I smiled at both of them, with the renewed courage to walk in like I owned the place. Yes, I could do this!

Through the pointed, arched doorway, we stepped into the opulence of splendor and elegance. The solid walnut doors were meticulously carved with the sign of Mercury. The staff didn't even look up at the five of us as they hustled past with last minute preparations. We might as well have been invisible!

I had studied the floor plans of the Palazzo Pisani Moretta many times to ensure all the details were perfect, but nothing prepared me to see it with my own eyes. I imagined myself as a medieval lady of the Italian royal court, colorfully dressed in a gown of many layers. My aching feet from the pain of my heels awakened me from fantasy. Now that we were here, nothing could stop us! I wished we had arranged for costumes. A rich, burgundy velvet gown with a mask of pearls and rubies would be perfect.

I gathered my adventurers toward the entresol. From this vantage point, we could watch the scene unfold below. Up the marble inlaid stairs, we marveled at the wall-to-ceiling colorful frescos from famous Baroque artists—the likes of Angeli, Diziani, and Tiepolo. The staircase was like a symphonic movement, spiraling us up toward the gods. My head was spinning like a top from all the exquisite detail. Even the chandeliers were Murano crystal, reflecting the light from hundreds of candles. The Palazzo Pisani Moretta was a masterpiece.

Mel, Olivia, and I went off to the ladies room before the other guests started arriving. We left the boys on the entresol. At the bottom of the stairs, we went inside a door I thought was correct. Inside stood one of the tiniest women I had ever seen. She was in a black uniform, complete with a white linen apron.

"Oh, *mi scusi.* I am sorry to have disturbed you!" I blushed. This was not the ladies room!

"Ah, Ms. St. James and ladies, welcome. You must be very special because a nice and handsome gentleman left you some beautiful gifts with instructions. Please follow me."

Had I found the portal to another world? I could not believe this! We stood speechless yet unquestioning, following our guide through a maze of doors; deeper into the palace we went. In the second room, we stopped before three ornate masquerade ball gowns. I knew which was mine before I even saw my name embroidered on it.

My dress was rich, jade-green velvet, cushioned with diamonds, sapphires, and pearls. It was unparalleled to the burgundy dress I had dreamed of previously; this dress was fit for a queen. Mel's dress was also unmatched, a contrast of black velvet inlaid with rubies. Olivia wore a rich sapphire blue gown that complemented her fair skin brilliantly.

Who had gone through all this trouble for us? I had a feeling Brian and Chris were behind it. I petitioned our petite escort for answers. "Please, can you tell me who gave us these heavenly dresses?"

She lifted her finger to her lips, in the universal sign of secrecy, then disappeared as quickly as she came. We were left contemplating the mystery as we slipped into the beautiful attire. Olivia couldn't resist asking, "Do you think these rubies are real?"

In utter disbelief, we shrugged our shoulders before breaking into hysterical laughter. Who was the mysterious donor of these beautiful gowns? Were they ours to keep? Off we went to be admired by the boys.

What seemed like moments since we had arrived at the Palazzo was actually well over an hour. The lounge was a sea of celebrities. I could make out my valiant protector, Mark, standing before us with a wink. We tried to make it back to the landing above to surprise Brian and Chris in our splendor, but no such luck. Johnson Price was standing just outside the door of the lounge, talking to the very famous Sloan. He reached over as I passed for a hug and a quick kiss on the lips. In the world of celebrities, everyone moves quickly. I turned around to look for Mel and Olivia, whom I had lost in the fray of guests.

Riveria Richardson was making a beeline toward me. He was a known philanthropist and talented musician. He was a favorite of Stuart's, and his band's latest album had just gone platinum. "Anna, please promise to save me a dance."

"You know I will, Riveria. It's great to see you."

"Anna, might I say the same about you? I am thrilled you're here."

At the center of it all was the amazing Antonio Lunas. Campbell Phillips had just arrived too, causing quite a stir. She was a famous singer and an actress in many romantic movies—not to mention, very eye-catching. Heath had just arrived with his date on his arm. He greeted me the Italian way with cheek-to-cheek kisses.

"Wow, you look amazing, Anna. You are beautiful," he said emphatically.

The guests arrived in their eighteenth-century-medieval-masquerade attire. I was glad to be dressed the same. Our guest list read like a page out of *People* magazine, and I greeted my way back to Brian and Chris. They had mysteriously followed suit with their own medieval costumes, looking devilishly handsome.

Brown Davis, the famed musical composer, accompanied Antonio Lunas, who was on his PRS Lunas guitar that glistened with each movement. Antonio was dressed in what could only be "The Antonio Lunas medieval twist." It was a modern performance fit for a royal family. Brown Davis filled the Palazzo with soft jazz from his gleaming, white saxophone as the guests continued to stream in.

All around us was a blaze of burgundy, gold, red, green, and blue. The sparkling of rubies, emeralds, sapphires, and diamonds cast kaleidoscope refractions on the wall that swayed to the beat of the music. I was caught up in the rhythm and sway of the evening.

Antonio and Brown continued on stage, dazzling the crowd. Had I just had breakfast with Antonio that morning? Seeing him entertain below was more like a fantasy; yes, this was a dreamlike world.

Out of the corner of my eye, I spotted Stuart step out onto the ballroom floor with Mystique as his date. Her smile beamed for all to see as she was dressed as Marie Antoinette. They looked spectacular! I had seen them many times before, but tonight I found myself hanging over the edge to stare down at the two of them.

Stuart was dressed like the boys, in Venetian knee breeches that made him look strong and athletic. The Zoccoli shoes were a nice touch for his grand entrance and a far cry from the melted Sperry Top-Siders he loved so much. He looked older than his date, but tonight he was the handsome host in a room full of stars. I was proud of him and realized just how much I loved this man. It wasn't the same as I felt for Jean Michel, but maybe I could find that with Stuart someday.

It seemed he must have read my thoughts. Stuart glanced up at me from below, smiling in his charismatic way and waving for all to see. Of course he had known I would be here! I felt the room's attention turn toward me. Before I could run and hide, there were cameras taking shots from every angle. So much for being discreet, Stuart! I could just imagine what the morning's headlines would say.

Stuart jumped up on stage; after all, it was his party! Before I knew it, Stuart Manning and Patrick Dillion were jamming to "Purple Haze" and

"Foxy Lady" alongside Antonio. Stuart was looking more like himself, standing among legends.

When the music stopped, Stuart grabbed the microphone for an introduction. "Welcome! I would like to thank you all for coming to Venice."

The room exploded with applause. He went on, "I would also like to make a toast to a brave and amazing woman. Anna St. James, thank you."

Now the cameras were really working overtime. I accepted his gracious gesture with a slight nod. The Palazzo came alive. From the landing, I admired contemplatively the man I'd known for years. I had watched him completely transform from widowed billionaire to loving father and now, thriving philanthropist. He continued speaking into the microphone for all to hear. "Anna, may I have the next dance?"

My first reaction was to shake my head no, but with all the people staring at me, I had no choice. Self-consciously, I made my way down the grand staircase with every single eye in the Palazzo trained on me. "Look natural," I prayed with each step. I could see Brian and Mel in the sea of people below, giving me a nod of approval. Chris kindly stepped in to escort me down the staircase, just as I worried my knees might buckle. Stuart took my hand and led me to the dance floor.

"Anna, my dear and wonderful Annabelle, I knew you would be here tonight. Do you like your dress I picked out? The green matches your eyes perfectly."

I was speechless and swept up in the dance.

"Anna, this is not like you to be at such a loss for words."

Stuart continued with a smile, "So, I succeeded in surprising you this evening? I'm glad. Now, I'm going to say something, and please let me finish. Okay?" I nodded.

"Anna, thank you for always caring, for standing by my side when I did not make it easy. I hope you know how much you mean to me. I have loved three women in my life: Vanessa, Sabrina, and you, my dear Anna. Please never forget that."

He pulled me closer into his arms. I had no words. Once the dance was over, I managed to say something. "Stuart, you know I love you too. I always have. There is a piece of my heart that will forever belong to you. Truly, thank you for everything."

I squeezed him in the ribs to lighten the conversation, "So, you knew I would come, huh?"

"Annabelle, how long have I known you?" He asked, smiling down at me.

All I could do was laugh and give him a kiss on the cheek as he claimed another dance. Once the dance was finished, Stuart leaned over and kissed me in front of everyone. I worried what Marie Antoinette might think! I stood there, totally astonished, as he whispered in my ear, "Anna, I will see you in the morning."

Riveria was waiting for the next dance, and it seemed like a stream of partners thereafter. Stepping away to take a short break, I turned to check on Stuart. What kind of man hosts a party in Venice for over two hundred guests and foots the bill himself? Better yet, how had I come to be employed by such a man? It was still a mystery to me. What an adventure he had taken me on!

I was in Venice, a city of magical proportions, yet that moment of loneliness still haunted me. A longing for home and the life and love I had lost overwhelmed me. I wished to share this surreal experience with someone. What was Jean Michel doing after we went our separate ways? Had he gone back to Mauritius with Bridgitte? I still got butterflies at the thought of him. What was the fascination that lured me deeper into this world? Why was I not able to leave Stuart Manning? Maybe it was out of a strange sense of obligation. Or maybe it was the jet fuel running through my veins since the day I took my first flight as a three-month-old infant. Could I love Stuart the way I had loved Jean Michel?

I needed to get some fresh air and fast! On my way toward the door, a voice I could never forget caught my ear. In a beautiful French accent, someone whispered into my ear. "Anna, *excusez-moi*, I knew you would be here this evening."

I wanted to lean back into those strong arms and just close my eyes in disbelief. "My beautiful Anna, may I have the pleasure of this dance with you?"

This was the voice that kept me up at night—the voice of Jean Michel Durand. "*Je t'aime pour toujours.*"

He held me fast in his arms before I could say anything. How I remembered being mesmerized by the intensity of those eyes. Oh, yes, my handsome Jean Michel had a voice I could never forget. He was more familiar to me than I was to myself. The dance ended much too quickly, and I felt a bit dizzy. I never wanted to let go.

I didn't have to try. Chris and Brian were on either side of me, giving Jean Michel a cool greeting before protectively swooping in. "Anna, we're leaving right now. Excuse us, Jean Michel."

Olivia and Mel were waiting for us in the water taxi. Brian and Chris were unusually quiet the whole way back to the Hotel Excelsior. When I could find the words I asked, "What was that about? Are you angry?"

Chris finally broke the silence. "Anna, both Brian and I were there in Monte Carlo on that awful day you were taken. We heard nothing from Jean Michel until the night they found you, and he was there for the mission. We kept thinking he would come back into your life, but he didn't. He hurt you. Do you understand that? We lived through that incident too, not knowing if we would ever find you and feeling responsible for what had happened."

I did understand. "You could do nothing to stop what happened that night. In fact, the whole reason we had the motorcycles was to distract me from my breakup with Jean Michel. Don't you remember the tollbooth? I'd never laughed so hard in my life. Thank you for that memory. You are both amazing, and I love you, but I have never stopped loving Mich."

I parted ways with the couples for some time to think. My heart was still beating wildly from seeing him earlier. His voice and his eyes captured me in the same way they had that fateful evening back in Paris.

Once inside my suite, I could feel a slight breeze off the ocean. The breeze led me toward the open French doors of my balcony. There was a cool mist rising off the evening Adriatic. Did I leave the doors open, I wondered? With a step forward, I bumped into an entry table covered in flowers that hadn't been there before. Not a square inch of the table surface was visible beneath the many bouquets. Still dwelling in a bit of fear, I picked up my phone to call Mark when a white card in the arrangement caught my eye:

Tonight was magic. You have always taken my breath away, from the first time we met, my Anna, mon amour, ma vie. Can you ever forgive me? I am looking forward to many more nights filled with the magic we share together. I never want to let you go again.

Yours, always and forever,
Mich

Jean Michel was back. He was the only man I had ever truly loved. Suddenly, there was a knock at my door.

Chapter Twenty-Four

COMING FULL CIRCLE

Sometimes you don't know when you're taking the first step through a door until you're already inside.

—Ann Voskamp, *One Thousand Gifts*

tuart knew we would try and crash the party—that much was clear. So much for being sneaky! He had us fooled. I had not dared to think Jean Michel would be among the guests. He was the best of all surprises. Since that first evening in Paris when Stuart introduced us, I was a goner. Our trip to the South of France assured me there would never be anyone else.

Last night was a wonderful surprise, and yes, the knock on my door was the only true medicine for my broken heart. I wasn't sure if I would ever see him again after our dance, but the flowers made me hopeful. The gift of Jean Michel standing at my door was more than I could bear. His arms were outstretched in the promise of what was to come.

"I love you, *mon Cherie*. I knew I could not spend another minute without you in my life. When you were taken, it was as if my heart spilt in two. Can you ever forgive me for not being there for you?"

I felt only warmth and love for the man standing in front of me. "I was heartbroken when we last saw each other. I tried to pick up the phone to call you a hundred times, but I couldn't go through the heartache again."

I continued. "I never got the chance to thank you for saving my life, so I'm doing it now. The mercenaries you sent came just in time."

He stared intently into my eyes. "I went crazy trying to enlist the help of everyone we knew. I was there with the mercenaries when they found you. I was there when Stuart cradled you in his arms, saying how sorry he was and how he loved you."

He looked distant for a moment before taking my hands in his.

"I thought you had moved on with Stuart. It wasn't until he called with an invitation to the ball that I finally knew the truth. Can you ever forgive me?"

Could my heart burst? How could he have ever doubted our love? He was the only man for me.

"Anna, Stuart wants us to meet with him sometime today. Will you come with me?"

We were in each other's arms as the sun rose that morning with the promise of our future. I was hopeful, knowing that with Jean Michel by my side nothing was impossible.

"Jean Michel?" I asked, treasuring his closeness to me.

"Do you have any idea how much I love you?"

He softly leaned over to give me the kiss that had first swept me off my feet. That first night in Paris after the ambassador's dinner seemed so long ago.

Stuart called that morning to ask if we could have breakfast together. It seemed early after hosting the masquerade ball the night before. No doubt he was exhausted from hosting! We invited him up to my suite for breakfast sitting out on the balcony overlooking the magic of the Adriatic Sea. Stuart looked tired, more than I had seen him look in a long time. He came straight over to give me a kiss.

"Jean Michel, Anna, I need to say a few things before I will answer your questions. Please be patient with me. Anna, you came so suddenly into my life. It seems like a lifetime ago when we shared the flight that changed everything. Something about you shined from our first encounter, even as you were faced with a crisis. I think a part of me fell in love with you then and there.

"Now, Jean Michel, hear me out on this. I have loved three women in my lifetime. One was the love of my life, then my little Brina, and the other is you, Anna. I knew from the beginning that Jean Michel was the one for you. We are a privileged few who experience a love like this.

"You two belong together. There was never any doubt about that. That is why Vanessa and I asked you to be Sabrina's godparents. That is why we asked you, Jean Michel, to take over the foundation to continue the work of helping children around the world. Yesterday, Jean Michel accepted the job as Director of the Manning Foundation, effective immediately. I can think of no finer man to continue our work.

"Anna, you have been all over my case, worrying about me when I look tired. I have not been well for some time. I apologize for not telling you sooner. A few months ago I decided I had best see a doctor. The diagnosis is a rare form of Leukemia. It has spread throughout my entire body, with a life expectancy of no more than a few months at this point. Now, Anna, calm down. I have come to terms with this. It breaks my heart that I will not be there for Sabrina, but I know of no finer couple to raise her than the two of you. She loves you beyond reason. Yes, this means you need to get married quickly. If Jean Michel had not come to Venice, I would have married you myself. Settle down, Jean Michel. Yes, you heard me right. I would have been honored to marry Anna."

I started to stand up to interrupt when Stuart went on.

"Anna, please, let me finish. I have more to say. I'm not proud of how I have lived my life these past few years. I have made amends for that, knowing I will be with my beautiful Vanessa soon. I would like you both to give me your word on a few things. I already had all the legal papers drawn up a few months ago, but as you know, it's been an interesting last few years.

"My entire estate is in both of your names: Mr. and Mrs. Jean Michel Durand. But there's one stipulation on that. I want Sabrina to grow up in a normal environment. I want her to have siblings and, someday, to come alongside the two of you to set up orphanages all over the world. I want her to know you as her parents, but also to know how much Vanessa and I loved her. She brought an inescapable joy into our lives, one that I will never forget.

"I hope to see orphanages on every continent in the world, growing and nurturing the children our hearts fell in love with in Africa. I know with my wealth comes problems, but I think you both can handle it. It would honor both Vanessa and me for you to pick up where we left off. Oh, and one more thing. Please see that Conor and Liz serve on the board of the foundation, along with Brian, Melanie, Chris and Olivia.

"Well, don't just stand there; say something!"

I was consumed in tears of bittersweet grief and thankfulness. Jean Michel had met with Stuart earlier, but it was only concerning the foundation. He was equally shocked. Stuart had brought us together on that fateful night in Paris, and even in his precious final days he was doing the same. Above all, he entrusted us with Sabrina, his love of all loves. I could not imagine our lives without Stuart, and I would honor his requests until the end of my days.

We left Venice the following day. Stuart requested no special treatment. He wanted to live life as he always had, even under the shadow of an incurable disease. Jean Michel and I would stay at the estate once we got back to Los

Angeles. Sabrina was beside herself in joy at our homecoming. Oh, she was one thoroughly loved girl.

Jean Michel and I planned a wedding in five weeks. We were hoping for Stuart to give me away. Two weeks before our wedding, Stuart quietly passed away. The media went crazy with references of Vanessa's untimely death and its possible ties to Stuart's death of a broken heart. We knew differently. Mr. Stuart Manning had left us all better people. I found a note scribbled by his bedside:

Anna,

I know you will find this note. I am so proud of you. I trust you will love Sabrina as your own and she will grow up to be as wonderful as you are. She will have both Vanessa's beauty and yours. I love you, my dear Annabelle. I always have. Vanessa and I will be celebrating with joy on your wedding day to Jean Michel. Thank you for never leaving my side. You were the first person to truly know me and trust me, as I trusted you. We will meet again.

Yours always, in love,

Stuart

I sat at his bedside, washing away my tears as I smoothed out the note on my lap. I would keep it forever. Yes Stuart, till we meet again—I love you. Jean Michel came in and sat by my side, giving me the strength to move forward. We would make it together.

About a week later, we had a memorial service out on *Sonoma SMS* to honor an amazing man, Mr. Stuart Manning. I would never forget him, and I would strive to do everything he had set in motion. I had been given an *exposure to a billionaire* in the richest sense.

Jean Michel was at my side, holding our beautiful Sabrina. He set her down briefly. When she looked up at the two of us, she said, "Papa, Mama . . ."

EPILOGUE

ur love story had really begun in the magnificent Cote d'Azur, and there it continued as we stood side by side. A love that knew no limits grew within our home under the watchful eyes of those treasured friends who had come and gone. High above, on our special perch overlooking the sweeping ocean below, was our beloved Chateau Eze. This was a day to celebrate and remember a man whose legacy would not be forgotten. It was being lived out on the two little legs of our precious Sabrina, who stood between us as the sun made its final descent over the Mediterranean Ocean.

ACKNOWLEDGMENTS

The list is long of all those who have helped make this dream become a reality. Thank you to my husband, Doug, who has stood by my side in love and support; we did this together. Thank you to my son, Jason, and his wife, Liz, along with their girls, Maddie, Paloma, and Lucie Lee, for all the prayers, technical advice, editing, and input. Thank you to my beautiful daughter, Kellee, her husband, Ram, and their two sons, Luka and Tristan. You have walked this adventure with me for years, encouraging me, giving me advice and steady help, listening endlessly through my thought process as the story unfolded. This was truly a team effort from the very beginning. Thank you to each of you, with my love always. My cup runneth over.

To my sister, Janet Turner, your constant love and support throughout the years is priceless. Our adventures growing up gave us such a thirst for travel. I love you, sis.

To Karen Wayt, thank you for listening, for laughing, and for being one of my "besties" throughout life and to Bob Wayt for graciously reviewing the editing process of Exposure to a Billionaire.

To my Sistas:

Melanie Dobson, you inspired, encouraged, and held my hand throughout this process. No words can properly express my heartfelt thanks, but suffice it to say I could not have done this without you, without the constant advice, counsel, and gentle leading. You have taught me much with your big heart for others. Thank you.

Mary Kay Taylor, your smile touches everyone you come in contact with. You are the reason I met such a wonderful and supportive group of women, who now are all part of my extended sisterhood. Thank you for helping, praying, and loving me throughout this process, my special Chica.

Jodi Stilp, thank you for your time and effort editing while cheering me on. Your quick mind was much needed and your suggestions were always spot on. You are the best.

Diane Comer, thank you for your friendship, love, and support. You are a wealth of wisdom. Our adventure together continues.

Julie Kohl, thank you for your real and loving support. You have touched my heart more than you know. You are such a gem, Roo!

Orlena Ballard, you are amazing. I love doing life with you. Thank you.

To my new sister, Shirley Hancock. You are beautiful inside and out. It was your gift of insight in connecting people that made this happen. Your knowledge and tireless energy is amazing. You love so well. I feel like I have known you my entire life. Thank you.

Pam Vredevelt, you blow me away! Our adventures are just beginning, but thank you for connecting me to Morgan James Publishing and for your wise counsel, direction, and friendship.

To Lauren Ruef, could I have a better content or word editor? Thank you for all the fun insight and great work you did to support me. You are the best!

Thank you to my parents, Roger and Marilyn, who instilled in me at a young age a love for travel and adventure. The world was always an open book. What a gift I will always cherish.

Also, thank you to my in-laws, Herman and Genevieve Menke, who gave me a love for France. Genevieve was my most fervent encourager, always asking for one of my stories to read. I am forever grateful we could spend our summers in Normandy with the entire Menke clan! What wonderful adventures and memories.

To my Menke brothers and wives, you all are amazing!

To my lifetime friends, Christian and Ans Leger, your friendship and support throughout the years has touched my heart.

My deepest appreciation goes out to all my fellow flight attendants, pilots, schedulers, mechanics, caterers, drivers, and ground personnel. Most important, I would like to thank my passengers. Without each of you, I wouldn't be where I am today.

To Casey Powell who saw something in me all those years ago giving me a rare start into the world of corporate aviation. We have had many adventures.

Rod and Carol Wendt, your friendship is one of a lifetime. I certainly saved the best for last. It has been a delight to work for you and your family, but more important, I look forward to many more adventures with you in the coming years.

Chris Weidman, you are my brother from another mother, and your friendship is treasured. Thank you for your technical aviation input, too. We have seen the world.

Jo Lito, you are the best! You mentored me into this crazy world of corporate aviation. Yes, I learned from the best!

Cory Nelson, you are the best in the business. Thank you!

To Kristina Bauer-Selten, Susan Parry Silva, Darcy Pearson, Karen Cassens, Valerie Denny, Susy Odegaard, Fran Wilkins, and Sara Culver Truby. You women inspire me beyond belief. Thank you from the bottom of my heart for allowing me to serve in this industry over the years and for making me look good doing my job. I will forever cherish the friendships, the laughter, the heartaches, and the impossibly long days that have made me appreciate and look forward to my next chapter: coming home! Cheers to the wonderful journey in the skies of corporate aviation.

Thank you to Morgan James Publishing for taking my hand and leading me down this new, lifetime adventure. Terry Whalin, David Hancock, Jim Howard, Megan Malone and Angie Kiesling, thank you for listening to me, answering my endless questions, and gently guiding me down the path of publishing. I could not have done this without you.

To Meg Daines who meticulously used her incredible skills to research and sketch maps for each chapter. What a labor of love. Thank you.

I would also like to do a big shout out to an organization called Hear the Cry. Mike McDonald, you inspire me beyond belief. I love what Jesus is doing through you. Thank you. Please go to www.hearthecry.org and check out what is happening all around the world. A percentage of each book sold will go to this organization that helps children around the world.

Most important of all, thank you to my Lord and Savior, who has led me on my path, experiencing the journey of a lifetime.

Colossians 3:17: "And whatever you do in word or deed, do it all in the name of the Lord Jesus, giving thanks through Him to God the Father."

ABOUT THE AUTHOR

Ann Menke began her journey into the world of corporate aviation in the late '80s as a flight attendant seeing the world. She has trained and mentored flight attendants, as well as pilots, over the years. The daughter of an Air Force officer, she has a love of travel that started as far back as she can remember. Her family lived in many different places, including the Canal Zone, Panama, which only furthered her love of travel. She also spent vacations exploring Central and South America. Ann began writing stories from the time she could hold a pencil in her hand and is an avid reader. She has been married to her husband, Doug, for thirty-five years. Their two children are both married, and the Menkes enjoy coveted time with their five grandchildren. The family has spent many special summers at their home in Normandy, France. Ann currently resides in the Pacific Northwest.

"Traveling—it leaves you speechless, then turns you into a storyteller."
—Ibn Battunta

CPSIA information can be obtained
at www.ICGtesting.com
Printed in the USA
FSOW02n1723280416
19793FS

9 781630 477585